"If I refuse?"

Nicoletta brought one of her tiny hands to her breasts and exhaled a trembling sigh.

"If you refuse me, *amore mio*, I will indulge myself in such an unbridled orgy of bloodletting that not a single mortal will be left alive aboard the *Atlantic Princess* when England appears on the horizon.

"Two thousand crew and passengers. Even I have never savored so rich an experience.

"To drink in the light of two thousand mortal souls. Ah, the ecstasy. Think of it!"

David tasted the bile rising in his mouth. Nicoletta had seduced him by being a virtuoso in the ways of love, but her real genius was for evil.

By Michael Romkey
*Published by Fawcett Books:*

I, VAMPIRE
THE VAMPIRE PAPERS
THE VAMPIRE PRINCESS

# THE VAMPIRE PRINCESS

## Michael Romkey

FAWCETT GOLD MEDAL • NEW YORK

A Fawcett Gold Medal Book
Published by Ballantine Books
Copyright © 1996 by Michael Romkey

Library of Congress Catalog Card Number: 95-90698

ISBN 0-449-14937-4

Manufactured in the United States of America

First Edition: February 1996

10  9  8  7  6  5  4  3  2  1

To Matt, for his intensity;
To Ryan, for his ambition;
And to Carol, for her love.

# PART I

◇

# Venus Rising

# 1

✦

# The Dock at Midnight

THE NIGHT WATCHMAN zigzagged toward the guardhouse, the yellowish beam from his battery-powered lantern panning back and forth across the dock.

The first half of Yu's shift had been pleasant enough. A crew of workmen had stayed late to finish a job, which kept it from becoming lonely on the dock until later in the evening. Besides, the hours between sunset and midnight belonged to friendly ghosts, so the watchman was never afraid.

It was a nightly ritual of Yu's to drink a cup of green tea in the guardhouse exactly at midnight. The tea helped keep the night watchman awake. It also fortified him against the horrors of the second part of his shift.

The second half of the night was reserved for malevolent ghosts, witches, and black magic. The intermittent harbor traffic would stop after midnight, the wind would die, and even the rats would vanish into their hideaways, leaving the darkness so quiet that the watchman sometimes imagined he was the last person left alive in all the world.

It was an unlucky job, but it was the best that a man who had used up all his luck could expect.

Yu regularly burned hell money to pacify his departed ancestors, but it was not their spirits haunting the dock. His forebears had been peasant farmers in southern China—not sailors swept overboard by freak waves, murdered in gambling disputes, or crushed to death by cargo containers broken loose during storms and tossed around the deck like

3

lethal toys. There were many ways to die at sea, most of them violent. The night watchman knew this from experience. He had been in the merchant marine until he exhausted his good fortune by surviving a typhoon in the South China Sea.

Go to sea again, the palm reader told him, and you will die.

And so Yu the sailor became Yu the night watchman.

The main thing was to keep moving after midnight. If he kept walking up and down the dock, an eternity would pass, but the stars would eventually begin to slide in the heavens. After another eternity, the sky would begin to lighten in the east and the dark power would be broken. The day guard would finally come to work—late, typically, still rubbing the sleep from his eyes—and the night watchman would be free to find his bed.

The dock was cluttered with equipment, shipping containers, and junk salvaged from crumbling ships, making it impossible to walk more than a short distance without having to veer around some obstacle. Yu circumvented a hotel-size gas range pushed over on its front and threaded his way through a dozen green acetylene tanks on two-wheeled carts. He stopped for a few moments to play the lantern's light on a mass of copper wire wound into a snarled coil. Yu wondered how much wire was lying there on the dock. Games like this helped the night pass more quickly, though the trick did not work so well after midnight.

Easily ten kilometers, the watchman decided.

Derelict ships towered over the dock on either side, pressing down like steel mountains that might collapse at any moment. The mercury-vapor security lamps installed every two hundred feet did little more than accentuate the darkness. The light cast webs of tangled shadows that merged effortlessly with the night, a vague deterrent to thieves, a halfhearted reminder that the dock was not completely deserted.

Yu nearly tripped over a single link from a ship's anchor chain. The chain, cut into pieces to make it easier to haul away, had formerly belonged to the freighter moored to the seaward side of that dock. Wrecking crews had stripped away significant portions of the hull, leaving little more than a steel skeleton above the waterline. The watchman turned the lantern on the metallic bones a moment, then quickly lowered it, not wanting to attract the ghosts lurking within the ship.

Far out in the harbor, the foghorn began to croak its low, bleating cry, a homing signal as well as a warning to pilots trying to navigate the darkness. The watchman peered into the black void. It was impossible to see, but he could feel the cold, clinging dampness coming at him through the night. Soon the fog would boil over the docks, blanketing the abandoned ships in thick gray wool.

Yu hated the fog more than anything else. It hid the corroded hulls until he was close up on them—then made them jump out from the swirling mists. He dug a clove cigarette out of his jacket. The aromatic smoke cheered him, as did the pathetic brightness of the match, which disappeared with a hiss when he tossed it into the black water between two ships.

A furtive movement caught the watchman's attention. The lantern's beam settled on an enormous wharf rat. The greasy rodent stared back at the light, transfixed for a moment before it squealed, turned, and scuttled back up the braided metal cable, the way it had come.

The watchman followed the rat with the lantern's beam until the creature disappeared onto the ocean liner's main deck, five stories above the dock. The light crawled along the bow until it came to the ship's name painted in faded red-and-gold letters.

*Esprit de France.*

The fact that the watchman could not read these words gave them mysterious, maleficent power. They seemed to represent not only the ship's name, but a sorcerer's incantation for capturing ghosts within the rusting ruin, disembodied spirits who could be placated only with steaming bowls of blood.

The *Esprit de France* was the largest ship moored to the dock, and its size alone made it alarming. The ocean liner was so huge that Yu could describe it to his wife only as being like a vast floating city. Yu looked up at the scales of rust flaking from the hull, and it made him think of an ancient dragon hunkered down in the brackish back-bay water, sleeping with its belly buried in the harbor mud. The dragon was quiet now but capable of great violence if aroused.

The watchman thought about the ghosts of the countless passengers who had died on board the once-great ocean liner. To pass away far from home, with your spirit condemned to wander for eternity—horrible, horrible. It would take more than a single bowl of blood to satisfy these spirits' furious hunger.

Yu thought about the ghosts of the six smugglers who had used the abandoned hulk as a place to process Chinese heroin before it was towed to the salvage dock. The criminals were killed in a shoot-out with the Singapore Constabulary. Their ghosts were trapped aboard the ship, too. Yu was certain of it. The watchman had heard them moving about up on the deck, shuffling back and forth with spectral satchels of contraband.

Yu's nightly duties included going onto each ship for a cursory inspection, but he had not yet been able to bring himself to include the ocean liner on his rounds. What if he became lost in the cavernous ship? The ocean liner had thirteen decks—a most unlucky number—and hundreds of rooms. The foreman had used a can of yellow spray paint to make a line on the floor that the watchman was supposed to follow up endless flights of stairs to the Promenade Deck. The foreman had been quite specific in his warning: Do not wander away from the marked path, he had said, or the watchman would become lost inside the ship. But that would never happen, Yu thought, because he would never be foolish enough to set foot aboard the haunted ocean liner.

The watchman switched off the lantern to conserve batteries.

The abandoned hulk loomed larger in the darkness. As if stirred by the watchman's fear, the ship tugged against its mooring lines. The steel cables gave out a low, trembling groan as they tightened against the wooden pilings. *The dragon knows that its death is near,* Yu thought with a shudder.

It was good that the ship would be cut up soon for scrap, freeing the trapped souls, melting down the metal so it could be used to make bulldozers and shining new automobiles. The salvage crews would start tearing the ship apart any day now. It would not be too soon for the night watchman.

Yu heard the automobile approaching along the access road when it was still quite far away. The car's headlights flashed for a few seconds on the *Esprit de France*'s three angled smokestacks, which reminded the watchman of tilting tombstones in a Christian cemetery. Car doors opened and shut. Yu heard a few words of conversation, but the words were too far away for the watchman to make them out. He could not see the visitors, but his ears told him that they were coming onto the dock.

The watchman climbed up on a forklift and shined his lantern through the debris until the visitors came into view. A young Chinese businessman squinted irritably when the light hit his face. With him was a tall round-eye. They walked briskly toward him, each man swinging a leather briefcase. It was obvious from their bearing that they had the authority to be on the dock. Still, Yu would have to ask them to come to the guardhouse to sign the visitor's log.

The men continued down the dock until they reached the bow of the ocean liner. Round-eye stared up at the rusting monster reaching ominously over him in the darkness, walking backward, trying to take in the entire ship. Impossible, since Round-eye was so close, and the ship so big—

big as a mountain, with its sprawling mass cloaked in darkness.

The watchman saw the first wisps of fog begin to creep over the dock. Ghostly fingers reached up around the edges of the decking as if the spirits of drowned sailors were trying to pull themselves out of the water. Yu was suddenly glad he was not alone.

Round-eye, his head thrown back as he stared up at the ocean liner, uttered a single word. The fact that the word was spoken in Chinese was almost as surprising as the word itself.

*"Piau lian,"* Round-eye said.

Beautiful.

The astonished watchman grabbed the forklift's roll cage as if to keep himself from falling.

*Piau lian?*

Round-eye thought the decayed, rusted derelict was *piau lian?*

*"Hun mei,"* the other man said to the round-eye, but it was obvious to the watchman that he was only indulging the foreign devil.

Madness, Yu thought. To speak of the ghost ship as *piau lian* was round-eye madness of the worst sort.

Round-eye seemed to suddenly notice the night watchman and yelled something. Yu didn't hear what. He was too frightened to listen. He already knew what was coming.

Yu stood on the forklift for a moment, watching the visitors' impatience grow, too frightened to move, too frightened even to breathe. But then he felt himself moving, climbing down off the forklift, walking obediently toward the distinguished visitors.

It was midnight, perhaps a few minutes past. Yu would not have his cup of green tea in the guardhouse. His tea ritual was broken, and that in itself was bad luck.

The fog was already rolling over the dock in great smothering billows, merging the world of the living with the world of the dead, making it possible for the inhabitants of either side to cross freely back and forth across the frontier.

Pointing the way for the visitors with his lantern, the night watchman moved grimly up the gangplank, leading them into the cold and dripping darkness of the sleeping dragon's belly.

# 2

✧

# David Parker

**D**AVID PARKER PULLED the Jaguar into a secluded spot between two stands of sea grape high as a man's head. The intimate pocket of greenery concealed the convertible from the road, which was sparsely traveled by that time of night. The white sand sloped sharply away from the road, flattening into a plateau that extended to where the high tide broke, then took a second dip down to the wet, chocolate-colored sand that melted into the surf's gentle club-soda fizz.

The woman in the car with David was not Nicoletta, though there was hardly anything unusual in this. Nicoletta was not jealous when David went out with other women. Quite the contrary. She encouraged him to find other lovers, to be promiscuous, but for her own reasons.

"It's been a lovely evening."

David met Dominique Neva's eyes and smiled.

"Yes, but only because the pleasure of your company has made it so."

Dominique responded to his soft, low voice as if the words were caresses. Of course, she didn't know about Nicoletta. Dominique wouldn't have understood, though God only knew that David himself didn't understand Nicoletta and her strange, disturbing demands.

Dominique wore black. The sleeveless gown was cut low enough in back to reveal tanned skin all the way to her waist, the tawny brown flesh unbroken by bra line, mole, or blemish. Her jewelry was equally elegant in its simplicity:

a single strand of pearls around the neck, a silver bracelet on the left wrist. The beaded shawl around Dominique's shoulders kept her warm during the night drive. Still, David could see the effects of the cool air on her arms, on her breasts.

David had taken Dominique to cocktails at the exclusive Jupiter Colony Club, then to supper at Armand's in Jupiter Beach. Afterward, they'd driven slowly down the coastal highway and parked on A1A just outside the village of Juno Beach. David had been telling Dominique about the new opera he was writing. He did not confess the trouble it was giving him, for that would have required him to find the words to frame the shadow Principessa Nicoletta Vittorini di Medusa had thrown over his life.

Nicoletta deeply inspired David, but the art his muse brought forth was invariably filled with brooding darkness. David had begun to suspect Nicoletta of pouring poison down his creative well. Since becoming Nicoletta's lover, David's musical creations had all been misbegotten creatures, deformed, hideous, monstrous children even their parent had trouble loving. He was close to abandoning the opera project. Who in their right mind would want to hear a production so filled with anger and despair, a musical tale of depression, murder, suicide? Indeed, David was beginning to consider giving up composing altogether, although he had scarcely admitted this to even himself.

"You look uncomfortable," Dominique said, laughing quietly as she tugged loose David's bow tie.

If he did, his thoughts, not his clothing, were responsible. David was perfectly at ease in the tuxedo, one of three he owned, each exquisitely tailored to suit his long, angular frame. He'd let his hair grow long, and the wind played in it, blowing it gently around his narrow face.

The full moon had risen several hours earlier, when David and Dominique were having supper beneath the teal-colored canvas canopy at Armand's, looking out across Jupiter Inlet at the curious red lighthouse. By the time David parked the Jaguar at the beach, the moon was suspended high in the sky, a celestial lamp bathing the night in soft, otherworldly glow. Dominique's skin shined like satin in the blue moonlight. David closed his eyes a moment and considered what it would be like to brush the smooth skin of her neck with his fingertips, with his lips.

"Do you like me, David?"

David unfastened the top button of his heavily starched white shirt and leaned back in the seat, admiring Dominique. She could have easily been a model, though she was far too wealthy to have ever had to think about earning a living.

"I like you very much, Dominique," David replied, which was true.

Dominique bit her bottom lip and trembled almost imperceptibly. David had already noticed that she experienced a fluttering sensation in the pit of her stomach whenever she looked into his smoldering eyes. That was how it had been ever since he'd made the change. Women were unable to resist him—the chaste, the married, the accomplished sexual athletes, even the women who liked only other women. David Parker had but to desire a woman, and she was his for the taking. Because he was a gentleman, David had disciplined himself against abusing his seductive powers. Still, he was capable of stumbling during moments of weakness—especially if Nicoletta was somewhere nearby, singing depraved bacchanalian hymns his ears alone could hear. The spirit was willing, Nicoletta had taught David, but the body, though imbued with immortality and superhuman strength, was weak when it came to resisting the earthly temptations of the flesh.

"Would you like to kiss me?"

So easy, David thought, smiling to himself—smiling a little sadly. David had pushed the Hunger near the limit of his endurance. It demanded satisfaction now, satisfaction David could postpone a little longer but not refuse, its ominous necessity overpowering his sensual want.

"You may, if you want to, David. You may kiss me."

David leaned forward, took Dominique's face between his hands, and drew her to him.

"I would like to kiss you more than almost anything else in the world," he said.

Their embrace was long and filled with fast-rising passion. Dominique opened to David, rising to him, completely ready, completely willing, the banked fires of her desire bursting into open flame.

"Make love to me, David," Dominique whispered in his ear.

Making love first—first, before the other thing—was David's private ritual, but he doubted the Hunger would allow it this time. He had held the banshee at bay too long. The terrible need clawed at him now from the inside out, like a starved dog in a frenzy to tear itself free from the confines of a burlap bag to get at the lamb tethered nearby.

David kissed Dominique again, this time with passion bordering on violence. His lips found her neck. He bit at her silky flesh with his teeth, drawing her skin into his mouth with his own quickening breath. The myriad impressions comprising the young woman's essence flooded David's senses: the salty-sweet taste of her skin; the rare perfume in her hair; the hot, moist sensation of her irregular breathing against his ear; Dominique's memories of other lovers; the rich ache of her longing for David. And this more than all the rest: the seductive song Dominique's blood sang as it danced and whirled through the tight, secret passageways that penetrated her lithe body in the most intimate ways imaginable.

The dull ache in David's upper jaw sharpened as his blood teeth distended, a sensation as unpleasant as having red-hot needles stabbed through his upper gums. Only the comforting pounding of Dominique's heart calmed David enough to stop him from crying out from the pain, from the sudden horror of recognizing the beast he had again become.

David Parker understood very well what he *was*, yet for some reason he was always profoundly startled when the

Hunger took possession of him, leaving him feeling like a man who wakes up one morning to find his hands inexplicably covered with blood. When the Hunger took over David's body, as it invariably did every fortnight if he refused to feed its peculiar need, it transformed him so that he was no longer a composer or even a man, but a predator—or so Nicoletta would have it.

Of course, not all members of David's race subscribed to the belief that vampires were killers by nature. The *Illuminati*, the benevolent brotherhood to which David had belonged before he went away with Nicoletta, had counseled him that one law stood above all others in governing conduct in both the vampire and mortal worlds: *Thou shall not kill.*

Nicoletta had sought to convince David otherwise.

The vampire princess was the moon to the *Illuminati*'s sun, her cruel rages the antithesis to the benevolent stewardship the *Illuminati* felt toward the mortal race. Human beings were inferior to the *Vampiri*, Nicoletta believed, mere cattle that existed to satisfy the vampire's needs and pleasures. Mortals were to be killed without a moment's consideration or regret.

The *Illuminati* considered Nicoletta an outcast, a criminal. They would have gladly destroyed her to stop her centuries-long killing feast—Nicoletta laughed whenever she talked about the many times they'd tried—but she was far too powerful for even the *Illuminati*. The beautiful girl-woman form her physical body took concealed an ancient and powerful evil that seemed as invincible as Death itself.

David had fallen in love with Nicoletta without knowing the darkness concealed within her twisted soul, a darkness he was only beginning to understand. He had been an eager student for Nicoletta's first lessons. She was a master of the hunt, an unparalleled authority at the art of finding and seducing beautiful lovers. While a vampire could have any mortal lover he desired at the snap of his fingers, Nicoletta introduced David to hundreds of delicious ways to prolong a courtship, to draw out the push-pull attraction of sexual opposites until each affair became a beautiful and wondrous waltz whirling dizzily through the sweetest of nights. There were twenty-seven ways to kiss a lover; Nicoletta taught them all to David. There were thirteen ways to caress the back of a lover's neck; these, too, David learned, an enthusiastic adept in the art of love, training in the bed of the greatest lover of them all.

Yet David had abruptly balked when Nicoletta attempted to move on to instruct him in the poetry of killing. There were many ways to end a mortal life—some long and cruel, some quick and merciful—and Nicoletta was an accomplished expert in them all. The vampire princess knew as much about inflicting pain and death as she did about eliciting the most exotic forms of pleasure.

Nicoletta tried to convince David that the act of lovemaking between a vampire and a mortal was incomplete unless the passion climaxed with the mortal being drained of blood, of life, but this was further than David could go. Even if Nicoletta's clever arguments forced David to accept the premise that killing was the ultimate expression of *Vampiri* being, he could not bring himself to commit this most final, and bestial, of acts.

Dominique moaned and thrust herself upward. "David!" she gasped, sensing what he very nearly wanted—not just her body, not just her blood—and offering it to him, offering him *everything*.

It was always the same, which made it all the more difficult for David to stop himself from killing. His lovers offered their bodies to David, but not just their bodies. They offered their blood, their lives, their souls.

David—and the Hunger—required no further encouragement.

With a quick, certain thrust, David sank his blood teeth deep into Dominique's tender neck. The rapture he experienced as the first blast of her hot blood sprayed into his mouth made his body shake with ecstasy. Beneath him, Dominique stiffened, her breath changing to irregular, frantic gasps. She was enjoying it almost as much as

David, yet she felt only the pleasure and not the ferocious power that accompanied the multiple-orgasmic explosions that coursed through the vampire's body with each swallow of blood.

David drank in Dominique's blood, he drank in her youth, her strength, her memories. And when the blood had rendered him drunk to the point of delirium, his soul broke free from his body and flew up from the earth at an impossible speed, his unfettered intellect racing through the universe, seeing things only God could see, apprehending in a glance the clockwork that governed the birth and death of entire galaxies and their innumerable worlds and alien civilizations.

*This was what it was to be a vampire, an immortal, all-knowing being, a living god!*

Power!

Freedom!

Knowledge that extended light-years beyond the patchy, paltry meanings that could be sketched using language's pathetically inadequate semiotics!

And yet this was but the first movement, the prelude to the ultimate bliss, to the boundless universal consciousness David could share only if he was courageous enough to take the terrible final step into the eternal silence.

A dim thought took shape in the back of David's mind, a perception so ephemeral that it barely registered in his consciousness.

*Nicoletta was right.*

Like the slowly roving eye of a motion picture camera's lens, David's attention returned to the softly yielding form beneath his arching body.

*Nicoletta was right.*

How delicious it would be to drink and drink and drink, to follow the swirling red whirlpool down into its mysterious center, to vicariously experience the blissful stillness of Dominique's death—then rise up quickly at the last possible moment, like a swimmer emerging from the depths with his breath long spent, bursting back into life, a phoenix, an immortal, a god who knows everything there is to know about life and death and everything between!

David felt the coldness creeping into Dominique's fingertips. He saw the familiar shadow fall dramatically across her soul—a shadow strangely similar to the one Nicoletta had cast over his own life.

David reminded himself that he must release Dominique, to stop while there was still time for her to live, but Nicoletta's voice was suddenly in his mind, drowning out his own voice, telling him to kill the bitch and be done with it, to pass through the final portal to real knowledge.

No! David shouted in his mind. No!

Nicoletta's taunting words broke off into a long shriek of insane laughter. All misery brought Nicoletta pleasure, even David's.

My dear God, David thought, why have you abandoned me? Why have you let me become so like *her*?

David began to sob, but still he did not withdraw his deeply seated teeth from Dominique's neck. He continued to suck the blood from her punctured throat, plunging deeper and deeper still into the abyss of Dominique's terrified soul, his guilty ecstasy increasing as they rushed together toward the last impenetrable darkness, toward the final and most unknowable mystery of all.

# 3

✧

# Lord Godwin

LORD GODWIN STOOD before the window with his hands locked behind his back, frowning as he stared down at the Thames in the predawn gloom.

Godwin Lines, Ltd., was located in St. Katharine Dock, a neighborhood that was once the hub of the British Empire. Through the docks of St. Katharine, Wapping, and Surrey—and past Limehouse Reach, the West India Docks, and the Millwall Docks on the Isle of Dogs—the riches of the world had sailed when Britannia ruled the waves. St. Katharine Dock was built in 1828, one of engineering genius Thomas Telford's projects, a series of warehouses arranged around three basins on the Thames's northern bank. During its heyday, the dock was crowded with traders, sea captains, and burly workingmen hauling wine and wool into the warehouses.

St. Katharine Dock closed in 1968, but the buildings had since been made over into pricey offices. This was an idea that very much appealed to Lord Godwin—taking something old and worn out, fixing it up, and finding a new use for it. Godwin bought one of the nicer properties in St. Katharine Dock as headquarters for his new transatlantic ocean liner company. Godwin Lines, Ltd., was situated between an art gallery and an architectural practice in what had originally been a shipping company's office. The building was red brick and dark wood, stark and sparsely elegant, more utilitarian than Victorian in its fashion. Lord Godwin commuted to the office in the speedboat tied up to his private dock. The helicopter on the roof catercorner from the satellite dishes was for longer trips to Heathrow Airport and Windmere, Lord Godwin's country house.

The antique photographs hanging on the walls in Lord Godwin's office showed the evolution of the transatlantic passenger trade, from the early days of steam power through the golden age of the ocean liner, which climaxed just before World War II and collapsed immediately thereafter. Occupying the place of honor behind Lord Godwin's desk was an oil painting of his great-grandfather, Queen Victoria's First Lord of the Admiralty. On the credenza beneath the portrait were photographs of Lord Godwin's favorite horse, his sailboat, his parents, and his estranged wife, Lady Camellia Godwin, as well as several showing him posed with various notable figures, including several prime ministers and Prince Charles, a friend from childhood.

Six feet three and whippet thin, Lord Godwin had a narrow, aristocratic face with a high, prominent brow and a warrior's sharp, deep-set eyes—piercing china-blue eyes that stabbed like a duelist's blade when he was displeased. His mouth was firm, his chin strong. In profile he resembled portraits of the Duke of Wellington painted around the time of the Battle of Waterloo. Wellington was, in fact, a distant relative, and a Godwin had been one of the great general's aides-de-camp when he defeated Napoleon.

The sound of the front door opening and closing downstairs interrupted Godwin's bleak meditation. He looked at his watch. It was the janitor arriving for work.

Godwin turned away from the window. He sat down at the conference table in front of his black IBM notebook computer. The table's cherry wood surface, lovingly waxed by its owners for the past two centuries, glowed with a rich inner light. Godwin recognized no incongruity between the sleek new computer and the antique table. To Lord Godwin, the entire point of having money was that it gave you the opportunity to enjoy the best of both the new and the old.

Which was, after all, the point of the *Atlantic Princess* project.

Lord Godwin pushed the computer's resume/suspend button. The Microsoft Word document popped up the computer's flip-up color screen. The letter to Keiko Matsuoka was meant to set the context for Lord Godwin's argument that Miss Matsuoka and her syndicate of wealthy Japanese investors should join him as investors in the *Atlantic Princess*.

". . . The novelty of flying has worn off," Lord Godwin read, finding where he'd left off. "Traveling by commercial jet today provides passengers with all the comfort and elegance of a bus trip. Even the Concorde has become passé."

Lord Godwin's fingers began to fly over the keyboard. He'd made this presentation so many times, he could lay out the groundwork almost without thinking.

Well-to-do travelers were ready to consider options to air travel between Europe and the United States, but presently there was only one. The *Queen Elizabeth 2* was the last passenger ship making regular—albeit limited—transatlantic crossings. Yet the *QE2* was getting long of tooth, and the economics of shipbuilding precluded launching anything to equal, much less surpass, the *QE2* in comfort and luxury. However, an extraordinary opportunity had come along that was simply too good to ignore. The *Esprit de France*, the most elegant ocean liner ever launched—as well as one of the largest—had been in a Singapore dry dock since 1966, tied up in an international court battle between the creditors of its various former owners. The suit had finally been settled, however, and Godwin Lines, Ltd., had bought the *Esprit* for a song, as it was headed for the scrap heap. The titanic ship was being outfitted in Japan and was about to be rechristened the *Atlantic Princess*.

The "new" *Atlantic Princess* would be a floating pleasure palace of unequaled splendor. Each cabin was being individually decorated with alabaster bathtubs, antique silver tea services, crystal ashtrays, art deco furniture, Dalí prints, the finest silk sheets. The best chefs were being hired, the best orchestras retained, the best wine ordered for the *Atlantic Princess*'s capacious on-board wine cellar.

"The *Atlantic Princess* will set a new standard in luxury travel," Lord Godwin typed on his computer. "Indeed, the ship will make forever obsolete the term 'jet set' as a label for defining the most fashionable mode of transportation.

"All available cabins have been booked for the *Atlantic Princess*'s maiden voyage. Occupancy for the twice-monthly crossings now stands at an impressive ninety-two percent for the entirety of the *Atlantic Princess*'s first season."

Enough crowing, Lord Godwin thought, leaning back in his chair. Now, the tricky part. He had to explain the problems without making them sound bad enough to scare off Miss Matsuoka and her investors. He couldn't lie. A Godwin never lied, even though for the first time in his life, Lord Godwin wished that he could.

He picked up the fax that had caused him so many sleepless nights and regarded it balefully.

**FasFax High-Speed Facsimile 18:22:03 3193556283**
Godwin Lines, Ltd.
12 St. Katharine Mews
St. Katharine Dock
London, E1
U.K.
Telephone: 171-222-6283


**To:** Lord Bryce Godwin
**From:** Bob O'Conner
**Subject:** *Esprit/Atlantic Princess* project

*Personal and confidential*

   The ship was in much worse shape than McKinnley & Johnson represented. Despite M&J's claim to the contrary, the stacks are probably corroded beyond re-

habilitating. The steering gear is inoperable and probably
will have to be replaced. The inboard and outboard
screw shafts on both the starboard and port sides
are rusted solid in their bearings, though I think I could
eventually free them. It was impossible to assess the condition of the turbines without breaking them open.
Years of inactivity have probably rendered the engines
beyond repair, though this isn't an issue if you still intend
to replace them with diesels.

I discovered an unreported gash in the starboard
bow at H Deck level. The damage runs from the chain
locker through the cofferdam into the fuel oil tank approximately parallel to the No. 1 hatch. (I don't know
how M&J could have missed this in their survey.)
My guess is that the tugs pushing the ship into dry
dock hit some underwater obstruction. The relative lack
of corrosion in the fuel oil tank after I had the saltwater
pumped out indicates the damage is recent.

As you already know, the ship's wiring will have
to be entirely torn out and replaced. M&J has been unable
to locate the *Esprit de France* wiring diagrams. It will
be extremely difficult—though not impossible—to do
the work without the original plans.

The ship's plumbing is also basically shot. The plumbing
diagrams are at least intact, although they're in French.

The Yomatsu Shipyard is incapable of completing
the refitting, lacking both equipment and personnel.
The overhead cranes don't have the horsepower to lift
the old turbines out of their holds. The yard crew here
may be adequate for prep and final cosmetic work,
but there are serious deficiencies in the engineering
and electrical staffs here.

The project appears to be at least a month behind schedule. It's difficult to say, since Scott Campbell, M&J's
site project manager, has been less than forthcoming
with information since you notified M&J you intended
to fire them. Campbell said he might be able to locate
some "missing" M&J work files if I guaranteed his
job. If you decide to proceed, it may be expedient

to negotiate something with Campbell. However, I will not—repeat *not*—work with the dishonest son of a bitch.

As I see it, you have four options:

1. Cancel the project.
2. Continue the work at Yomatsu, if you can get them to install a more powerful crane. Installing a new crane will delay the project at least twelve months. You'll also need to bring in a lot of technical help—I know some good ex-navy men from Norfolk and San Diego we could have on the job with twenty-four hours' notice.
3. Continue work at Yomatsu, but rebuild the old steam turbines instead of replacing them with diesels, thus getting around the crane issue. As mentioned above, the turbines are questionable, but it's impossible to know without tearing them apart. They spared no expense when they built ships of the *Esprit*'s class back in the '30s and '40s, so there's a chance they can be saved. Retrofitting the turbines with the new Bergin superchargers might even get you a ship that is more economical to operate than one powered with diesels. Be aware, however, that M&J has already contracted with Volvo to buy the new marine diesels. You might be able to buy your way out of the contract.
4. Have the *Esprit/Atlantic Princess* towed to Osaka. Osaka has the best yards in the Pacific, but you'll have to wait six months for a berth opening.

Although I haven't had a look at the M&J books, my off-the-cuff prediction is that the final tab will run far past the $400 million M&J told you to budget. If you plan to stick to the original timetable, crews will have to work around the clock, which could easily push the project to $800 million.

I'll take over this job if you really want me to, but I can't in good conscience recommend that you do anything at this point but cancel the work and cut your losses.

You'll also want to talk to your lawyers. Even my cursory inspection has turned up numerous examples of M&J's negligence, incompetence, and malfeasance.

Best regards,

Bob O'Conner
Chief Engineer, USN (retired)
Allied Naval Architects, Inc.

Lord Godwin dropped the fax and went back to his letter to Keiko Matsuoka.

"Instead of installing new Caterpillar diesels, our engineers have suggested rebuilding the old steam turbines. This should strike a resonant chord with our more environmentally conscious passengers—and these days, who is not concerned about the environment? An added benefit is that this will cut millions of dollars from the project's price."

Interesting Miss Matsuoka's venture-capital group in the *Atlantic Princess* project was crucial. Britain's economy was going through a shaky spell, and the bankers in the City, as the London version of New York's Wall Street was called, had cold feet when it came to visionary—translation: *high-risk*—projects. Lord Godwin had been turned down by the big investment banks in the United States that had an interest in maritime ventures. The latest disappointment had been over the collapse of a Crédit Lyonnais loan only weeks after Lord Godwin completed the tricky negotiation. The French bankers had expressed special interest in the project, which seemed appropriate, since the *Atlantic Princess* had first sailed under the Gallic flag as the famous *Esprit de France*. Godwin had been getting ready to fly to Paris to sign the papers, when the government canceled the loan. The French finance ministry was seeking to stem the tide of red ink flowing from disastrous investments in MGM, Olympia & York, and the late British publisher Robert Maxwell's enterprises. The *Atlantic Princess*'s prospects for success were simply too uncertain, the Crédit Lyonnais official told Lord Godwin over the telephone. As a parting shot, the banker reminded Godwin that the French government had done nothing but lose money on the old *Esprit de France*, so perhaps not getting involved in the ship's new incarnation was for the best.

The unpleasant truth of the matter was that Lord Godwin had gone very far out on a limb with the *Atlantic Princess* project. The original budget had been a staggering $400 million, of which he'd personally guaranteed $200 million, entailing every last shilling he could put his hands on. Unfortunately, the incompetence and negligence of his original nautical architects resulted in costs bloating almost beyond belief. It was going to take nearly $800 million to get the ship ready to sail and in Miami to pick up its first passengers. Lord Godwin faced certain foreclosure if he couldn't enlist new investors. Miss Matsuoka's group might be his last chance to pull himself back from the brink of disaster. But there were worse things worrying Lord Godwin than his own bankruptcy. Many other investors and contractors, involved in the project because they trusted Lord Godwin's reputation, would end up broke, too. Lord Godwin would rather die than bring disgrace on his family's name.

"I recently hired Chief Engineer Robert O'Conner to personally supervise day-to-day operations in dry dock," Lord Godwin wrote. "Chief O'Conner is a board-certified naval architect. Before retiring from active duty, he was responsible for refitting numerous mothballed ships for service, including the U.S.S. *Iowa*."

Lord Godwin frowned in the blue glow of the computer screen. The Japanese had surrendered to the Allies on the deck of the *Iowa*. Mentioning the *Iowa* was probably in questionable taste. But bringing the *Iowa* out of mothballs had been a huge project, the largest ever, in fact, before the *Atlantic Princess*. Chief O'Conner's involvement with the *Iowa* proved that he was up to the job with the *Princess*, unlike McKinnley & Johnson. Surely Miss Matsuoka would understand the context and not take offense.

Lord Godwin didn't even want to consider what would happen if his courtship failed to consummate a financial relationship with the Matsuoka Group. The Americans had an odious phrase to describe what he was about to become financially unless Keiko Matsuoka bailed him out: dead meat. Lord Godwin fiddled with the brightness control on his computer screen and wondered why so many metaphors for failure involved food: *Your goose is cooked. You're in the soup. You're toast. You're in hot water.*

Were those the sorts of things people were already saying about him? Did people think his goose was cooked?

"Lord Godwin?"

He looked around to see Miss Wilson, his executive assistant, standing in the door. He had been so lost in thought that he hadn't heard her come in.

"Good morning, sir. Would you care for a cup of tea?"

Lord Godwin gave Miss Wilson a crisp, businesslike smile. He never allowed his subordinates to notice when he was out of sorts.

"A cup of tea would be lovely, Miss Wilson," he said, though not nearly as lovely as getting Keiko Matsuoka to commit $400 million to the *Atlantic Princess* project.

# 4

✧

# The Diary of Principessa
# Nicoletta Vittorini
# di Medusa

THE FAMILIAR RESTLESSNESS has leached back into my soul. Like bad water seeking its level, the ache is forever in my heart, a hole in my soul, a darkness in my noon, an infected wound that refuses to heal no matter how close I come to drowning myself with the only medicine that takes away the pain.

Bellaria, Bellaria, forever lost to me, my Bellaria.

The New World has its charms, but like a plant pulled from its native ground, its roots left to dangle too long in the sterile air, I have come to yearn for the renewal that only symbolic interment in the rich, nurturing soil of my forebears' ancestral land can bring.

> ... *great Odysseus,*
> *who sat apart, as a thousand times before,*
> *and racked his own heart groaning, with eyes wet*
> *scanning the bare horizon of the sea.*

I stood alone on the balcony, scanning the bare horizon of the night sea, watching the long, curling swells rushed up on the beach, arching forward as they tumbled in upon themselves, the deep, muffled rumble transformed into a foaming hiss as the ocean spread itself flat and silver over the dark tidal flat. It was not Odysseus's Ithaca that has racked my own heart to groaning, but Bellaria. My birthright is lost to me forever, yet is this not the true essence of yearning—the acute longing for something that is ultimately unattainable?

The night breeze rustled through the coconut palms. Somewhere far out at sea, beyond the horizon, a sail snapped in the wind. I imagined the captain looking up from his wheel, startled by the sound. Or perhaps the crew was in the middle of a tack, trying to make landfall from the Bahamas before daybreak. I listened but heard nothing more. They were too far away for even my sensitive ears, although the night was quiet except for the wind and waves.

Bellaria is lost, but there is always Italy. My villa there awaits me, and my art collection, my rare manuscripts, my Egyptian and Babylonian artifacts—so many things to divert me on the long, lonely nights. Of course I will not be alone if I decide to take David with me. That, however, remains to be seen.

In the garden behind the walled mansion, lying upon a chaise longue beside the pool, Veronica Pauli sighed in her sleep. I turned away from my solitary remembrance of things past and walked swiftly through the mansion, listening all the while to the sound of breath moving in and out of her body, soft counterpoint to the waves and the wind in the trees.

Who can resist the pleasure of watching their lover sleep?

She was as lovely and helpless as an infant. The wind rubbed itself softly against her silk robe. It caressed her blond hair and played in the tiny petals of the tea rose she held lightly in her sleeping hand. The flower's delicate perfume floated gently to me, disguising the humid, fecund earthiness always present in the tropical air.

Overhead, beyond the dancing palms, the moon was a thin fingernail of ivory light. Insubstantial wisps of clouds moved steadily across the glittering sky, creating the illusion that it was the stars that the wind was blowing. It would rain at dawn, though the clouds would disappear quickly afterward, the wind driving them off to wherever it is clouds go when they vanish from the sky.

Veronica shifted in her sleep. Her left hand came up to her throat, feeling unconsciously for the silver St. Christopher medal. She was not a religious woman. The medal had been a gift from a sometimes boyfriend, a joke. She was afraid to fly out of Aspen because of the wild winds that tear through the mountain passes. The St. Christopher medal was supposed to protect her when she took off in her father's private jet. She'd forgotten to take it off when she got to Palm Beach.

I took a step nearer.

Veronica startled in her sleep as my shadow touched her face.

"Quiet, my love," I whispered, and slipped gently into her sleeping mind. "It is only Nicoletta."

Veronica was dreaming about being chased through the dark forest, pursued by a swift, shadowy shape that swooped and danced through the trees as if riding upon the wind. A light sheen of perspiration glistened on her golden forehead and in the hollow of her neck. My heart began to race.

I knelt beside her.

Veronica whimpered. She tried to awaken, but I wouldn't allow it. She struggled against the force of my will, but she was no match for me. It was pointless to resist.

"There is only one place you can go to escape me, my darling," I said quietly. She could flee only into the eternal night of death, her sole refuge. Veronica turned her lovely face away from me, her heels digging into the nylon cushion. She was afraid in her unconscious mind, but the other familiar emotions were there, too—the excitement, the anticipation, the sensual craving.

"Surrender," I whispered, teasing her ear with the tip of my tongue.

Veronica gasped, twisting her body, arching her back.
*Surrender.*

The thundering blood in her veins pounded in my ears, drowning the more distant sounds of night beside the ocean. I pressed my feverish mouth against Veronica's, her lips cool and moist. I kissed her deeply, and she kissed me back, taking me into her dream.

Our hearts began to beat with the same hurried rhythm. Soon we would be truly united.

My kisses fluttered like butterflies down her delicately curving neck.

We pressed against each other, one body, one mind, one soul. Together we waded deep into the warm waters of a dangerous river. Wave upon wave of pleasure flooded into us as currents and shadows swirled swiftly around us, grabbing us, pushing us, turning us this way and that, threatening to sweep us off our feet.

*The time has come, my love.*

Veronica's eyes opened wide, and she stared up at the night sky, the window into the eternal darkness that is the secret heart of creation.

For that instant I let her come into me as I had been in her, sharing my preternatural awareness. The experience jolted her like an electric shock. Veronica's nervous system was utterly unprepared for my hypersensitive awareness. Her mind whipsawed back and forth as she tried to regain her balance amid the sudden flood of sensation— the conversation between the Haitian maid and her lover in the servants' quarters of the estate next door; the way her silk robe felt against my bare skin; the smell of hothouse strawberries ripening in the refrigerator; the sound of a crab stripping flesh off a dead fish on the beach; the obscure but discernible rhythm made as the wind brought the palm trees' drab green fingers to life, pushing them up and down, up and down, inhuman hands beckoning Veronica to rise up out of her body and go into the eternal darkness. Such a rich and variegated catalogue of impressions for

Veronica to juggle, the voluptuous *Vampiri* banquet of the senses!

"It is time, *amore mio*," I whispered, feeling my lips move against her pulsing neck as I spoke.

Veronica's body arched beneath mine as I drove my teeth cruelly into her neck, cannulating the carotid artery, tapping the fountainhead of her being, gulping the steaming gusher with tremendous relish. I heard myself moan, but it was as if I were listening to someone else from afar. The blood consumed me as I consumed it, and everything else in the world became very far away.

Veronica's arms and legs became rigid and her spine bowed. Her jaw locked open, first from the shock, then from the force of pleasure so sharp and quick that it robbed her of her breath. Her right hand tightened reflexively around the rose, the thorns biting into her flesh, releasing tiny bubbles of blood, black pearls that shined in the pale moonlight. She began to shiver, her body quaking from un-imagined sexual pleasure that mingled with an equal measure of stupid animal terror. I allowed the pleasure to wash over her like a warm, opiated sea, but I also made sure she was acutely conscious of her mortal body's reaction to being drained of its blood. If she was to relinquish her mortal life to me, then I thought it only appropriate that she see it drawing away from her, like a passenger who stands at the ship's railing and watches the shoreline recede into the horizon.

*Look, my love. Observe the final moments of your life and understand how near Death stands to you.*

Animal dread tainted her blood with the faintly bitter aftertaste of adrenaline. Her skin began to feel clammy against mine. I drank more deeply still. Veronica's blood pressure fell dangerously low as her body sank into hypovolemic shock. Only when her heart began to palpitate wildly did I force myself to release her for a final moment of grace. I can be merciful when it suits me.

The smooth, blemishless skin on Veronica's young face puckered slightly. I could feel the fast-traveling chill penetrating her bones, numbing her. Yet at the same time, what transcendent joy I had given her! I had paid her for her blood with ten mortal lifetimes of ecstasy compressed into a deliciously prolonged few minutes. She had risen with me higher and deliriously higher on wave after wave of ecstasy, each climax thrusting her upward toward the start of yet another orgasmic plateau. She had not been cheated in our bargain.

I cradled Veronica in my arms like a baby. Rapid blood loss had left her euphoric even without the narcotic help of the powerful tranquilizing chemicals that passed into her through my saliva. Had I not helped keep her mind in focus, she would have been but dimly aware of what was happening. She motioned with her hand for me to continue, the gesture uncoordinated and drunken due to the lack of oxygen in her brain.

I lowered my blood-smeared mouth to her neck again and began to suck.

Veronica made a small, frightened whimper, a pathetic animal sound, like a rabbit caught in a trap. The dark specter of death, barely noticed at first, was drawing closer now, and with alarming speed, bringing with it the unfathomable, palpitating terror of that featureless black horizon that extends into eternity—the bleak, indifferent nothingness reaching out to gather her into its arms and swallow her whole.

I let her see it all then—the corrupt intercourse awaiting this golden being once Death had gathered her into his icy embrace. I, who have seen everything in my long, savage life, allowed Veronica to behold each image as plainly as if she were observing a series of photographs: her mutilated body; the flies; the lines of ants marching up her lifeless arm by the time the maid had arrived to work at six-fifteen—late, as usual. The gaping policemen who would snicker and point at her nude body, hiding the unspeakable lust they felt at beholding her beautiful, nude corpse. (Unspeakable to them, but not me!) The swabbing of her genitalia for traces of semen. (Not this time, boys!) The autopsy, the lazy "Y" incision, the removal of her vital organs for inspection and weighing. The hasty, sloppy stitches up her belly as she lay on the cold steel table, staring at the light with sightless eyes. Then on to the mortuary, with its sundry insults, into the box, her embalmed face waxy beneath the makeup, for a final showing before she went into the ground. Alas, even the best embalming job only delays the inevitable rot. I let her see that, too, for it is what I like best about death—the awful, inexorable corruption of the grave, transforming what was once a strutting, arrogant human being into the reeking putrescence that is the true basis of mortal existence.

A single word materialized in Veronica's mind, her final conscious thought before dying: *Please!*

I had to release her to laugh. She lay limp in my arms, like a blond Cleopatra in her death swoon.

> *I am dying, Egypt, dying.*
> *Give me some wine, and let me speak a little.*

But Veronica was incapable of speaking further, the poor darling. The only wine we had to share was her blood, and I had yet to drink my fill of it. Her body began to shake. Her throat made a harsh rasping sound, like gravel thrown against the tin roof of a vineyard shed. After that there was nothing but the startling pure quiet that rings as clear and bright as a silver bell the moment a life has ended.

I held Veronica's still body in my arms, drawing the last precious drafts of blood from her body like a hungry babe that greedily suckles at its mother's breast.

I went into the pool house when I was finished, where I found what I needed in a drawer behind the bar. The knife was for cutting limes. I tested its serrated blade against my finger, feeling the chilly sharpness of metal slicing into my skin. A line of red appeared, followed by a rapidly rising bead of blood. I stuck my finger into my mouth, the taste of my blood as heady as hundred-year-old cognac. I pulled my finger out of my mouth and looked at it. The wound was already healed.

Surprising though it may seem, there have been times when my body's uncanny ability to heal itself has proven annoying. There was the night I spent lying on my back in a filthy Tangiers hotel room, while the image of the Madonna was tattooed into the milky white skin of my left breast. I awoke the next night to discover, to my profound distress, that my skin had purged itself of the decorative inks, undoing the artist's painstaking masterwork. Alas, the tattoo could not be re-created: the artist, brilliant even in the haze of his heroin addiction, was already dead.

By the time I returned to Veronica, the powerful healing enzymes in my saliva had already done their work on her neck wound, closing the two small punctures, leaving only the blue-black discoloration surrounding the wounds that soon would be gone, too.

I slashed viciously at Veronica's throat with the knife, back and forth, back and forth, cutting so deeply that her head was nearly severed. It would have been foolish to leave the authorities a mystery in the form of a body drained of its blood with no apparent wounds. The police would examine the bloodless corpse and conclude her throat had been cut elsewhere and her body hastily dumped beside the pool.

I climbed behind the wheel of David's red Jaguar convertible and drove across the bridge to Lake Worth on the mainland, throwing the knife into the water on the way. I recrossed the intercoastal to Palm Beach, turning toward our rented mansion overlooking the sea.

David was in the drawing room playing the piano when the limousine pulled into the courtyard. I could hear the long, sweeping passages cascading through the darkness, music venting the passion in his tortured soul.

I came in the front door, dropping my purse on the floor

for the servants to pick up when they returned in the morning. The double doors to the main salon were closed. I reached out my hand and realized the instant before my fingers touched the cool metal that they were locked.

"David?"

The only answer was the sound of Liszt—mad, frenzied music, music possessed with genius and madness and diabolical complexity.

"David, open the door."

Still no reply.

I blinked, and the salon doors flew open, along with the French doors that line the wall along the side of the room looking out over the ocean. The wind rushed into the villa, billowing the curtains, making my long gossamer dress and my hair float around me, transforming me into a vision charged with the electricity of immortal power.

David sat staring at me. His hands remained poised over the keyboard, but the music had stopped, the aftertones continuing to reverberate from within the grand piano. The only light in the room came from the candelabrum on the piano. The flames sputtered and danced, but I did not allow the wind to extinguish them.

I reached out my hands. "Come to me, my love."

David turned on the bench to face me squarely, but he did not get up.

"Surely you are not still angry with me, my love?"

I had killed his last little plaything, the voluptuary billionaire's daughter, when he refused to finish the job. For some reason that upset him. Perhaps David had been planning all along to kill Dominique Neva himself, though I doubted it. Heaven knows he toyed with her long enough to have snuffed out her life a dozen times.

"I have something important to tell you," I said when David continued to pout in silence. "I have become weary of America and its shallow attempt at culture. I have decided to return to Italy as soon as I can arrange passage aboard a fitting vessel."

As you know, Diary, I have been planning my return to Europe for some months and have already booked the best cabin aboard the *Atlantic Princess* for her maiden voyage across the ocean. I had not bothered to mention any of this to David, of course, it being my habit to tell him only what I want him to know. No one understands better than I do how little one can trust a lover!

There was no mistaking the look in David's eyes. I seldom have to penetrate his mind to know what he is thinking. David Parker is the most transparent vampire I have ever known.

"You will like Italy," I said a little cruelly, sticking the knife in him and twisting it.

"You will enjoy seeing the treasures I have collected during my wanderings, David, shipping them always back to Italy. I am especially proud of my art collection—my da Vincis, Rembrandts, Michelangelos, and van Goghs. And my artifacts. One entire vaulted room in the cellar is filled with pharaohs' golden death masks inlaid with enamel and jewels, Inca sacrificial daggers, and Babylonian idols. But best of all is my scriptorium. My library is equally fit for a princess, or a philosopher, or a vampire—which is appropriate, as I am all three!"

"Actually, I wonder if it might not be better for you to go to Europe without me," David said in a quiet voice. He regarded me warily, but I said nothing, interested to see how much nerve he really had. I stared at him, my face an inscrutable mask. What he would have given to know *my* thoughts, Diary!

"I've been giving it a lot of thought lately, Nicoletta. I really think it would be better if we—well, you know."

I refused to help him, but continued to keep my eyes locked onto his.

"I'm sorry, Nicoletta. There really isn't any point in our trying to pretend this is working. Go to Italy without me. We'll both be a lot happier. I'm staying in America."

Still I said nothing, but turned with a merry laugh and

left him there, staring at my back with a perfectly balanced combination of disbelief, fear, and hatred on his face.

Progress, Diary!

If I can get David to hate me, the battle is half won.

# 5

✧

# Keiko Matsuoka

THE BONE CHINA cup clicked delicately against the saucer as Keiko Matsuoka set it down. "I appreciate your coming to Jakarta to brief me on the problems, Bryce."

"There are always problems in a project this big." After a beat Lord Godwin added uncomfortably, "Keiko."

"Yes, I suppose so." Keiko's stare was as unyielding as her smile. "Why don't you fill me in? I'm preparing the quarterly report for my investors."

Lord Godwin slid a computer disk across the conference table to Keiko. "Here is the latest spreadsheet. We're running a bit over budget."

Keiko inserted the disk into her laptop computer and scrolled down through the document. "Thirteen percent over budget, to be precise."

"We'll make some of it up on the back end. The expenses spiked because we decided to remodel the passenger areas at the same time we worked on the mechanicals. It compensated for some of the time we lost getting the turbines operational."

"Which will allow you to meet the scheduled launch date?"

"I'm afraid that that will be impossible."

"If you miss launching on the fifteenth," Keiko said with even patience, "you will be unable to make it to Miami in time to do the final preparations for the maiden voyage."

Lord Godwin nodded gravely.

Keiko leaned forward until her small breasts pressed against the conference table. "What are the ramifications, Bryce?" she asked in the same patient voice. Keiko was careful never to lose her temper unless it was absolutely necessary. Anger was a potent tool, but only if used sparingly.

"I suppose we have no choice but to postpone the maiden voyage. We'll upset a bloody lot of influential people, but it can't be helped."

"You know, Bryce, when I first visited you in London you did an exceptional job of making me believe in a project some of the smartest people in business said could never succeed."

"It will still succeed," Lord Godwin said, thrusting out his handsome jaw.

"No, Bryce, you're wrong. Your pockets aren't deep enough to hold out while the haut monde gets over its upset at having you disrupt their social calendars. The *Atlantic Princess*'s credibility—and our money—rides on that ship sailing from the Port of Miami with its passengers on the appointed date."

Lord Godwin started to say something, but Keiko cut him off.

"I simply will not permit you to miss the launch date." She turned off the computer and snapped its lid shut, squaring the flat white rectangle on the tabletop in front of her. "Get that ship into the water, or else, Bryce."

"Keiko," Lord Godwin said, holding up his hands.

"I have a no-risk arrangement with my biggest clients. They will not allow me—or you—to lose their four hundred million."

"They're not going to lose their money."

"I can see that the time has come for me to bring you more fully into the picture concerning your investors."

"What do you mean?" Lord Godwin asked, blinking.

"The Matsuoka Group's original investors held a forty-five percent equity stake in François Semiotics when it went belly-up two years ago. That little spot of trouble forced me to recruit new partners for my venture capital fund. Fortunately, I was introduced to some very wealthy gentlemen who are not afraid to take risks. They are, however, unwilling to tolerate failure."

Lord Godwin leaned forward, his face blanched, his voice sepulchral. "Who are your fund's investors?"

"That's a question you would have been wiser to have asked earlier, before my partners became *your* partners," Keiko said, leveling a manicured finger at Lord Godwin's chest. "But then, in my experience even the best business-people tend to overlook such details when they find themselves in desperate straits."

*"Who?"*

"The Yakuza."

Lord Godwin's hand came halfway to his mouth.

"The wonderful thing about a private fund, especially one that invests in foreign companies, is that there's no reporting of any kind. The money goes quietly into a new venture's bank account for four or five years, the company goes public, and the principal and profits come home, freshly laundered, if you manage the details properly. Which is, of course, a perfect investment strategy for the Japanese Mafia."

Lord Godwin sank back in his chair and closed his eyes.

"I can get help for you, Bryce, if you need it. Let me know if you have any trouble with the people at the Yomatsu shipyard—the unions, inspectors, what have you. You'll appreciate my associates' special skills."

"Bloody hell," Lord Godwin muttered weakly to himself.

"Sail from Miami on the appointed day, Bryce, make lots of money, as promised, and the Yakuza will stay in the background, like good silent partners."

Keiko opened her attaché case and put the computer inside it.

"But if you fuck this up, Bryce, it will be very bad for both of us."

Lord Godwin sat shaking his head, in denial as much as disagreement.

"I like you, Bryce. I have faith in you. Get us over this rough stretch of road, and we'll all make a lot of money."

Keiko pushed back her chair and stood, the meeting over.

"I'll let you in on a secret. The French government is considering privatizing Air France. If I can put that deal together, we'll get you another ship like the *Atlantic Princess* for the Pacific, which is where the real money is, and have an absolute lock on the top tier of international travel. I know you come from old money, Bryce, but your equity stake in a venture like that would make you rich beyond your wildest dreams. But for now you'd better get busy. Trust me: the *Atlantic Princess*'s maiden voyage is one deadline you do *not* want to miss."

Keiko strode to the door, opened it, and went out into the hall without looking back.

"Bon voyage, Bryce," Keiko called over her shoulder.

# 6

✧

# Nicoletta's Diary II

**D**AVID HAD GONE out for the evening, and yet our rented villa was not entirely deserted when I returned home just before midnight. I detected a presence in the house the moment I stepped out of the limousine. I had intended to change my clothing and go back out dancing, but I decided to trust instead in what providence had delivered unto me. I sent the driver away, telling him his services would not be required further that night.

There was an envelope waiting on the foyer table. I slit it open with my fingernail and removed the note written in David's hand.

My dear Nicoletta: I sincerely apologize for being so difficult recently. You are right. The time has come for me to become what I have become, if that makes any sense.

It made more sense than anything David had said in a long time.

Although it will be several nights before the Hunger is upon me again, I have gone out to hunt—and not because I *have* to, but because I *want* to. I know you will understand that!

Indeed I did.

I have arranged a little surprise for you. I hope that it will help you forgive me for being such a fool lately. All my love, David.

"Well!" I exclaimed. This was progress indeed.

I went into the library, threw the note into the fire burning in the grate, and got out two glasses and a bottle of absinthe. The clock was chiming midnight, but the night was only getting started.

"I was beginning to think you'd changed your mind about tonight."

My visitor was sitting in the overstuffed chair beneath a brass floor lamp in the corner of my bedroom. When I came in, he was reading the new de Sade biography I had bought the evening before at Barnes & Noble. He was good-looking, with a high, intelligent forehead and firm mouth. His wire-rimmed glasses made him look professional, although without completely disguising the Dionysian gleam in his blue-green eyes. He had taken off his blazer and hooked it over the side of the chair. The white Ralph Lauren Polo shirt nicely displayed his upper body, which was tanned and well-muscled. I could see the hair on his chest—black and silky—through the shirt's open collar.

"I had another affair I needed to attend first."

"I imagined as much," he said, smiling with the left half of his mouth. Closing the book on his lap, he reached backward for the pocket of his jacket, found a Polaroid, and looked at it lovingly before offering it to me.

The photograph showed me, naked, handcuffed hand and foot to a four-poster in the antebellum great house at Arlington Plantation in Jerusalem, Mississippi. That had been a night to remember! David must have found the photograph among my papers and given it to my handsome gentleman caller. It seemed rather out of character for David to be giving strangers pornographic pictures of me, but then, David's note had assured me that he was turning over a new leaf—a most welcome new leaf, Diary.

I slipped gently into the man's mind. His name was

Mark Gray. He owned a furniture factory in Dallas, where he had a home. He also kept an apartment in Rome and a condominium in Palm Beach, the latter near enough to our villa for Mark to have left his Ferrari parked in the underground garage at the condominium and walked over.

Gliding through his thoughts, I saw that Mark Gray was almost as much a sensualist as I. He had played the role of satyr so many times that I was surprised he had not grown horns and goat's hooves. His mind was filled with musky remembrances of nights depraved enough to have pleased as jaded a bawd as the emperor Tiberius—or Principessa Nicoletta Vittorini di Medusa. I almost regretted that I would be returning to Europe in a few short weeks. It would have been fun to accompany this mortal on his sticky debauches.

Then I found what I had been seeking—the memory of a magazine filled with amateur photographs of men and women engaged in various intimate acts. One of the photographs showed Mark, performing on a circular bed with a beautiful young woman, their bodies glistening with olive oil. David had mailed away my Polaroid in response to Mark Gray's magazine advertisement for lovers.

How deliciously bad of David!

I poured absinthe into each glass and went to stand in front of my gentleman caller. The sexual tension became instantly palpable. I breathed in his manly smell: warm, soapy, with just a lingering hint of cologne. And his blood! If Veronica Pauli's nectar had been Nouveau Beaujolais, Mark Gray's was a zinfandel, full of spice and ripe for the drinking!

"You are even lovelier than in the photograph, my dear. And even younger. You are eighteen, aren't you?"

How strange to hear myself spoken of as young! I sometimes forget. I, who saw the High Middle Ages flower; I, who inspired Renaissance painters; I, who witnessed the discovery of the New World.

"I have been very bad," I said in a little-girl voice.

Mark Gray licked his lips, which had suddenly become

dry. A hint of perspiration appeared at the edge of his hairline. "Tell me more," he said a little hoarsely.

"I have been more wicked than you can possibly imagine," I breathed, lifting my hands to my breasts, gathering the material of my dress in my fists. I was wearing a black cotton jumper with a shirred empire waist and horn buttons that ran from the neck to the ankle-length hem. I began to pull at the cloth with a slow, gentle tension. The top button popped open.

"I have let men . . ."

The next button popped.

"Do things to me . . ."

And the next.

"One, two, three, a half dozen of them. Whatever they wanted. All night long."

The remaining buttons sprang open, one of them tearing free, arcing across the room. I stood before Mark Gray with my dress opened to below my navel, feeling his breath on my skin. A light sheen of perspiration glistened on my belly, golden in the lamplight, the sweet, honeyed smell of my sweat a heady perfume to my lover, as intoxicating as smoke rising from an opium pipe.

Mark Gray's hands came up and brushed lightly, playfully, over my breasts. He began to unfasten my bra's front closure, his fingers warm, dry, and steady.

"You know what happens to wicked young girls," he whispered.

I nodded as the two halves of the bra fell open, releasing my breasts to his hands. A dreamy look came into his eyes before they closed and his mouth found my breast. My nipple grew hard in his mouth. I could feel the slight serrations in his front teeth as he bit playfully at my flesh, sending shivers up my spine. The familiar ache began to throb in my upper jaw, but I pushed *that* urge back down inside of me, concentrating instead on the similar ache between my legs.

I clasped my hands around Mark Gray's head, pushing him harder against my breast as he came forward out of the chair, forcing me backward onto the floor, one hand ripping my dress the rest of the way open.

I took my various pleasures with Mark Gray, an accomplished lover who did not disappoint me. When I had finished with him two hours later and he lay back on the bed, exhausted, I sank my teeth into his neck and gorged on his rich blood.

I slipped again into his mind, as I often do with my playthings, after I had swallowed three liters of his blood, exsanguinating him to the brink of circulatory collapse and death. He had started to hallucinate. His dying eyes were frozen open, watching the ceiling as it began to revolve around his head, picking up speed with each rotation. His soul was caught in the whirlpool, and the spinning cyclone dragged him quickly down into the silent abyss. The room became suffused with green light, then everything went suddenly black.

His heart stopped beating.

Mark Gray was dead.

The silence gathered us both into its arms. I felt the familiar exhilaration as death swooped me up and left me hanging suspended in the twilight region between where life leaves off and whatever else there may be begins. For a few seconds I enjoyed absolute peace, the only peace a vampire can know. And then, like a sprinkle of sugar dissolving in a cup of hot tea, the moment was gone and I was back in my immortal flesh.

I pulled my blood-smeared mouth from his neck and stared off into space, satiated yet hungry for more.

It was only then that I chose to consider the danger I had smelled lurking in the night for some minutes. My instincts warned me to flee, but as I remain a creature of intellect, not instinct, I chose to wait like a patient theater patron for the curtain to rise.

And then I saw it all: the cunning—the delicious cunning!

*"O powerful love! that in some respects makes
a beast a man, in some others, a man a beast."*

I looked down at Mark Gray's lifeless body. It would be
a pity to waste the remainder of his blood. I bent low and
clamped my teeth back into his neck, sucking the delicious
elixir from his body, my mind filled with Shakespeare.
(Perhaps someday I will allow scholars to "discover" the
play he wrote about me, Diary!) I was pulling the last
thickening dregs from Mark Gray's corpse, when a gaso-
line-fueled explosion blew open the doors to the room, followed by a scorching wind.

I looked up and watched the flames race up the carved
wooden panels of my door, dancing across the ceiling like
the angel of death's unfolding wings. Unless you have been
in the heart of a blaze, it is impossible to appreciate how
loud a fire can be. It crackles; it roars; it shrieks and moans.

(This is all grist for your mill, Diary. It is a good thing
for us both that I had the foresight to keep you hidden
away in the safe house I secured on the West Palm Beach
side of the Intracoastal Waterway, put safely away with my
collection of passports and tickets for the *Atlantic Princess*.)

I pushed Mark Gray's corpse away from me, listening to
the muffled, disjointed rumble as it collapsed in a limp
heap on the floor. At the window I drew back the burning
curtains. The window was covered with wrought-iron grill-
work, over the top of which the steel hurricane shutters had
been closed and barred from the outside. I did not burst out
of the pathetic barricade, though I could have done so easily enough. Instead, I went out into the inferno of the up-
stairs hallway. Flames swept around me like a burning
river. My silk robe had become a robe of fire. I smelled
burning hair and flesh—mine, all mine. The tapestries
hanging from the walls, the Chinese carpet, and the antique
furnishings all fueled the blaze.

With my eyes closed against the painful brightness, I
walked toward the stairs, my steps neither fast nor slow, listening to the sirens of emergency vehicles already racing

down Ocean Boulevard. There was a splintering sound above me. I raised my hand and blocked the flaming beam as it pitched down from the ceiling.

The staircase was intact, but the wooden risers—the carpeting was burned completely away—glowed like coals in a fireplace. The stairs were too far burned to support my weight, so I rose up into the air and floated down to the entry hall.

Two firemen wearing breathing masks broke open the front door with their axes. They tried to come into the foyer, but the heat was too much for them. I did not allow them to see me as I drifted between them.

Outside the inferno, the night air was refreshingly cool against my seared flesh.

David cowered in the bushes by the pool house. I did not look in his direction, but I let him see what he had done to me. The fear pulsing out of him was as thick as the smoke boiling up from the house. He was more afraid of me at that moment than he had ever been. I presented an appalling vision: my eyebrows and eyelashes singed off, my hair burned away, my skin and lips blackened and horribly burned.

Fire is by far the worst death, Diary, for those who can die.

I left David to stare after me, wondering whether I would die—and pondering what I would do to him if I didn't. Dear David! He wanted to kill me so much that he had even been willing to sacrifice a mortal life. At long last we had arrived at the inevitable crossroads. David was learning to kill, at least by proxy—and to be a vampire.

I walked between the fire engines, stepping over hoses, and exited the compound through the open gate. The first cars full of gawkers were arriving as I crossed Ocean Boulevard and went through the gate that led down to our private beach. I walked across the sand and into the soothing waters of the Atlantic. I walked until I could walk no farther, then swam in strong, swift strokes that carried me farther and farther away from the shore.

The sea is Mother to us all. I have lived by the sea almost all of my long life, and I have never been happy when I was away from it.

The choppy surf gave way to deep ocean swells as I continued to swim. I took a mouthful of seawater and swallowed. I let the water spill into my mouth and swallowed again and again. The Mother was in me, and I was in her, and we were as one, of blood, in blood, the essence of everything.

I stopped moving my arms and legs. The moon was directly overhead as I rolled over onto my back and slipped beneath the waves. I could see the moon's light underwater, but it grew gradually dimmer and then disappeared altogether, leaving me in the cold, wet darkness.

Down I sank, deeper and deeper into the lightless sea, a companion to the dark, slithering horrors that live at the bottom of the ocean. Something big and fast brushed by me, its rough skin scraping mine. Farther still I sank, the weight pressing down on me until at last I stretched my body out against the cool ocean floor. Sea worms and sightless crabs crawled over me, tending me, watching over me in my repose. The tidal currents picked at my body in whispers, carrying away bits of burned flesh, food for the fishes.

It was nearly dawn before I rose up out of the waves and shook free my long, luxuriant coils of black hair over my skin, as white and soft as a newborn babe's. I levitated there, watching the lighted outline of the city by the sea, the water frothing and boiling at my feet, a living tableau of Botticelli's *Venus*.

I was borne up by the sea. I was born by the sea. I will dwell by the sea forever.

# 7

✧

# Dr. Anderson

THE FULL FORCE of the South Florida heat slammed into Carrie Anderson only when she finally stopped running. It was nearly seven in the evening, but the temperature was still above ninety, the sun's slanting rays cutting across Miami Bay with brutal directness. Carrie stood at the railing, struggling to get her breath, sweat trickling down her arms, dripping off her fingers, spattering the deck like heavy summer raindrops.

"You're sagging, boss."

"Not sagging," Carrie gasped. "Dying."

Carrie wiped the perspiration out of her eyes with the back of one wrist. She had been living aboard the *Atlantic Princess* for a week. Every day after work she ran twelve laps on the ship's quarter-mile jogging track. Her eight-minute-mile pace was respectable, even if she wasn't anywhere near being in Brooke Morris's league as a runner. Not that it mattered to her that Brooke was in conspicuously better physical condition. Carrie wasn't competitive about running or anything else—except academics.

From her first day in kindergarten through the final day of her medical residency, Carrie Anderson had had to be the top student in each class or it made her almost physically ill. Maybe it was the product of having two teachers for parents, maybe it was just her own peculiar brand of ambition. Of course, being the best at anything has its price. Now, with her education finally behind her, Carrie was beginning to discern the dim outlines of an entire

50

world she had somehow missed all the years she'd kept her formidable concentration focused on school.

Did it matter to Carrie that Brooke was younger? That her firm body was swifter, stronger, as limber as a dancer's, and perfectly tanned?

Carrie typically left those sorts of questions unasked, though if she'd thought about it, she would have admitted it did matter, if only in a certain limited way. Why else would she be trying to outrun someone nearly ten years her junior in the stifling Miami heat?

Running was itself proof Carrie had perceived that her personal puzzle was missing pieces. She had taken up the sport during the final year of her residency, when she had suddenly—and with an appalling degree of surprise—discovered one morning while looking in the mirror that she was well into her thirties, showing the first telltale signs of aging, and almost emphatically single. Her biological clock had been ticking, but Carrie (a physician!) somehow had not noticed until that late date.

It was only due to an inconsequential encounter—an inept, embarrassingly brief affair following a disastrous introduction to gin and tonics at a student-faculty mixer—that Carrie was no longer technically a virgin. Her lack of experience notwithstanding, it was an absence of time, not interest, that had retarded her love life. Her studies had consumed her nights, her weekends, her holidays. Now that that was all over, Carrie found herself feeling rather like a passenger who has arrived too late at the railroad station: She was eager to climb on board, but the train had already left the station with the other passengers, leaving behind only the kind of loiterers and matrimonial transients anybody with any sense at all avoids like the plague.

Strange that none of this had mattered to Carrie Anderson, the brilliant medical student. What peculiar pirouette of logic made any of this significant now that she was Carrie Anderson, M.D.?

Fortunately, Carrie was still young. And attractive—in a

low-key, cerebral sort of way, she thought, regarding the
sweat-streaked face reflected back at her in a glass porthole.
And fit, of course. Not as fit as Brooke, but fit nonetheless.
As a physician, she had an obligation to serve as an example
to others. Why, she'd just run three miles with Brooke Morris in a hair under twenty-one minutes! It had nearly killed
her, but she'd kept up with the younger woman.

There was still time. The clock was ticking, but there
was still plenty of time, wasn't there?

Carrie's Achilles tendons were already beginning to
stiffen as she popped open a can of Canada Dry sparkling
water from her cooler and sank onto the deck, dangling her
legs over the edge of the ship. Brooke joined her. For a few
minutes they sat watching the work on the dock as the sun
slipped visibly lower over the Miami skyline. Eight stories
below, a crane was winching heavy pallets of supplies up to
the No. 2 hatch, which was three levels below them on the
main deck between the forward observation lounge and the
foremast. The big crane looked like a toy from their van-
tage point on the Sports Deck.

Carrie had finished her pediatrics residency that spring.
She'd intended to take the summer off before joining a
group practice in Des Moines in October. She changed her
plans after a medical headhunter contacted her, looking for
a physician to work for three months as the junior member
of the *Atlantic Princess*'s staff. Dr. Phil Hunt, a general
practitioner from Chicago who'd taken the senior job in the
ship's infirmary as a prelude to retirement, had convinced
Carrie the shipboard job would be a great working vacation.

Filling out the *Atlantic Princess*'s medical staff were
Brooke Morris and Della York, both registered nurses.
Brooke, a twenty-six-year-old Miami native, was paired
with Carrie as a team. Della, who was close to Phil Hunt's
age, was on Dr. Hunt's team—the Silver Team, he jokingly
called it, because Phil and Della both had gray hair. Carrie
and Brooke, both blondes, became the Gold Team. It was

only after Carrie joined the Gold Team that she found the first strand of "silver" in her own hair.

"I hate running on a track."

Carrie took a long drink of carbonated water. "I disliked it at first, too, but I've gotten to like it. It's hypnotic going around and around."

"Lap rat. Will they let us use the track when the paying customers are on board?"

"We can run before seven in the morning or after eight at night." Carrie held her wet T-shirt away from her back so that the air could get at her overheated skin. "We're not supposed to lounge out here with the passengers during the cruises."

"Don't let Lord Godwin hear you call them cruises."

*Cruise* was a word they'd been instructed to avoid. A cruise was a slow, aimless trip around the islands, according to Lord Godwin's taxonomy. The *Atlantic Princess* made voyages or transatlantic passages, not cruises. Carrie had spent an hour a day in class with other inexperienced members of the crew, learning the proper seagoing terminology. Port, not left; starboard, not right. Bow, not front; stern, not rear. Ship, not boat. Voyage or transatlantic crossing—never *cruise*. That word was anathema to their employer.

Down on the dock, stevedores were attaching the crane to a special metal platform holding a blue Mercedes-Benz. There was a garage for automobiles on the F Deck, deep inside the ship.

"Nasty-looking bruise."

"Yeah." Brooke pulled back the leg of her running shorts and ran her fingers over the purple bruise on her hip. "Compliments of Captain Franchini."

"That's flagrant harassment. You should file a complaint."

"Nah."

"Brooke!"

"Lord Godwin may be a good guy, but who is he going

to back a week before the *Atlantic Princess*'s maiden voyage: some chick nurse or his ship's captain?"

The *Atlantic Princess* was honeycombed with so many storerooms and obscure mechanical compartments that each member of the crew had been issued photocopies of the sectional blueprints. It would be too easy for someone to lie in wait for an unsuspecting woman to happen by—especially if the someone was a pig like Franchini. The captain was a well-known Neanderthal. All the women aboard the ship knew to stay away from him.

"Good evening, ladies," a voice behind them said as Carrie was about to pull rank on Brooke and insist she report the incident with Franchini. "It looks as if it's going to be a super sunset."

It was Cyril Ogden, the ship's British purser. Cyril dragged a deck chair across the rubberized jogging track and positioned it in front of the railing next to Carrie. Brooke offered Cyril one of Carrie's cans of mineral water, which he accepted with thanks.

"How are preparations coming along with you two down in the infirmary?"

"We're a little rushed, but we'll be ready in time. How about you?"

Cyril rolled his eyes. "Never in my career have I encountered such a debacle over reservations. I spent the day ringing up people who have gotten whatever they've wanted for their entire lives to inform them that they are *not* going to be aboard the *Atlantic Princess* when she sails. I wouldn't wish some of the phone calls I've had on my worst enemy."

Carrie and Brooke made sympathetic noises.

"And then there was the unfortunate matter of some reservations that were turned over to a Johnny-come-lately, supposedly due to unspecified computer problems." Cyril snickered. "Not bloody likely. The tickets were mailed to Alexander Fox. You understand what *that* means."

Carrie and Brooke looked at each other blankly.

"Don't tell me that neither of you has heard of Alexander Fox."

Carrie and Brooke shook their heads in unison.

"Where have you two been hiding for the past few years?"

"Medical school," Carrie answered truthfully.

"He has something to do with computers, doesn't he?" Brooke offered.

"You might say that," Cyril said in an arch voice. "Alexander Fox is one of the biggest names in Silicon Valley, and a very, very wealthy man. To his discredit, it seems he is also something of a hacker. It appears that he found a way to break into the ship's reservations computer and purloin reservations he was otherwise unable to obtain for the sold-out maiden voyage."

"How could he do that?"

"With a modem and telephone, Carrie. It's difficult but not impossible, if you know what you're doing. I've been over it all with Jack Ketch. Our chief of security agrees that the only likely explanation involves computer skulduggery."

"It sounds pretty unlikely to me," Carrie said. "It's not as if Fox is some kid sitting up all night in his parents' basement, looking for mischief to get into with his PC."

"Then you don't know Alexander Fox," Cyril said with a wicked laugh. "He has a well-earned reputation for being an eccentric genius—difficult, egotistical, a rule breaker."

"What's Jack going to do about it?"

"What can he do? Fox has the tickets. He was too clever for us to trace the crime back to him. From a practical standpoint, Jack Ketch believes our best recourse is to retain Fox as a consultant so that he can help us keep anybody else from purloining reservations in a similar fashion."

Carrie could not keep from laughing.

"It is rather rich, isn't it?" Cyril agreed.

"The henhouse has been raided, so the ship's top cop thinks the best solution is to hire the Fox."

"One must be pragmatic, Carrie, if—"

Cyril's words were cut short when the air was split by a sharp snap, like the first crack of what will be a deafening roar of thunder. Carrie looked down in time to see a load of cargo crash down onto the dock. The pallet, which was loaded with kitchen supplies, split open. Tin cans rolled away from the wreckage in all directions.

The crane's broken cable rose into the air with a slow, sinuous movement, drawing a graceful S against the fading blue sky. The cable drifted higher still with an almost languorous motion, turning lazily, then suddenly picking up speed. It was almost too late to react when Carrie realized the inch-thick rope of braided steel wire was whipping straight toward them.

Carrie dropped her drink and threw herself backward. Somehow, she managed to kick Cyril over backward in his chair. She liked to think that she'd tried to save him, but it all happened so fast that she was never really sure whether the maneuver was intentional or not.

Brooke's shrill scream disappeared beneath the much louder shriek of metal against metal as the cable struck the railing. The top bar bent but deflected the cable, which whipped against the outside wall of the officers' quarters, showering Carrie with sparks and leaving a long, ugly gash in the white paint that covered the steel outer bulkhead.

And then, as suddenly as it had started, everything was quiet.

Carrie found herself lying on the deck, her heart pounding. She looked to one side and saw Brooke.

"Are you all right?"

"I think so," Brooke said, her voice quavering as she sat up.

Down on the dock, men were shouting and running in all directions, but nobody there seemed hurt. The cable was swinging harmlessly back and forth in the air, tethered to its long metal arm. The railing where they had been sitting was bowed like a highway guardrail that has had a speeding truck bounce off it.

"Cyril?" Carrie asked, turning.

The purser lay sprawled on his back on top of the collapsed canvas chair, headless. Arterial blood was pumping from his neck, spraying the white-painted bulkhead. The headless body was quivering with random muscle spasms.

Carrie got slowly to her feet, her eyes following the irregular curlicue spray of red toward its inevitable destination. Cyril's upright head rested at the edge of the Sports Deck jogging track. The open eyes stared straight into Carrie's, a look of inexpressible horror frozen on his features. The eyes seemed to move, following Carrie as she took several uncertain steps forward. Carrie had the sickening sense that Cyril's mind continued to be aware, that he was conscious of what had happened to him. The bluish lips trembled, either random nerve impulses or the fatally wounded purser attempting to speak.

"My God," Brooke said, the words barely distinguishable. Her eyes were fixed on the severed head, her own face a horrified mask. She'd gotten to her feet and was backing away unsteadily, nearer and nearer the railing.

"Brooke!" Carrie snapped.

Brooke met Carrie's eyes.

"Get ahold of yourself."

Brooke nodded.

"There's nothing we can do," Carrie said.

Carrie had to force herself to look at doomed Cyril's face a second time. She could tell by his eyes that Cyril was mercifully gone now. The eyes were blank, the pupils slightly askew. His suffering was over.

Carrie turned toward the pounding footsteps, holding her hands out in front of her.

"Everybody stay back!" she ordered. "There's been a terrible accident. None of you can go any closer until the police arrive."

# 8

# The Fog

LOUIS ANDRÉ DID not fear Baron Samedi, *loa* of the graveyards, or Legba Grand Bois Chemin, guardian of the passage between this world and the next. There was only one invisible Louis André dreaded—his old *baka*. Fortunately, Louis had found a way to rid himself of the creeper.

Louis André was a *tonton macoute*—not one of the political thugs left over from the Duvalier regime, but the real thing, a traveling sorcerer who wandered from village to village toting a bag filled with medicinal plants, black candles, dried toad, black cat, bat, and all the other ingredients that were indispensable in the casting and removing of spells.

The *tonton macoute* was good at his work. He knew how to placate the *loas* when they were angry, how to make charms to ward off *loup-garous*, the witches who sucked children's blood. For a fee, Louis could cure most illnesses brought on by spells that weakened the *gros bon ange*. For customers who could afford to pay a little more, he would turn hexes inside out and backward, leaving the misfortune to fall upon the heads of the original perpetrators.

During the early part of Louis's career, before he got a *baka* and at last possessed true power, the *tonton macoute*'s customers were mostly women—stay-at-home *placées*, good-time-girl *jeunesses* who couldn't stay with the same man for more than a week, *bousins* who sold their bodies to any man with money. Mostly, Louis sold them love potions made from hair clippings and dried hummingbird flesh, magic to get a man, to keep a man, to drive away a man in order to make room in bed for someone new.

Just as a carpenter must learn to hammer with his left hand as well as his right, Louis became proficient in black magic as well as white. The dark side was where his real talent lay—the root of his power and trouble.

Louis was a master of the magic that brings bad luck, illness, and death. For the right amount of money, he could be hired to sprinkle graveyard dirt around an enemy's home, causing impotence and blindness. Or he would dig up the bones of his client's enemy's father and add it to the mixture, a potion that would drive a man or woman quickly to suicide. Louis was also an adept zombie master, though the art of zombie raising had fallen into official disfavor and was subject to the harshest sort of punishment from the government's bullyboy *attachés*. There was no one in Haiti better than Louis at separating the *gros bon ange* from the *corps cadavre* to make a zombie, who in turn made an excellent servant, until the inevitable rot set into its flesh.

Of course, there were many *tonton macoutes* who could accomplish these feats in one fashion or another. To hold true power, Louis needed Legba Grand Bois Chemin to grant him a *baka*. Louis prayed to Legba for years for a creeper, but the *loa* ignored Louis until one night Louis did something that was evil even by his own loose standards.

A half-blind old woman named Maman Marie hired Louis to remove the hex a neighbor had put on her goats to stop them from giving milk. When Maman Marie got out a battered cigar box and fumbled for a silver coin for Louis to bury—part of the ritual to turn around the magic—the *tonton macoute* was startled to see that the box contained nearly one hundred dollars in American money, more money than Louis had seen at one time in his entire life. Late that same night, drunk, Louis slipped back to Maman Marie's house and strangled the old woman in her sleep.

The next night—All Saints' Day—found Louis in a graveyard many miles from Maman Marie's village. The voodoo ceremony was in honor of Baron Samedi, god of graveyards, the first spirit Legba drew up out of the waters of death. Louis wore a new suit of black and purple, Samedi's colors paid for with Maman Marie's money, and a carved wooden phallus hanging from a rope around his waist. At midnight Louis separated himself from the woman he was tangled with beneath a mango tree and went to the altar carrying a small package. The hour after midnight is the most powerful time to perform black magic, and Louis had brought Legba a gift the *loa* would have to notice. The others watched in awe and terror as the *tonton macoute* undid the twine holding the bundle and peeled back the rags covering the murdered old woman's severed right hand.

The others backed away from Louis as he began to dance between the graves in slow, looping circles to a beat heard only inside his own head. One at a time the drummers joined in, their rhythm infecting the other revelers until they were all whirling around the graveyard, their heads thrown back in ecstasy.

Louis danced himself into a trance, dislocating his *gros bon ange* from where it was attached to a man at the nape of the neck, so that Legba Grand Bois Chemin could climb down the Great Tree and enter Louis's heart, once the path was no longer protected by the great good angel of Louis's soul. When Louis felt the heavy sensation of weight press down on his shoulders, and the rush of strength flow into his body, he knew the *loa* was coming into him. Legba took Louis with *la prise des yeux*—the taking hold of the eyes, a style of possession that left the sorcerer fully aware of everything that was happening to him.

It was then that Louis saw his *baka* for the first time.

The creeper lurked at the clearing's edge, watching Louis from the shadows, its eyes a matched pair of glowing red coals. Louis heard the *baka*'s wheezing laughter as Legba began to move Louis stiff-legged toward the bonfire. The fire crackled and roared, it danced and leapt, the spirits within trying to draw Louis into the blaze, to seduce him like *bousins* beckoning him to come into a pleasure house. This was lost on Louis, of course, for it was Legba who controlled his body, yet Legba himself was not indifferent to the fire demonesses. Legba may have lived in water, but he was fiery by nature. The *loa* went to the bonfire and reached into it with his hands—Louis's hands—to draw out two burning branches upon which the most seductive fire spirits danced.

Louis still had the scars to help him remember that night. He hadn't felt the pain then, when his body belonged to Legba, but later, after the *loa* had left him, the agonizing torment of those slow-healing burns!

The *baka* went with Louis when he left the cemetery shortly before dawn. It performed many tasks for Louis, going into the underworld—where it dwelled with the invisibles when not serving the *tonton macoute*—to bring back dead souls to do Louis's bidding. With the *baka*'s help, Louis André became a powerful sorcerer. Within a year of his murder of the old blind woman, he owned a small, pleasant house in Port-au-Prince, where he counted wealthy merchants, numerous captains, a dozen colonels, and even a general among his clients.

Louis's only problem was the greedy *baka*, which required the life of one of the *tonton macoute*'s relatives every year in payment. At first this was of little concern to Louis, who came from a large family and had many brothers and sisters, aunts and uncles, nieces, nephews, and cousins. But as the years passed, Louis's family began to shrink at an alarming rate. The army, disease, and the *baka* moved the André family quickly toward the brink of extinction. Eventually, Louis's remaining relatives guessed what was going on and were among the Haitians most eager to climb aboard a rickety boat and hazard the passage to life in the Promised Land.

The *tonton macoute* began to worry after the *baka* devoured the last of his known blood relatives. If there were no more Andrés to give the *baka*, the creeper would satisfy its fiendish desire with Louis.

There had to be a way to rid himself of the *baka*, Louis reasoned, if only he could figure out the right magic. The *tonton macoute* consulted with the island's most eminent sorcerers, spending all his money and performing many dark deeds before he learned the secret.

Louis sacrificed a black rooster at sunset and put it into a ritual pot called a *govi*, along with locks of his hair, fingernail clippings, rum, and spring water. He washed his clothing in the *govi*, then wore it for forty days. At the end of the forty days, Louis ate a meal from the pot, which made him violently ill. An astonishing mixture came up from Louis's stomach: centipedes, lizards, a scorpion, part of a snake. Louis gathered as much of the mess as he could in a rum bottle that he buried in the yard outside Maman Marie's former house at the next new moon, sprinkling the ground with water that had never been held in any kind of closed container.

The *tonton macoute* summoned the *baka*.

It didn't come.

Louis was free of it—he was almost certain that he was free of it.

Louis decided to join the exodus to Florida. Louis knew of a cousin and at least two nieces in Miami. They would guarantee Louis a few more years in the unlikely event that the *baka* reappeared to demand its annual payment. And Louis had heard that one of the nieces was pregnant. A lucky break! A baby would give Louis a fourth year, if the *baka* came back.

Louis was the only person the *loas* awoke when the fog swallowed the overcrowded sailboat, covering the sleeping passengers like a damp blanket thrown over so many corpses in a Port-au-Prince alley. The fog was an outward manifestation of the invisibles, the swirling mist the breath of Baron Samedi rising up from the world of the dead.

It was important to keep yourself from becoming wet, especially wet with dew. The soul lived in the head, just as spirits lived in the water, and a wet skull was a magnet for maleficent entities. Dew, fog—the one was as bad as the next, Louis André thought, winding the red handkerchief more tightly around his head. Both waters came from nowhere, from the sky, from the invisible realm of the *loas*, the voodoo gods.

The only thing more dangerous than letting your head get wet was being outdoors at noon. This, too, Louis had been forced to endure in the preceding three days, though the straw hat that he'd worn seemed to have protected him. The body casts no shadow at noon, leaving you temporarily without the protection of your *gros bon ange* at midday. Spirits try to take advantage of the midday mortal weakness, swooping and diving through the air, gibbering to themselves as they search for bodies to steal. Why, hadn't an invisible possessed Henri de la Bruyère almost at high noon the previous day? Some of the passengers had tried to hold Henri down, but Louis could see that it was pointless. The raving man eventually succeeded in throwing himself into the water, where he immediately drowned, dragged down by the spirit in his head and the spirits lurking in the menacing blue sea.

That morning the fog seemed almost benign, though Louis knew better. The mist made everything quiet, muffling sounds, covering even the slow breathing of the sleeping passengers jammed into the boat. There was no wind, which was of no consequence, since the craft had lost its only sail in a storm their first day out. Even the ocean swells became hushed, as if pressed down by the weight of Baron Samedi's dense breath, which the first dim light of dawn was turning the color of wool stained with charcoal dust.

Louis heard something in the fog. He turned his head, inclining his ear, to better hear.

The sound was deep and rhythmic, like the heartbeat of a huge whale. Too big to be the *baka*, Louis thought, though it brought little sense of relief.

The throbbing grew louder with alarming speed. Louis heard others stirring from their sleep behind him, but he was too terrified to take his eyes off the place in the fog where the sound was coming from, a monstrous heartbeat, the deep pounding of the *loas*' own voodoo drums. The fog had begun to glow with an eerie incandescence, a reflection of the fiery nature of the angry god hidden behind the mists. Perhaps the sound Louis heard was the heartbeat of Legba himself, the god stalking the watery wastes, Louis's old *baka* creeping along at the Legba's side, both of them searching for Louis, come for the soul he owed them—his soul.

Somewhere high overhead Louis heard three bright, brassy notes, like the chimes the archangel will ring to signal Judgment Day.

Louis stood up—pointlessly, since there was nowhere to go to escape—his head thrown back as he gaped up at the towering prow of the *Atlantic Princess* as it suddenly materialized out of the fog. Water parted gracefully on either side of the ocean liner's bow as it split the waves, moving straight down on the crudely made sailboat—relentless, inexorable, inescapable. The unmistakable mark of Death was upon the ship, its metallic skin festooned with the figures of the souls it had claimed, and the dimmer outlines of the souls it had yet to reap, their eternal energy burned up in the leviathan's belly to drive the floating city of death across the haunted waters. Not even the most desecrated graveyard where Louis André had practiced his black arts could rival the atmosphere of evil emanating from the vessel. The ocean liner fairly reeked with evil, the stench as overpowering as the smell of burned rubber and flesh from a "necklacing" victim in Port-au-Prince. Louis had been a powerful *tonton macoute*, so it was perhaps fitting that death, when it finally arrived, visited him as such a sinister and overpowering apparition.

A more experienced crew aboard the *Atlantic Princess* might have noticed the faint vibration that rippled through the hull when the liner hit the refugees' boat. A more experienced crew certainly would have waited longer after leaving port to switch the ship's radar over into long-range navigation mode. They were only ten miles out of the Port of Miami, steaming at full speed through the foggy, early dawn light, trying to make up for time already lost. The voyage had barely started and the bridge crew's nerves were already frazzled. They had been preparing to cast off the mooring lines the previous evening when the U.S. Coast Guard unexpectedly denied the *Princess* permission to sail. The delay disappointed the passengers and attendant press and deflated the gala bon voyage party. Captain Franchini stayed on the bridge all night in a purple rage, ordering that the ship leave port the minute clearance was granted, as it finally was, at four that morning, when the Coast Guard was at last satisfied that there really were enough life jackets on board for all the passengers and crew.

The collision sent Louis flying through the air. The screams, the throbbing of the ocean liner's engines, the jagged noise of splintering timbers—these things all seemed curiously faraway to Louis as he tumbled weightlessly through the mist, sounds that emanated from a world the *tonton macoute* had already left behind. Louis was on his way to another world, Legba's world, where his old *baka* would be awaiting him. Louis could almost hear the creeper laughing its wheezing laugh at the thought of having Louis to feast upon.

Louis André wasn't even dead yet, but he already had one foot in hell. Of course, the sorcerer had just time to think, feeling the rising heartbeat of the *Atlantic Princess*'s engines deep in his belly, that had been true for many years.

# PART II

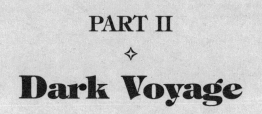

# Dark Voyage

# 9

✧

# The Captain's Dinner

THE PHOTOGRAPH LAMINATED on Dr. Carrie Anderson's identification card bore only a fleeting resemblance to the face she saw staring back at her from the gilded full-length mirror in the *grande salle à manger.*

The ID showed a studious-looking young woman with pale blue eyes and a shock of unruly hair. A pleasant enough face, but certainly not one to turn heads. The woman in the mirror—an elegant, almost ethereal beauty with an expression of mild astonishment on her painted face—could hardly be the same person. Carrie was almost ready to believe herself the victim of an elaborate hoax, to think that she was peering into a fun-house mirror contrived to make her appear neither fat nor thin, but beautiful.

She wore a white gown with a low-cut back and plunging front that exposed more of her breasts than she was accustomed to revealing away from the beach. The dress didn't even make it to her shoulders, leaving her to wonder what trick of the dressmaker's craft kept the bodice from falling to her waist. Bobbie, one of the hairdressers in the *Atlantic Princess*'s salon, had taken her wild tangle of hair, which Carrie usually wore pulled back in a ponytail for lack of anything better to do with it, and piled it high in a way that was disheveled yet chic, like a Gibson girl from the 1890s.

The mirror betrayed no sign of the familiar image of the sober Dr. Carrie Anderson, whose analytical mind was as clear and cool as spring water on the verge of becoming ice. Instead, Carrie saw a creature whose primary substance was not intellect, but flesh—lithe and tawny, part lioness, part gazelle. The most startling thing of all was that Carrie actually *liked* the woman she saw in the mirror.

This must be what it's like when the caterpillar meets itself after becoming a butterfly, Carrie thought. The fact that the caterpillar had not planned to become a butterfly, or even imagined it could undergo so startling a metamorphosis, was entirely beside the point. Perhaps beauty was more than just skin deep. This change, this discovery, this unfolding of an unsuspected secret other life—it seemed more than a mask to be discarded at the evening's end. Yet if this beautiful creature was more than just the disguise of a moment, if she was as real and insistent as Carrie's familiar other self, then which was the genuine article, and which the forgery?

Beyond the entry and down the two symmetrical staircases that curved gently around like a nautilus shell, the *Atlantic Princess*'s main dining room—the *grande salle à manger*—was beginning to fill. Tradition dictated that the captain's dinner be held the second night out of port. The formal gathering was the premiere social event of every transatlantic voyage. The men wore tuxedos, the women gowns and their best jewels. The officers and certain crew members, including the ship's doctor, were expected to be in attendance.

"You look stunning tonight, Dr. Anderson."

Mandy Robsard instantly noticed the distracted expression in Carrie Anderson's eyes. Something was troubling the doctor. And then Mandy knew what it was. Carrie was not nearly as self-possessed as she pretended. She was nervous about the evening ahead, Mandy thought with satisfaction. Mandy, on the other hand, was utterly fearless. She had to be. It was the secret of her success.

"Thanks, Mandy. You look rather stunning yourself."

Mandy ran her hands lightly over her hips, admiring the way her drop-dead-perfect body filled the black sequined gown. She'd invested a lot of time in her body and was used to having it admired. Although her primary job was as editor of the ship's daily newspaper, she doubled as one of the *Atlantic Princess*'s aerobics instructors. She'd signed on for both jobs without informing her employers that she planned to desert the ship as soon as they got to England because of her *real* job, but that was classified information, private, her own business.

Mandy was acquainted with Carrie, although they weren't close friends. She had run with Carrie and Brooke a few times, although she greatly preferred working out to music in the gym. She thought running was a bore.

"Aren't these dresses fantastic? Lord Godwin has thought of everything."

"Good thing. If I had to rely on my own wardrobe, I'd probably be wearing jeans and a white clinic coat tonight."

"Love your hair. And you should wear makeup more often."

Carrie turned her head from side to side, studying Bobbie's handiwork. "I feel like Cinderella on her way to the ball."

"Then I hope you meet Prince Charming."

"I wouldn't be here at all if I didn't have to be. Dr. Hunt would be a lot more at home with this crowd of debutantes and polo players. I wish I could have gotten him to switch shifts with me."

Mandy laughed. "Phil would hate being here even more than you do."

"That hardly seems possible."

"Why, Dr. Anderson, are we just a wee bit nervous?"

"Petrified. I'll be happy to get through tonight without using the wrong fork or committing some other unforgivable faux pas."

"Just relax and have a good time, Doc. Can't you give yourself a pill or something?"

"I'm afraid not."

"Too bad. My God, have you ever seen so much purple

hair? They must go through blue rinse by the truckload in the ship's salons."

"Actually, the passengers are a lot younger than I expected. There are a lot of people in their fifties, forties, thirties. I've never seen so many photogenic profiles at one time in all my life. This must be what it's like to live in Beverly Hills."

"The beautiful people," Mandy said, allowing a trace of sarcasm into her voice. "The haut monde. I'm surprised the press isn't along for the ride. This is tabloid heaven."

"Lord Godwin is adamant about protecting his passengers' privacy."

"Sure he is, but I'd have thought *Hard Copy* or one of the other aggressive gossip rags would have smuggled a stowaway on board."

"It would have to be a stowaway, between the cost and unavailability of tickets. Anyway, you're here. You represent the press."

"Yeah, right," Mandy said, giving Carrie a sideways glance. "The ship's newspaper isn't exactly the *National Enquirer.*"

"Thank heavens for that."

"Actually, I'm not working tonight. A passenger's companion is feeling a little under the weather, so I was drafted to take her place and fill out the table."

"Lucky you."

"Lucky me," Mandy said. "My date for the evening is Monsieur Salahuddin. From the look on your face you must have seen the piece *60 Minutes* did on him."

Carrie shook her head. "I don't have time to watch television."

"He's an Iranian arms dealer and up to his elbows in profiteering from the unending troubles in the Mideast. That's how he made his money. *Lots* of money. I don't even know why he's sailing on the *Princess*. His yacht is nearly as big as this ship."

"You're exaggerating."

"Well, only a little." Mandy's voice dropped to a whisper. "You should see the woman he's traveling with. A complete bimbo."

"I have seen her, Mandy, and she's not ill tonight, at least not as far as I know. She does, however, have one of the nastiest black eyes I have ever seen."

Mandy blinked. Information like that was pure gold. "He hit her?"

"She says she tripped over a pair of shoes and whacked her head against a doorknob. You did not hear any of this from me, by the way. Doctor-patient confidentiality and all that. I'm telling you only so that you'll know to stay out of Salahuddin's reach."

"Bet on it." Mandy checked herself in the mirror a final time, dipping her chin for a surreptitious check of her roots. She had a horror about showing dark roots. "Well, Doc, we're getting to be fashionably late. I'd better find my table. Have fun tonight."

Mandy scanned the room as she descended the staircase, hoping to find Salahuddin and have a word in private before supper. Dinner with Salahuddin was an unexpected bit of good luck, something to put in the bank for later, when her present project was completed.

"Just be careful," she heard Dr. Anderson call after her.

Lighten up, Carrie, Mandy thought.

Alexander Fox stood in the doorway, watching the beautiful woman in the shoulderless white gown make her way carefully down the stairs.

The *grande salle à manger* was filled with beautiful women, but it was also mainly filled, period. Fox stood with his hands in his pockets, scowling, ignoring the people streaming around him. Crowds were high on Fox's list of dislikes, along with shopping malls, poorly scripted computer codes, fast food, driving behind people who didn't know where they were going, American beer, waiting in lines, and dealing with fools in general.

Fox checked his watch. Plenty of time to skip cocktails in the dining room in favor of a trip to the lounge for a dry

Tanqueray martini, up, with two olives. Besides, he didn't see the couple he was interested in in the room below. Since Fox had contrived to sit at their table—nothing having to do with computers was beyond his reach—he'd have plenty of opportunity to study them up close during supper.

The Veranda Grill was deserted except for the bartender. Fox got his martini and took it outside onto the deck that overlooked the pool and fantail. There, Fox could be completely and quite enjoyably alone for a few minutes to think about his next move.

Jack Ketch smiled wolfishly at Carrie Anderson. "Good evening, Doctor," he said, extending his hand.

"How do you do, Mr. Ketch?"

"I couldn't be better," Ketch said. "Now."

Carrie's hand felt warm and firm. No doubt her body was too. He'd seen her running laps around the Sports Deck with the little blond nurse. Ketch worked out daily too, but with the free weights in the gym. The scenery there was better, he thought, thinking of Mandy Robsard sweating in her skintight bicycle shorts and thong. It was funny how seeing a woman in the right kind of clothes was even sexier than seeing her naked.

Jack Ketch was one of those men for whom middle age seemed to be made. His silvering hair gave him a distinguished appearance, and the years had softened his hatchet face, toning down its predatory aspect. He wondered if the attractive Dr. Anderson was attached. She wore no ring on her left hand, not that it would have mattered. One of the things that interested the former policeman about working on the *Atlantic Princess*—after the money, of course, which was quite good—was the opportunity to meet an endless procession of beautiful women. Ketch liked women. He liked them so much that he'd been married three times, each marriage ending because he could not keep himself from wandering. Ketch had never seen Carrie Anderson with makeup on before, and the mascara and lipstick had worked a magical transformation, turning her from a pass-

ingly pleasant wildflower into a gorgeous rose whom Ketch
wanted very much to pluck.

"I don't mind admitting to you"—Carrie nodded to an
elderly man who winked at her as he passed by—"that I'm
about as comfortable in this dress as Queen Elizabeth
would be on Rollerblades."

Ketch had a short, sharp laugh.

"I suppose it's all part of the job," Carrie went on, her
smile pinned firmly in place.

"You'll be fine, Doctor. Just relax and enjoy."

"You're the second person to tell me that tonight."

"Then it must be good advice."

Carrie's laughter was genuine. "I'll make you a deal. I'll
try to relax and enjoy the evening if you promise to come
to my rescue if I start to babble while trying to hold up my
end of the polite conversation."

"It's a deal. Listen," he said in a low, confidential voice,
moving closer to her so they wouldn't be overheard. "I'm
an old hand at this. The secret is to remember that people
are endlessly fascinated with their own achievements, problems, and opinions. If you can manage to let them talk
about their wonderful selves and sit back and smile politely,
they'll think you're the best conversationalist they've ever
met."

"That's scandalously cynical!" Carrie said, pretending to
be shocked.

"I've been around the block enough times to know how
things work. Stick with me, kid, and I'll teach you a thing
or two."

And indeed he would, if she'd let him.

George McCormick recognized Jack Ketch, the chief of
security aboard the *Atlantic Princess*. Lord Godwin had introduced McCormick and his wife to Ketch in the casino
earlier and they'd all had a drink together. McCormick had
liked Ketch well enough, though he was not inclined to
trust policemen very much, including ex-policemen.
McCormick didn't know any criminals who had become

police officers, but he'd known plenty of policemen who had ended up as crooks.

The woman talking to Ketch was a stranger, but a ravishing stranger at that. An actress, McCormick thought, though not one he recognized. A Hollywood starlet, perhaps, a plaything brought along on the trip to amuse an older man, a director or producer having a fling or a midlife crisis. No one knew better than George McCormick how much wickedness there was in the entertainment world. He'd sown his share of wild oats, but that was all in the past now.

On McCormick's arm was his wife, allowing herself to be expertly squired through the crowded room. Nancy McCormick had been having trouble remembering things lately. They had an appointment with a specialist when they got back to the States, something McCormick was dreading. It was difficult to admit, even at age eighty, that the good times were nearly over. George McCormick had developed a visceral understanding for Dylan Thomas's poem about raging against the dying light, though the silver-haired impresario was too suave to do his raging anywhere except within the privacy of his heart.

"Jack, how are you?" McCormick said, his Virginia accent as present in his voice as it was the day he went away to prep school as a boy.

"Fine, George." The two men shook hands.

"You remember Jack Ketch, Nancy. Lord Godwin introduced us in the casino. Jack is the officer in charge of ship security."

"Of course I remember," Nancy said, but George could see the uncertainty in her eyes.

"May I introduce Dr. Carrie Anderson? Dr. Anderson, George and Nancy McCormick."

"Enchanted," McCormick said, for a moment becoming forgetful himself and imagining he was again on the sunny side of fifty.

"You look very lovely tonight, my dear," Nancy McCormick said, holding Carrie's hand protectively between hers, exuding a matronly aura of talcum and violets.

"May one pay that sort of compliment to a young woman these days, especially a young woman doctor?"

"Oh, George! I keep reminding George that new acquaintances don't always understand his sense of humor."

"That's quite all right. And, yes, one may pay a young woman doctor that sort of compliment, at least *this* young woman doctor."

McCormick helped his wife into her chair while Ketch did the same for Carrie.

"I feel like we're in very good hands tonight," McCormick said to his wife. "Here we are, seated with both the ship's physician and head of security at our table."

"That's all very well and good for us, dear, but it's Ricky whose welfare concerns me."

"Ricky is our grandson," McCormick explained.

"He insisted on running off tonight to something called the T Club. He's only ten, hardly old enough to be off on his own for the evening. Do you think he'll be all right with that group?"

"Nancy is an incorrigible worrier," McCormick said, patting his wife's veined hand.

"He'll be perfectly fine, Mrs. McCormick," Ketch said. "Mona Smith, the woman in charge of the program, watches those kids like a hawk."

"The T Club is totally supervised," Carrie said. "It's set up to make preteens feel as if they're being treated as teenagers, but it's still really just glorified group baby-sitting."

"He'll be as safe as he would be at home in his own bed," Ketch said.

George McCormick smiled reassuringly at his wife, but the distant look in her eyes told him she'd drifted off, her mind going wherever it went with such distressing frequency.

From his place at the head table, Captain Vincenzo Franchini kept careful watch over the wealthy and famous personages arriving in the *grande salle à manger*, especially the ones who happened to be female.

Captain Franchini considered himself a great lover and an even greater connoisseur of female beauty. Though Franchini was short for a man, he preferred tall, statuesque women. According to Franchini's classification system, beauty depended principally upon size and symmetry. Just as no small house or ship could be truly beautiful, neither could a small woman possess the bodily presence required to make a completely satisfactory impression. Only tall women could have the sort of eurythmy that transcended mere harmony of proportion.

The way a woman bore herself was also integral. Nothing dissipated the spell cast by physical beauty faster than physical awkwardness. A truly beautiful woman moved with graceful rhythm. She walked into the room with the flowing sweetness of honey.

Manners, too, were crucial. Vulgar speech, poor etiquette, crude behavior of any sort—these were to beauty what an off-key tenor was to opera, a jarring disharmony that ruined everything. Comparing a comely woman with exquisite manners to an equally comely but socially unpolished woman was like comparing a cloud to mud; the difference was not merely in the form, but in the essence. A Venus, the ultimate personification of beauty in Franchini's female classification system, possessed unmistakable soignée, an attitude of sophisticated elegance that cannot be taught, but, rather, wells up from within, the fruit of good breeding and careful education.

Captain Franchini's alertness earned him the honor of being the first in the *grande salle à manger* to see the living embodiment of female loveliness float through the doors and look down on the room, a goddess materialized upon the altar for the multitude to worship.

Franchini, raising a glass to his lips, stopped in midmotion as an electric thrill shot through him, leaving his nerve endings tingling. He'd known she was aboard, but she'd been a recluse since the ship left its harbor. The waiting had served only to make the moment more acutely pleasurable.

"Behold, the living Venus," Franchini said to himself quietly when Nadja Bisou entered the room, lifting his eyes worshipfully toward the living idol.

Nadja Bisou looked down on the dining room, listening as an electric buzz rushed through the crowd like a wind rushing across the waters. It was as though someone had turned on a bright light in a dark room; heads now were turning reflexively toward the light, as if commanded by a power beyond their understanding or control, a force directed entirely by the movie star.

A man at the foot of the stairs turned away from his wife and began to clap. The applause moved quickly through the room, the noise building to a gratifying roar.

The energy that flowed into Nadja from the crowd's adulation was almost palpable. She could feel it warming her, as nurturing as the sun's life-giving rays. She fed on her audiences' affection, drinking it in the way vampires drink in blood, disguising her unbridled lust for it only with the greatest of difficulty. Nadja felt herself grow stronger, the definition of her tall, sculpted body becoming sharper and even more beautiful.

Yes! she thought to herself, looking down at the worshipful crowd through half-closed eyes, greedily soaking in their expression of admiration. The actress acknowledged the applause with a nod and graceful wave. She began to descend into the crowd of ordinary people, an angel descending to earth to dispense grace among mere mortals.

She was the only woman in the room wearing a short dress, a tight, scanty sheath covered with hand-sewn red sequins that sent spears of ruby-colored light shooting around the room as she floated down the stairs. There were many beautiful women present that night, but none had made an entrance half as dramatic. The fact that this, like most things in her life, had been carefully calculated was of no consequence whatsoever. She no longer conformed to the rules others made. Great artists were beyond that. Nadja made her own rules.

Nadja began working her way through the room, exchanging hugs and kisses with various friends and acquaintances. This was not a typical crowd of fans. Many of them had even more money than she, no mean feat. But none had her fame, or her beauty, and certainly none of them had ever won an Oscar. Though she never would have admitted it, Nadja Bisou was proud of the fact that she had not inherited her money but had earned it with the skillful use of her body abetted by her shrewd mind. The illegitimate daughter of a French hotel maid and a Soviet diplomat, Nadja Bisou had invented herself. What Wall Street tycoon or English lord could say that they had been born with nothing and created an entire world and a fortune to go with it out of the strength of their own will?

There were, of course, other assorted celebrities aboard the *Atlantic Princess*, the sort whose names appeared in newspaper "people" columns, garden-variety glitterati. The great ship's inaugural voyage was, after all, the social event of the season. Nevertheless, Nadja Bisou knew she was in a class by herself, a goddess elevated high above those who were merely rich and famous, in a way that was more than just symbolic. Through her movies she had even achieved a kind of immortality. Who else among the passengers aboard the *Atlantic Princess* could make such a claim?

Carrie thought Bisou was even more beautiful in person than she was in the movies. The light danced like amethysts in Nadja Bisou's famous blond hair, making it sparkle and glitter nearly as brightly as her sequined dress. Her mouth was full and painted the deep red of ripe cherries. The actress's Slavic cheekbones were high and prominent. Her large turquoise eyes sparkled and flashed beneath the twin penciled arches of her eyebrows.

The actress stopped two tables from Carrie's. A woman, someone whose face Carrie recognized although she did not know her name, stood up. She and Nadja hugged and exchanged air kisses. Nadja's face registered the consideration of some request. Bisou nodded. Yes, yes, yes. She would think about it. But what had she been asked? To attend some charity dinner? To consider a role? To an assignation later that night? The rumors about Nadja Bisou's diverse love life were so widely known that the details had reached even Dr. Anderson's unworldly ears.

The movie star was only one table from Carrie's now—close enough for her to see that the actress's skin was clear and bright, like a photograph of a fashion model taken under hot bright lights, the flaws later airbrushed away. Except there were no flaws in Bisou's skin. She had to be—Carrie did some quick mental arithmetic—close to forty if not a bit past it. There was no evidence that the plastic surgeon's scalpel had visited her face. No slight enlargement of the mouth, no need to wear the hair carefully arranged to cover almost invisible scars along the scalp line. Skin like Nadja Bisou's was a genetic gift.

Nadja chatted with a man while his wife, who didn't get up from her chair, did a slow burn beside him. Nadja seemed completely indifferent to the other woman's hostility, lowering her eyes a moment to meet the woman's glare before she returned her full attention to the man. Her brilliant smile dimmed not so much as one watt in the course of tacitly acknowledging that the woman wanted to scratch out her eyes.

Nancy McCormick got to her feet and met Nadja Bisou between tables, the two women taking each other's hand.

"Darling," Mrs. McCormick said, and kissed Nadja Bisou on one cheek. "George and I were delighted when we heard you were on board. Where have you been hiding yourself?"

"I've had the most frightful headache," Nadja said, touching the sides of her head with her fingertips and letting go of Nancy McCormick to go embrace her husband.

George McCormick introduced Nadja to Carrie and Ketch. Carrie was too stunned to do more than nod, though Ketch took the movie star's hand with great relish and kissed it, which should have looked silly but somehow didn't.

"You should consult with Dr. Anderson if you are unwell," Mr. McCormick suggested.

Carrie smiled weakly and forced herself to take several slow, deep breaths. She needed to get a grip. Yet how could she, when Nadja Bisou was sitting at her table?

Mandy Robsard's words echoed inside Carrie's head. Maybe Carrie should have given herself a pill.

"You can have all the tokens you want. Just come back if you need more."

"Thanks," Ricky McCormick said, accepting the paper cup filled with copper-colored coins.

"It's kind of fun to find a game you like and learn to beat it," the woman said from behind the golden bars in the teller's window. "You can win free games here, just like at a mall arcade."

Ricky had quickly become bored with the T Club. There were about thirty other kids there, but he didn't know any of them. The deejay was playing music Ricky liked, but he was too shy to ask any of the girls to dance. Besides, he didn't know how. Apparently none of the other boys did either. They avoided the dance floor as if it were paved with hot coals, preferring to stand in the corners or bug the deejay, who let them into his booth to look at the electronic gear and CD collection. The girls, on the other hand, stayed on the dance floor, dancing in groups. When a pretty young woman tried to organize a dance lesson designed to entice the boys onto the dance floor, Ricky decided it was time to split and slipped unnoticed out the door.

Captain Nemo's Arcade was two doors down the hall from the T Club. Ricky had the place to himself when he wandered in. He played Mortal Kombat for a half hour, then tried out a half dozen more video games before he discovered the Pinball Wizard Room.

Lord Godwin had a passion for pinball and had made sure that the ship's arcade offered a serious selection of the best machines. There were thirty machines in the room, everything from vintage fifties games to the latest high-tech models with digital sound and blazing lights. The old machines were from Lord Godwin's private collection. He'd pulled off a minor coup in 1981 when he heard Philippine President Ferdinand Marcos had decided pinball was evil and decreed that all machines be destroyed; Godwin was able to buy several hundred rare vintage machines for pennies on the dollar.

Ricky played Vampira, one of the newer games, for half an hour, then moved over to an older machine called Jungle. He quickly figured out how to rack up bonus points, and after his fifth token he began winning "free" games. Jungle kept him enthralled for more than an hour, but by then some of the kids from the T Club had discovered the arcade, along with some bossy teenagers. Ricky poured his remaining tokens into the pocket of his jeans and decided to find something else to do.

The captain's dinner was only about half over, Ricky noted, checking his watch. Thank God he hadn't had to dress up and go to that! He had at least another two hours to roam the ship. Ricky had told his grandparents that he was going to the T Club, but he hadn't said he was *staying*.

Ricky was getting to go to Europe because his parents were getting divorced and his grandma was worried that he was depressed. The divorce bothered Ricky, but it wasn't that big a deal. His father had never been around much anyway. If anything, he'd seen more of his dad once he started splitting his vacations between his mother's and father's homes.

Ricky went outside and leaned over the railing. The wind was in his face, and he could hear the faraway rush of water parting around the ship's hull. How deep was the ocean beneath the *Atlantic Princess*? A mile? Five? Ten? Images of great white sharks, electric eels, and killer whales swam through Ricky's mind. Even when he tried to scare himself, it was impossible for him to work up much of a sense of fear aboard the ship. The *Atlantic Princess* was too big for him to feel threatened by the monsters of the deep. Being aboard the ocean liner was like going to sea in a floating city.

Ricky went over to the light outside the stairway and took a ship's map out of his back pocket. That's how big the *Atlantic Princess* was: Every passenger was given a map to help them find their way around the cavernous vessel. This would be an excellent time to go exploring, with the grown-ups and probably most of the crew tied down at the captain's dinner.

Ricky turned the map around in his hands, orienting himself. On one side was a cutaway diagram of the ship and its thirteen decks as viewed from the side. On the reverse side were smaller deck-by-deck diagrams. The areas outlined in red—red-designated areas were restricted to crew members—interested Ricky the most. The chain locker— that sounded neat. Is that where the anchor chain was kept? There was a parking garage deep in the ship's bow. That would be worth seeing. Ricky was into cars, and he suspected there might be some Porsches and Ferraris to check out aboard the *Atlantic Princess*.

Ricky carefully folded the map, stuck it in his back pocket, and started down a staircase that led into the deepest bowels of the ship, wondering what mysterious secrets he might encounter in the restricted decks below.

# 10

✦

# Nicoletta's Diary III

**I** WAS BORN on Bellaria, in the eastern Mediterranean. On maps, Bellaria is a comma writ backward. The island's main body is the sort of irregular circle a child might draw, with a tapering peninsula that curves away to the southeast, a tail pointing toward the modern state of Israel. The island is a little more than half the size of Rhodes, its landmass occupying only three hundred and fifty square miles.

Bellaria is an idyllic place. Blessed with a climate of perpetual spring, the unceasingly moderate weather is never too hot or too cold, too wet or too dry. The low mountains forming the island's spine are richly forested with pine, cypress, juniper, and cedar. The rolling hills comprising the rest of the isle are unsuitable for intensive farming, but provide lush pastures for sheep and horses.

Bellaria is noted for its vineyards, its groves of fruit trees, its fertile coastal fields of vegetables and flowers. These, in their turn, keep the island's famous apiaries brimming with rich, aromatic honey. The forests are filled with deer and wild boar, the sea and rivers with fish, the sky with fowl. Little wonder that illiterate Christian peasants believe Bellaria once contained the biblical Garden of Eden.

The Greeks, the wise architects of our Western civilization, ruled Bellaria for five hundred years. Succeeding them on the island, as elsewhere, were the Romans, who possessed the isle for nearly a millennium. The ruins of a dozen Greek and Roman temples can still be found on Bellaria, including the magnificent Temple of Apollo, one of the best-preserved Doric structures in existence, second in splendor only to the Temple of Concord in Sicily's Valle dei Tempi.

Tunisian Berbers overran Bellaria in 905. The island remained in Muslim hands until 1190, when Duke Leonardo di Medusa besieged Bellaria for the King of Naples during the Third Crusade. Richard I, *Coeur de Lion*, had recently captured Cyprus, Acre, and Jaffa, but fell short of his goal of returning Jerusalem to Christian rule. Duke Leonardo was more successful in his campaign. The Neapolitan warrior lured the Berber navy into a sea battle and annihilated them, then stormed Bellaria and sacked the Muslim fortress. The King of Naples named my ancestor Prince of Bellaria and our island became the Kingdom of Naples's easternmost outpost.

My great-grandfather laid the cornerstone to Castle Misilmari upon the ruins of the Berber citadel, which had been built upon the ruins of the Roman citadel, which had been built upon the ruins of the Greek citadel, which had no doubt been built upon the ruins of the citadel built by whatever lost civilization held the island before the dawn of recorded history.

Castle Misilmari took shape on a high hill overlooking Bellaria's natural harbor on the eastern coast, occupying the declivity where the isle's comma head and tail were joined. Beneath the fortress's battlements, the land fell away in a gradually sloping crescent that ended in a narrow strip of white sand, with ample area in between for the port city of Misilmari to take root and grow. Mountains came down to the shore in the distance to the southwest and northeast—Mt. Mistras and Mt. Mikinai—protecting the castle's flanks.

Castle Misilmari boasted one of the finest libraries outside Rome. Our scriptorium housed thousands of rare volumes of classical learning. Many of these priceless books and scrolls had been preserved since antiquity by the Arabs, until their libraries were captured during the Crusades and subsequently shipped to Castle Misilmari to help satisfy the di Medusa family's thirst for knowledge.

The Misilmari scriptorium nearly proved to be too rich a treasure trove of learning. Philip IV considered turning away from the Muslim East to instead attack Christian Bellaria, all in hope of carrying off the di Medusa library! Philip was, of course, utterly without scruple. The French king had already installed his puppet pope, the bogus Clement V, in Avignon, and suppressed the Knights Templar— good allies of the di Medusa family—and put their Grand Masters to death so that he could confiscate their wealth. Philip openly lusted after the contents of Castle Misilmari's scriptorium. Fortunately, the King of Naples convinced Philip that there was far greater loot to be captured in the Holy Land, and so Bellaria was spared.

There were two towns on Bellaria: Misilmari, the island's only city; and Riesi, a fishing village on the island's north shore.

Although the island nominally belonged to Naples, Misilmari was an international city. Walking through the bazaar, one was as likely to encounter a Greek, Turk, or Syrian as someone from Naples. The air in the markets and wharves was filled with polyglot chatter. While the residents of Riesi were mostly Italian and Greek, the population of Misilmari was a jumbled combination of Italians, Greeks, Persians, Jews, Syrians, Arabs, Slavs, Berbers, Lombards, Tartars, and Negroes, all come to do business and grow rich on the frontier between East and West.

The city was divided into four quarters. The Neapolitan Quarter was behind Castle Misilmari, affording it the most protection from attacks by sea. This district had the grandest villas and was the least crowded. It was here that the Neapolitan merchants and administrators who served my family lived. The Greek Quarter was to the southwest, on the sunny side of the castle. This quarter housed the best physicians, apothecaries, and teachers, most but not all of

them Greek. The Christian Quarter was northeast of Castle
Misilmari. It was a fairly rough-and-tumble district, where
assorted Lombards, Frenchmen, and Spaniards dwelt; not
an especially unsafe district to be in after dark, but far from
being as desirable as the Greek and fashionable Neapolitan
districts.

The final neighborhood was the Khalisa Quarter. *Khalisa*
is Arabic for "pure." When the Berbers were driven out,
the Khalisa Quarter was where the island's remaining
Muslims congregated. By the time I was born, the Khalisa
was pure in name only, the neighborhood's Muslims greatly
outnumbered by Persians, Syrians, Jews, and Negroes. The
Khalisa was the least desirable district in which to live—it
was closest to the harbor and contained the warehouses and
wharves, as well as the city's markets, bazaars, and shops.
It was, however, the liveliest quarter in the city. The
Khalisa was a tangle of noise and traffic, a place where cut-
purses, prostitutes, and moneylenders mingled with warriors, sailors, and wealthy Arabian merchants.

The Khalisa's cobbled streets were narrow and winding
even by the city's medieval standards. A visit there was an
experience for the senses—especially the sense of smell.
Jostled by the pressing crowds, nearly assaulted by merchants selling rugs and silver bracelets and Gypsies wanting
to tell my fortune, I would smell oranges, fish, the delicious
aroma of roasting coffee beans, *torrefazione*, dung, garlic,
sweat, roasting chicken, flowers in the flower-seller's cart.

I would wander in the Khalisa when I needed to clear
my mind after too many hours at my studies. The sights,
sounds, and smells never ceased to refresh, and the danger
there thrilled me. I grew up in dangerous times, and despite
Bellaria's natural beauty, it was a dangerous place, though
perhaps not as dangerous as most. As *principessa* of the island, I never left Castle Misilmari without an armed escort.
To an adventurous youth, danger and adventure are indistin-
guishable.

My family had treated Bellaria's diverse residents with
equanimity, borrowing a page from the ancient Romans,

who allowed the peoples they subjected to keep their gods and their customs, so long as they rendered unto Caesar that which was Caesar's. Yet the danger lurking in the Khalisa was of a more insidious variety than we suspected. Far better it would have been for the di Medusa family to have put aside the velvet glove and ruled instead with an iron fist, for in our misguided benevolence we unwittingly nurtured vipers.

I was a precocious child, as thirsty for knowledge as any of my forebears were.

At age ten I had read enough of Aristotle—in the original Greek—to decide that henceforth I would believe in only those truths that I could verify through empirical observation and experimental proof. This was after I started to read the Bible in Latin, and discovered the absurdity of island lore linking Bellaria and the Garden of Eden. As it says in Genesis:

> *The Lord God sent him forth from the Garden of Eden, to till the ground from which he was taken. He drove out the man; and at the east of the Garden of Eden he placed the cherubim, and a flaming sword which turned every way, to guard the way to the tree of life.*

My family's castle guarded Bellaria's eastern shore, not angels wielding God's fiery sword. Indeed, there were no flaming swords to be found anywhere on the island, a fact I verified during a systematic survey of the island's topography when I was eleven. And, of course, Bellaria was not divided by the rivers Pishon, Gihon, Tigris, and Euphrates. Even someone with a superficial education knows those rivers are found in ancient Mesopotamia.

Bellaria had its share of wise men, and these were my teachers. I learned astronomy from my father's astrologer. I learned chemistry and pharmacy from Castle Misilmari's alchemist, a mysterious German named Magnus Hebrus, whose hair and beard were shock white. The island monastery was home to the revered Thomas of Misilmari. Brother Thomas served as my tutor in philosophy and supervised my overall education during his daily visits to the castle. Though remembered now only by antiquarians and classical scholars, Brother Thomas was one of the most renowned savants of his day. His translations of Aristotle from Arabic greatly influenced St. Thomas Aquinas's *Summa Theologica*.

Scholars from Athens and Alexandria were regular guests at Castle Misilmari, some traveling months over dangerous seas and bandit-infested land routes to visit my family's scriptorium. We even entertained a few Arab visitors. It was only fitting, my father said, since it was the Arabs who had preserved so much of the classical wisdom that the superstitious Christians had labeled as heretical and attempted to destroy after the Roman Empire collapsed in the West.

Under Brother Thomas's enlightened tutelage, I studied the seven liberal arts—the *trivium*: grammar, rhetoric, and dialectic; and the *quadrivium*: arithmetic, music, geometry, and astronomy. And, of course, alchemy, the precursor of chemistry, with Magnus Hebrus, who devised the first table of the elements. I even began to write my own *summae*, an encyclopedic treatise I envisioned as encompassing the entirety of mortal learning.

My *summae* was to remain regrettably uncompleted.

On the thirteenth morning of the fifth month of my fifteenth year, I awoke to find a squadron of Muslim men-of-war standing to outside our harbor, riding the waves like a flock of gulls, the galleys' low black prows bobbing up and down all the way to the horizon.

My father ordered the defensive chain be pulled across the harbor's mouth, effectively locking out the belligerents' ships. His cannoneers limbered up their weapons. Though primitive, the guns were deadly enough to fire again and again at an easy target. The enemy ships quickly raised their sails and disappeared beyond the horizon. The men on the battlements cheered as if they were witnessing a great victory, but I knew the ships would return soon enough.

My father sat up most of that night, talking to his captains and his brother, my uncle Rocallo. Various strategies were discussed. It was agreed that invaders might succeed in landing their troops on Bellaria, though certainly not in the harbor. The enemy's options would be limited even if they succeeded in getting ashore. The castle was thought impregnable to land attack. As long as the citadel's cannon commanded the harbor, supplies could be brought in that would make it possible to continue a siege indefinitely.

I was allowed to sit in attendance through this long conference, though I kept far back in a corner, virtually invisible in the shadows. I knew it was not my role to participate, but to listen and learn. Later, when the candles were burned down and the various strategies had been proposed, debated, and refined, my father indicated that I should remain behind as the others left him.

"What do you have to add, little *principessa*?" he asked, pouring me a small glass of mullioned wine.

"You know I am unschooled in the ways of war, Father, but . . ."

"We knew there would be a 'but,' Nicoletta," my father said with a smile. "Brother Thomas keeps us well informed of your studies. You have spent considerable time of late reviewing Julius Caesar's *Gallic Wars.*"

"Very well, my liege." I bowed my head. "I disagree with Uncle Rocallo on the subject of Artinoos."

I had cut straight to the heart of the most sensitive issue. Artinoos was the most powerful merchant on Bellaria and related to most of the Muslims on the island. He was also their unofficial leader, as my father would not allow them to have an actual mullah stirring up trouble in the Khalisa. My uncle and Falcone, the captain of our men-at-arms, had almost come to blows over Artinoos during the war counsel.

"I side with Falcone," I said. "Artinoos should be brought into the castle and held hostage. Treat him as an honored guest, if you wish, Father, but keep him where he can do you no harm. Let Bellaria's Muslims know that Artinoos will be put to death at the mere suspicion that they are providing aid and succor to the invaders."

"Taking Artinoos hostage would brew controversy in the Khalisa at the time we need it least. Our brother is correct. The prudent course is to treat our Muslim citizens with deference, lest they forget they are our friends."

"I know the Khalisa, Father. They will respect best a show of strength. Moderation will be interpreted only as weakness. You should force Bellaria's Muslims to convert to Christianity so that they will have as much to fear from the sultan as your Christian subjects."

"And what of those who refuse?"

"Those who refuse to renounce the Prophet should face summary execution."

My father looked at me a long while before speaking, as if taking a new measure of me. "We are surprised to hear such harsh advice from our young daughter."

"Harsh circumstances require harsh action, Father."

"A man's faith is his most precious possession, daughter. I cannot force so many of our good citizens to surrender that which is most dear to them. And even if I did, I doubt more than a handful would choose conversion over death."

"Then so be it."

My father walked to the hearth and jiggled one andiron with his foot, causing the fire to kick up again, a shower of sparks ascending the chimney like firebirds released from a cage.

"Would you have a tyrant for a father, Nicoletta?"

"Better a live tyrant than a dead saint."

"Do not chop logic with us, Nicoletta," my father said sharply. "Need we remind you that it is not our own head we most fear losing, but yours?"

"I beg your grace's pardon," I said as I kneeled.

"These matters weigh heavily upon us and put our tempers to trial," my father said, raising me up. "Come. The hour is late, a time fit only for owls and ghosts. Off to bed with you. May your dreams provide a sweet escape from the heavy troubles of the waking world."

My father fell ill soon after that. The midsummer winds had shifted around to the north, bringing a pestilential miasma from the Turkish mainland, or so my father's Greek physician claimed. My father began to speak of a persistent headache. Days passed, the headaches lingered. He grew progressively weaker until one morning he lacked the strength to rise from his bed.

It is hardly possible to relate to a modern sensibility the sense of raw anxiety that pervaded the entire island when the king fell ill. Lorenzo was more than our leader. My father was our shield and our sword against the enemies who would flay the skin from our living bodies. Some peasants feared the very grapes in the vineyards would fail to ripen with the king ailing, that the procession of seasons would stagger without God's holy warrior to watch over us, maintaining the cycles in the seasons, and the secret, half-forgotten rhythms in nature worshiped in pagan times.

My father's illness created a delicate problem. With King Lorenzo incapable of vigorous governance, much less decisive military action, the di Medusas' rule of Bellaria was more vulnerable than at any time since my great-grandfather sailed from Naples to conquer the island.

The Roman emperors had the most practical attitudes about preserving imperial power. They never hesitated to do whatever had to be done, regardless of whether the blood that spilled on their feet belonged to a father, mother, sister, brother, wife, or some more distant relative.

At fifteen, I was too much the naïf; I knew too little of the world to be able to appreciate the merits of the unflagging boldness that shies from no act, no matter how unspeakable. Yet even now my heart is not so devoid of mercy that I would be able to kill my own dear father—even if I knew he was certain to die anyway—in a Machiavellian bid to capture political power and save our kingdom. Or so I tell myself, though it has been many centuries since I have had a moment's remorse about killing anyone.

Magnus Hebrus, my father's alchemist, sent an apprentice to my chambers to request an urgent private audience with the *principessa*. I followed the apprentice—a thin young man with singed eyebrows who stank of sulfur—deep down inside the castle to where the alchemist kept his lair.

I found Magnus bending over an alembic of boiling liquid, his face bathed in weird green light. Magnus's usual interests were elements and minerals, yet he seemed to have developed a sudden interest in biology. Lined up on the bench were six wicker cages holding rats. It was apparent even from my cursory inspection that the vermin were part of a progressive experiment. The rat in the first cage exhibited the full vigor of life, standing on its hind legs, grooming its face with its front paws. The rodent in the sixth cage was dead, lying on its back with its feet up in the air, its mouth open, a tiny pink tongue protruding past ugly yellow teeth. The creatures in the intervening four cages demonstrated progressive stages of distress.

At Magnus's elbow was a human skull, the skin mostly rotted away from its time in the crypt. A significant portion of hair—black and flowing, like mine—remained attached to the grisly object. The foul-smelling artifact had evidently belonged to a woman, someone who had died young, before her hair turned gray.

Magnus gave the apprentice a cross look. The young man scampered out of the room, leaving us alone.

"There is something I must ask you to bring me," Magnus said without preamble, turning from the bubbling beaker. The alchemist was not the sort of man who wasted time with idle pleasantries.

"As you wish, Master Magnus. You have but to ask."

The alchemist pushed a stray lock of his long hair back behind an ear. His good eye glittered with malice. "Bring me a clipping of your father's hair."

I was not easily shocked, but what Magnus asked stunned me.

Magnus snorted and looked down at me past his crooked nose, regarding me with a baleful look as I stared up at him. "I am no witch, *Principessa*."

"Then why, pray tell, do you make such a strange request of me? Surely you know how some ignorant and superstitious person would regard your request."

"I believe that your father is being slowly poisoned."

I felt like a ship's sail when the wind suddenly disappears, the canvas gone slack, the ropes limp, the wooden prow sinking heavily into the water.

"If I am right, *Principessa*, a sample of King Lorenzo's hair may help me identify the poisoning agent. If I can do that, then perhaps I can find an antidote or devise an antidote. I will leave it to others to concern themselves with who is responsible for such a treason, if that proves to be the case."

Magnus leaned forward and looked closely into my eyes. "How are you feeling yourself, *Principessa*? Have you been experiencing headaches or any sensations of intestinal distress?"

"No!" I grasped the alchemist's table to steady myself, startling the rats. The ones that were still capable squealed in alarm.

"You must be extremely careful, *Principessa*. Watch what you eat, what you drink, even what you touch. A skilled poisoner can be very subtle. I know of one who poisoned the inside of a pair of kidskin riding gloves. The victim absorbed the poison through her hands and died very soon afterward in great agony."

"But how could the sultan manage such a crime? Only Christians serve in Castle Misilmari."

"He would need an accomplice," Magnus said. "Perhaps if we can identify how King Lorenzo is being poisoned, the materials and methods will point toward the traitor." He laid his hand on a huge leather-bound book with Arabic writing on its spine and an ivory skull inlaid into its cover.

"Poisons have been the subject of my experiments here of late. This ancient poisoner's bible is part of the scriptorium's locked files."

"What locked files?"

"The ones in the secret alcove."

"What secret alcove?"

Magnus's only answer was an inscrutable smile. "Using this evil book as a guide for these rats, I have sought a substance whose effects on its victims are similar to those we have seen in our king."

"And that relic from the tomb?"

"A Sicilian courtesan poisoned several years ago with arsenic. I have discovered a way to detect trace amounts of certain poisons in the hair, where residues become concentrated. That is why I need a sample of your father's hair. I wish to analyze it."

"All right," I said. "I will do as you ask."

"One more thing, *Principessa*. You must not breathe a word of this to anyone. Our only hope of success is that they do not know we know."

"It seems a wiser course would be to tell as many people as possible so that the entire castle would be on its guard."

"That might encourage the poisoner to put a quick finish to what has been a long and circuitous drama. Your father is strong enough to give us a little time. I calculate he has at least another week."

I blinked back the tears, reminding myself that I was a student of philosophy, that I had learned to control emotions. I had to retain control, if not as a philosopher then as a *principessa*.

The walls of Castle Misilmari had ears that remained hidden even from me. At least that is the explanation I have concocted to dismiss the sequence of events that followed swiftly on the heels of my interview with Magnus Hebrus.

The alchemist was trampled to death by a runaway team of horses the next morning during a visit to the Khalisa to collect a shipment of supplies.

The alchemist's apprentice survived the "accident," but his body was found floating in the castle moat at nightfall. He had become overwhelmed with grief, or perhaps complicity in his master's death, and flung himself from the battlements. Either that, or he was silenced by Magnus's assassins to prevent him from telling what he might have seen or heard that morning in the Khalisa.

But that was only the prelude to the coming requiem. Just after vespers the next evening, Brother Thomas administered the last rites to my father.

"Do not divide the loyalty of our people with a fruitless search for poisoners who will disappear like water sinking into the sand," my father said as Uncle Rocollo and I leaned close to hear his almost inaudible whisper. "The traitors have done their work. Now, you must remain strong and look toward the greater menace."

"Poisoners?" my uncle demanded with nervous rage.

"Yes," Father whispered, his voice as transparent as a mist floating over dew-soaked grass. "I turned to Magnus for help—"

"Traitors!" Uncle Rocallo cried.

"Begging your worship's pardon," Mikarios, my father's Greek physician, said, reaching out to restrain Rocallo without quite touching him. "This agitation can bring no benefit to our august patient. Can you not see how this conversation wearies him? He needs every bit of his strength, sirrah, to keep Death at bay."

Rocallo withdrew with an embarrassed apology. He stood outside the chamber door, conferring in angry whispers with Falcone, the captain of the guard, until Brother Thomas went out and led them both away.

I fell asleep holding my father's feverish hand. I was awakened when the watchman called midnight. My father's hand was cool and dry. I thought his fever had broken, and I silently praised God. I'd made a hundred desperate promises to the Lord since Magnus's death, that I'd give up philosophy, that I would take the vows of a holy order, if only my father were spared. And now—Hallelujah, Jesu!—the crisis was past.

I quietly called for the serving girl to bring a candle into the bedchamber.

"Father?"

The maid hurried in from the antechamber, but stopped at the foot of the bed, the candle shaking, tears rolling down her cheeks.

I had made a most regretful mistake.

My father, King Lorenzo Vittorini di Medusa III, was dead.

I arose after a sleepless night, put on mourning clothing, and went down to the great hall, where my father's body lay in state.

As was the custom of the time and climate—embalming being almost unheard of in Europe until the Americans showed up during World War I—my father's corpse was to remain unburied for but a single day. At sundown, his noble corpse would be carried to the Castle Misilmari chapel and, after the funeral Mass, be interred beneath the chapel in the di Medusa family crypt.

While the islanders lined up outside the closed portcullis to pay their respects, the first three hours after dawn were reserved for the family alone. In my grief an hour passed before it occurred to me to wonder why Uncle Rocallo was not beside me, mourning his brother the king. Rocallo was not noted for the swiftness of his mind, but I had never known him to show his older brother disrespect. Had the poisoners who had killed my father turned their attentions to my uncle?

I motioned one of the guards over—not one of those in the honor guard around my father's bier, but a sergeant stationed at the door. The man was nicknamed Tondo because his belly was round, like a circular tondo painting.

"Have you seen my uncle?" I asked, putting my hand on Tondo's arm to save him the trouble of trying to genuflect before me.

"I thought you knew, *Principessa*."

"If I did, I would not ask."

Embarrassment rendered Tondo's ruddy complexion even more red, so that his head resembled a big red apple with an unruly thatch of yellow straw on top. "You will be happy to hear, *Principessa*, that Lord Rocallo is at this moment busy torturing the traitors who poisoned King Lorenzo."

I do not know what Tondo thought about me running out of the great hall—probably that I thought I might miss out on the fun. Holding my black skirts high, I flew down the steep stone stairs that wound around and around, corkscrewing into the castle's nether depths.

The dungeon had been seldom used during the years of my father's rule. On Bellaria, petty criminals were punished with fines, which in turn enriched our state's coffers. More serious infractions were dealt with by banishment from the island, and, in a few extreme cases, beheading, a quick and just retribution for murder and rape. Indeed, my father's court should have been renowned for its humanity in an age when those who stole bread, fished in the lord's river, or missed church could have their skin flayed, be broken on the rack or wheel, have their eyes gouged out, their faces branded with red-hot irons, their bodies pulled or hacked apart. One could rarely enter a European city when I was a girl without seeing the rotting corpses of hanged men and women swinging from gibbets outside the city gates, the walls festooned with heads on poles and quartered bodies impaled on spikes.

The guards at the dungeon gates were too startled at my sudden appearance to try to stop me as I burst past them to see the nightmare transformation my vengeful uncle had worked in the hours since my father's death.

The dungeon was far beneath the ground, unlit by natural light, cold, damp, the air as brackish as the water in a strangled bog. The ceiling was low and broken by many vaults that divided the room into numerous claustrophobic chambers. The meager light that came from the flickering

torches seemed to multiply the shadows rather than illuminate the grim scenes of human misery and debasement.
Here and there in the blackness were firepots filled with hot
coals that glowed eerily, like the eyes of demons peering
out at the damned. The coals in the braziers were not to add
warmth or light, but rather to augment certain cruel tor-
tures. Heating over them were branding irons and metal
rods of various shapes, designed to be inserted into places
where they would cause unimaginable agony.

Where had so many cruel instruments of pain come
from? Had they been there all along, or had they simply
materialized—a gift from Lucifer—when the opportunity
for so much wanton cruelty suddenly gave them purpose?

The prisoners cried out to me to have God's mercy on
them—the ones who had not had their tongues torn out
with red-hot tongs or slit down the middle. A single small
voice separated itself from the moaning and wailing. "Help
me, *Principessa* . . ."

I did not know the scullery maid's name, but I recognized her face, though how this was possible I do not
know, since her nose and ears had been cut off. Around her
waist was an iron girdle that was chained to the floor. She
held her upturned hand in appeal to me—the hand a hand
no more, but a swollen, bloody pulp of mangled flesh. A
heavy metal box was attached to her left hand, from it protruding the parts of numerous screws and gears designed
with fiendish brilliance to reduce a human hand to a useless
lump of torn flesh and splintered bone.

My uncle was in the middle of the dungeon, bending
over something on the floor.

"*Principessa*, help me . . ."

One of the torturers—a Spaniard from the Khalisa—
stepped out of the shadows, wrapped his massive hands
around the scullery maid's neck, and began to choke her.
Before I could order him to release her, I heard the sickening sound of cartilage crushing. The maid's eyes bulged so
much that they nearly came out of their sockets. I will

never forget the pitiful expression on her face, staring at me, begging me for mercy in her last moment of life.

"Rocallo!" I screamed, feeling the veins bulge in my forehead.

My uncle stood stiffly at the sound of my voice, clenching and unclenching his fists with his back toward me. He shifted his weight from his left to his right foot and back again, as though in response to some fiend possessing his body, a shuffling golem responding not to hearing his name but rather to the howling of his own bestial wrath.

"Rocallo!" I shouted again, hearing anger and despair in my voice. "What in the name of God have you done?"

My uncle turned around. I will never forget the look on his face. His eyes were filled with a wild, fanatical light, as mad as the eyes of the Prophet's opium-eating warriors. And his smile—his chilling smile was one of the most horrid things I have ever seen.

Rocallo's blouse was unfastened at the neck, the sleeves rolled up. The bodice was stained crimson, and dripping, as were his hands up to his elbows.

"Mikarios," Rocallo said, trembling as he spat the physician's name from his mouth as if it were loathsome offal.

The outline of the physician's body emerged from the nightmare scene like a picture coming slowly into focus. He was on the floor at Rocallo's feet, his head turned to one side, a mask of indescribable pain and horror frozen on his blankly staring face. Mikarios's body had been cruelly broken. His elbows and knees were bent at unnatural angles, his repose impossible according to the rules of ordinary human physiology.

Mikarios's body seemed to be draped over a pillow on the stone floor in a pool of blood that continued to spread, touching Rocallo's boots. The longer I forced myself to stare at the grim visage, the more details emerged. Mikarios was bent over nothing but his own entrails. Rocallo had disemboweled him, slitting open his belly and dragging out Mikarios's intestines—no doubt while Mikarios watched, though Death had mercifully released him.

"Mikarios was the traitor who poisoned your father," Uncle Rocallo said, pleased with himself.

Poor Mikarios. Who can know if he had really been involved in the plot to poison my father? Not even I, with all my preternatural powers, though my intuition tells me he was innocent of any crime against my family.

The physician's intestines seemed to be moving under him as I stared at his broken body in mute horror. At first I thought it a trick of the flickering torchlight. But no, they *were* moving with a wet, creeping motion. Mikarios's greasy, bluish bowels—their surface brightly tattooed with the red lines of blood vessels—continued to leak from his body. I knew Mikarios was dead, and that his body possessed no will of its own, yet his intestines seemed strangely alive, a writhing mass of snakes covered with bloody mucus that slithered toward the legs of their murderer.

The dungeon, damp and cold a moment earlier, was suddenly hot and airless.

I remember a vague impression of falling. One of the torturers—the Spaniard?—caught me before I collapsed on the stone floor. I realized this when I awakened in my apartments and found the two bloody handprints on my dress.

I summoned Rocallo to my rooms after the funeral Mass. It took him nearly an hour to respond, but that only gave me more time to master my temper. He arrived with Falcone trailing behind.

"What, pray tell, do you think you accomplished in the dungeon?"

Rocallo's proud smirk dissolved into an expression of uncertainty.

"He learned the identity of the traitor who murdered your father," Falcone said when Rocallo seemed unable to find his voice.

"Mikarios was the poisoner," Rocallo said. "I do not

doubt that others were involved. They will be caught and suffer a similar fate."

"Who employed Mikarios to poison my father?"

"What do you mean?" I could see the thoughts turning over in Rocallo's slow mind. It was like kicking over rocks and watching centipedes scramble.

"Employ simple logic," I said, knowing full well that such elementary exercises were beyond Rocallo, who could hardly read. Unlike my father, who had grown up on Bellaria and was, like me, rigorously tutored in the classics, Rocallo spent his youth in Naples under the mistaken idea that he would receive a more sophisticated education in Italy.

"What had Mikarios to gain by poisoning my father if not twenty pieces of silver for playing Judas? Surely you do not think the physician hoped he could make himself king of Bellaria?"

Rocallo and Falcone just stared at me.

"If Mikarios was the poisoner, which I doubt, he must have been in the employ of the sultan, who hopes to sow chaos among us by killing our king. But the poisoner, whoever he or she is, would not have communicated directly with the sultan. The traitor must have worked through the sultan's agent on the island, probably someone in the Khalisa who may well know crucial details about the Muslim invasion plans. Did Mikarios reveal the identity of this agent before you killed him, Uncle?"

Rocallo looked at the floor and said nothing.

"Why do you question that Mikarios was the poisoner, *Principessa*?" Falcone asked. "He confessed his crime."

"Because torture is crude and unreliable, Falcone. What poison did Mikarios use?"

Rocallo and Falcone exchanged a confused look.

"Did he concoct it himself, or was it supplied by one of the sultan's agents?"

They could not answer because they did not know.

"Don't you see the mistake you have made? A prisoner

will confess to anything if you put him in enough pain. You have learned nothing of use."

"I learned who killed your father."

I laughed bitterly. "Put to torture, *you* could be made to confess to my father's murder, Uncle."

"Never!"

"I know you are a brave man, Falcone, but I could say the same of you."

Falcone, to his credit, did not bother to deny something so obvious.

"A skillful interrogation, Uncle, would have ferreted out corroborating evidence, established an inexorable chain of logic and fact detailing precisely who was involved; why; what they did and when; how much they were paid; what poisons were employed; and how they hoped to make their escape. And even more important than that, when and how our enemies intend to capitalize on our king's death."

Rocallo stubbornly shook his head.

I moved to within several inches of my uncle and stood looking up at him through narrowed eyes. "Furthermore, Uncle, if Mikarios was the man who poisoned my father, he died much too quickly. I would have killed him by inches over the course of many, many weeks, so that his final days would themselves seem an eternity in hell."

I turned away from them then, leaving them dumbfounded. They were not bad men, but they were simple men. Rocallo and Falcone were soldiers, not philosophers. Their role was to fight, not rule. They had stepped beyond their usual arena, only to discover themselves quickly lost.

"It is too late to worry about any of that now," I said, looking out over the harbor. "We must turn our attention to the future. Our energies would be better spent preparing for the invasion, which must now be imminent."

"Let me worry about Bellaria's defense, Niece."

I whirled around, my eyes filled with fire.

"Need I remind you, Lord Rocallo, that I am *principessa* of Bellaria?"

"You need remind me of nothing, *Principessa*," Rocallo

said, bowing his head slightly. I very much wanted to slap the patronizing smile off his face, but I managed to keep my temper in check—barely.

"It pains me to frame this in a crudely legalistic argument, Uncle, but I became regent of Bellaria upon my father's death."

"I am afraid I have no choice, niece, but to rule as regent until you reach your majority or marry."

I looked again to Falcone. I could see the turmoil behind his eyes. He was weighing us both in the balance, and I suppose it was to his credit that he had not decided to instantly side with an old friend. When I spoke I addressed my words to Falcone, a polite way of telling him I appreciated the position he found himself in—and that I would be grateful if he gave me reason to be.

"It is fortunate that I know my uncle loves me, Falcone, or else I would think that his words smack of treason."

"If you were older, Niece, you would realize you are too inexperienced in worldly matters to see us safely through these dangerous times."

"I may be inexperienced, Uncle," I said, my eyes still on Falcone, "but I have a quicker mind than anybody on this island save Brother Thomas. Superior strategy formulated by a superior intellect will save us from defeat at the hands of a numerically superior enemy." I shifted my eyes to my uncle. "Just as it would have saved us from the blunders you made in the dungeon."

"A girl who faints at the first sight of blood is not capable of leading us into battle," Rocallo scoffed.

The change in Falcone's eyes was subtle but unmistakable. I had nearly convinced him, but my one fleeting expression of weakness was to prove my undoing.

Falcone turned and walked to the door, looking back at Rocallo. "Excuse me, my liege, but we have much to do."

Rocallo grinned at me, then followed.

I awoke to the smell of smoke and burning pitch. Throwing a cloak around my shoulders, I ran out onto the balcony overlooking the courtyard. Thick black clouds were boiling out of the doors and windows in the storehouses built against the castle's eastern wall. A watchman stumbled out of the west storehouse, gasping for air and coughing.

Falcone was running across the courtyard at a trot, carrying his sheathed broadsword in his strong right hand.

"I couldn't find the fire, sir," the watchman said when he'd momentarily stopped coughing. "It must be in the cellar."

"Falcone!" I shouted.

The captain glanced up briefly, waving me off with evident irritation. He had no time to coddle a frightened girl in the midst of an emergency.

"They must have dug a mine beneath the wall!" I shouted.

Falcone stopped abruptly and stared up at me, realizing I was right.

"To arms!" Falcone shouted. "The Muslims are upon us!"

As if in response to the captain's order, there was a deafening roar as an entire section of battlement collapsed, releasing a cloud of smoke, dust, and sparks that quickly reached my balcony, making it impossible to see anything. I heard their shrill, trilling battle cry of the Prophet's warriors.

I grabbed a small battle-ax from a display of armor in the hall outside my apartments, then threw open the door to a room filled with cowering serving women. "To arms!" I cried. "It's better to die fighting than be raped in front of your dying husbands and carried off as concubines."

None of them budged, though their wailing increased. Women! I thought with disgust. No wonder Falcone had thought me incapable of ruling the island.

The courtyard was chaos. Everywhere I looked my men were being overwhelmed and butchered. The enemy continued to stream into the castle through the breach in the wall. I could hear the portcullis being raised and the boom of a battering ram against the main gate.

Falcone stood on the chapel stairs. "Rally on me, men!" he cried. A dozen desperate soldiers, a pathetic remainder of our once-strong garrison, pressed close to their captain. Some of them were already grievously wounded, but I could see they were cheered by his presence, as if the force of his personality alone could protect them against the overwhelming odds. He saw me in the doorway. I raised my ax in salute to his bravery.

"Let us show these heathens a little Christian steel," Falcone shouted. "Forward for Christ and Principessa Nicoletta!"

Falcone led his men at full tilt into the onrushing horde, swinging his two-handed broadsword above his head in a wide, deadly arc.

It was the last I saw of Falcone.

Our cause was plainly lost. The only question for me was whether I should follow Falcone's example and escape defeat by dying in battle. As tempting as that was to me at the moment, capture would be the even greater humiliation.

I was slipping along a covered walkway on my way to the scriptorium when I saw Rocallo. He was standing alone in a doorway across the courtyard, a vague, befuddled expression on his face. A company of warriors in turbans spotted my uncle and started toward him. Rocallo may have been a fool, but he was no coward. Raising high his sword, he stepped forward smartly and met the approaching typhoon of flashing steel.

In the scriptorium, I dashed to the fireplace and pulled down on the gargoyle's right wing. It didn't budge.

The sound of feet running down the hall outside the scriptorium froze my breath. But the feet ran on by, followed a moment later by an even greater number. I heard the Muslims' battle cry and the crash of metal against metal.

I pulled the gargoyle's wing with all my strength. There was a dull click somewhere within the stone wall. The wing dipped downward, cocking the counterweights that swung the stone wall out several feet, a space wide enough for a single person to slip into the passageway beyond. I only just managed to get a candle started before the counterweights completed their circuit and swung the wall closed behind me. A second after that, the invaders crashed into the scriptorium, but by then my presence was safely concealed by a thick stone wall.

The passage was cold and damp. The walls were covered with moss, the floor slippery, angling steadily downward through the living rock for what seemed an impossible distance before it finally leveled off. I hurried along, my candle sputtering in the darkness, unarmed now except for the dagger I carried inside my dress. I drew out the razor-sharp silver spike and held it in front of me with my right hand.

The smell of the sea grew steadily stronger as I felt my way along the precarious subterranean passage. Soon I could hear it, too. Tiny sea creatures scuttered out of the way of my feet and peered out at me from the cracks and crannies in the walls. Better crabs than rats.

And then I remembered.

My *summae*!

The treatise was back in my apartments. There was no question of my going back. The hidden door opened only one way. My father, my kingdom, my *summae*—I had lost everything!

The tunnel ended in a natural sea cave whose entrance was completely hidden during high tide and virtually invisible the rest of the time. I found a small sailboat in the cave, as my father had promised many years before in preparing me for what even then he knew might one day come to pass. The single mast was unstepped so it could clear the low ceiling. There was a box aboard containing sundry supplies and garments, along with two wooden caskets filled with jewels, treasure enough to pay my way to safe haven—all the way back to Naples if need be.

"Wise Father," I whispered.

I began to cry then, tears not of grief but of rage. If Falcone and the garrison had chosen to follow me instead of my dim-witted uncle, all of this might have been avoided. If I had been born my father's son, they would have followed me.

"Damn them all!" I said to the sea, knowing that she would bear me even as my own subjects had thrown me down because an accident of birth had brought me into the world a female. But what of my sex? I thought of the women cowering together in the castle, too cowardly to wrestle away for themselves any small measure of control over their destiny, even if it was but the power to choose to die.

"Damn them *all*!" I swore again, and this time I meant them all—every man and woman among them.

I stripped off my shoes, threw them into the boat, and hiked up my nightdress. I managed to push the boat down the tongue of sand into the water, scrambling in after it. I lay flat in the boat so it could drift clear of the overhanging branches and vines that had so perfectly masked the sea cave. The tide was too high, however, and the boat became stuck, so I dragged my way, hand over hand, through the verdant tangle.

Castle Misilmari and the surrounding town were lit by flickering lanterns and campfires, but there was no general conflagration. The invaders were smarter than that. There was nothing to be gained in destroying what they had so easily conquered. And the scriptorium would be safe, since unlike my fellow Christians, the Muslims respected learning and never sacked libraries in the cities they conquered. They might even find a place on its shelves for my *summae*. Perhaps I would be fortunate enough to retrieve it myself after I reconquered the island.

I waited nearly an hour before stepping aboard the mast, hoping the tide would carry me farther from the shore and any Muslim men-of-war that might be riding anchor in the darkness.

It was a moonless night, and studying astronomy had made the constellations seem like old friends, the only friends I had besides the sea as I set out alone from

Bellaria. I turned the prow north toward the mainland. It was a beautiful night for sailing, though a tempest would have better suited the turmoil in my heart. Instead, there was only a clear sky, a gentle wind, and a *principessa* traveling *à la belle étoile*.

The benevolent sea carried me away from the dangers that lay behind me. As for the dangers that lay ahead, I would attend to them as they arose.

# 11

✧

# Table Talk

NANCY McCORMICK WAS staring at the flowers.
It was a lovely arrangement. Balanced. Graceful. In no way overdone or vulgar. Indeed, the buds and greenery in the crystal bowl at the center of the table were a bit understated. That was the mark of real artistry, her husband liked to say: understatement. One held back enough to hint that more complex truths lay beneath what could be glimpsed on the mere surface of things. It was true whether you were talking about theater, music, or flower arranging.

Nancy had a passion for flowers. She would put on a sun hat and gloves and lose herself for hours in her gardens. Begonias. Daisies. Baby's breath. And of course roses. Nancy McCormick's roses were famous in Richmond. Tulips in the spring. The hothouse in winter—it wasn't *really* gardening, but at least provided fresh-cut flowers for the house. Fortunately, winter didn't last long in Virginia, unlike in New York City, where she and George had been compelled to spend too much of their time when he was still producing Broadway shows.

Nancy looked up from the flower arrangement and—who were these strange people? The fact that she had become accustomed to sudden and dramatic mental lapses hardly made them any less terrifying.

*"A certain amount of memory loss is unavoidable and normal."*

She remembered the doctor's words well enough, even if

111

she couldn't recall his face, where she'd seen him, or when. Nancy knew the problem extended far beyond what could be labeled "a certain amount" of forgetfulness. She almost looked forward to her appointment at the Mayo Clinic when they returned from the Salzburg Festival. The truth would be difficult, but in a certain sense not knowing was even worse. The Mayo doctors would examine her, and then, with faces as solemn as judges', pronounce her sentence, mouthing the dreaded A word.

The night suddenly came back into focus, Nancy McCormick's awareness of place and context returning as quickly and unexpectedly as they had departed.

Nadja Bisou, the movie star, was trying to cajole George into producing her Broadway debut. Bisou needed neither George's money nor his expertise. It was his good name she hoped to use, Nancy thought, though George would never let anybody take advantage of him that way, not even someone as beautiful as Bisou.

Nadja Bisou's most recent films had not been successful. The actress was an exceptionally beautiful woman, Nancy thought, studying Bisou's perfect skin as the actress flirted with George. How perverse that Hollywood could consider Bisou "old"! The theater had a more forgiving nature. Nadja Bisou would make a wonderful Lady Macbeth, Nancy thought, if her talent had enough depth for serious acting.

Nancy's husband caught her eye. He flashed Nancy a silent appeal for her to rescue him from the actress.

"When can we expect to see you again on the big screen, Miss Bisou?"

"I've decided to take a hiatus from filmmaking, Mrs. McCormick." The glitter in Nadja Bisou's eyes was anger disguised. "There are so few good parts for women these days."

"We seldom go to the movies anymore," Nancy said, wistfully fingering her pearls. "They're either too violent or too juvenile—or both."

"Motion pictures have degenerated to mere spectacle, although they never were much more than that."

Nancy and the others at the table turned toward the small child-woman resting her delicate hands on the back of an empty chair. She was strikingly attractive, and her Italian accent gave her voice a musical quality. It was almost as if the girl were singing, Nancy thought, giving the newcomer a friendly smile.

The sound of conversation and the Strauss waltz the orchestra was playing in the background seemed to drop away all at once, leaving the *grande salle à manger* silent and empty except for the darkly beautiful woman.

She was small, barely more than five feet tall, with hair as black as a raven's wing swept up on her head. She had the face of an antique doll, her skin was a translucent white, the color of ivory, the color of sun-bleached bone. Carrie's first impression was that she could hardly be more than sixteen. But her eyes gave her away. The woman's eyes—their color the iridescent green common in cats but seldom seen in humans—were entirely too knowing to belong to a child.

She was even more beautiful than Nadja Bisou, Carrie thought, though her beauty was of a more subtle variety. If Nadja Bisou possessed the kind of beauty that hit a man in the forehead like a two-by-four, then the younger woman's beauty was the sort that pierced a man's heart like one of Cupid's golden arrows, the blade so sharp, the pain so sweet, the victim would continue to stagger forward for some distance, unaware that he'd been mortally wounded.

The woman wore a long-sleeved gown of black watered silk with a slight train that pulled along on the floor behind her. The dress was scooped in front to reveal the tops of her breasts, which were full and as creamy white as her face. Her magnificent emerald necklace echoed her Tyrrhenian eyes, with an emerald cocktail ring and earrings to match.

There was nothing cruel about the angle of the stranger's

slightly raised left eyebrow, and no hint of scorn in her Mona Lisa smile, yet Carrie sensed an unmistakable chill to the tiny young woman's perfection, as if a brilliant artist had carved her out of icy stone. And what was it about her that made Dr. Carrie Anderson feel so ill at ease? Maybe it was that Carrie disliked being reminded of so many unpleasant truths about herself: that her biological clock was ticking; that she had neither husband nor child; that she was suddenly—and why did it continue to be such a surprise?—getting older in ways that no honest person would call better.

Or maybe it was something else, Carrie thought, watching the darkly beautiful child-woman, a sensation in the pit of her stomach that felt unaccountably and unacceptably close to desire.

George McCormick had not written poetry since his days at Harvard, yet looking down at the dark young woman made him want to pen lines of verse. If McCormick were to describe her in a poem, he would invoke images of the moon, visions of dark queens found within a deck of tarot cards, ravens, weeping willows, midsummer nights spent wandering aimlessly, lost and alone amid ruined Grecian temples and whose oracles fell silent in ancient times, when the old gods died.

It took McCormick several moments to notice the young man standing slightly behind the woman. Hardly a suitable companion for such a beauty, McCormick thought. The man was tall and extremely thin, with the hint of dark circles under eyes that held a look that seemed quite close to open despair. With his sunken cheeks and long hair, he would have been at home amid a small circle of esthetes; surrounded by millionaires, movie stars, and royalty in the *Atlantic Princess*'s *grande salle à manger*, the woman's consort appeared merely alienated and pained.

"Today's films are mere spectacle," the petite beauty repeated, smiling serenely at McCormick. "And spectacle is, of course, the lowest and least artistic form of drama."

"Most people today would find Aristotle's standards too rigid," McCormick said, picking up her allusion to Aristotle's *Poetics*.

"Perhaps if the moguls in Hollywood were as well read as you, sir, they would be capable of drawing finer distinctions. Permit me to introduce myself. I am Principessa Nicoletta Vittorini di Medusa."

George McCormick accepted her proffered hand and lightly touched his lips to it, breathing in her intoxicating perfume.

"And this is my companion, David Parker."

A real Italian, Nadja Bisou thought, listening to the woman's accent. There were so many phonies aboard the *Atlantic Princess*, but Nadja's ear was infallible.

Nadja thought Principessa Nicoletta was extremely sexy, if you liked child-women. Nadja did.

Drugs, surgery, exercise, outlandish diets—Nadja Bisou had tried them all in her pursuit of eternal youth. None of these things had made the years melt away faster than a beautiful young lover!

Ketch stood up straight and tall, smoothing his tuxedo.

There was something rare and special about Principessa Nicoletta, something beyond what Ketch could put into words. There didn't seem to be anyone else in the room—in the world—but Nicoletta when Ketch looked at her.

And her beauty!

Beauty was a much-overused word, Ketch thought, once you saw someone like Nicoletta. Besides, words could only approximate what you saw with your eyes, not how it made you feel in your belly. And looking at Nicoletta made Ketch feel like a stallion who had been shut up too long in his stall.

She couldn't possibly be as young as she looked.

Not that it mattered to Ketch.

\* \* \*

"May I ask if you are David Parker the pianist and composer?" George McCormick asked.

"I am," Parker said listlessly.

Carrie had thought Parker's hand felt unnaturally warm. Perhaps he was ill. That would explain the feverish look in his eyes.

"We had the very great privilege of attending the premiere of your opera in New York," Nancy McCormick said.

"An outstanding work, Mr. Parker. I wish you could have been there."

"I had intended to be there, but I . . ." His voice trailed off.

"Mr. Parker has been ill," Principessa Nicoletta said.

"I'm sure Dr. Anderson is an excellent physician, if she can help."

"Flattery will get you everywhere, Mr. McCormick," Carrie said with an embarrassed laugh. "But really, Mr. Parker, if there is anything I can do to help you, please do not hesitate to drop in to the infirmary anytime to see me."

David looked at Carrie without speaking for so long that she felt her face turning red. No matter how sick the man was, it was no excuse for the overtly hungry look in his eyes.

"Thank you, very much," David finally said. The act of expressing these simple words visibly depleted his meager reserves of energy. "Perhaps I shall take you up on your kind offer."

"I hope you will do us the honor of performing for us sometime during the voyage, Mr. Parker," Nancy said.

"Perhaps," he said laconically.

"Oh, do say you'll play something, David," Principessa Nicoletta said brightly. "Perhaps some Mozart."

Carrie watched what little blood there was in David's bloodless face drain away. Nicoletta had inflicted some invisible hurt on David Parker. Perhaps he hated playing

Mozart, although Carrie could not imagine anyone disliking Mozart's music.

"The audiences love your opera," Nancy said. "As did we."

"Very much so," McCormick added. "And rarer still, the critics love it."

Parker did not answer. His eyes seemed to study intently some invisible flaw in the tablecloth.

"There are so few truly serious musicians in America today," Principessa Nicoletta said. "I told David he should flee America before he discovered that he was the last serious composer left there."

"But America is filled with people who care passionately about music," Nancy protested mildly.

"We are going home to Europe," Principessa Nicoletta said in a dreamy voice, ignoring Nancy McCormick. "Europe is the mother of Western culture. How can David aspire to create immortal art unless he drinks deeply from the one true wellspring of culture?"

"I'd say Europe would be more properly described as the cenotaph of Western culture." The eighth and final member of the dinner party arrived. He motioned for the others to remain seated and pulled out his chair.

Carrie was relieved that Principessa Nicoletta was able to laugh at the stranger's rude remark—a musical laugh, though there was something strange about it, a shifting, diminishing melody written in a minor mode.

"Would someone please define the word 'cenotaph'?" Ketch asked lightly.

"A cenotaph is the stone used to mark a tomb," Nicoletta explained.

"I'm George McCormick." McCormick's smile looked somewhat forced as he extended his hand to the latecomer. "This is my wife, Nancy."

"Hello, all. I'm Alexander Fox."

Oh, my God, Carrie thought, smelling the gin on his breath even from where she sat. Not *him*.

\* \* \*

Fox cut his steak, nodding at the blood that oozed out onto the plate. Rare, exactly as ordered.

"You know, Mr. Fox, I've recently become an admirer of your talent with computers."

"Thanks," Fox said, cutting off another piece of steak, his eyes going back and forth between his dinner and Jack Ketch. The ship's security chief had been shooting him funny looks ever since he sat down. He obviously knew. "Maybe we can have a drink sometime," Fox said with a grin, deciding to twist the knife to punish Ketch for his heavy-handed coyness. "I might be able to give you a tip or two about keeping the *Atlantic Princess*'s computer system safe from tampering by unauthorized individuals."

"I'll look forward to our private chat."

Ketch's smile was arctic. Fox guessed Ketch would like nothing better than to put him in handcuffs and kick the shit out of him. The ex-cop had a bad record when it came to roughing up suspects. The last incident had been serious enough to force Ketch into early retirement. Fox knew all the details. He had Ketch's confidential personnel record downloaded onto the laptop computer back in his cabin, along with files on most of the passengers and crew.

"I saw you this morning up on the Sports Deck," Fox said, looking past Ketch to Dr. Anderson. "You much of a runner?"

Carrie shrugged and looked away.

It was the third time Fox had tried to start a conversation with Dr. Anderson, but she wasn't having any of it. Fox guessed Ketch had told her how Fox had hacked into the ship's reservation system to "steal" reservations. Her opinion of him would be different if she knew the truth.

Fox glanced at David Parker, who sat staring off into space. He hoped Parker didn't share his interest in Carrie Anderson. He liked the doctor, even if the feeling wasn't mutual.

And what of Principessa Nicoletta Vittorini di Medusa? She worried Fox on several levels. You could hardly lift a finger without creating an electronic record that someone clever could trace, yet Principessa Nicoletta had the most unnaturally blank life of anybody Fox had ever run a search on. If it weren't for a handful of database hits—which could have been plants, if she were very clever—Fox wouldn't have believed she existed at all.

Principessa Nicoletta caught Fox looking at her and gave him a smile that made his stomach tingle. It was almost as if she knew what Fox was thinking, although he was, of course, far too practical to believe in any of that ESP stuff.

"Ladies and gentlemen," said Captain Franchini, rising to his feet. "It is one of the most sincerely proud moments of my life to welcome you, as your captain, aboard the *Atlantic Princess*."

Applause interrupted the captain, who acknowledged it with a sharp little bow. The cordless microphone in his hand assured that even the most elderly people could hear the flourishes of Captain Franchini's voice in the far corners of the cavernous, fern-festooned dining room. He looked taller than usual in his crisp dress whites, the effect aided by the lifts in his shoes.

Franchini's eyes found Nadja Bisou. He wanted especially to impress her. And the little beauty at Nadja's table. Principessa Nicoletta Vittorini di Medusa. They had never met, but Franchini would remedy that soon enough. Perhaps they would become more than friends? Though she was small, there was something quite alluring about her. Yes, she was most definitely in need of the captain's special attention.

Franchini noted Dr. Anderson's glare. American women—they baffled Franchini. They led the sexual revolution, but now they considered it harassment when a man told a woman she had a shapely derrière or nice breasts. It made no sense.

"Rather than make a few remarks, as is customary during the captain's dinner, I would, with your kind permission,

like to make a brief toast and cede the floor to the man we
have to thank for being aboard this magnificent ship tonight."

Captain Franchini held up his hand to forestall the applause until the completion of his introduction.

"The word that best describes our host on this voyage is
'visionary,' for what is a visionary besides someone with
the genius to see beyond the horizons of ordinary mortals,
the ken of his sweeping gaze taking in nothing less significant than the outline of the future?"

"Hear, hear!" cried several English-accented voices.

"Ladies and gentlemen, it is one of the most profound
honors of my life to present to you the gentleman who
charted the historic course for this vessel, rescuing her
from an ignominious end in a Far East scrap yard and
personally escorting her back into service as the most elegant ship to ever set out across the North Atlantic. I give
to you the man history will one day recognize as the sav-
ior of the most refined and exclusive mode of passage between the continents of North America and Europe. Ladies
and gentlemen, *mesdames et monsieurs*, Lord Bryce
Godwin."

Mandy's hand shot under the table to intercept Monsieur
Salahuddin's wrist as his fingers began to creep around her
thigh. Drunken pig, Mandy thought. She had tried to be
nice to the Iranian, thinking it could pay dividends later on,
but she'd about had it. If he tried to grope her under the
table one more time, she was going to deck him.

"Excuse me," Mandy whispered to the purple-haired
dowager seated next to her, pushing back her chair. If
Godwin was going to make a speech, this was as good a
time as any to powder her nose. She'd already had enough
of his duplicitous propaganda inflicted upon her.

The audience in the *grande salle à manger* rose as one
to celebrate Lord Godwin. The roar of applause was so
loud it was almost alarming, the noise multiplied beyond its

natural volume by the rich wood paneling, the hammered metalwork, the etched glass.

The ovation lasted nearly five minutes, a seeming eternity. Saving the former *Esprit de France* from the smelting furnaces had transformed Bryce Godwin into the living patron saint of transatlantic travel for wealthy aficionados.

Lord Godwin waited for the applause to die down, first patiently, then with evident embarrassment. He was not the kind of man who craved displays of approval. Lord Godwin had gambled his fortune and honor on the *Atlantic Princess*. He prayed only—and he did pray—that his luck would hold long enough to make good on the corners Keiko had forced him to cut in order to get the ship out of dry dock in time for it to make its sold-out first voyage.

"Ladies and gentlemen, please! Ladies and gentlemen!"

Lord Godwin saw a thin young man get up and slip away from his table. It was David Parker, the brilliant but reclusive composer. The display really was going on far too long.

"Ladies and gentlemen, please!"

Lord Godwin had to call for order a half dozen times before the audience at last fell into respectful silence.

"I welcome you aboard the *Atlantic Princess*. But more important than welcoming you, I salute you, for you have chosen the sea over the sky, the gentle roll of the ocean swell over the jarring bump and shudder of the midair turbulence one encounters while trapped within those abominable contraptions known as aeroplanes."

Renewed cries of "Hear, hear!" and "Bravo!" erupted around the room, followed by a second sustained ovation.

Lord Godwin struck the perfect tone, Keiko thought. A pompous English lord was exactly what the ship needed to give it the proper brio. Especially with so many rich Americans on board. Americans were such snobs! They were nearly as bad as the Japanese.

Of course, the real money with this sort of ship was to

be made in the Pacific Rim, where the wealth of the twenty-first century would be concentrated. Lord Godwin had already said he wasn't interested in helping with Keiko's plans for a sister ship to the *Atlantic Princess*, which would sail out of Los Angeles or San Diego, but she'd think of a way to convince him. And if she couldn't, her silent partners could. That would all come later. They needed a successful maiden voyage and then a successful first year. If Godwin could get them through that, Keiko could take it from there—with or without him. There were other English lords to be had on the open market if circumstances required that Bryce be forced out of the picture.

"I salute you, fellow voyagers, because in booking passage upon the *Atlantic Princess* you have told the world that you refuse to be herded through an airport like cattle in a stockyard, ultimately driven into a claustrophobic aluminum cylinder in order to be hurtled through the troposphere at unnatural speed, packed cheek by jowl with your neighbors on either side, afforded less space than was granted immigrants traveling in steerage one hundred years ago."

More cheers, whistles, and cries interrupted the speech. The atmosphere had become as raucous as a baseball game or soccer match. It was as if the old home team, Money and Social Standing, had finally managed to overcome several generations of disrespect to stage a world-championship rally aboard the *Atlantic Princess*.

"Let others hurry. Let others rush through airports, jostled by crowds, only to stand and wait for their luggage, assuming it actually arrives, battered and scuffed, carried not by careful porters but hurled into conveyance systems that chew it up and spit it out. But not you. No, my dear friends, you will never again allow yourself to be treated in such tawdry fashion, now that an alternative exists. And let me just briefly emphasize that the alternative now does exist, despite the United States Coast Guard bureaucrats, who unnecessarily delayed our sailing by proving themselves unequal to the task of keeping straight the mountains of paperwork that they required us to submit."

"Give 'em hell, Lord Godwin!" a voice with a thick Texas twang called out, much to the crowd's amusement.

Lord Godwin draped his long frame across the podium. Brushing a long forelock of hair away from his distinguished brow, he gave his audience a smile that bespoke all the qualities the *Atlantic Princess* was designed to reflect: breeding, class, money, unflappable self-assurance.

When the latest eruption of applause subsided, Lord Godwin lifted his champagne glass head high. A flurry of motion throughout the room accompanied the tinkling of crystal and china as voyagers picked up their own flutes.

"I propose the first toast to you, and to your impeccable taste in having chosen to be here tonight aboard the most refined and opulent ocean liner to ever traverse the trackless depths of the North Atlantic."

Keiko Matsuoka raised her champagne glass to her lips.

The lights went out, plunging the *grande salle à manger* and every cabin, office, and compartment aboard the *Atlantic Princess* into darkness.


Ricky McCormick pushed open the steel door marked CREW ONLY, jumping when it banged against the metal bulkhead, making a sound like a hammer hit on a steel drum that echoed through the cavernous parking deck.

There were only a few lights on in the room, dim red bulbs covered with glass domes that were in turn protected by metal cages. The shadows and the eerie red light made the room appear even spookier than it otherwise would have. Ricky almost turned around and left, half expecting the devil himself to pop up beneath one of the glowing lamps, brandishing his pitchfork.

The outlines of cars were clearly visible in the strange ruby-colored gloom. Porsches, Jaguars, Mercedes—was that a vintage Ford Cobra?

Ricky went down the stairs, walking quietly to keep the soles of his sneakers from slapping loudly against the corrugated metal steps.

The cars were densely packed in the hold, with narrow aisles between the vehicles barely wide enough to allow Ricky to pass. Most cars were parked bumper-to-bumper, so that Ricky had to make his way slowly along until he found a space wide enough to squeeze through to the next aisle. The goal, of course, was the Cobra in the center of the garage, with stops along the way to check out several Corvettes and Ferraris.

Ricky was sliding between two Mercedes when the lights went out, frightening him half out of his wits.

Keep cool, he told himself, vowing not to go exploring again without a flashlight.

Ricky was trying to orient himself in the darkness, thinking that the door was somewhere behind and above to the left, when the door slammed shut, leaving him too frightened to move, too frightened even to scream.


Mandy Robsard was returning from the powder room when the *Atlantic Princess* lost its electrical service, plunging the hallway leading back to the *grande salle à manger* into total darkness.

"Jesus Christ!" she exclaimed, by no means the only person to express a startled expletive. She reached into her purse for the penlight she always carried, along with a notebook, pen, and container of Mace. The ship must be in even worse condition than she had thought, although this was one instance when she almost would have gladly been wrong—especially with the *Atlantic Princess* fast approaching the middle of the North Atlantic Ocean.

Somewhere in the darkness a woman sobbed.

"For heaven's sake, calm down," a stentorian voice ordered.

Mandy turned away from the dining room. She had no more time for the blue-haired ladies at her table. Or for

Monsieur Salahuddin. She flashed her penlight once briefly, then began to hurry toward the exit onto the open deck. Mandy had work to do—her *real* work.

# 12

✧

# Nicoletta's Diary IV

THE LAND ROUTE to Constantinople led straight into the Taurus Mountains. The lush, rolling coastal hills—a precinct of vineyards, pastures, and groves of fragrant cedars—gave way to twisted, stunted pines and brown stubble. We climbed steep, dangerous passes, rising toward the distant Anatolia plateau. The desolation became so great that it was like riding through hell, a dead land where nothing lived save snakes, scorpions, and the occasional vulture that drifted overhead, patiently awaiting our transubstantiation into carrion. Our horses carried us across mile after mile of blasted wasteland, with neither water to drink nor trees for shade.

My captain was an expatriate Frenchman named Jacques Diderot, the scion of an aristocratic family who had fled to the Latin East years ago after killing a royal favorite in a duel. Diderot's sword was for hire, but not his honor. A deal once struck remained a deal until he'd fulfilled his end of the bargain, or died in the trying.

My guards paid little notice to the grim countryside. They were much accustomed to the hard travel and the privations of war. Our horses seemed less immune from despair. My own mount was a magnificent black stallion named Mars, bred for charging through stirrup-high grass with an armored warrior on his back. He plodded along with his head down, sulking, showing no sign of the high spirits that had led the horse trader who'd sold him to me to caution that no woman could control such a beast.

Diderot had warned that the journey would be arduous, but it was far more trying than I had imagined. I was an excellent horsewoman, but I had never spent day after day upon a sweating stallion, trying to outride the sultan's marauding Muslim cavalry. Instead of an eiderdown mattress, I slept on the stony ground. I looked on the ordeal as an opportunity to harden myself physically in the way the rigors of studying philosophy had hardened me mentally. Conquering Bellaria would require strength of mind, and I was determined to prepare myself.

When we were not playing cat and mouse with the Muslim cavalry, the trip was excruciatingly boring. How I longed for a book from the Castle Misilmari scriptorium! A good book was the one precious commodity my otherwise foresightful father had forgotten to supply in the sailboat maintained as means for a desperate escape.

I fought off ennui by sketching out plans as we crossed Anatolia. I gave the matter furious consideration and decided that there was no way I could accomplish my aims without the assistance of a worthy husband. Bitter gall that I, whose trouble had been authored by meddling men, should have to rely upon a man—and an unknown man at that—to achieve my revenge.

I would return to Naples and marry well, with the help of my king and kinsman. My husband would have to be a lord with great wealth and many men-at-arms, a chivalrous warrior who would never permit such an affront to the honor of his wife's family to go unpunished. With the King of Naples's blessing—and the loan of part of his fleet of war galleys—we would return to Bellaria and drive the Muslim invaders into the sea.

Though I had never been given to fantasy, I found myself lapsing into reveries where I imagined myself standing on the battlements of the recaptured Castle Misilmari, holding aloft the severed head of Artinoos for my men to cheer. These visions were so vivid that I could feel the oil in the dead man's greasy hair and see the harbor, where the corpses of my enemies—blackened and bloating in the hot

Mediterranean sun—bobbed like corks on the water, food for flocks of sea birds that swooped down to tear off strips of rancid flesh, while below, in the water, the fishes, snails, and eels burrowed into their bellies.

Late one afternoon we rode into a field of poppies that fell away in front of us, the beginning of a wash that led to a wide, muddy river flowing slowly in the far distance. Our exhausted horses smelled water and began to strain against their bits, wanting to run to the first open, moving water we'd seen in two weeks.

"This is a good place for trouble," Diderot muttered, looking right and left as the horses, which we could barely rein in, cantered down between the bluffs.

I neither saw the archer nor heard the arrow that simply appeared in the middle of Diderot's neck. He opened his mouth, but the only thing that came forth was a spray of blood. He tumbled backward off his horse, which continued to run along with the rest of our company, now traveling at full gallop.

Doubling my hands around Mars's reins, I darted a look over my shoulder. Diderot's horse shot past me, pounding toward the river, fast now that it was free of its armored rider.

The archer stood high in his stirrups with a bow in his hands, the string vibrating after its release. I was just realizing that he must have gotten off a second shot, when the horse and rider on my left went down in an explosion of flying dirt.

"Ride for your life, my lady," a yellow-haired soldier nicknamed Mustard yelled, then wheeled his horse to meet a trio of the attackers riding hard down on us.

I dragged against the reins and somehow managed to bring Mars sharply up. The stallion pawed the ground and reared, turning around in a quarter circle before coming down off his hind legs. The smell of blood had overcome the smell of water, and the charger seemed to know what was expected of him. What I wouldn't have given then for a battle-ax or spear! Though we were outnumbered twenty to one, I was so furious over Diderot's death that I would have gladly forfeited my own life if I could have but struck down one of the shrieking bastards.

"Save yourself, *Principessa*!"

It was an Englishman named Robert. His left arm was nearly severed at the shoulder, his jerkin drenched with the rich flow of arterial blood. He lifted his sword with his fighting hand. For a stunned moment I thought he was going to strike me down, but instead, he slapped Mars's rump with the flat of his blade. The horse reared again, then leapt forward with such force that I was nearly thrown from the saddle.

Mars ran as if he were leading the final lap of the race for the golden apple in the Hippodrome. I gripped the saddle with my knees and pressed my head down along the stallion's neck for speed, and to make a smaller target. The gully twisted and turned. As we rounded one particularly tight curve, I turned Mars up the steep bluff, hoping to throw them off our trail. I felt his feet slip as he struggled for footing in the loose, sandy soil, then dig in and hurl us forward as if horse and rider had been shot from a catapult. We galloped a furlong, then leapt a crevasse.

I threw a look behind me. Only two of my pursuers made it up the bluff, and one man's horse was balking at the crevasse. The other made it across, though, and kept coming.

My lone pursuer's horse was smaller than mine but quicker, a nimble Arabian. He'd hurled away his spear, shield, and helmet—his prey being a mere woman. Only luck or being the better rider would save me, and despite my skill, I was hardly foolish enough to think I could best someone who had lived his life in a saddle.

I turned Mars down the next gully and raced for the river. Getting across the river was the only chance I had.

A grove of cottonwood trees stood between me and the water. I had my eyes on the trees as I spurred Mars for one final burst of speed, thinking how I could cut through the trees to get to the water the fastest. The hardscrabble ground gave way suddenly to river sand. The changing ground beneath his feet made Mars falter, the falter turning into a stumble. I had the sickening feeling in the pit of my stomach of things letting go. Before I knew it I was flying through the air, Mars flying with me, the animal screeching in terror for the both of us.

I do not know how long I was unconscious. The Muslim was standing over me when I opened my eyes and groaned.

He extended a hand and said something in a guttural dialect.

I slapped his hand away and got to my feet by myself. The world began to whirl. I closed my eyes and the whirling stopped. When I opened my eyes again, the soldier was walking toward me, leading Mars by the reins. I have never been particularly sentimental about animals, but I was glad to see the creature alive. I had only myself to blame for our upset. I should never have tried to spur him into the sand.

My captor babbled and motioned to my saddle. He evidently intended me to remount and accompany him back to camp. I looked at the man, with his long beard, his leathery skin, and his patched robe. He did not strike me as the sort of man who would postpone the pleasures of the moment in the hope of getting a ransom at some indefinite point in the future. He was, however, extending me a certain courtesy in not raping me on the spot, which is what I had fully expected.

I gripped Mars's saddle and prepared to mount the stallion. The soldier gripped the stirrup in both hands to make it easier for me to guide my boot into it.

"Thank you for showing me such courtesy," I said.

He understood my tone but not my words. His beard arranged itself in a smile.

I shoved the dagger into the man's belly, pushing it until the blade was in him all the way up to the hilt. I saw the surprise in his eyes, then the incomprehension, then finally the sick understanding that he would be dead in a matter of moments.

He was barely taller than I. The dirt was caked so finely into the lines around his eyes that I wondered if he had ever washed his face. Yet it was not a bad face, rustic and weathered but pleasant enough. He looked more like a farmer than a warrior, and perhaps that is what he had been before joining the Jihad. His lips parted and he began to say something, but the words caught in his mouth. His breath told me that he had eaten wild onions earlier that day. I wondered if the blade of my dagger would smell like wild onions when I took it out of his stomach.

I had been able to put my blade into him because it was the last thing he expected of me. I was, after all, only a woman, and a small one at that. A sweet young girl, barely strong enough to lift the books she loved to read, hardly someone anyone would regard as *dangerous*.

I looked at the man through narrowing eyes. He thought I was too frightened to stay with the men and fight. He thought I had run away. He wouldn't have followed me into battle, either. I would have almost preferred rape to seeing the contempt he held me in for the mere fact that I had been born female!

"You men are all the same," I said, hearing the rage in my voice.

I jerked the blade upward. There was a tearing sound, the ragged cutting of robe and flesh that didn't stop until my dagger lodged against his sternum.

Blood gurgled in the dying man's throat.

I looked deep into the dying man's frightened eyes and grasped the dagger with both hands. I gave the knife a cruel twist, thinking of his guts winding around the blade and being cut into pieces, freeing a hemorrhage within his belly.

"I will see you in hell," I hissed, my face so close to my enemy's that I could have kissed him as he died. He groaned. His eyes grew cloudy and went slightly askew, staring past me at nothing.

I put one hand against his shoulder and shoved. He fell at my feet. I leaned over and wiped the dagger's blade on his jerkin.

Mars was at the water's edge, slaking his thirst.

"That is enough for now, my friend," I said, patting his neck before I climbed into the saddle.

I spurred the horse and he waded into the river, carrying me safely across. We emerged into a field of oats. I allowed Mars to browse for a few minutes, then put him into a gallop.

It had been a momentous day. Despite the disaster of losing Diderot, my escort, and—worse still—my boxes of jewels, something of incalculable importance had occurred that would serve me well in the difficult times ahead.

I had learned to kill.

I lived like a bandit, traveling by night, hiding by day. When I crept into villages after dark to steal food, I feared the peasants' dogs more than the enemy soldiers, but there were plenty of them, too. I managed to make off with a man's caftan and a ratty velvet fez, into which I tucked my long hair. With my face and hands suitably caked with grime, I could go into town after sundown and pass for a young man hurrying on an errand, if I kept away from the lamps.

I traveled like this for many nights, reckoning by the stars as if I were still in my sailboat. I knew I had to be getting close to Constantinople. Unfortunately, the closer I got to my destination, the more active the enemy cavalry became. The sultan had his eye on the last jewel in the Byzantine crown, and, with the city nearly surrounded, was preparing to pluck it.

I was riding along one night, probing for a way past the enemy encampments, when I heard a troop of horses pounding down on me from a long, sloping hill of newly mown hay. Mars was too exhausted from hard use and poor feed for us to make a run for it. I jumped off the stallion and got him to lie down in the sweet alfalfa, a trick we had had ample opportunity to practice.

A Muslim cavalryman came over the hilltop so fast that I thought his steed was going to launch itself into the sky and soar toward the stars like Pegasus. A double column of riders galloping two abreast came next, the flowing white robes the riders wore over their full suits of armor shining in the moonlight. My heart leapt when I saw that the chest of each man was decorated with a large Roman cross. These were not more Muslim horsemen, but Christian Crusaders.

I jumped upon Mars and cantered toward my salvation.

The Muslim must have mistaken me for one of the Crusaders and thought himself surrounded. He tightly reined in his horse, turning first to face his pursuers, then back to me. The others were nearly upon him, drawing out their long double-handed swords as they rode.

To his credit, the Muslim decided to face his death chivalrously. Instead of trying to continue fleeing on his blown horse, he jumped down off his mount and drew his blade. His pursuers would have to either cut him down like a dog, or one of them would have to serve as the Christian champion and face him in man-to-man combat. If the Crusader died in single combat, a second Christian would have to take his place. If the Muslim's skill was great and his strength even greater, he could theoretically defeat the forty men facing him and ride away free.

The leader of the Crusader column—a tall warrior on a black stallion nearly as fine as Mars—was the first to reach the enemy, and the first to accept the challenge. The quality of Seville steel, honed so sharp that it would cut in two a silk scarf dropped onto the blade, is well known; it was, however, no match for the might of a two-handed broadsword swung by a powerful knight. The Crusader drove the man back and back again, until the Muslim finally lost his grip on his sword and saw it fly away like a silver-winged night bird, carrying his life with it.

The Muslim fell to his knees and pressed the palms of his hands together before his chest. I could not tell whether he was saying his last prayer to Allah or supplicating the knight for mercy. I was about to cry out for his death, when the knight's sword flashed in the moonlight. It was odd to see how long the warrior's headless body remained upright, spraying a fountain of blood into the air in an almost comical fashion.

The host of Crusaders turned its attention toward me. As I fought to keep Mars from rearing, the others pulled up around me, their high-strung warhorses shaking their heads and pawing the ground as if impatient for more action.

"Hold, brave warriors," I cried, pulling the Turkish fez from my head and shaking out my hair so that it fell curling around my shoulders, reaching all the way to the saddle. "I am a Christian lady. I place myself in your protection."

Their leader, the knight who had so recently fought as their champion, made his way through the others on his charger. He lifted his visor and peered at me. I saw within his steel helmet a handsome face, with a strong chin and mouth and a neat black mustache. At first the expression on his face was completely blank, but after an uncomfortable moment he began to laugh as if he'd just witnessed the most hilarious jest.

"At your ease, my brave lords," he said, his Italian colored with a Venetian accent. "You may safely sheathe your swords. It is only a woman."

I started to reach for my dagger, but stopped myself. I was a stranger in a strange land, and these men the only allies I was likely to find.

"We must ride east, not west, if you are to safely reach Constantinople," Bassanio said. "Nicomedia is in the Turks' hands. The land route is closed. But I know a captain in Zonguldak who can get you there across the Black Sea."

He looked at me with an easy smile.

"And you need not worry about pirates. The Byzantine Navy is much more efficient than the disorganized Greek and Latin fleets. They have kept those dogs in check. The sea-lanes between Zonguldak and Constantinople are open and safe as can be. Trust me, you have nothing to fear."

And I did. I trusted Lord Bassanio implicitly.

* * *

Every city has citizens who live on the margins of society and the law; in Zonguldak, there was nothing but margin. The city, as ugly as its name, was a no-man's-land between the warring Christian and Islamic worlds, a twilight land of desperate refugees, criminals, beggars, cripples, pirates, Gypsies, mercenaries, slavers, prostitutes, and parasites. Zonguldak was a ditch, a low spot between the East and West where the dregs washed in from Europe and Asia, collecting in a festering pool of corruption and evil. Had Magnus been able to extract the essence from the worst elements of Misilmari's Khalisa, distilling it to its purest form in a crucible, Zonguldak would have been the poisonous result.

"It might as well be Baghdad."

"You must remember that we are in the East, Principessa di Medusa," Bassanio said, having overheard me. "The onion-shaped domes on the larger public buildings, the distinctive Moorish archways—these are all characteristic of the architecture in the Latin East."

"But it is a Christian city," I said, repressing the impulse to turn the statement into a question.

"Nominally Christian, *Principessa*, though the architecture has more of Mecca than Milan about it. The city is a polyglot of people and languages, including Christians, Muslims, Zoroastrians, Coptics, and even the handful of Hindus and followers of the Buddha. The Byzantine Empire has always been influenced by the corrupt and degenerate Orient."

Our horses could barely squeeze through the city's streets, which were crowded with people and starved-looking pariah dogs. Raw sewage trickled down the middle of the street. Garbage was heaped in tall mounds in front of buildings, a breeding ground for rats and vermin. I wrapped a scarf across my face against the stench. If there is a more unhealthy place on this planet, I have never visited it. I did not have to ask to know that plagues depopulated Zonguldak at regular intervals.

I reined Mars to keep him from stepping on a twisted cripple who had fallen in front of us. Lord Bassanio barked angry words of Persian to a watchman, who began to beat the poor cripple with his cudgel. The man scrambled to his feet and scuttled into the crowd with a crablike run.

"Lord Bassanio!" I cried in shock.

"He wanted you to step on him, *Principessa*. If you broke a bone or two in his body, you would be compelled to compensate him in gold."

I stared at Bassanio as if what he said were utterly preposterous.

Bassanio laughed and shook his head. "The ways of Zonguldak take some getting used to, Principessa di Medusa. That man was not born crippled, you know. Many of the beggars in here have disfigured themselves. The more pathetic they are, the more successful their begging. Why, many of them take their children and intentionally—"

"Stop!" I put up one hand as if that could block the purulent city from my mind.

For a moment the brutality of life overwhelmed me. The world was ruled by unreasoning, war-loving men, a charnel house where stupidity, violence, and horror was inexorably replacing science, philosophy, and art. There was no escaping the ugliness of it all, not even for a philosopher princess.

# 13

✧

# Night Moves

**R**ICKY McCORMICK STOOD absolutely still, waiting for the lights to come back on. When they didn't, he began to say a little prayer over and over in his head. *Please lights, please lights, please lights ...*

It was hard to tell how long he'd been standing in the dark. Maybe just a few minutes, but it seemed a lot longer. He told himself not to panic. It wouldn't do any good to start bawling like a baby, no matter how scared he was. It might even make things worse. They wouldn't come looking for him down in the parking hold for a long time, maybe not till they got to England. They'd think he'd fallen overboard.

He was going to have to get himself out of this. He would simply work his way back out the way he had come. No big deal. It would be like playing blindman's bluff, the Olympic version. He *thought* he knew approximately where the door was in the cavernous room.

Ricky began to slowly feel his way, his hands on the automobiles' chilly metal bodies.

"Shit!" he said, hopping on one leg. He'd barked his shin trying to get between the car bumpers.

The sound of Ricky's voice echoed back to him from the dark void. But there was something else. He thought he heard something besides his voice, the faint sound of movement all but masked beneath the engines' drone.

Ricky could have almost sworn there was someone—or something—out there.

137

But who could it be? Who else would be there in the darkness? A stowaway, angry that his hiding place had been discovered? Or maybe someone who had followed him into the hold, one of the bad strangers children were warned about?

Ricky crouched down behind the automobiles. The throbbing of the ship's engines seemed to grow suddenly louder as the dark made Ricky's ears more sensitive. The deep, throaty rhythm was the heartbeat of a giant mechanical monster, *ca-chung, ca-chung, ca-chung*, like the ghost noise in the Edgar Allan Poe story Ricky had read called "The Telltale Heart."

Was that a faint sound in the distance? A scuffle? The stealthful shuffle of a stalker's foot against the metal deck?

The atmosphere of menace in the room became so great that Ricky could almost feel it pressing its clammy deadman's hands against his face. He began to crawl backward on his hands and knees, trembling with fear.

The presence seemed to be drawing nearer. How could he—it—move through the room with such speed?

Ricky was squeezing himself under a Lincoln when the dim red lights came back on. He slowly raised himself up and peered through the window of the car. There was nobody there—nobody he could *see*. Then, remembering something from the movies, he ducked down and looked under the cars for his pursuer's feet. It worked better in the movies than in real life, though, since there were too many tires for Ricky to see very far in any direction.

Silently, cautiously, Ricky stood all the way up. He saw nothing—and no one seemed to see him.

Ricky slid his body onto the car trunk, crabbed across it, and lowered himself down into the next aisle, expecting the bad guy to jump up at any second and tear after him. But there was no one. Ricky repeated the operation against the next row of cars, eyes wide, ears straining, constantly looking all around. He saw no one, but the nearer he came to the stairs leading to the exit, to safety, the greater his fear became. He moved faster and faster until he was throwing himself across the cars, too frightened to care about scuffing the wax on so many beautiful automobiles.

Ricky was already running when his feet hit the deck after coming down off the last car. He was just beginning to dash up the stairs, when someone grabbed him from behind.

"Let me go!" Ricky shouted. He flailed his arms and kicked his feet, but whoever it was was much bigger and stronger than the boy. A hand across Ricky's eyes made it impossible to see anything but a few broken glimpses of the weak red light at the top of the stairs, mocking him about how close he'd come to escaping.

Ricky felt hot breath against his neck.

Ricky sucked in a sharp breath to rend the air with a shriek of pure animal terror, but the fear went out of him before he could scream. The boy felt suddenly and inexplicably at peace. It was as if he were cradled in his mother's arms instead of some fiend's. Ricky felt the way he did after a hard day of play, when he'd had a hot bath and was lying in bed on the verge of drifting off to sleep.

Ricky tried to fight it, but it was too strong for him, overpowering his body and his mind. A warm cloud of pink cotton candy seemed to envelop Ricky's awareness. He drifted off into a happy dream, mercifully oblivious of the pressure on his neck as the vampire's razor-sharp teeth broke through his skin and penetrated his jugular vein.

"It seems we are to have a few unscheduled moments of romantic candlelight," Lord Godwin said when the lights went out. The joke elicited nervous laughter.

The candelabra kept the diners in the *grand salle à manger* from becoming overly alarmed, though that would hardly be the case with those few passengers who had skipped the captain's dinner. They would require additional soothing, Lord Godwin thought.

Bob O'Conner, the *Atlantic Princess*'s chief engineer, got up from his table and disappeared through the kitchen exit. It was impossible for Lord Godwin to judge how serious

O'Conner thought the problem was from looking at his face. The American's usual expression was a scowl, though Lord Godwin found the man easy enough to deal with once he got past O'Conner's gruff exterior.

It startled Lord Godwin to see that the emergency lights designed to illuminate the *grand salle à manger* stairs were not lit. The deck lights were out, too. This was particularly disturbing, since it indicated failure in the doubly redundant backup generator and battery system that were supposed to ensure key lights were illuminated "no matter what" in an emergency.

"It's only a fuse," Lord Godwin extemporized sotto voce to the man on his right, the retired board chairman of General Motors. "Mr. O'Conner, the chief engineer, has gone to sort it out."

Lord Godwin was almost thankful that Keiko Matsuoka was blackmailing O'Conner. (Was there any key person involved in the project Keiko *wasn't* blackmailing? Her "special resources" included a videotape of Captain Franchini cavorting with an underage Florida girl.) O'Conner had tried to quit when Lord Godwin informed him that they would have to make whatever compromises were necessary for the *Atlantic Princess* to meet its original sailing date. However, the ever-resourceful Keiko took O'Conner aside for a little chat. Lord Godwin tried not to listen, but the gist of it was plain enough. O'Conner's oldest son was, like his father, a career navy man. The son, the captain of a missile cruiser, had committed some indiscretion, the nature of which remained unclear to Lord Godwin. Whatever it was that Keiko knew, it was enough to keep O'Conner on board the *Atlantic Princess*.

"I'm sure that—"

Lord Godwin was interrupted by the lights coming back on. A relieved sigh went through the room, followed by a smattering of applause.

"The waiters must be trying to cue me that it is time to conclude the toasts so they can serve coffee."

The laughter was still nervous, but less so than before.

"I would beg you to remember, ladies and gentlemen, that this is the maiden voyage of a great ship that has been completely refitted. There are bound to be a few minor problems. I will take the opportunity now to thank you in advance for your forbearance in the face of one or two insignificant annoyances that will, I trust, be hardly worthy of your notice."

A sympathetic murmur went through the *grande salle à manger*.

Lord Godwin remained standing. He had one more toast to make. He looked down at Keiko Matsuoka and forced himself to smile.

Keiko Matsuoka smiled back benignly, enjoying Lord Godwin's secret humiliation.

"I would be remiss if I failed to introduce someone without whom my dream of saving this marvelous vessel would have remained only that: a dream. I don't have to tell you that I had no trouble finding skeptics when I went looking for partners in this project. That is, until I had the good fortune to meet Keiko Matsuoka, the financial genius who manages the Matsuoka Group."

Lord Godwin painted a glowing picture of Keiko's brilliant career, tactfully omitting the trouble that led to her taking in the Japanese Mafia as partners. When he was finished, she rose, made a formal Japanese bow, touching her hands to her thighs, and sat back down, politely declining his invitation to make a few remarks. Keiko felt no need to flaunt her authority over the pompous Lord Godwin.

Keiko looked around the room, making mental notes about potential investors for her group. She was very much in her element in the dining room full of millionaires and billionaires. Their number included the idle rich, who'd inherited their money and had little idea what to do with it besides spend it. These parasites, however, were in the minority. Most of the men and women aboard the *Atlantic Princess* were financial warriors like Keiko. They had earned the privilege of being aboard her ship with their shrewd and ruthless business victories. As the Japanese knew better than anybody, business was war.

Keiko's eyes lingered a moment on Nadja Bisou, the movie actress. Keiko had no interest in investing in Hollywood. The Yakuza would kill her in a minute if she ever had a write-off like Sony's.

Her gaze shifted to another woman seated at the table, the small, beautiful woman with olive skin and the eyes of a gazelle. Who was this?

Principessa Nicoletta Vittorini di Medusa noticed Keiko's attention and smiled.

Keiko would have to ask Bryce to introduce them. The tiny aristocrat looked exactly like the kind of person who had lots of money to invest and the self-assurance to invest it aggressively.

*"Excusez-moi, monsieur."*

Max Burr took one glance at Chef Charles L'Ouverture, sniffed, and turned back to peer through the window in the door leading from the kitchen into the *grand salle à manger*. Chef Charles could go hang as far as Max was concerned. He certainly wasn't going to let that fop order him about, even if it was the little Frenchman's kitchen.

The thing most people noticed about Max was that his mind and his body seemed to belong to different people. He was extremely bright, spoke half a dozen languages, and had even been a member of the Royal Shakespeare Company for a short time in his youth. Though in casual conversation he allowed bits of his native cockney to show, he could convincingly affect the voice of a Scottish laird or a member of the East German proletariat when the situation demanded it, and with enough flair to be convincing.

Max's body, however, was somewhat less nimble than his mind, at least to the casual glance. He stood five feet eight and weighed two hundred and sixty-five pounds. Though he was nearly as broad as he was tall, his body didn't contain much fat. He might have passed for a gorilla, if there'd been hair on his face or head, which were both shaved clean as a baby's bottom.

When Max grinned, nearly everything above the neck moved—ears, forehead, scalp. He had a disarming smile, even with the gap between his two front teeth. For counterbalance, his scowl was menacing enough to clear a stadium of soccer hooligans. In his wing collar, morning coat, and striped pants, Max looked like a safecracker masquerading as a butler, or perhaps an ex-boxer moonlighting as a gangster's bodyguard. He'd been all three—burglar, majordomo, boxer—though he'd never been a criminal in the ordinary sense. Max's petty felonies had all been committed in the service of the law, or something like the law, if you bent the rules a bit.

Max Burr had taken Cyril Ogden's place as purser after Ogden was decapitated. He'd had a bit of convenient help, of course. His employer had arranged the whole thing, getting him aboard the ship and giving him the perfect job to serve as a cover. He'd worked in a bank, knew all about currency laws, and had a good head for numbers. The purser job was a lead-pipe cinch.

Max had been sitting in the projection room when the power went out, enjoying a private screening of *Interview with a Vampire* with an American named C. K. Smith, who seemed to know everything there was to know about vampire movies. The original plan called for Max to go down to the dining room and pick up their man as he was leaving supper. When the lights went out, Max decided it wouldn't hurt to have a look right away. You never knew. Someone as smart and dangerous as their boy was capable of just about anything.

Max heard a waiter approach and backed out of the way in time for the man to push through.

Max was familiar with his man's face from the photographs, though the blighter had hidden in his cabin suite since the *Atlantic Princess* set sail.

"Bloody 'ell," Max muttered to himself. His man wasn't at his table.

"Monsieur Burr, if you please! I must insist."

"I was just leaving," Max said, giving Chef Charles a lengthy look at the gap that showed between his front teeth.

Max Burr left the ship's main kitchen by a service entrance and went to look for David Parker.

The orchestra switched from chamber music to dance tunes after dessert was served. It was a pleasant change for George McCormick. He liked Mozart and Bach well enough, but his personal tastes ran toward Gershwin and Ellington and the sophisticated big-band jazz orchestrations of his generation.

The stewards cleared away the dishes, and the waiters brought coffee and port. The space in front of the orchestra began to fill with couples turning gracefully in a fashion that seemed to McCormick to be light-years removed from what now passed for dancing. McCormick took a last sip of coffee, patted his mustache, and stood.

"If you will all excuse us a moment, I would like to dance with my lovely wife," he said, beaming as he moved to pull back her chair.

"I'd rather not, George, if you don't mind terribly much."

McCormick found himself in an uncharacteristically awkward position, hands on the back of his wife's chair, smile stiffly pinned in place, the others' eyes upon him. He couldn't remember a time Nancy had refused an invitation to dance. She loved dancing.

"Don't be too disappointed, dear. It's just that I feel a bit tired this evening. Perhaps Dr. Anderson would do you the honor?"

"I'm afraid I'm not much of a dancer," Dr. Anderson warned as McCormick steered her onto the dance floor.

"Nonsense, my dear," McCormick said, making every effort to preserve his usual gallant bonhomie, when what he really wanted to do was take his wife back to their cabin suite and make her lie down and rest.

"I'd never danced so much as a step until last week,"

Carrie said, concentrating hard to follow McCormick's lead. "Lord Godwin arranged some training sessions for the more socially retarded members of his crew. We went over finger bowls and fox-trots and so forth. I haven't had to cram so hard since med school."

McCormick laughed. She was a charming young woman, and completely unlike what he would have expected in a lady doctor. But then, he knew his ideas about that sort of thing were hopelessly obsolete.

"Is Mrs. McCormick feeling entirely well? I hope you don't mind my asking. Being nosy about people's health is one of the occupational hazards of being a doctor."

"Nancy is not at all herself this evening, I'm sorry to say. In fact, she hasn't been herself for some time now." McCormick felt a tightening in his throat. He didn't know why he was admitting to a new acquaintance something he'd scarcely admitted to himself. Perhaps it was because she was a doctor. People were supposed to confide in doctors.

"She goes through spells when she doesn't seem to be living in the present moment," Dr. Anderson said, leading the conversation even as McCormick was leading the dance.

McCormick nodded.

"And she has trouble remembering things—where she put her keys, or even why she was looking for her keys in the first place."

McCormick nodded.

"And there are moments of what seems to be general mental confusion."

"Either you are a very good physician, Dr. Anderson, or the prognosis is painfully obvious."

"Has she seen a doctor for testing?"

"She's going to the Mayo Clinic when we get home from Europe."

"An excellent idea. It isn't necessarily Alzheimer's, Mr. McCormick."

"Really?"

"It could be a tumor."

"My God!"

"Many tumors are treatable."

"You never know how truly unimportant money is until you discover it can't buy you the only thing you want," McCormick said after a pause.

"May a wet-behind-the-ears medical doctor offer a piece of unsolicited advice to someone much wiser and more experienced? Don't waste a single minute thinking about what you have to lose. Be grateful for what you've had, and have, and will have."

"That is very good advice, Dr. Anderson. I think you're wiser—"

"Excuse me."

McCormick turned to see who was tapping him on the shoulder.

"Mind if I cut in?"

Almost before McCormick—or Dr. Anderson—knew what was happening, Alexander Fox had taken hold of Carrie's hands and was whirling her away. Careful to wipe all traces of worry from his face, George McCormick hurried back to his wife.

As long as he kept his mouth shut, the odious Fox was a passably attractive man. He may have spent most of his time in front of a computer, but he'd apparently compensated with plenty of exercising outside. The skin on his pleasant face and strong hands glowed with a healthy tan. His shoulders were wide and strong, his stomach flat. Where Carrie's hands rested on Fox's arm and back, she could feel well-toned muscles beneath his clothing. On his left wrist was a Timex Ironman runner's watch identical to the one Carrie always wore, though she'd taken it off for the captain's dinner.

Fox wore wire-rimmed glasses. His hair, which had probably always been finely textured, was beginning to thin on top. Instead of trying to hide his approaching baldness—

men tended to be even more vain than women about their hair, in Carrie's limited experience—Fox had an athlete's crew cut that was combed to stand up on top. There were a few flecks of gray in his hair and mustache, the first signs of approaching middle age.

"Am I doing okay, Dr. Anderson? It's been a while since I've hit the dance floor."

"Was that a glimmer of modesty, Mr. Fox?"

"Does modesty seem out of character for me?"

"Oh, I don't know," Carrie said, affecting a nonjudgmental attitude about the loathsome Fox. His only response was a grin. He was apparently immune to what others thought of him, a social turtle with an impervious shell.

"I did my turn in dance class in the eighth grade as punishment for sneaking out of the house at night. How I detested that class! I suppose that everything, even dance class, serves a purpose, if you wait long enough to discover it."

"What a lovely sentiment."

"I am not much on sentiment, Dr. Anderson."

"For some reason, that doesn't surprise me."

"You don't like me, do you, Dr. Anderson?"

"I don't know you well enough to say I dislike you." Her tone was suitably cool and detached, but her face was burning. The song ended and Carrie abruptly excused herself and beat a hasty retreat.

"If you haven't made up your mind yet, then there's still hope for me," Fox called after her.

Not in a million years, Carrie thought.

Mandy went up through the Queen Elizabeth Lounge. The room was deserted with everybody down at the captain's dinner. It was eerie to be in a place that was always filled with people and noise and find it quiet and empty. She hurried out onto the Promenade Deck and climbed the exterior stairs two stories higher to the Sports Deck.

Her destination was the No. 2 funnel, the middle of three smokestacks on the *Atlantic Princess*. The funnel was connected to the No. 3 and No. 4 boilers, which sat on the H Deck thirteen stories below. The stack was located between the satellite dishes forward—the electronic gear sat on what had originally been the squash courts—and the helipad aft.

Mandy had earlier overheard two ship's officers discussing something of interest, the latest in a growing list of leads to check out. She took out her penlight and shined it along the base of the slanted funnel, examining the angle where the heavily riveted stack was attached to the deck. She'd walked nearly halfway around the funnel before she found it—a small but distinct crack in the metal.

She took a step backward and looked up at the funnel. The black cylinder towered more than forty feet above the Sports Deck, the top deck on the ship except for the bridge. A wisp of white smoke trailed dreamily out of the funnel.

How much did the stack weigh?

The answer might be in the copy of the ship's plans Mandy had locked in the steamer trunk in her cabin, along with the other evidence she'd been collecting. Tons, for sure. She'd have to think of a meaningful way to describe it. If she wrote that the funnel weighed, say, fifty tons, people would have no frame of reference. She'd say it weighed as much as one hundred elephants, or a 747 jumbo jet, or whatever.

Looking up at the funnel, which was not unlike looking up at the Rock of Gibraltar, inspired Mandy to take a step or two backward. It horrified her to think what would happen if the fatigued metal gave way and the funnel came crashing down on the Sports Deck. It would certainly flatten anything it fell on, including the helipad and the Queen Elizabeth Lounge beneath it. Mandy didn't think the funnel would capsize the ship as it rolled overboard, but it would smash the hell out of whatever it hit on the way down—not to mention any passengers who might be in its path, a titanic steamroller.

Mandy took the compact Nikon camera from her purse and popped up the flash. She was aiming the camera at the crack in the funnel, when she heard a footstep behind her.

Strong hands grabbed Mandy before she could turn, one clamping tightly over her mouth, preventing her from screaming.

The Nikon shattered when it hit the deck, the canister of high-speed thirty-five-millimeter film clattering across the helipad, spilling out a shiny ribbon of film.

# 14

✧

# Nicoletta's Diary V

**I** WAS ATTENDED BY two dark-skinned Turkish handmaidens, who bathed me and massaged fragrant oils into my skin until I drifted into unconsciousness. I was awakened by the touch of a small hand against my cheek. I sat straight up and looked around in alarm, forgetting at first where I was and how I had gotten there.

The room was softly illuminated with the flickering glow of Persian oil lamps. It was night. I had slept all night and straight through the day.

The handmaiden who had awakened me hid her mouth with her hand and giggled. The second handmaiden came into the chamber, hurrying around the room with a taper, chattering in Turkish as she lighted candles, evidently urging me to get up and get dressed. They helped me get into a flowering Oriental silk gown drawn from their master's stores of finery, combed out my thick, long hair, and braided flowers into it.

There was a quiet knock at the door. It was a servant, an Arabic fellow wearing a caftan, fez, and Persian slippers. He must have wondered what I was laughing at, but when I saw his fez, it reminded me of my weeks of traveling through Turkey disguised as a boy. The fellow hid his consternation—servants had their eyes put out or worse for showing disrespect in those days—and motioned that I should follow.

The Moorish characteristics of Lord Bassanio's walled villa gave it an exotic aspect, as though it were the setting

for the *Arabian Nights' Entertainments*. The hall floors
were covered in opulent Turkish carpets, the walls were
draped with Oriental tapestries resplendent with silver and
golden threads. The sumptuous furnishings I saw in the
rooms we passed must have been looted from the homes
and palaces of eastern potentates, booty brought home from
the Crusades. Indeed, Bassanio's villa was not so much a
home as a treasury. Even by lamplight I could see that the
corners of the rooms were cluttered with statuary, bolts of
rare cloth, silver and gold plate, carved Indian chests of
teak inlaid with ivory, Persian silverwork.

My escort led me downstairs into the great hall, where
Lord Bassanio sat alone on a raised dais in a throne or-
nately carved and gilded with gold, with red velvet cush-
ions to make it comfortable. For what king had such a chair
been made? How many hands, Christian and Muslim, had
passed it on its way to Bassanio's villa?

"I again thank you, my lord, for your protection and hospitality. You are a model of chivalry in these barbarous
times."

"It is I who must thank you for your example," Bassanio
said modestly. "You are a brave woman to have ridden
across Anatolia unescorted." A gong rang somewhere off in
the villa. "May I accompany you to supper, Principessa di
Medusa?"

We lay on couches Roman-style and feasted on a dinner
of exotic delicacies, entertained by tumblers, magicians, and
a troupe of Indian minstrels who played drums and strange,
many-stringed instruments from the East that made exotic,
hypnotic music.

Valerian and Townsberry were present, along with several other notables. Zonguldak's worthiest citizens had been
invited to welcome Principessa Nicoletta Vittorini di Medusa to their city, although to a man they had oily, disrep-
utable countenances. I would not have trusted any of them
to have sold me so much as a rug. Bassanio introduced the
ladies—I use the term loosely—at the banquet to me en

masse as the wives of his men and friends. They did not have the look of wives about them, but rather of lowborn courtesans done up in cheap, gaudy finery.

We ate course after course of food. Our cups were never allowed to be empty. Not wanting to become drunk, I quickly determined the best course was not to drink at all. As midnight approached, I found myself the only sober person in the room, the servants included. One of the serving girls was too inebriated to realize her tunic had fallen far enough down her shoulder to reveal her breast. The guests made great jest of this, though the poor girl was too drunk to understand. She carried a golden bowl filled with a confection shaped and colored to resemble miniature apples.

"They're called Eve's apples," said Bassanio, who was as deep in his cups as the others. "A specialty found only in Zonguldak. You must try one."

Bassanio's heavy insistence was almost enough to make me suspect I was about to be the brunt of some wine-sodden practical joke. Yet, as I did not wish to offend his hospitality, I took one of Eve's apples from the bowl and bit into it. It was difficult to tell why the others had been so greedy to get at the candies. The outside was sugary sweet, but the inside was more the color of molasses, chewy and sweet but with an unpleasantly bitter aftertaste. Bassanio watched me until I finished the treat, then broke into a big grin.

"Very good," I lied.

"But very rich," Bassanio said, slurring his words. "You must be careful not to eat another this first time. It would make you ill."

I promised not to.

Bassanio's chamberlain clapped his hands and the room began to pulse with slow drumming.

"You're in for a real treat," Bassanio said, moving over next to me, sitting down heavily. "A troupe of blackamoor dancers. They're supposed to be Egyptian, but they're Africans, if you ask me. I'll wager you never saw anything like it on Bellaria."

Servants moved throughout the room, taking torches down from the walls and extinguishing them, leaving only dim oil lamps to light the room. It was a warm evening. The Moorish windows were open and a breeze caused the lamps to flicker, filling the room with shifting, sinuous shadows that almost seemed to move in time with the drumming.

It was about then that a peculiar feeling of languor began to take possession of my body. I began to feel warm and lazy, but at the same time I became acutely aware of everything I saw and heard. I don't know when the first dancer slipped into the room because I was staring at the flame dancing on the tip of an oil lamp. It seemed to actually be alive, a miniature burning angel that jumped and turned for my personal entertainment.

The hypnotic drumming became more insistent, until I heard it not only in my ears but in my stomach. The slow, steady pulsing caressed my body, echoing the rhythm of my heart.

My eyes were idly following the moving shadow that materialized into a woman. She was as black as ebony and completely naked, her dark skin glistening with olive oil. I could not take my eyes away from her. Her supple breasts were round and full, curving slightly upward at the nipples, whose outlines were hard and sharp against the softer chocolate skin surrounding them. Her belly was flat, her waist tiny, the sinuous motion of her full hips almost more than I could bear. Indeed, I caressed her sleek black body with my eyes, unmentionable thoughts taking shape within my slow-moving mind.

Other dancers had slipped into the room. Some were men, some women, all with naked, oiled skin and shaved heads.

The couch I was lying on was covered in silk. Strange that I hadn't noticed that before. I rubbed my hand back and forth against the warm, smooth material. It was as if I were caressing the dancer's body, feeling the electric sensation move through my palm and up my arm. I shifted my hips slightly so that I could rub the inside of my knee and thigh back and forth against the silken couch. Such a simple thing, so subtle a motion, yet it set my entire body tingling with sensual pleasure.

The guests, who had been crude and noisy throughout the banquet, wordlessly watched the dancers, breathing through their mouths, their eyes hungry.

"I hope you do not object to the dancers' nakedness, Nicoletta," Bassanio's voice whispered in my ear.

"No." My voice sounded dreamy and very far away. "But are they not ashamed?"

"They are opium eaters. The drug makes them depraved beyond caring what they are made to do."

I knew of such creatures from studying ancient Greece. The lines of the *Odyssey*, which Brother Thomas had me memorize as a girl, floated through my mind like clouds drifting across a summer sky.

*My men went on and presently met the Lotus-Eaters,*
*nor did these Lotus-Eaters have any thoughts of destroying*
*our companions, but they only gave them lotus to taste of.*
*But any of them who ate the honey-sweet fruit of lotus*
*was unwilling to take any message back, or to go*
*away, but they wanted to stay there with the lotus-eating*
*people, feeding on lotus, and forget the way home. I myself*
*took these men back weeping, by force, to where the ships*
*were, and put them aboard under the rowing benches and*
*tied them fast, then gave the order to the rest of my eager*
*companions to embark on the ships in haste . . .*

I dimly perceived that I had been drugged, yet I could not seem to make myself care. I felt too lazy to protest, too languid to get up to leave. What did any of it matter? I had become a lotus-eater. The dancers intrigued me. Their nakedness moved me in an entirely new way. It was sinful, but what did I care about sin? I was being carried along in a warm, soft current.

I think I may have fallen asleep for a moment, which is common for those who use opium. I remember open-

ing my eyes and seeing that the dancers had paired off
in every imaginable combination: woman and man;
woman and woman; man and man. The drumming had
quickened and the dancers began to spin and whirl. Bodies
touched and separated. Flesh slapped against flesh, feet
stamped against the floor. The dancers were streaked with
sweat, their breath coming now in deep pants.

The room had become hot with the heat generated by the
dancers' bodies, a dozen naked black furnaces heating the
night with their passion. I felt a trickle of perspiration run
down my brow, but I was too enervated to wipe it away.

The dance had become far more than implicitly erotic.
Hand to breast, pelvis to pelvis, pelvis to buttock. I rubbed
my hand back and forth against the silk couch and watched
the naked bodies grind together, glistening with oil and perspiration, fingers touching, probing, caressing, soothing,
tongues flickering along the edge of an ear, an arm, a thigh.

A body pressed against me from behind. Bassanio. He
draped his arm over mine. His hand began to caress my
breast through my silk dress, his hand, the silk, my flesh—
all three merged into one delirious, delicious sensation.

Lost in their opium-induced trances, the dancers moved
into the inevitable next plateau of their performance. One
dancer leapt into her partner's arms, wrapping her legs
around his waist. I watched his manhood disappear into
her—an enthralling sight! I had seen animals copulate, but
never a man and a woman. His partner began to roll her
head in ecstatic circles, crying out with pleasure at each
thrust of his hips.

Two women fell to the floor near my couch, one with her
body pointed this way, her partner just the opposite. My tu-
tors had provided me with an excellent education, yet I realized then that I knew nothing.

Bassanio had insinuated his other arm underneath me,
which he began to slowly move down my belly. I did not
resist him. There seemed no urgency to do anything but
submit to my building inner passion.

One of the dancing girls climbed up on our table, shoving food and dishes out of her way, lowering herself down on her side. Her eyes were on my eyes, her mouth slightly parted, tongue playing around her lips. She parted her legs and reached around from behind, parting the petals of her rose, spreading its glistening petals to reveal its heart, its secret.

Bassanio had hiked up my skirt and was pushing my legs apart. My gown was drenched with sweat, and my own breath coming in deep, irregular pants. The touch of his hands, at once rude and caressing, made me tingle with a pleasure I had never experienced. Like a lotus blossom unfolding to the strong, irresistible fingers of the sun, I felt myself opening.

"Keep your head, man."

The voice belonged to Valerian. The words sounded oddly slow and muffled, as though my ears were filled with honey. Strange that the greed in his voice was so prominent. It was always there, of course, despite his efforts to disguise it. I could hear the drink in his voice, too, but not the languorous, sensual tones that had overcome the rest of us. Valerian was too clever to become a lotus-eater like the rest of us, his heart consumed by endless calculations of profit and loss. The poor, shallow man. If the bowl of Eve's apples had been within my reach, I would have offered him one to eat.

"She'll fetch a better price if she's still a virgin, Bassanio." I closed my eyes to better enjoy the delicious sensation of Bassanio's tongue licking my neck.

"It'll make no difference, Bassanio." This was Townsberry. "There are no virgins left. Nobody would believe you if you tried to say she was one."

Saying nothing, Bassanio rolled me over onto my back, ripping my silk dress open up the middle. The air felt good against my naked skin. I looked slowly around at the circle of leering men, a lotus-eater conscious only of the warm, glowing ecstasy that had not yet been satisfied.

I had eaten of the honey-sweet fruit. I was unwilling to

take any message back, or to go away, or to do anything but stay with the lotus-eating people, feeding on lotus.

Bassanio climbed on top of me, pushing himself between my legs.

Bassanio's man Valerian was next, not wanting to miss out on my rape, if Bassanio was determined to deflower me. Townsberry came next, then the others.

My head throbbed when I awoke, but the pain in my skull was nothing compared to the pain between my legs—and the spiritual pain caused by my shame.

I lay in bed in the heavily curtained room, feeling rage build within me even as passion had the night before, my anger pushing the shame out of my heart. It would do no good to cry and mourn the loss of my maidenhood. My virginity was gone. Neither shame nor remorse would bring it back.

Only the consolations of philosophy could lift up my spirit. The humiliation I'd been forced to endure would break me only if I allowed it. I was a Stoic, and Stoics remained indifferent to extremes of pain as well as pleasure—both of which I had been drugged and forced to endure the night before.

What had happened to me at Bassanio's orgy had only one practical consequence, I concluded, drying my eyes against my pillow. The circle of enemies on whom I would one day revenge myself had grown larger. That was all the previous night signified. That and nothing more.

I expected to be made to participate in subsequent entertainments, but I proved to be wrong. I was left unmolested for the next fortnight, locked in my chambers, where I was visited only by my two handmaidens.

I awakened on the morning of my forty-third day of captivity to downcast eyes and mournful expressions. My handmaidens treated me with special tenderness as they brushed out my long hair and braided it in a single plait intertwined with wildflowers. They bathed and oiled my body, sprinkling it with fine perfume. My eyes were painted with Egyptian mascara. I was dressed in a simple silk dressing gown that tied around the waist with a cord. Velvet slippers were put on my feet.

Someone knocked on the door. The older of the two handmaidens, whose name was Mardian, opened the door.

I'd expected Bassanio, but it was Valerian. I drew myself up straight and gave him an imperious glare, wishing more than ever that I still had my dagger.

"Come," he said brusquely. He turned to the two guards standing close behind him. Chains and irons hung from one of the men's hands. "If she gives you any trouble, clap her in shackles."

I hurriedly kissed the handmaidens good-bye, their tears telling me I would not be returning. I most likely was being turned over to the sultan, who would either behead me or—worse—force me to join the concubines in his seraglio. I followed Valerian downstairs and out into the courtyard. The guards walked at either side of me, the irons clanking ominously as I desperately tried to think of a way to escape.

We approached a closed carriage hitched to a team of four horses. Bassanio was waiting, and he opened the door as we approached. Valerian climbed in. I stopped and looked up at Bassanio, imagining how much pleasure it would bring me to see his severed head impaled upon a pike.

"I will convey your fondest regards to the sultan," I said, pleased to hear how calm and even my voice sounded.

But Bassanio only laughed. "The sultan has no interest in you, my lady. If you were the *prince* of Bellaria, your life might be of some value to His Excellency. Unfortunately for us both, you are but a *principessa*. You are no threat to him. You could never hope to raise an army and try to take back the isle he took from you. You are, after all, only a woman."

My hand flashed out and struck Bassanio hard across the mouth before he could react.

"Bitch!" he shouted, pulling back his fist.

"Bassanio!" Valerian barked. "Your uncontrolled passions have already depreciated her value."

Bassanio touched his fingers to the corner of his mouth and brought them away bloody. "You'll pay for your impudence," he sneered. "Mark my words. You'll pay today, and you'll keep on paying for as long as you live!"

Seeing the blood I'd drawn filled me with a strange exultation. But it was not enough! How I wanted Bassanio's blood to spray into the air and collect in great crimson puddles on the ground! I stepped boldly near my enemy, looking up at him, my eyes locking on to his. One of the guards grabbed my shoulder, but he did not pull me away. I was, after all, only a woman, and no real threat to Lord Bassanio.

If only I had my dagger!

"I've watched better men than you die, Bassanio. I've *killed* better men."

Bassanio took an involuntary step backward. He was not so brave after all, I thought with a smirk.

"Come on," Valerian said, as impatient as the stamping horses. "We're going to be late if we don't leave now."

The guards took my arms and lifted me into the carriage, much to Valerian's irritation, who warned them not to bruise me. I sat across from Valerian and glared at him as we rode through the crowded streets of Zonguldak. The ride was not long. The driver opened the door and dropped the folding step. The guards got out in front of me. They made as if to help me down but continued to firmly hold my arms so that I could not run away.

We'd come to the warehouse district along the waterfront. Above the rooftops, I could see the bobbing masts of the merchant ships and men-of-war moored in the harbor. Some of the ships in the harbor were bound for Constantinople and then Naples, but I knew they would not be carrying me with them. I'd escaped the Muslims in Bellaria and survived the ride through an entire country filled with marauding Muslim warriors, serpents, and treacherous desert only to lose my freedom to a Christian Crusader. The irony was most unpleasant.

A whip cracked. Someone began to scream piteously. The whip cracked again.

We followed Valerian toward a large building with iron rings set into the stone walls. People were chained to the exterior walls. Others sat in the street, their heads and hands locked in heavy wooden yokes. A group of perhaps ten naked women were crowded into an iron pen. A varlet who looked like he worked in a tannery was entertaining himself by poking the caged women with a stick, laughing as they screamed with pain and anger.

Valerian strode in through the huge open door, leading us into a dim, stinking room filled with moans and crying.

We had come to the slave market.

I had an hour to consider how Seneca, Epictetus, Marcus Aurelius, and the other great Stoics would have confronted such a fate. By the time my turn came around and rude hands grasped at me, I had adopted the serene indifference of someone who has trained her mind to remain calm regardless of what fate brings. I was stripped naked and lifted onto a block of limestone. The stone was cold against my bare feet, its surface worn smooth by the innumerable poor wretches who had passed that way, people who had fallen so low in the world that they no longer could be counted as people at all, but as animals to be sold to the highest bidder.

My prospective buyers circled like sharks, like dogs around a bitch in heat, inspecting me with their eyes and their hands. The auctioneer was a one-eyed giant who carried a cudgel to threaten customers and slaves alike. He allowed me to be pawed for several minutes, but then ordered a stop.

"Back away, you pariahs," he snarled, grabbing the wrist of the lowborn knave who had been fondling my breast. He shoved the cur backward into the jeering crowd. "She's a highborn lady with skin that will bruise as easily as a peach. I'll not have you manhandling her."

The slave trader rubbed the cudgel's knobby end against my belly to draw attention to my milky skin. I shrank from being touched, an involuntary reaction that elicited a merry roar from the crowd.

"If you want to bruise her, my boys, you'll have to buy her first, and then you can bruise her in whatever ways you want! The bidding starts at one hundred gold pieces."

The crowd exhaled a collective groan. Most of the buyers were merchants, farmers, and petit nobility. One hundred gold pieces was enough money to buy and outfit an entire trading ship, far beyond the means of someone who owned a handful of slaves to tend fields and carry slop buckets.

"You filthy pack of blind jackasses," the slave trader yelled, shouting down his customers. "Don't you know quality when you see it? Why, her father was a king, a lord born to the ermine. That was before the sultan set his greedy eyes on Principessa Nicoletta's kingdom. We know what happens when that devil takes it into his head to conquer some fine province that is rich, fat, and easy for the taking."

There were more angry shouts, but this time the hostility was directed at the sultan. They all knew the Muslim warlord would add Zonguldak and the remainder of Turkey to his satrapy as soon as Allah moved him to do so.

"I appeal to your finer instincts, gentlemen. Only the cruelest circumstances could drag such a fine maiden to this place of sorrow. What say you? Who will pay one hundred gold pieces so that Nicoletta can go free? It's only fitting and right that Lord Bassanio should be repaid for saving her from the sultan's grimy hands."

The laughter and derisive shouts expressed the crowd's disbelief that Bassanio had saved me from anything.

"All right, then, you filthy goat-suckled scum," the slave

trader bellowed. "I can see there's not a gentleman among you. Begging your pardon, Count Valerian. Excepting you, your worship."

Valerian nodded.

"If you don't want to ransom this *principessa* so she can return home to Italy, then consider bidding on her for less noble reasons." I kept my eyes straight ahead as I felt the slave trader's rough fingers climbing my thigh. "She'd make a fine whore for a gentleman. Hell, boys, she'd make a fine *wife* for a gentleman—a gentleman with one hundred gold pieces."

Someone behind me bid. A fat man in a turban raised my price another ten gold pieces. A cruel-eyed whoremonger with a forked beard shouted next, then a Greek the auctioneer called Themistius. The bidding for me settled into a contest between the whoremonger and Themistius. What little value is set on human life! I used to wear jewels worth more than a thousand gold pieces, but now I listened in shocked fascination as the price for my life escalated ten gold pieces at a time.

The slave trader finally rapped the cudgel on the side of the auction block, and the crowd broke into applause. It was over. Themistius had won the bidding war, buying Principessa Nicoletta Vittorini di Medusa for three hundred and twenty gold pieces.

Themistius had a neat, short-cropped beard and a pleasant face. He didn't smell bad either, which set him apart from most of the other men in the slave market. He helped me into my robe, averting his eyes as if he were as ashamed as I was of my nakedness.

"You'll catch your death, *Principessa*," he said, throwing a heavy woolen cloak around my shoulders. "Pull the cowl up over your head. There. That will protect you from prying eyes when we leave. Shall I call you *Principessa*? Perhaps that would be too painful a reminder."

I did not answer, momentarily too overcome with shame

at seeing myself sold at auction like an animal, like a common slave.

"Yes, no doubt that is the case," Themistius went on, carrying on the conversation for both of us. "I will simply call you Nicoletta until things get sorted out. Would that be all right with you?"

The streets were as crowded as ever and smelled so bad from animal and human waste that I nearly gagged. Adding to the chaos, a shepherd was driving his sheep down the middle of the street. The animals were terrified of the people and the noise and kept trying to run, which was impossible, since there was no place to run except into the crowd. The result was a sort of moving brawl, with sheep and people battering themselves and each other as the fleecy procession made its way up the street by fits and starts.

Themistius found a doorway to pull me into until the bizarre parade passed. "If you are a Christian man, sir," I ventured, looking up into his friendly coffee-colored eyes, "you will help me get back to Naples. My uncles will reward you handsomely for my freedom."

"Pray do not think me so blind to the plight of a lady in distress that I can think only of my reward," Themistius said, removing his hand before he spoke, too humble to look me in the eye. "You must believe me, my lady, when I say that money is the furthest thing from my mind."

I could hardly believe my ears. Only after walking among the lowest of the low had I come to meet a good man in that city of the damned.

"Now, please come. The streets are not safe for a *principessa*."

Villains masquerading as heroes, heroes going about in the guise of peasants—the world was filled with irony and surprise, I thought, following Themistius toward his home.

The street where Themistius lived was barely wide enough for the two of us to pass side by side. Ropes crisscrossing overhead were draped with laundry belonging to the occupants of the buildings' upper levels. Old men and old women loitered at the open windows, looking down on us with detached interest.

Themistius's home was more shop than house. The entry led into an office such as a scribe or moneylender might use for conducting business. Crammed into the space were three old-fashioned stand-up desks, and at each a clerk bent over ledger books and piles of paper.

"This is Nicoletta," Themistius said simply. I was grateful to him for not embarrassing me by indicating to the clerks how far the Fates had ordained me to fall. "She will be staying with us for a short time."

I nodded to the clerks.

"Come," Themistius said, drawing back a curtain. "Let me show you where you can rest. You are no doubt tired after this morning's experience."

I followed him down a dark, narrow hallway and up three flights of rickety stairs. There were several doors at the top of the stairs, the one at the end open. Inside was a small, well-scrubbed bedroom. The window shutters were open, admitting a slanting shaft of brilliant sunlight. Outside, the neighborhood laundry fluttered in the breeze like a display of colorful flags. The street and its stench were far below.

The room was quite modest by the standards to which I was accustomed, yet at that moment it seemed like the most wonderful room in the world. When I stepped into the tiny bedroom and looked around, I saw a safe haven, a refuge from pigs like Bassanio and Valerian, a stopping-off place until I left for Naples. My escape from the Muslims on Bellaria, the treacherous ride across Turkey, and the indignities I'd suffered at the hands of Bassanio and his men—all those receded into the background at an astonishing speed as I looked around my clean, sunny, serving-girl's room. From a very great height I had fallen into the depths, but the worst was behind me. Fortuna's wheel was spinning in an upward direction. Principessa Nicoletta Vittorini di Medusa was again in possession of her own destiny.

"Nicoletta?"

I turned around, so grateful that I could have thrown my arms around my deliverer.

Themistius's dark eyes had taken on an expression of deep intensity.

"Nicoletta," he repeated after a long pause, licking his dry lips. "Take off your clothes."

We set out the following day in a ship that wallowed heavy in the water with its cargo of Eastern spices. There were four traveling in our party: Themistius, myself, and two clerks whose duty—so far as I could determine—was to ensure that I didn't murder the Greek in his sleep.

We sailed west across the Black Sea, getting close enough to Constantinople for me to see the spires of its great churches upon the horizon. I burned with rage to see the Byzantine city as a slave. As the captain veered the ship northward, Themistius ordered the clerks to take me to my cabin. He must have guessed I was contemplating jumping overboard and swimming for Constantinople.

We reached the Danube and sailed up its mouth some miles before docking in a city guarded by a black tower. Themistius paid the German prince a visit in his tower while the cargo of spices were off-loaded. I went along, following between the clerks, forced to walk an appropriately humble distance behind Themistius. Since he had not deigned to speak to me since raping me, I knew nothing of our ultimate destination. I half expected the Greek to turn me over to the German—who neither bathed nor cleaned his teeth—to serve his stinking pleasure. This, however, was not to be. We spent the night in the tower and left the next day on four good riding horses, our baggage trailing behind on two pack animals. Accompanied by a mounted guard of hired soldiers armed with crossbows, we cantered down a road that led straight into the mottled, murky gloom of a dense forest of ancient oaks.

The Germanic forest swallowed us the way the night devours the day. The forest's cool darkness was a world apart from the sunny isle where I had lived until my precipitous fall from grace. We often rode for hours without seeing more than the smallest patches of blue overhead. This was a moody, bewitched country. No doubt a druid or two could still be found in these parts, offering human sacrifices to their ancient tree gods, hanging bronze amulets from the low-hanging boughs of sacred oaks. The Romans had been unable to stamp out their pagan cult; I had no reason to believe the Christians had been any more successful.

We rode for days, until I began to despair that I would ever again see the sun. At length the forest path transformed itself into a narrow road that climbed the foothills leading into the Carpathian Mountains. The beech and oak trees slowly gave way to conifers as the air began to thin. I knew something of the region from the maps I had studied in my father's scriptorium. The Carpathians are a crescent-shaped mountain range that gave birth to the Vistula, Order, Tisza, and Dnestr rivers. This was the ancient Roman province of Dacia, which had come to be known as Transylvania.

There were few people in this wild, uncivilized corner of the world, a place torn by violent wars and blood feuds that were horrific even by the standards of the Dark Ages. Before the arrival of the sultan's slave armies—and mercenaries like Bassanio—the native people had to fight against an endless series of conquerors: the Lombards, the Avars, the Bulgarians, the Cumans, the Mongols.

Transylvania was one place in the Christian world where the Muslim invaders had been held in check. While the Islamic soldiers' fanaticism usually enabled them to sweep over their enemies in battle, an inexorable wailing tide dedicated to Allah, they were no match for the savage frenzy of the Transylvanian warlords who had been bred from a millennium of endless warfare.

We made camp beside a wild river that cut through a slashing gorge. There seemed to be no way across, though I knew that there had to be one, for the road continued along on the other side of the river until it disappeared in the trees.

Themistius was seated cross-legged on a Persian carpet, drinking the Turkish coffee to which he was addicted, when one of his hired Germans dragged me into his pavilion. Themistius motioned for me to sit across from him and offered me a cup of the thick, bitter coffee. I had not noticed how numb my fingers had become with cold until they were wrapped around the steaming cup.

Themistius regarded me warily for many minutes before speaking.

"You are no doubt wondering where I am taking you. I'm sure your mind is full of foolish ideas. You probably think I'm carrying you off to work in some remote and stinking brothel, where you'll be made to rut in flea-infested straw with a dozen men every night."

"No."

"I did not invite you to speak, so——"

"You paid too much gold to see me used as a simple whore," I said, talking over the cur's voice. "I surmise you have something more ambitious in mind for me."

"I suppose I should admire your spirit, and your intelligence. Your quick mind is unusual for a woman. Your quick tongue, however, is all too typical."

I repressed the impulse to throw the coffee in the Greek's face. Far better to keep it to warm myself.

"You are to wed a powerful Transylvanian king."

I took another sip of the coffee and wondered what manner of lie the Greek was telling me.

"I'm glad to see you've decided to be reasonable." He looked past me and nodded. I heard the guard Themistius had ordered to stand by shuffle away into the night. "There will come a time when you will decide that you owe me a debt of gratitude, Nicoletta. I was able to arrange an excellent match for you. Not so good as if you were on the throne in Bellaria, but not bad at all considering your circumstances."

"And what circumstances are those, pray tell? Are you referring to the fact that I, *principessa* of the Kingdom of Bellaria, have been dealt with in the most treacherous manner imaginable by nearly every man I have had the misfortune of coming into contact with since my father's death? Are you referring to the fact that to satisfy the greedy machinations of devious, lowborn swine, I have been kidnapped, raped, and sold into bondage?"

Themistius's coffee-colored eyes became hard. "You might put it that way, *Principessa*, although I would advise against it. Your royal blood is precisely what made it possible for me to arrange your betrothal to a Transylvanian king. If your blood were any less blue, you would be lying on your back in a whorehouse right now with some scabrous peasant between your legs, beautiful though you well may be."

The hostility went out of the scoundrel's eyes. "It might have been different, Nicoletta. I lost my heart the moment I first laid eyes on you in the slave market. I entertained a fleeting hope that you might consent to become my wife. I would still turn my back on the gold if you would agree to marry me."

I shot the Greek a look of imperious contempt. "I would rather die."

"I thought as much," Themistius said, his tone close to despair. "You are too proud, Nicoletta. Royal blood may not flow through my veins, but I would make you a good husband."

"It has nothing to do with your bloodline. You are a rapist and a slaver. My enlightened father would have put you to death for your crimes had you made the mistake of plying your wares in Bellaria."

"Your enlightened father is dead," the devious Greek said, returning to the commercial detatchment that had allowed him to treat me not as a human being but as a piece of property to be bought and sold at a profit.

There was nothing I could say to that, so I said nothing.

"Do not overlook the graciousness of the opportunity I have afforded you, little Nicoletta. Even someone as young, strong, and healthy as you would wear out after a few years of rough trade. It would be a short, brutal life. You should fall down at my feet and thank me."

I laughed merrily, as if he had made a jest.

"Serve me another cup of coffee, Greek, and tell me about this king to whom I am supposedly betrothed. Does he know that you raped me?"

"Don't joke about that. Not *ever*."

"What made you think I was joking?"

"You play at a game that will get us both broken on the wheel. Radu Vlachs is too shrewd to expect that you are coming to him without a certain amount of shop wear. He knows about Bellaria, of course, and is duly impressed with your valiant escape. So impressed that he is quite willing to overlook the fact that you bring no dowry to the marriage."

The sound of his own voice seemed to restore a measure of Themistius's courage.

"Besides," he added with a raffish grin, "I'm sure Radu Vlachs is willing to allow certain accommodations in order to make a match with a cultured and highborn Italian lady. Otherwise, he would have been satisfied with one of the provincial sluts who pass for ladies in Transylvania."

"Radu Vlachs," I said, trying out the name against my ear. It sounded guttural, sharp, foreign. "Tell me about him, Greek."

"The people call him the Hammer. They love him very much. He is a valiant warrior and a great king, the victor of many terrible struggles with the Prophet's armies."

"Why do they call him that—the Hammer?"

"His preferred weapon is the heavy battle-ax. He is apparently a large and extremely powerful man. With a battle-ax you batter your enemy to death even as you cut him to pieces. It is a terrible weapon in the hands of someone who has the strength of a bear."

Themistius paused to take a sip of coffee.

"His province has been on the verge of being overrun by the Muslims for generations. Now, after a long series of bloody victories, the Hammer has finally driven the enemy back. For the first time in centuries his people have breathing space and time for something other than killing the sultan's men and burying their own dead. Now that he no longer has to spend his every waking moment in war counsels, Radu Vlachs has turned his mind toward—please do not laugh—civilizing his fiefdom.

"The king yearns to be far more than a bloodthirsty warlord. I do not deny that he is a little rough around the edges. His manners are crude, his castle not up to the standards of comfort to which you must be accustomed. There are no parterres, garden ponds, or trompe l'oeil murals on the ceilings. Not yet, at any rate, but you could change that, *Principessa*. Indeed, he wants you to change that."

Now the Greek was calling me *Principessa*! I thought that we must be close to Radu Vlach's kingdom if Themistius was beginning to treat me with respect.

"You are certainly wise enough to recognize that Radu Vlachs is something of a visionary leader in the benighted mountain provinces. He looks forward to the day when the enemy's armies are forever routed from the Carpathians, and his people can found schools and libraries and drag themselves up from the mud and the blood, from the barbarism forced upon them by years of warfare. He is looking for a queen who will be mother to his children, but he is also looking for a queen who will be mother to his kingdom's culture."

"How did I come to be chosen for the singular honor of becoming Radu Vlachs's consort?"

"The king sent his emissaries far and wide to arrange a match. I met one in Constantinople. Alas, what prince would send his daughter to the Carpathians? There were a few, of course, but most of the girls were not beautiful, *Principessa*, and none were as well educated as you. When I heard of Bassanio's good fortune in finding you, I knew you were a perfect match for the Hammer."

So, I thought, looking away from the Greek, the truth was still that I was being treated as nothing more than a head of prime livestock, to be bought by the discriminating trader and resold to the highest bidder.

"I do not try to make things sound better than they really are, *Principessa*," the Greek said, divining the thoughts fleeting through my angry mind. "It was this or a few unspeakable years in some fetid Asian brothel. You really should be grateful."

I looked back at Themistius, my eyes flashing.

"I must counsel you against making the Hammer look like a fool for treating you generously. Despite his intentions to introduce a measure of culture in his court, he is entirely capable of slitting both our throats. Radu Vlachs is famous for his murderous rages in battle. I would not do anything to unbalance his humors."

The Greek coughed and lowered his voice, though needlessly, I thought, for there was no one in camp with us except his clerks and the hired German guards.

"There are also political reasons to exercise caution. The Hammer's brother, Duke Vlad, heartily disapproves of his brother's decision to marry a foreigner. He thinks your Italian blood is weak and will dilute their race. Duke Vlad and his faction are your enemies. They will watch for signs of weakness, *Principessa*, and should they find any, they will exploit them to the fullest. You have already seen for yourself what can happen when the powers fail to unite behind the strongest leader."

The Greek leaned forward, his voice falling to a whisper I had to strain to hear.

"My best advice to you, *Principessa*, is to play the part you were cast to play in this tragic drama. You are no longer a virgin, but it would be suicide to let Duke Vlad suspect as much. You cannot begin to imagine how brutal these Transylvanians can be when given the excuse."

Themistius got to his feet, paced back and forth in the pavilion, then threw himself down on the rug in front of me.

"As much as you hate me, *Principessa*—and as sick as it makes me in my heart—you must understand that the least hint of dishonor will condemn us both to slow deaths too horrible to contemplate. Even though you are a woman, you must see the logic in what I say."

I clamped my jaws together, determined to resist this latest insult, the rudest affront of all.

"Allow King Radu Vlachs to restore you to the position to which you were born. You may have come through the Zonguldak slave market, Principessa Nicoletta, yet you can still become a queen. The ignominy of what transpired in Zonguldak can—and *must*—remain secret, or we both die."

The queen of a barbaric kingdom in the Carpathians—I was not fool enough to relish the prospect, yet it held intimations of power and possibility. Even this might serve my greater purpose, if I could remain a Stoic through the ordeal of being bred to a barbarian warlord. Perhaps it was vengeance that worked in mysterious ways.

"Duke Vlad will meet us at noon tomorrow at the frontier of the Hammer's province. I will be paid my expenses and a modest finder's fee," he said with a smile, "and return the way I came. Vlad will escort you the rest of the way to Castle Vlachs."

There was a faint noise behind me, the muffled brush of a boot against the ground. Someone lurked outside the curtained pavilion's entry. It had to be the guard hovering nearby, for Themistius was too clever to be spied upon in his own camp. It was wise of the Greek to be so mistrusting of me. He understood what I was capable of doing to him, given the opportunity.

"And so I must put it to you plainly, *Principessa*: Can you find it within you to see the merit in this match? Because if you cannot, we must break camp now and ride like the devil out of these mountains."

"I am perfectly capable of seeing the logic in the arrangement you offer, Themistius," I said with a Stoic smile.

"I only hope one day I can properly repay you for all you have done."

I got up then and left the Greek alone, looking after me and wondering what I'd meant.

# 15

✧

# First Kill

**H**E KNEW IT was too late to do more exploring. Any nosy adult he ran into would give him the third degree, demanding to know what he thought he was doing, wandering the ship at that time of night, grilling him about whether his parents knew he was out alone at midnight.

And that would be a *laugh*.

His parents weren't on board the ocean liner. He hardly thought of them as his parents, if the truth were to be known. They were really more like an affectionate, distracted aunt and a detached, remote uncle he saw only at holidays and for a token week or two when his boarding school closed down each August. Even when he was at home at break, Mother seemed to always be away at a tennis tournament or house party. And Father—well, not even Mother ever had any idea where Father was most of the time, and that was why she'd divorced him, wasn't it?

Besides, there was the matter of the flashlight—he didn't have one.

After the earlier misadventure, he didn't want to go wandering off into the gargantuan ship's far recesses without a backup light. With any luck at all he would be able to buy one in one of the *Atlantic Princess*'s shops in the morning. Until then, he'd stick to the better-traveled parts of the ship.

All of that aside, he still didn't feel like going to bed.

His little "nap" earlier in the evening had left him feeling completely awake, even to the point that the nerves in his fingers and feet tingled with the most extraordinary sensitivity. This was how it must feel to drink too much coffee, he thought. Everything seemed more sharply in focus that night. Sounds were louder, colors brighter, smells more distinct, more meaningful to his suddenly keen animal senses. And his mind! Ricky McCormick's mind was *sharp as a knife*.

Ricky strolled alone down the deck, thinking about— things. His parents. The privileges his grandparents granted him because they were worried that he was depressed about his parents' divorce. The guilt his grandparents felt because their son had turned out to be such a rotten father for Ricky.

On a night like this, Ricky thought, standing at the railing and looking up at the diamonds glittering against the black marble sky, on a night like this it all seemed so *obvious*. It was like the time at school when he'd been accidentally handed the answers to a fiendishly difficult geography exam.

Ricky was on the Sun Deck, the highest passenger-occupied deck on the ship, where the best cabins were located. His grandparents' cabin suite was situated just aft of the first of the *Atlantic Princess*'s three angled smokestacks. The suites were among the most expensive on the ship, though since Ricky had been around money all his life, it didn't impress him much. The only cabins on the ship better than his grandparents' were the three *appartements de grand luxe* at the very front of the Sun Deck. Occupying the *grand luxe* suites were Keiko Matsuoka, one of the people who had money invested in the ship; Lord Godwin, who basically owned the ship, from what Ricky could tell; and Monsieur Salahuddin, whom Ricky's grandfather had said had "earned a fortune in blood money," whatever that meant.

Ricky turned when the elevator door opened behind him. The car was empty. He stepped inside and pushed each button on the elevator's control panel so that he could stop at each floor on the way down to the B Deck and look around.

It had been a long, strange night. The events in the

parking garage had left him both elated and frightened. The lights had gone out. And then there was the odd sensation that someone was with him in the hold, stalking him. Ricky hadn't been able to find his way out. What happened after that was unclear, like a dream he could not quite recall. He must have sat down—either to hide, because he was afraid, or to wait for the lights to come back on, or maybe even *both*—and fallen asleep. The next thing he'd known, the electricity was back on and he was climbing the stairs toward the door. At first he'd felt feverish and weak, as if he were getting sick, but after a few minutes this curious energy surged into him, making the night come to life. And so he'd gone back to wandering the ship, starting at the top this time, keeping to the well-lighted public areas, just in case.

At the very top of the ship was the bridge, of course, which was where the captain, pilot, navigator, and other officers steered the *Atlantic Princess*. They didn't sleep on the bridge though. The officers' cabins were on the next level down, the Sports Deck. The Sports Deck had a jogging track that ran all the way around the ship. The tennis courts were behind the No. 1 stack, followed by some satellite dishes atop the roof of the indoor squash and racquetball courts. Next came the No. 2 stack, then the helipad, the No. 3 stack, and a big open area leading back to the mainmast, which was seated about three-fifths of the way to the ship's stern. That's where the Sports Deck ended—just past the mainmast, above the Veranda Grill and the outdoor pool.

Beneath the Sports Deck was the Sun Deck, with cabin suites and entrances to the racquetball courts and men's and women's gymnasiums. The McCormicks' cabin and the three *appartements de grand luxe* were on the Sun Deck.

The elevator door opened at the Promenade Deck.

Ricky looked out. Someone was going into a room, shutting the door behind quietly. He couldn't tell if it was a man or a woman. Ricky pulled his head back into the elevator as the doors began to shut.

The Promenade Deck had the widest outside deck, and was so named because it was where passengers were supposed to "promenade." The Forward Bar and Observation Lounge were at the front of the ship on this deck, followed by more cabins, the dreaded Children's Playroom, a chapel, writing rooms, the Queen Elizabeth Lounge—from which children were expressly banned—the library, and various cabins, smoking rooms, and observation lounges.

Next was the Main Deck, Ricky thought as the elevator stopped and its door opened. He started to stick his head out of the elevator but pulled it back in quickly when he saw a tall, thin young man striding down the hall toward him. Ricky pushed the close button. The door shut before the man could reach it.

The Main Deck was just cabins anyway. If you wanted to look out at the ocean beneath the Main Deck, you had to do it through a porthole. The most interesting feature of the Main Deck was near the bow, where the foremast was set. Two-thirds of the way up the mast was the crow's nest, which was actually a little room at the top of a high ladder. Ricky would have very much liked to visit the crow's nest, which was usually unoccupied, although he had yet to devise a way to get to it without being seen from the bridge.

The elevator door opened at the A Deck. The A Deck was basically boring from what Ricky had seen of the ship's diagrams. Just more cabins. He pushed the button to close the elevator door with scarcely a look into the corridor.

The B Deck was as far as the elevator would take him in that part of the ship. There wasn't anything to interest Ricky on the B level, just passenger cabin suites, though there were some places worth visiting farther down.

The C Deck was where some of the crew had cabins. Also, the crew dining room was on the C Deck. The main dining room, the *grande salle à manger*, was also located on the C Deck, but that was back in the middle of the ship, between and below the No. 2 and 3 funnels. Though the kitchen for the *grand salle à manger* was sensibly located behind the dining room, the crew's kitchen was one deck beneath the crew dining room, on the D Deck; food and dishes went up and down between the levels in dumb-waiters. Ricky had learned this by studying the detailed diagram of the ship he'd found printed in a booklet in the writing desk in his cabin.

The more interesting parts of the ship were in the bow. The F Deck, for example, was where the cars were parked. The G and H decks held cargo. Ricky was keen to explore these areas, imagining them filled with huge wooden crates, stacks of suitcases, and steamer trunks the size of coffins.

Beneath the H Deck was the Engineering Deck. This was the lowest deck in the ship. There was more storage there, and something called the chain locker, which sounded worth seeing. The boiler and engine rooms were on this lowest level, where the constant presence of crew members would make it impossible for him to explore on his own. Ricky would have to ask his grandfather to arrange a tour, which would be less exciting than seeing these chambers on his own but better than not seeing them at all.

Ricky pushed the hold button and strolled out into the B Deck corridor. The hallway was quiet as a tomb. When he closed his eyes, he could feel the almost imperceptible swaying as the ocean liner plowed through the Atlantic swells.

A shriek from the end of the hall made Ricky jump.

A woman emerged from the stairway and began to run down the corridor, her long blond hair and a red scarf streaming behind her. A man in a tuxedo emerged from the stairwell and gave chase.

Ricky backed into the elevator and pushed the close button. He'd never seen adults play tag before, but he knew drinking made people do funny things.

The elevator carried Ricky back up to the Sports Deck, where he disembarked, strolling slowly toward his grand-parents' cabin suite, feeling vaguely unfulfilled. He looked up at the stars, which still glittered with the same peculiar brightness. Probably because they were in the middle of the

Atlantic with no streetlamps to pollute the sky with second-hand light.

The lights were all off in the McCormicks' suite, Ricky saw as he walked past, his sneakered footsteps silent. His grandparents would have a cow if they knew he'd gone back out after they went to bed. There were lights on in other cabins, of course. It would be cool to find a place on the ship where there wasn't much light, a place where the stars would be really spectacular.

The helipad.

It would be perfect, Ricky thought. They turned the lights on up there only for landings. Of course, they were way too far at sea to be within any helicopter's range. It would be a blast to lie on his back on the helipad and look up at the sky. Maybe the ship had a telescope he could borrow? He'd have to ask tomorrow.

Ricky took the stairs behind the No. 2 stack two at a time. He was walking across the helipad—his face tilted up to the glittering expanse of diamond-sparkled blackness above—when he tripped on the body in the darkness and went sprawling.

Carrie opened her eyes and blinked. Someone was at her cabin door.

She sat up and swung her legs out of bed. The luminous dial on the alarm clock said that it was only twelve-thirty. She'd been asleep a little more than an hour. Since she usually woke up at four to get ready for her work shift at five, she had gone straight to bed as soon as she had returned to her cabin after the captain's dinner.

"Who is it?" She switched on the light and looked around for her robe.

"Phil Hunt."

Uh-oh. She grabbed her robe and wrapped it around her on the way to the door.

"What's up, Phil?"

"Some kind of accident up on the helipad. Somebody's been hurt pretty bad."

"You want me to look after Mrs. Reston?"

Marie Reston, their first coronary case, had come into the infirmary in the early evening. Considering the age of many of the passengers, Carrie wouldn't have been surprised if there were more.

"Not exactly. I want you to go topside to handle this."

Carrie stared.

"As a special request from Lord Godwin."

Carrie gave Dr. Hunt an incredulous look. The older physician's face betrayed nothing. One thing medicine will do is teach you to have a good poker face, Carrie thought.

"Your experience in emergency medicine is a hell of a lot more current than mine."

"If you say so, Phil."

What the hell was going on? Didn't Lord Godwin trust Phil Hunt? And if he didn't, why did he hire him as senior physician? He was a capable doctor from what Carrie had seen. Or was Lord Godwin more concerned about Mrs. Reston than whoever was hurt up on the helipad?

"You'd better hurry, Carrie. We can discuss it later." Dr. Hunt closed the door behind him.

Carrie pulled on a pair of jeans and a T-shirt and slipped into her Nikes without bothering to find socks. She'd thrown her white clinic jacket over the chair by the door. She pulled the jacket on, grabbed her bag, and hit the hallway at a dead run.

U.S. Coast Guard Seaman, First Class Joseph Rameriz sat at a gunmetal-gray table in Thomas Point Station, Bermuda, looking at satellite photographs through a magnifying glass.

When Seaman Rameriz was assigned to the Coast Guard's International Ice patrol, he imagined having to spend months aboard a claustrophobic icebreaker in the heaving Arctic Ocean. Nothing could have been further from the truth. His current job took him to sea only on weekends, when he went fishing. And if being stationed on

Bermuda was not quite as good as duty in Hawaii, it was a decent second.

Seaman Rameriz helped watch 45,000 square miles of North Atlantic shipping lanes for icebergs, using a combination of airborne radar, satellite maps, meteorological reports about weather and currents, and computer modeling.

Rameriz's pet project was tracking an ice monster named M-27. Two years after it calved from a glacier in Greenland, M-27 was still nearly two miles long. Like most icebergs, six-sevenths of M-27's volume was beneath the surface. Still, the iceberg towered more than two hundred feet in the air, its toe extending one thousand feet beneath the waves.

"Chief Burnham? Take a look at this, sir."

"That big mother been giving you nightmares again, Rameriz?"

"No way, sir. I'm safe and snug on Bermuda. It's the captains crossing the North Atlantic who are having nightmares about M-27. Look here. She's drifting closer to the shipping lanes. I thought we might want to put out a special warning, sir."

Chief Burnham picked up Ramirez's clipboard. "Nah," he said after giving the reports a quick once-over. "She's not making much speed. I'd be surprised if that big white pig caused anybody much worry for the next forty-eight hours. We'll include an update in the regular advisory. Do the paperwork."

"Aye-aye, sir," Seaman Rameriz said.

The advisories were updated every twelve hours. That was probably good enough, Seaman Rameriz told himself. Ships stayed in the shipping lanes, more or less. Nobody in the merchant marine got majorly lost anymore. Even the most unseaworthy Liberian rust buckets had satellite-aided navigation.

Seaman Rameriz went into the radar room and bent over the scope, his face awash in emerald light that flickered every time the rotating beam touched one of the specks of light that represented bounce-back from a treacherous mountain of floating ice. M-27 was the biggest and brightest one of them all. You couldn't do anything with a monster like that except stay the hell out of its way. They'd used icebergs for bombing targets during World War II. The bombs never even fazed them.

Seaman Rameriz thought about what it would be like to look up from the deck of a tramp freighter and see M-27 looming over your ship. It would be like having somebody drop Mt. Everest on your head.

David Parker sat at the grand piano in their suite, staring at the keys.

"Play something, darling."

He did not respond or in any way indicate he had heard.

"The night is still young," Principessa Nicoletta purred. "If you are disinclined to entertain me with music, then perhaps I shall go out and find one or two playthings with whom to amuse myself."

David looked sharply at Nicoletta. "Don't even joke about that."

Nicoletta laughed merrily. How could he ever have been entranced by the sound of her laughter, the smell of her perfumed hair, the touch of her fingertips against his face?

"I am not joking, *amore mio*. I plan to have a great deal of fun before this magnificent ship reaches its destination. The question is whether I do it now or later."

If Nicoletta's powers were not so formidable, he would have thrown her into the ocean. Maybe the next best thing would be to throw himself into the dark, sweeping waters. He might not have the power to end Nicoletta's dissolute life, but at least he could bring an abrupt halt to his own failed existence.

"If you would agree to make an earnest attempt to learn the secret joy of killing, David, I might agree to limit the amusement I find for myself aboard the *Atlantic Princess*."

"If I refuse?"

Nicoletta leaned back in the daybed and regarded David through dreamy eyes. "If you refuse me, *amore mio*, I will indulge myself in such an unbridled orgy of bloodletting that not a single mortal will be left alive aboard the *Atlantic Princess* when England appears on the horizon."

Nicoletta brought one of her tiny hands to her breasts and exhaled a trembling sigh.

"Two thousand crew and passengers—the ecstasy of reaping such a nonpareil harvest might be enough to carry me away to heaven on the rapture-driven wings of crimson angels. Even I have never savored so rich an experience. To drink in the light of two thousand mortal souls. Think of it!"

David slammed his open hand down on the keyboard, filling their salon with ugly, discordant noise. "How can you say such things!" he shouted, grabbing at his hair with both hands as if to tear it out.

Nicoletta fixed him—*pinned* him—with a malevolent stare that set his skin to crawling. "Pray do not be such an incorrigible weakling. I find it unbearably tedious."

David did not dare take his eyes off her as she walked slowly toward him, brushed the fingers of her left hand lightly through his hair, and continued on, trailing her hand behind her along the piano. She was capable of killing him in an instant if the whim took her. Sometimes he wished she would.

"I am weary after so much conversation at the captain's dinner. Play something nice for me, David, and I will not go out killing tonight."

Nicoletta's smile was wicked.

"Play some Mozart for me," she said with a little laugh, knowing how much the request hurt David, for Wolfgang Amadeus Mozart was one of the *Illuminati* and had been David's mentor before Nicoletta seduced him away from that benevolent order of vampires. The *principessa* leaned back against the corner of the love seat, eyes again shut, lying very still, as if she were asleep, or, better yet, dead.

David turned back to the Steinway. After a few moments' hesitation he lifted his hands and began to play.

\* \* \*

The halogen floodlights blinded Dr. Carrie Anderson as she climbed toward the helipad, her free hand firmly clamped on the iron railing.

"Hold up, there."

Carrie squinted at the silhouette barring her way, letting go of the railing to raise her hand and block the light. It was one of the ship's security officers.

"I'm Dr. Anderson," she said. "Please get out of my way."

"It's all right, Jeff," Carrie heard Jack Ketch yell.

Carrie climbed the rest of the way onto the helipad. She saw a half dozen people on the deck now that she was no longer looking up into the blinding lights. They were gathered around something on the deck near the No. 2 stack. Ketch was walking quickly toward her, his hand on a boy's shoulder, though whether to comfort him or to keep him from fleeing, Carrie could not tell. George McCormick was on the boy's other side. Mr. McCormick was wearing slippers and a robe over his pajamas. Ketch indicated for Carrie to meet them at a ventilator, where their line of vision would be shielded from whatever was happening behind the No. 2 stack.

"What's the story here?" Carrie asked, pushing her hair out of her face. The wind was brisk that high up on the ship.

"This is Ricky McCormick," Ketch said. "You know Mr. McCormick, of course."

"Hello, Mr. McCormick. Hi, Ricky."

"Ricky found someone who has been injured rather severely," Ketch said.

"Then I'd better see to them," Carrie said, her impatience showing.

"There will be plenty of time for that later." There was no mistaking the meaning in Ketch's voice.

"Mr. McCormick thought Ricky might need a sedative or something. You're a pediatrician, right?"

Carrie nodded.

"He's had quite a shock," Mr. McCormick said, though

it was obvious that he had, too. He put his arm protectively around the boy.

"I'm okay," Ricky said.

"Good, but let's just have a quick look, anyway." Carrie took a silver examination light from her pocket and, stooping a little, shined it in the boy's face. His complexion was an unnatural shade of white. She shined the light in his right and then his left eye. The pupils were a little slow to respond. His forehead felt clammy to her hand. She put her fingers against his neck. The pulse at the carotid artery was elevated but steady.

"You hanging in there with us?"

Ricky nodded.

"Good. I think you may be suffering a mild case of shock, Ricky," Carrie said, addressing her remarks to the child rather than to his guardian. "I want you to go back to your cabin and sit up in a chair with a blanket around you. Keep nice and warm, even if the blanket makes you sweat. Do you understand?"

Both the younger and elder McCormicks nodded.

"Try to stay awake until I get down to see you. I don't think it will be too long. Maybe you could watch TV. There's still something on TV to watch, isn't there?" Carrie asked helplessly. As absurd as it seemed, she had no idea what was on television at that hour, since she never watched TV.

"Sure," Ricky said.

"Run along now. I'll look in on you in a little while and maybe give you something to help you sleep."

"Okay," Ricky said, and nodded. His responsiveness was a good sign.

"Thank you, Doctor," Mr. McCormick said, almost as if she'd just saved the child's life.

"Not at all, sir," Carrie said. She made a swift, surreptitious examination of George McCormick. He looked worse than the boy. "If you'd like, I can give you something to help you sleep, too."

"That's an offer I might take you up on, Doctor."

The two McCormicks detached themselves and headed for the stairs. It appeared to Carrie that Ricky was leading his grandfather away, rather than the reverse. Which made sense. Children are a lot more resilient than adults.

"Dr. Hunt could have examined the boy as well as I."

"Knowing your background in pediatrics, we thought it would be best for you to have a look at the boy. McCormick is a pretty heavy hitter, you know."

"I'm sure you know you've insulted Dr. Hunt in the process," Carrie said, picking up her bag from the helipad.

"Let Lord Godwin and Captain Franchini worry about Dr. Hunt's bruised feelings."

"Fine." Carrie took a deep breath and let it out slowly, telling herself she had far more than Ketch's insensitivity to worry her. "Shall we get on with this?"

Ketch nodded and led the way.

The individuals huddled behind the No. 2 stack looked at Carrie as she approached them. Lord Godwin was there, pale and grim, along with the odious Captain Franchini, and a handful of other ship's officers, several of them looking as if they'd been asleep until recently.

"Give the doctor a little room," Ketch said gruffly.

At the center of the somber congregation was a seated figure with its back slumped against the No. 2. The body had been completely covered from head to foot with a white sheet. It was obviously an adult female, probably young and fit, judging from the contours of the sheet. Starting at the head there was an ugly red stain that had spread outward and down, pulled by gravity.

"How long ago was she found?"

"About twenty minutes," Ketch said.

"By Ricky McCormick."

"Affirmative."

Carrie looked up at Ketch and began to frown. "Is it a good idea for there to be so many people here? Isn't there a risk of losing or contaminating evidence?"

"You do your job, Dr. Anderson, and let me do mine."

Carrie returned Ketch's stare for a moment. She might be

the new kid on the block, but she'd been around enough to know that Ketch wasn't following standard investigative procedure. Not by a long shot. Lord Godwin refused to meet her eyes. She looked to Franchini. The little smirk on his face told her he was glad to see her put in her place. A woman doctor aboard his ship—Carrie knew Franchini had opposed Dr. Hunt's decision to hire her.

Carrie put down her bag and jerked on a pair of rubber gloves. She took the edge of the sheet in her fingertips and held her breath. No one had bothered to tell her one thing about what had happened, but she knew from the quantity of blood that it was going to be damned ugly.

# 16

✧

# Nicoletta's Diary VI

CASTLE VLACHS SAT atop a mountain set apart from the main backbone of the Carpathians, a lonely aerie punched straight up from the Transylvanian forest as if by Titans fighting in the underworld. From the south, the cliffs of Vlachs Mountain were perfectly vertical and unclimbable. The rock face was naked of vegetation except for what bits of lichen and moss could cling to windswept granite. Peregrine falcons were the only creatures who found the cliffs habitable. The Vlachs clan had adopted the falcon as their family symbol, their crest featuring a rampant falcon, its talons encircling the neck of a dying griffin.

Duke Vlad led our party around to the north side, where we began up a donkey track that zigzagged along a precarious series of narrow ledges. The final part of the journey required us to ride single file over a suspension bridge that could be easily cut by defenders under siege. Little wonder the Vlachian kings had been able to resist the Prophet's invading armies: Their fortress was impregnable.

The top of Vlachs Mountain had been leveled sometime near the end of the first Christian millennium to make room for the citadel. The castle that grew up around the original structure was no fairy-tale creation, but a squat, damp, drafty collection of rectangles built out of thick stone walls. Castle Vlachs had virtually no creature comforts—no library, no observatory, no alchemist's laboratory. It was a castle in the original sense, an engine of war, not a royal court.

Seen by a falcon soaring overhead, the fortress would have resembled a pentagram, with towers at the places where each of the five outer walls joined. The citadel, the oldest part of Castle Vlachs, occupied a ridge that sat in the exact center of the summit. The citadel was already more than four hundred years old when I first visited it and contained three hundred and twenty-six rooms, most of them crudely furnished. The nobles lived within the citadel proper or kept quarters in one of the five towers. The rest of the inhabitants lived in a warren of wooden, thatch-roofed buildings built against the main walls, the structures crammed on top of one another in every inch of available space.

A company of pikers in chain mail lined the road leading up to the main gate. They remained motionless, their eyes forward as my horse walked past. These were no ordinary garrison soldiers, but battle-hardened veterans. Every second or third man displayed some disfigurement from battle—a missing eye, a scar, part of a finger gone.

Two enormous gargoyles perched on the towers that framed the portcullis, monstrous winged devils with jagged teeth and long, serpentine tongues hanging past their chins. Their stone mouths were gutters through which burning tar and phosphorus could be poured on any invaders blessed enough to make it that far, only to be scalded to death within reach of the castle walls.

The cheering began even before I emerged from the tunnellike entry that opened into Castle Vlachs's central courtyard. It was a welcome surprise to discover the populace had turned out to welcome their new queen. Unlike Duke Vlad, the people of Castle Vlachs seemed prepared to love me. Wildflowers rained down upon me as I rode into the courtyard. Children were held up as I passed. Hands reached out to touch my skirts.

Duke Vlad was cheered, too. He was popular with the

people—not so popular as their new queen, perhaps, but a close second.

King Radu Vlachs—the *Hammer*—awaited me at the far end of the courtyard, standing on a simple wooden platform. He was a bear of a man, a hulking Slav who stood nearly six and a half feet tall. His hair was long and matted, and his untrimmed beard hung over his barrel chest like a tattered rag. The powerful arms jutting out from either side of his gleaming breastplate were bigger around than most men's legs. His armor and battle sword seemed inappropriate dress, but such was the fashion in the Carpathians, where men were accustomed to being called away from the hearth without a moment's notice to charge headlong into pitched battle with the Muslims.

One page held the reins of my horse while another helped me dismount. Two sour-smelling ladies-in-waiting led me up the rickety stairs to meet the Hammer upon this impromptu dais. I bowed my head, and as I began to go down on my right knee, as court etiquette required, King Radu reached out with his paw and stopped me, raising me up to stand beside him. He took my hand and held it aloft with his.

The crowd erupted in cheers.

"You bring a new light with you into my kingdom, *Principessa.*"

Radu Vlachs's halting Latin was as unpolished as his appearance, yet it was a welcome sign that he'd had some small measure of learning, an artifact of the priest who taught him his catechism. King Radu's church Latin would at least make it possible for us to communicate.

"Any light I bring into your Transylvanian province is but a reflection of your own greatness, my king."

*"Non,"* King Radu said. His stern eyes softened as he looked at me. "You are even more beautiful than was promised."

"You flatter me, my liege."

"And you flatter me by agreeing to become my queen. You must think my castle very crude."

"Quite the contrary, my king. When I saw this formidable mountaintop fortress, I thought *this* is my idea of beautiful. You have no doubt heard what befell the di Medusas on Bellaria."

"Aye," King Radu said, his voice sepulchral. The darkness that flickered in his eyes made me thankful I was not one of the Hammer's enemies.

Radu Vlachs escorted me into a vast dining hall, where the rustic lords and ladies were assembling for the welcoming feast. Themistius had told me the truth: There was no trompe l'oeil painting on the hall's barrel-vaulted ceiling, just the residue of centuries of soot from the fires in the enormous hearths at opposite ends of the cavernous chamber. King Radu and I were seated in the center of the hall on stone thrones that were remarkably uncomfortable even with a pillow and bearskin covering.

"I hope I am not being too indelicate, *Principessa*, if I mention setting a date for the wedding. I only broach the subject to save you the embarrassment of doing so yourself. No doubt the question is foremost in your own mind."

"I think it is very practical of you to do so, my king."

"Local custom dictates that we wait until the winter solstice to exchange vows. It is an old habit going back many generations. The priests do not much care for solstice weddings, saying they smack of paganism. I only hope the wait will not cause you much discomfort. Of course, if you wish to change our simple custom, I will order—"

"I would not think of altering your people's traditions."

Radu Vlachs again broke into a smile. I tried not to notice his teeth. I would have to think of a way to introduce basic hygiene without insulting the king or Duke Vlad and the other court conservatives. "Then it is decided," he said, glad to have so delicate a matter behind him. "A solstice wedding."

A servant kneeled before me, offering up a delicate goblet of Venetian glass filled with a wine that must have been brought to this remote province only at the greatest of trouble and expense. A serving girl appeared from behind my throne, gently lifting my feet so that she might slip an embroidered pillow beneath my heels.

I pushed the pillow away from my feet, shaking my head so that the girl would take it away. I also bade the servant take away the wine.

"Pray do not think me ungrateful, sire, but I do not wish your people to believe their king is taking a fragile plaything as a wife. I have become accustomed to spartan living since leaving Bellaria. To be truthful, I am no longer comfortable being pampered like a nightingale in a gilded cage. I prefer simple things."

Before King Radu could protest the trifling pleasures offered me, I stood and intercepted a page delivering flagons of ale to the nearest table. I lifted a vessel with both hands and drank. The chilled ale was potent and refreshing. I took a second drink to show I was not too good to share their plebeian brew. As I put down the flagon, I noticed Duke Vlad watching me, at his side two elder knights with flowing white hair and snowy beards.

"I can see that you are not entirely blind to the dictates of politics, Principessa Nicoletta," King Radu said in a voice meant for me alone.

"Not entirely," I said with a small smile.

"An appreciation for such things is fitting in a queen. I look forward to the benefit of your counsel."

That was a compliment! Perhaps Transylvania was not in all things backward.

"It is my deepest desire, Principessa Nicoletta, that you share your learned ways with my court," King Radu said, leaning closer. "We are a good and valiant people, yet we are simple and in some ways ignorant. Shine some of your light into Castle Vlachs, *Principessa*. A little poetry and music will lighten the days of a kingdom that has struggled for many generations just to keep from being annihilated."

I smiled up at King Radu, thinking that he was much different from what I had expected. Judging from his appearance, Radu Vlachs was a barbarian, yet the outward form concealed a mind that was capable of subtle distinctions. This king was no philosopher, but he might quickly become one, given the proper nurturing. The real question, of course, was not whether I could introduce King Radu to the pleasures of Aristotle, but whether I could get him to help me lead an army back to Bellaria.

"I was blessed to receive an excellent education, my king. It would be an honor to share what I have been taught with your subjects."

A woman emerged from the crowd as the king and I spoke, stopping a polite distance away, waiting for an audience. She was not dressed like the other women in the hall. Although her clothing was made from the same rude cloth, the garments had been sewn in an approximation of a style that had been popular in stylish courts when I was a little girl.

"This is Agripanella," King Radu said, motioning the woman forward. "She worked since childhood in the household of a priest in Cluj. The pox carried away the priest last winter. I was able to secure her services for you as body servant."

I motioned for her to rise.

"I await your pleasure, my lady."

I laughed with joy and clapped my hands. "You speak lovely Italian!"

"I grew up speaking three languages, *Principessa*: Daco-Romanian, the language of my native land; Latin, the language of the Church; and Italian, the language of Father Alister's native country."

"This is too thoughtful of you, my king," I said with a laugh, switching back to Latin. "Being able to speak in my native tongue with Agripanella will be like having a tiny piece of my home with me here in the Carpathians. I am deeply in your debt."

I saw from the corner of my eye Duke Vlad come walking toward us. The smile on his face was unnatural and frightening.

"I must thank my brother for safely delivering my new

queen," King Radu said, then added something to the duke in Daco-Romanian. Vlad ignored his brother and spoke instead to Agripanella, again in the guttural dialect.

"Duke Vlad says he has a most humorous story to tell you about King Radu," she told me, translating.

I glanced at Radu Vlachs. His face was an impassive mask.

"Duke Vlad wants to tell you the story of how his brother came to be known as the Hammer."

Agripanella looked nervously at King Radu, but he gave no sign that she should refuse Duke Vlad's order.

"King Radu captured seven hundred of the sultan's men in the Battle of Flastigur. The king gave an order that the prisoners—whose hands were bound behind them—be drawn up in a long queue on their knees alongside the Pastik River. King Radu went from man to man, smashing in each prisoner's skull with an armorer's hammer. All day he kept at his work, swinging the hammer again and again. He did not pause to eat or rest, but only to wade into the river from time to time to wash enough of the gore off himself so that he might continue. It was night when he finished. The river was red with blood and clogged with floating corpses. From that day forward, King Radu's fighting men have called him the Hammer."

I was careful to keep my face neutral. King Radu's eyes flickered toward Duke Vlad before settling again upon me. It was difficult to gauge the emotion behind the mask, but I thought what I saw was weariness more than anger.

"It was a glorious victory!" someone crowed. I had been so intent upon Agripanella's story that I had not noticed the delight the savage tale elicited among the others in the hall. They regarded the Hammer's butchery as one of the great moments in their history, an event to be celebrated, to be recounted again and again, a source of pride. Barbarians, I thought; they really were barbarians.

"The Battle of Flastigur was the first time I met the enemy after my father fell in battle against the sultan," King Radu said, monitoring my reaction as closely as was Duke

Vlad. "I was a young man, and new to the crown, and my heart was filled with rage."

"No wonder Muslims tremble when they hear the Hammer's name," I said with a controlled smile, skirting the trap Duke Vlad had laid for me, the first of many traps, I was sure.

King Radu turned to his brother and said something in their native language. Looking as if he were about to choke, Duke Vlad bowed to his king, shot me a hateful glare, and stalked off.

"I am sorry to have welcomed you to Castle Vlachs with such tales of Carpathian savagery. Perhaps it is best that you hear about us at our worst."

"I am a philosopher, my liege. A philosopher does not shrink from seeing things as they are."

"Then you must see that my brother does not favor the union of our families' bloodlines."

"We shall have to see what wonders time, a nimble wit, and a disarming smile can work on Duke Vlad."

Laughing, Radu Vlachs led me back inside the hall.

I established two schools, one for boys and one for girls. I put Father Dimitri, one of the few literate men in the kingdom, in charge of the boys' school, using a curriculum of my own devising. Agripanella was installed as headmistress of the girls' school. Though her own education had been severely limited growing up in a priest's household, she was too bright a woman to be wasted washing my clothing and brushing my hair.

Expecting the people to resist my girls' school, I discovered that few things were as expected in the Carpathians. King Radu's people welcomed the chance to educate their daughters, regarding reading and writing as feminine skills best suited to women and priests. Had King Radu not put his foot down with his lords—becoming the Hammer again for a few angry moments—the boys' school would have been a complete failure. As it was, the king issued a strict edict requiring his nobles' sons to attend class. Though

Duke Vlad and his favorites seethed, the royal edict summarily closed further discussion.

Radu fell more in love with me with each passing day. Curiously enough, I found that I did not loathe his attentions. With conquest, not romance, as my real concern, I could not have found a stronger or more courageous warrior for a mate.

At night Radu and I would sit in front of the roaring hearth, and I would tell stories about Bellaria. The isle had to seem like paradise next to Transylvania, where the winters were long, the living hard, and the past bloody. I planted my seeds as I went, content to wait a few years for them to flower. If all went as I had planned, sometime after we wed there would come a night when Radu Vlachs, lying beside me in the dark after making love, would begin to think about leaving his brother in charge of Castle Vlachs while he set out with his queen and a force of his adventurous warriors in quest of an idyllic life amid the vineyards and olive groves of the Mediterranean.

A peasant named Gareloch replaced Agripanella as my handmaiden.

Gareloch was a strange little gnome of a woman, half a head shorter than myself with a wild head of frizzy red hair. From the capacious pockets in her long woolen frocks she would pull all manner of strange things: blue-jay feathers, glass beads, tiny muslin bags filled with herbs and tied with a cast-off bit of rawhide—some of these talismans Gareloch carried to ward off evil. Gareloch was constantly signing herself against the evil eye. She started at the sight of ravens and owls and other peasant omens and was constantly on the lookout for ghosts and various hobgoblins, sprites, faeries, and wood spirits. She believed she had the power to foretell the future by casting a handful of worn bones she kept in her pocket. Although she allowed that her divining powers were still developing, she did have an uncanny ability to guess what the weather would be on the morrow.

Gareloch's ignorant peasant superstitions were hardly

unique. Without the benefits of philosophy and education, the citizens of Radu Vlachs's kingdom were extremely superstitious. I was too polite, and cautious, to criticize what I thought of their illogical belief in monsters and beasties.

One night I was sitting at my window, watching the moon rise, when the most beautiful sound came floating up to me from the forest below the castle. I had not heard the sound of a lute since Bellaria, and even then never heard it played with such grace and sensitivity. The haunting Dorian melody was bewitching, the song of a magical nightingale. As I listened, I fell into a sort of trance. The music seemed to be calling me, drawing me to it.

There were two of them. I could see them quite clearly in the moonlight as they emerged from the forest, following the road leading to Castle Vlachs. The woman sat upon a black stallion with the lute cradled in her hands, her fingers drawing from the instrument music sweeter than the most delicious lover's dream. She was tall and handsome, her hair as white as snow and even longer than mine. Her cloak was black silk shot through with threads of gold and silver. I could not make out her features from my great height, but I knew she would be a great beauty.

The man at her side rode an undistinguished brown horse, leading a pack horse on a tether. He was shorter than the woman, and his round body was wrapped in a dark cloak. His bearded chin was tilted down on his chest. Perhaps he was sleeping as he rode, lulled into a heaven of honeyed sweetness by his companion's magic lute.

I listened to the music for more than an hour as the travelers made their way up the tortuous path that climbed from the forest to Castle Vlachs. I was preparing to go ask King Radu to raise the portcullis, which was lowered each night at sunset, when I heard the distant rumble of the gatehouse machinery. Either the sentries or Radu Vlachs himself had been as charmed by the music as was I and had already ordered the raising of the gates.

"We have special guests," Father Dimitri told me in his

unctuous voice as I entered the great hall. "The blind old man who looks like a Franciscan is Johann the Poet. He has come to sing epics of the latest battles against the sultan."

"First bring them food and drink so that they may refresh themselves after their journey." My words sent a dozen servants rushing into action to make the newcomers comfortable, showing them what modest courtesies Castle Vlachs could offer.

The woman took a sip of wine but had no appetite. As Johann ate ravenously, attended by a page who told the bard what foods were on the dishes and served him what he requested, the minstrel set to work replacing one of the strings on her lute. She seemed quite shy, for she neither looked at nor spoke to anyone, not even Johann. I was wondering if she was a mute, if she owed her amazing facility for music to the fact that it was her sole means of communication, when she looked up at me. Our eyes met, and I immediately felt as if we had known each other all our lives. Her eyes were my eyes, the same Tyrrhenian blue hue, and seemed to reflect my own soul.

When Johann had eaten his fill, King Radu ordered silence from the jugglers and country musicians, who, as usual, were fighting to make themselves noticed above the shouting and barking dogs in the great hall. The old man stood in the middle of the hall and drew back the cowl of his robe. He reached out his hands and his face toward the roof beams, his opaque white eyes seeming to search for something that could be seen only in blindness.

"Johann was a fearsome warrior before the Muslims captured him and put out his eyes," Father Dimitri whispered to me.

Accompanied by the minstrel's lute, the bard began to chant his tale. At first his voice was tired, the voice of an old man, but as the epic unfolded, the words flowing from his mouth became smooth and resonant.

> *Tell us, Muse, of that treacherous day,*
> *When plots most devilishly vile,*

*Were hatched in traitorous conspiracy*
*To conquer the fairest isle.*

I sat bolt upright, my fingernails biting into my palms.

"I will tell him to stop," King Radu told me, leaning across Father Dimitri.

I shook my head, blinking to keep back the tears. "No, my liege. Let the bard pay tribute to honor my fallen kinsmen."

If I was unable to keep the tears back, there was no dishonor, for Johann sang so movingly of the di Medusa family's doomed struggle against the sultan that few of the warriors in the great hall had dry eyes by the time he finished. Emotionally exhausted, I excused myself immediately and went to my apartments, where I fell weeping into bed, sending Gareloch away with a backward wave of my hand.

Music from the minstrel's lute floated up to my room through the halls, through the stone walls, through my open window, a soothing balm to my aching heart. I fell asleep listening to the bewitching sound.

I awoke in the middle of the night, knowing someone was in my room—not Gareloch but someone else, and yet I was unafraid.

I sat up in the darkness, reaching for the lamp.

"Is it you?"

The soft golden light came up, and I saw that it was indeed the minstrel. I wondered how she had gotten past the guards, my handmaidens, and Gareloch so that I might awaken to find her sitting in my bedchamber, watching me sleep.

The minstrel looked back at me, returning my smile but saying nothing.

"I know you mean me no harm, but it is dangerous to come unannounced into the *principessa*'s private chambers," I said in a low voice. "Had I cried out, the guards might have harmed you before I could gather my wits enough to realize it was a friend."

The minstrel said nothing but moved to my bed and sat on the side of it. Her hair—it was so perfectly white that it shined like silver in the lamplight. I was as fascinated with it as Gareloch and the others had been with my raven-colored tresses, though I suppressed the urge to feel its silky smoothness between my fingers.

"Why do you not speak?"

The minstrel picked up my hand and held it between hers.

"You speak with your lute."

She smiled.

"You do not have your instrument with you. How will we communicate?"

The minstrel leaned slowly forward and kissed me. It did not seem an act of lewdness, but rather of friendship. She pulled my head toward her. I nestled my face against her perfumed, snowy tresses, silk against my skin.

Her lips were upon my neck. There was more than friendship in her kisses and caresses now, yet I did not reject them. I recalled the tenderness of my Turkish hand-maidens in Zonguldak. If the minstrel wished to seduce me, I was perfectly ready to take what comfort I could in her touch, knowing that her fingers would touch me as skillfully as they touched her lute.

The minstrel's lips opened against the skin on my neck like an exotic flower that blossoms only in the darkness. I felt her tongue's moistness, then her teeth nipping playfully at me. And then, without warning, the sharp prick of pain followed by an explosion of the purest form of sensual pleasure I had ever experienced.

I fell back against the bed and she climbed on top of me, straddling me with her legs, her mouth locked onto my neck as she gently began to suck the blood from my willing body.

\* \* \*

My feet were unsteady when I arose the next day. The sunlight hurt my eyes. I felt hot and feverish, although my stone-walled apartments in Radu Vlachs's castle were cold, damp, unhealthy. I picked up my looking glass and saw the unnatural blush in my cheeks. I turned my head and examined my neck, rubbing the tips of my fingers across the blemishless skin. There was a slight tenderness, but nothing more.

But what of the night before?

I had dreamed of a succubus. The minstrel's visit to my bedchamber, her caresses, the way her kissing my neck turned into a bite—hallucinations visited upon me by the fever.

I foolishly began to ready myself for the day and felt a sudden hollowness in my belly. I sat down hard on my bed, falling backward in a swoon. I did not awaken until Gareloch brought me my breakfast. I sat up but could not eat. I confess to being frightened, for illness in those backward days often led to death. Gareloch brought my chest of herbs and helped me mix a restorative potion. I drank the draft and lay back in bed, drifting off to sleep almost immediately. I spent the rest of the day and the night in bed, drifting in and out of sleep, harried by nightmares about ravens feeding upon my rotting corpse.

The fever was gone when I awoke the next day. The crisis had passed.

King Radu was touchingly solicitous of my health when I went down to the great hall. I assured him all was well with me, not knowing the change that had already begun within me.

The usual noisy collection of acrobats, dwarfs, and jugglers performing during supper bored me. I was impatient to see the minstrel, to have my eyes reassure me of what my mind already knew—that she was nothing more than an ordinary woman who had appeared to me in a capricious and meaningless fever-dream. The night dragged on like an interminable argument. The candles had burned more than halfway down when my impatience finally got the better of me.

"Where is the minstrel?" I asked Father Dimitri, trying to keep my voice casual.

"They are gone, *Principessa.*"

"*Gone?* Gone where?"

"Wherever it is that wandering minstrels and bards go, my lady."

King Radu overheard this exchange and noted my distress. "If it would please you, Principessa Nicoletta, I will send riders out to bring them back."

"It is just that I had hoped to have the pleasure of hearing them again. Never have I heard anyone coax such beautiful music from a lute."

Radu Vlachs called one of his men over and gave the necessary order, handing the man two gold coins as tokens of his appreciation for the poet and the minstrel, promising two more if they returned and yet another as reward for the messenger if he was successful. The messenger and a troop of escorts galloped out of the portcullis almost before I could thank Radu with a kiss.

The messenger and his escort did not return the next day. When they did not come back after a week, it was assumed that some bloody fate had befallen them and they would never return. Their disappearance renewed concerns that the sultan's marauding troops were once again lurking around the mountain kingdom's far corners, probing to find the first sign of weakness that would signal yet another all-out assault against Radu Vlachs's province.

"Despite appearances to the contrary, *Principessa,* danger is never really very far away in Transylvania," King Radu said to me one night in a heavy voice.

He was absolutely right.

A fortnight after the minstrel and bard disappeared from Castle Vlachs, I awoke after midnight to find the minstrel sitting beside me on the bed in my darkened room.

"They have found you!" I cried, sitting up and grasping her hands.

Giving no sign that she understood my words, the minstrel pulled me to her and wrapped her arms around me.

I cannot explain the joy I felt at finding my angel once again, or explicate the strange attraction—some would say *unnatural* attraction—I felt for her. All I can say is that the heart is its own master.

As we held each other, certain intrusive questions took shape in my mind. The minstrel's presence in my bedchamber that night argued that the previous visitation had not been the product of a fever dream, but a factual occurrence. So what of the rest of it—the memory of being bitten in the neck, the delirious pleasure I experienced as she drank of my blood, and the fever afterward? If the visitation and fever had been real, had the other things been real, too?

What nature of being was this minstrel? She had the ability to vanish into the Transylvanian forest more easily than the craftiest she-wolf, return unnoticed, and slip past castle guards so vigilant that hardly a rat could stir without drawing their notice. What was the source of her strange and darkling power? Could drinking blood somehow be the key? Whatever the explanation, it had to be subject to the empirical laws of science. To know these secrets would be to share in their power—power I might use to punish the enemies who had forced me from Bellaria and caused me so many indignities.

The minstrel began to kiss my neck. The touch of her moist lips sent shivers up my spine. I closed my eyes and was rolling my head to one side, when my will exerted itself. I pushed her gently away from me.

"Wait," I whispered.

Her blue eyes glittered in the darkness like a cat's. She showed no sign of impatience, no irritation or disappointment at having her pleasure—*our* pleasure—postponed.

"You know that I am yours," I said, "but before you take me again, there are things I would have you explain to me."

The minstrel said nothing.

"Can you understand my words? Is there not some way for us to communicate?"

The minstrel slowly smiled. "I can understand you, *Principessa,* and I will happily share my secrets with you, but I must warn you that words are inadequate tools for conveying the essence of my knowledge. To possess my powers, *Principessa*, you must experience them."

The minstrel's smile deepened, becoming even more mysterious. "You are an extraordinary woman, *Principessa.* You are not the least bit afraid of me."

"Only the ignorant are afraid of the unknown," I said.

I tugged at the drawstring that held my sleeping gown closed, loosening it until the gown fell to my waist. I lowered myself slowly backward onto the down pillows, never taking my eyes off the minstrel. Lifting my head slightly, I gathered my loose hair together and pulled it to one side so it wouldn't be in the way.

"Come," I invited her, "take of me what you will."

I was unable to get out of bed the next morning. The familiar fever was back in me, but sharper, harder, like a red-hot knife plunged into my brain. Again I thought I would die, although the agony I suffered made me almost wish I were dead.

Gareloch stayed at my side, changing the bedclothes when they became drenched with sweat, washing my brow with a cool towel, spooning a little water and broth down my throat when I was able to take it.

I awoke one day to see King Radu standing in my room, staring at me with a desolate face. Duke Vlad was with him, standing back in the shadows. His face was as grim as ever, but I could see the triumph in his eyes. He had warned his brother that I would never be strong enough to be queen in so harsh a country, and my sudden predisposition to fever had proven him right.

*If we are lucky, the wench will die soon enough. Then Radu can take a proper Carpathian queen at the solstice.*

Poor King Radu! He had shown me nothing but kindness. I was so heartsick to have disappointed the king that I did not at first realize I had somehow read Vlad's hostile thoughts, even though they had been composed in a language I was only beginning to comprehend.

I sat up in bed and looked at Duke Vlad, lifting up my hand, pointing at him. I intended to curse him for the ill health he wished me, but I lacked the strength even for this simple act. I fell back in bed, exhausted. At that moment I thought of my father, and how he had died by inches after being poisoned. I had come to know his agony, but would the experience make me stronger or merely dead?

Everything faded into darkness.

I had possession of my mind when I next awoke, but my strength was entirely gone. I could not even sit up without Gareloch's help.

"Are you afraid to die, *Principessa*?" Gareloch asked, bathing my face with cool water.

"I feel that what is happening to me is but a change, from one thing to something else."

"Do you want me to call for Father Dimitri?"

"Not the priest." I did not wish to speak with that hypocrite, but I also feared that he might suspect that I had been consorting with—what? A devil? An angel? I would have to go all the way into the great darkness to learn the answer to this question, which perplexed me more than the most difficult philosophical dilemmas I had wrestled with as a student back on Bellaria.

"How fares the king?" I managed to ask after a rest.

"He mourns for you, *Principessa*. He loves you very much."

"I am truly sorry that I have made him suffer. I do not wish to cause him more pain. Perhaps I can make it up to him someday."

"God willing," Gareloch said, and crossed herself.

I did not think that God would have anything to do with it, but I did not say as much.

* * *

A kiss on my forehead awakened me.

It was the minstrel, come back to visit me as I lay dying. I looked into her mind and saw that she was called Aedon, after the grieving woman Zeus had transformed into a nightingale. How strange it was that the minstrel and I had shared such intimacy without my knowing her name until then.

"I wondered if you would come before I died," I said, my whisper all the voice I could muster. "Do not worry, *amore mio*. I bear you no ill will. The fault is mine. I am too weak to accept the powers you tried to give me."

Faithful Gareloch sat in a chair, her eyes unseeing, bewitched by Aedon.

*Do not cry*, Principessa. *Just a short while longer, and you shall be as strong as I. One more kiss is all that will be required, my beloved, and you will be like me forever.*

The candle on the table next to Gareloch guttered and went out, leaving the bedchamber in complete darkness. And yet by some power unknown to me I could see in the dark—not clearly, but clearly enough.

*When you are a vampire*, Principessa, *you will see in the dark as well as in the light. And never again will you have to bend to suit the will of a mere mortal man.*

What was a vampire? The Slav word was unfamiliar to me.

Aedon's silky hair fell across my face as she kissed me again, on my lips, on my neck. I had never suspected that dying would be so sweet.

I spent the next fortnight completely insensate, trapped within a burning nightmare that refused to let me go. At one point I was dimly aware of Duke Vlad demanding that I be moved to the king's hunting lodge. Radu Vlachs reluctantly agreed, too good a king to allow the plague to take root inside his castle. King Radu tried to accompany me; his nobles nearly had to draw their swords to prevent it, finally convincing him of the calamity that would befall the province should their lovesick king succumb to the plague.

Faithful Gareloch alone remained with me, nursing me during my final illness. The first blizzard of winter arrived, piling snowdrifts deep around the hunting lodge. Outside in the forest, timber wolves howled to one another, the only company poor Gareloch had as she sat up with me through the long Transylvanian nights.

It was witching hour when my fever broke. I awoke and sat up in bed, my head filled with the prescient awareness of someone whose senses are no longer constrained by ordinary mortal boundaries. I heard the feathers rustle on an owl perched in a tree, waiting for a rabbit to venture from its burrow. Farther up the mountainside a wolf sat alone on an outcropping of rock, watching our lodge for signs of life. The Hunger rising within me pushed these perceptions from my mind, the empty gnawing seeming to double with every breath I drew.

"Gareloch," I called softly.

*"Principessa!"* My servant awoke in her chair with a start. She put her hand on my forehead and began to smile. "Your fever has gone down, and your eyes have cleared. You cannot imagine how worried I have been!"

"I am going to be all right," I said. Hearing my own hoarse words, I realized they were true. But the Hunger— how terrible my Hunger!

I put my trembling hand around Gareloch's shoulder and pulled her near me. The Hunger was raging inside me, a bestial howling that demanded immediate satisfaction.

"May I prepare you something to eat, *Principessa*?"

I looked into Gareloch's eyes and saw nothing but love and solicitude. Poor Gareloch! She had no idea what visions her kind words put into my tortured mind.

"You have not touched food for two long weeks, *Principessa*. You must be very hungry."

"Yes, Gareloch," I said, my voice a croak. "I am very hungry indeed."

After so many centuries and so many deaths, Gareloch's is the only one that causes me any remorse. Still, the taste of her blood that first time was delicious!

# 17

✧

# The Worm Turns

**"S**ORRY, SIR. YOU can't come up here."

Alexander Fox's attempt to look past the ship's security officer was useless. The halogen landing lights made it like looking into the sun. It was impossible to see what was happening on the helipad.

"I was just taking a midnight stroll."

The security guard stared. Fox knew that he was an unconvincing liar. He'd have to practice. He had been able to master anything he put his mind to, so there was no reason he couldn't learn to lie.

"Has there been some sort of accident?"

"I'm sorry, sir, but I'm not at liberty to say."

"I thought I saw my friend Dr. Anderson." Describing Carrie as his *friend* was a little optimistic, but Fox was optimistic about his chances with the attractive physician.

"You can't come this way, sir. You'll have to go back the way you came."

"Right."

"Good night, sir."

Jesus, Fox thought, turning back. Even the goons were polite aboard the *Atlantic Princess*.

The Garden Lounge was filled with exotic plants and birds. The room really was a garden of sorts, complete with golden carp swimming in a sunken pond in the middle of the room. The walls and ceiling were made of glass panels. The bar was along the rear wall. Opposite it, against the windows looking out over the bow, was the baby grand piano. David Parker sat at the keyboard, his head bent forward in concentration playing Liszt.

The bartender brought Keiko's drink. She sipped the champagne cocktail, testing it, and nodded her approval, dismissing the barman.

There were only a few people in the lounge. They chatted quietly, more intent on their conversations than the music. David was bent over the keyboard, oblivious of everything but his music, the complex, interwoven sixty-four-note runs flying from fingers like sparks, conjuring images of devils cavorting in a frenzied dance.

Listening to David, watching him, Keiko thought about how unfortunate it was for so beautiful a man to be trapped in an unsatisfying affair with a young mistress. Keiko was young, too, but she knew many things about satisfying men. She picked up her cocktail napkin and folded it into an origami swan, considering what it would be like to teach David the Rapture of the Yoked Oxen or the Frog-in-Heron's-Mouth.

Keiko finished her drink and threaded her way through the giant ferns to stand behind David. When the final chord was struck and the music continued to hang in the air like lingering incense, he slowly turned and looked straight in her eyes, as if he'd been aware of her presence all the time.

"You play like a man who is possessed," Keiko said, seating herself beside David on the piano bench.

"I am possessed," he replied in a low voice.

Keiko rested her tiny hand on his shoulder. Despite his thin, aesthetic appearance, his body was firm and strong beneath his jacket. The other passengers had departed while David was playing, and now even the bartender had disappeared. Except for the golden carp swimming in circles around the lotus flowers in their pond and the exotic birds dozing in their gilded cages, Keiko and David were completely alone.

"Possessed with what?" Keiko asked in a voice so soft, she wondered if she said the words or merely thought them.

"Passion," the vampire answered.

And then he kissed her.

Carrie pulled the sheet back and blanched. It was always more difficult when it was someone you knew, she reminded herself, taking several slow, deep breaths. Go slow. Remain detached. Be methodical.

The men had moved a discreet distance away from the body. Ketch, who had changed into a jogging suit sometime after the captain's dinner, was standing to one side, talking with a group of security officers. Lord Godwin was farther away, his back against the railing, staring off into the night, his carefully composed face not quite masking the stricken look in his eyes. Captain Franchini was beside Lord Godwin. Franchini stood smoking, one hand casually resting in the pocket of his white jacket, looking supercilious, as always.

The wind began to whip and snap the bloodstained sheet in Carrie's hand. She wadded it up, used her bag to weigh it down, and began her examination, beginning with noting the obvious things. Proceed from the general to the particular, that was the rule.

Mandy Robsard had been strangled from behind with a scarf. Her eyes bulged grotesquely in their sockets, which was common in strangulation. Her mouth was frozen open in a final scream that must have been silent, judging from the way the knotted scarf had crushed her larynx. Swallowing dryly, Carrie noted that the body had been mutilated. The killer had cut out Mandy's tongue, which was why it wasn't protruding from the mouth, as was usually seen in strangulation deaths. Blood from the wound continued to drool slowly from the open mouth, soaking the front of her dress—the party dress that Mandy had looked so lovely in a few hours earlier at the start of the captain's dinner.

Carrie had to look away for a few moments. The memory of their conversation in front of the mirror as they prepared to go into dinner was too fresh, the nerve it touched too raw. Carrie again found herself struggling to keep her composure, to escape the humiliation of breaking down in front of Lord Godwin and the others.

Like all physicians, Carrie had learned to make an accommodation with death, to treat it as a part of life, the end as natural and potentially beautiful as the beginning. But death was also Carrie's enemy, her daily adversary in her profession. It was especially difficult to lose to death when the victim was young. Mandy was only twenty-five or twenty-six, younger than herself, Carrie thought. And, like Carrie, single. It was probably a blessing that Mandy had no husband or children to grieve for her.

Carrie opened her medical kit and fumbled through it, looking for nothing in particular as she struggled unsuccessfully to keep herself from thinking about anything but the grim job at hand.

But what if Mandy Robsard had left behind a husband or an orphan, someone other than casual friends and aging parents to mourn the awful tragedy of her murder? Wasn't the primary function of life to create life, to perpetuate life? If so, then Mandy's death was doubly premature, the loss doubly bitter. Of course, Carrie thought, maybe she was really thinking about herself, projecting her own concerns on someone else's tragedy. Mandy's death made the reality of Carrie's own aloneness stand out in a particularly harsh, unforgiving light. Like her murdered friend, Carrie had let other choices get in the way of what now seemed like the ultimate priority in her life. How could something so crucial go unnoticed for so many years, only to loom over her now, the specter of failure in a place where Carrie had never even noticed there was a contest?

What the *hell* am I thinking about, Carrie thought, rebuking herself angrily. She had to get a grip on herself, to rein in her runaway thoughts before she fell apart completely. Carrie glanced at the others. Thank heaven none of them could see her mental turmoil.

Carrie forced herself to look again at Mandy's mutilated face. It was difficult to imagine anyone being capable of such an obscenity, yet it was plain that *somebody* was.

Carrie would tell Jack Ketch about Salahuddin, who had been at Mandy's table, and the "accident" that blackened Salahuddin's mistress's eye. Ketch could figure out whether the Iranian had anything to do with this horrible crime.

Something about the scene didn't make sense, Carrie thought, shining her penlight into Mandy's unresponsive pupil. Then it hit her: the blood. Though the sheet and dress were soaked, there should have been more blood present, a lot more blood.

Carrie tested the tension in the scarf with her index finger, easily slipping it between the material and the bruised neck. A ligature could serve as a tourniquet, cutting off bleeding, but the pressure had evidently been applied only long enough to bring about Mandy's death. The skin beneath the scarf was deeply discolored with ugly purple-black bruises. Whoever strangled the woman was strong and applied fierce pressure. The bruise turned slightly upward, front to back. The killer was taller than the victim and had stood behind her.

What else might explain the relatively minor hemorrhaging? Mandy might have swallowed some of the blood from the mouth wound, though that wasn't likely. Her body's reflexes would have worked against it.

Gently cradling the body, Carrie lowered it from its sitting position until it was lying on its side on the deck. She gently probed the mouth with a flashlight and wooden depressor. The tongue's removal had hardly been a surgical procedure. There were several inexpert false cuts, and tearing evident toward the incision's terminal end. The beginning signs of rigor mortis were setting in.

Carrie gently rolled over the body and examined the backs of Mandy's legs. Purplish lividity marks on the backs of the thighs showed where the blood had settled in the body following death. The lividity marks, along with the rigor, would put the time of death roughly around eleven-thirty, though it could have been as early as ten-thirty. Mandy must have left the captain's dinner early. As had Carrie, she thought with a shudder.

Carrie used a pair of scissors to cut all the way up the back of the dress and parted the halves. She was surprised to see more lividity marks on the back and upper shoulders.

Carrie caught Ketch's eye and motioned for him to come closer.

"The body was sitting up when I arrived. I assume that's how Ricky found it."

Ketch nodded. "He tripped over the legs in the dark."

"This body has been moved."

"What are you talking about?"

"It was flat on its back long enough after the time of death for blood to settle in the back. See?"

"I'll be damned." Ketch knelt and ran a forefinger over the heel of one of the shoes Mandy wore, then the other. "There's no sign she was dragged."

"A man could have easily carried her."

Ketch looked dubious.

"There also isn't enough blood."

"What's all that?" With a single gesture Ketch indicated the front of Mandy's dress and the pool of blood puddling on the deck beneath her mouth.

"That's blood, but it's not enough blood. If you were to cut out the tongue of somebody who is alive, blood would spray all over the place. My hunch is the mutilation was done after she'd been dead for a while. That would account for the relative lack of bleeding. I think she was killed somewhere around eleven, give or take. I'll know more definitively after we've had a look at the contents of her stomach. The cause of death was strangulation, using this scarf, which crushed the larynx, causing it to swell. Whoever did it was strong and taller than she was. Note the direction the bruise slants on the neck. The killer was probably a man. If the body was moved far, that also argues for the killer being a man. Not many women would be that strong."

Ketch nodded, leaning closer to study the neck, more comfortable than Carrie at examining the corpse of a murder victim.

"I think whoever killed Mandy stashed her body somewhere out of the way for half an hour, then came back, propped her against the smokestack, and cut out her tongue, probably throwing it overboard, though psychopaths—and I hope we're not dealing with one, though I wouldn't completely rule it out—sometimes keep parts of their victims' bodies as trophies, according to my abnormal psych instructor back at school. That would account for everything I see at first glance, meaning the lividity marks and the relative lack of blood, which is conspicuously less than one would expect from a normally pressurized vascular system. Did you notice that she had dinner with . . ."

"Did you ever think about going into forensic pathology?" Ketch interrupted with a crooked grin. "You seem to have a knack for this sort of thing."

"I prefer my patients to be living."

"Why do you suppose her tongue was hacked out?"

"God, I don't know, Jack."

"What's your woman's intuition tell you?"

"I believe in observation, Jack, not intuition, and especially not *woman's* intuition."

"Sorry," Ketch said without sounding as if he were.

"Maybe it's some kind of gesture. Either we're dealing with a lunatic, or somebody is trying to send someone a message. Doesn't the Mafia cut out stool pigeons' tongues to warn others to keep quiet?"

"You have an active imagination, Doctor."

"You need only look at the body if you need proof that there's something more than an active imagination at work on this ship."

"You've got a point there, Carrie." Ketch stood up with a groan and waved at his men. "Okay, let's get this body out of here."

"Wait a minute! I'm just starting my examination. I need to take the core body temperature. I also want to get a rape kit and take some swabs."

"Finish up in the infirmary. There's already been one

passenger up here snooping around. We need to contain this."

"Look, Jack," Carrie whispered as the others approached, "I hardly need to tell you that in any case of wrongful death you must never move the body until the basic examination has been finished. I've been here—what, five minutes?"

"Finish the exam belowdecks," Ketch said, his eyes suddenly cold. "We're going to get this mess cleaned up before the passengers find out and we have a panic on our hands. You've seen enough to sign a death certificate. Check out the body as much as you want once we get it out of a public area. We can't let this get out of hand."

Carrie took a step nearer to Ketch and looked straight up into his hatchet face, arguing in an angry whisper as his men formed a ring around them and the corpse. "I haven't done a thorough examination, and you haven't even taken the time to properly document the crime scene. I'm beginning to wonder if you are more interested in covering up this crime than investigating it."

"Don't *ever* tell me how to do my job, Dr. Anderson."

"Don't ever tell me how to do mine!"

"All right, let's get this down to the infirmary," Ketch ordered his men, ignoring Carrie.

"I do *not* authorize you to move that body until I have conducted the full and complete examination my responsibility as ship's physician requires," Carrie said, her own voice rising to match Ketch's. "You men get away from that body."

"Move the body," Ketch countermanded. "Now. That's an order."

"Do not move the body," Carrie said, nearly shouting. "And that's an order!"

"What seems to be the problem?" Lord Godwin asked without moving as two security officers rolled the corpse onto a lightweight body board while a third covered it with a navy blue blanket.

"Lord Godwin, it is an act of incompetence if not outright malfeasance to move this body," Carrie said, hurrying toward the Englishman and Captain Franchini.

"My dear doctor," Franchini began in the patronizing tone Carrie had heard him use with other women crew members. "Perhaps we can talk about this in private."

"You must tell them to stop—"

"Yes, I agree with the captain that it would be best for all concerned if we continued this discussion somewhere else," Lord Godwin interrupted. "Captain Franchini, perhaps we could repair to your stateroom. I think we could all do with some brandy after such a terrible shock."

Carrie jerked away from Lord Godwin when he tried to put a reassuring hand on her arm. She went back to her medical kit and slammed it shut, closed one clasp, fumbled with the second, decided to hell with it, angrily snatching up the case. To hell with Ketch, and to hell with Godwin and Franchini and their damned brandy. She was going to check on Ricky McCormick on her way back to the infirmary. At least she could do something for him.


They undressed one another and fell into the voluptuous satin sheets on the bed in the suite's master bedroom.

David was slow and tender, lifting Keiko gradually toward ecstasy. Keiko usually played the dominant role with the men she took to bed, but with David everything was turned around. She felt like a nimble sailboat at the hands of a skillful captain—so skillful that in the midst of their passion he was able to wordlessly communicate that there was something special he needed of her, something she had never given to a man. The precise nature of David's need became clear to her by degrees, but when at last she understood, it was as if she had always known it. What David wanted—no, *needed*—was a small, insignificant measure of Keiko's blood.

"Take whatever you want, my love . . ."

David's lips were against her neck, kissing, sucking.

"My blood," she gasped in a whisper as their passion built closer to crescendo. "Drink my blood."

Keiko felt the nip of his teeth, then something stronger, sharper, more insistent pressing against the flesh of her neck. It was almost more than she could bear when he continued to hold back, balancing her trembling upon the brink.

"Now, David!" she gasped.

Keiko shrieked and raked her red-lacquered fingernails across David's back as his teeth stabbed into her neck. Keiko arched her back and was carried away on an explosion of impossibly intense bliss.

"I see you found it impossible to hold the Hunger at bay a moment longer."

The voice—far away, velveteen, feline—floated toward Keiko. She lay suspended between two worlds, the woman's musical voice vibrating each nerve in her body.

"I knew the Hunger had to be strong in you after you ran away from that child without fully satisfying yourself. Oh, pray do not give me that horrific stare, David. I did not touch the boy."

Keiko felt David roll off her body. The pleasure coiling within kept her writhing against the warm tangle of satin sheets, her eyes closed tight.

"In any case, *amore mio,* this little Oriental doll is more to my liking than yours."

David sprang up from the bed. "Leave her alone, Nicoletta."

Someone was climbing into bed, but it did not seem to be David. Keiko opened her eyes and found herself inches from Principessa Nicoletta's lovely face.

"Don't, Nicoletta," David said, his voice no longer insistent but pleading.

Keiko felt Principessa Nicoletta's feverish lips press against hers. The tongue darting into her mouth was even hotter, a probing, flickering bird Keiko yearned to have fly all over her body. As if reading Keiko's thoughts, Nicoletta's kisses traced a path to her neck. Keiko pressed herself eagerly upward, open, ready.

Nicoletta's mouth found the place where David had bitten Keiko. Keiko felt Nicoletta draw away from the wounds momentarily, as if they shocked her, but she returned quickly enough, kissing the twin punctures with tenderness and even a simalacrum of pity. Never had Keiko experienced anything so intimate as when Nicoletta's tongue began to play around the raised edges of these tender, swollen perforations. Nicoletta began to lick and then suck at the wounds, gently at first, then with mounting urgency.

Keiko heard herself moan as she twisted and turned against the sheets, digging into them with her heels, clutching the rumpled, damp satin in her hands. She cried out as she felt the clotted wounds open anew and begin to seep blood into Nicoletta's sucking mouth.

"Nicoletta, no," David cried out.

Nicoletta released Keiko, pushing up on one arm.

Keiko opened her eyes to see Principessa Nicoletta looking down on her, her long tangled hair drawing a wild frame around her beautiful child-woman face, an enigmatic, half-mocking smile on her mouth. The vampire princess's half-hooded eyes told Keiko that Nicoletta could bring her pleasure far beyond what David had given her.

"Don't listen to him," Keiko begged. "Take my blood! Take it *all*!"

Keiko felt herself slam convulsively back against the bed. Nicoletta did not gently drink Keiko's blood, as David had, but sucked it hungrily, greedily, cruelly. Yet the princess fulfilled her part of the bargain. The pleasure David had brought Keiko had been beyond anything she had imagined possible, but it was only the prelude to this final ecstasy. There was pain now, too—the pain of having her life sucked out of her in one long, trembling embrace. It didn't matter. Like a drug addict who continues to jab needles into an arm disfigured with suppurating sores, the pleasure of the moment outweighed all other considerations. Only when Death was gathering Keiko into his dark embrace did Nicoletta pause.

"You are as lovely as a porcelain doll," Principessa Nicoletta said. She spoke with her lips against Keiko's wet neck, blood bubbling as she spoke. "You will make a wonderful vampire."

"You can't do *that*," David cried, nearly shouting.

"And pray tell me why not? She has the soul of a predator. She would make a far better vampire than you, *amore mio*. Of course, she would no doubt make things rather unpleasant for the other passengers aboard the *Atlantic Princess*."

"You're talking nonsense, Nicoletta," David said, his voice more controlled now, dismissive. "We'll be in Europe weeks before the transformation can take hold."

"The *Illuminati* have kept you ignorant."

"What are you talking about, Nicoletta? You know as well as I do that it takes six weeks."

"Perhaps for you, my love, but not for me." Hovering somewhere between life and death, Keiko listened to Nicoletta's chilling laugh. "I am very old, David, and the dark power is strong within my blood. I do not require six weeks to transform a mortal. I do not require six minutes. Open your eyes, Keiko."

Keiko did as she was told, although she was so weak that she could manage the feat only when Nicoletta supplied her with the strength by some mysterious means.

"Do you see the darkness drawing near?"

Keiko could only blink in reply.

"You need not go down into the eternal darkness, *amore mio*. I can give you life everlasting, Keiko Matsuoka, if you become one of the *Vampiri*." Principessa Nicoletta began to stroke Keiko's hair. "You are like me, a warrior. Our lives are nothing without honor and power—the honor and power that has been too often denied us because an accident of birth created us female."

"Do not do this, Nicoletta. Give her back to me and I will drain her dead."

"You would break your sacred *Illuminati* vow against taking mortal life just to prevent me from creating a beautiful companion?"

David hesitated a moment, his face a reflection of his inner torment before he finally nodded. "I will kill her, Nicoletta, if that is the price I must pay to keep you from making her one of us."

"But why would you choose to kill now, *amore mio*? Pray do not tell me you have become a jealous lover!"

"I have looked into her soul and seen only corruption and greed," David said, his voice bleak. "She would be a monster, Nicoletta, a monster just like . . ."

"Just like me, David?" Nicoletta's laugh was musical. "Yes, my dear boy. That is exactly the point. I am tired of your squeamish, warmed-over mortal morality. I yearn for the company of someone like myself, someone with whom I can share the joys of the hunt. Besides, in your heart you know that you would not be able to kill her. Let us not pretend it would be otherwise."

Nicoletta pulled down the right shoulder of her black evening dress, exposing the curving semicircle of the perfect white flesh of her upper breast.

"For the love of God, Nicoletta, I'm begging you not to do this. Stop before it's too late."

"Silence!"

There was a crash as David flew across the room, knocking over a chair and hitting the dresser.

"I will never forgive you for this, Nicoletta," David said, picking himself up from the floor. Keiko heard his steps retreating away from the bed. A door opened and slammed closed.

Principessa Nicoletta unfastened the black silk bra. She took her flesh between her red fingernails and squeezed until a rivulet of purple blood began to trickle from the nipple.

"Drink, *amore mio*," Nicoletta whispered. "Suckle at the breast of immortality."

Ricky had all the lights on in his bedroom, including the ones in his bathroom and closet. He'd managed to get his grandfather's umbrella and had it under the blanket; it wasn't much of a weapon, but along with the pocketknife under his pillow, it was the best he could do.

The actors in the police movie he was watching didn't really convey what it was like to see the body of someone who was murdered. Though he'd thought movies were realistic—and the more realistic they seemed, the more he liked them—he realized that a television or movie screen cannot transmit the horror you feel in real life when you see a dead person. The woman up on the helipad—her skin had been the same sickly shade of white as a frog's belly. He thought about how her eyes had protruded grotesquely from her head, with her mouth frozen open, the blood ooz-ing over her lower lip.

But it was not the memory of what he had seen that frightened Ricky the most, but what he had *not* seen. What if the killer had been lurking in the shadows thrown down around the No. 2 and 3 funnels? What if the killer had heard the sound of Ricky's sneakers coming up the metal stairway, forcing him to retreat before he was finished with his terrible work?

And, worse yet, what if the killer thought—incorrectly—that Ricky had seen him? It would hardly matter that Ricky hadn't seen anything but the dead woman's body. If the killer saw Ricky, he would want to get rid of him just to be sure.

Ricky moved his tongue around slowly in his mouth, pressing the tip against his teeth. Would the killer cut his tongue out after he was dead—or before?

He rolled over, buried his face into his pillow, and began to cry, but quietly so that he wouldn't disturb his grandpar-ents. He'd upset them enough already.

The big ocean liner had seemed like a wondrous play-land to Ricky at first, but now it was more like a sinister maze, a catacomb where a killer could easily hide. . . .

Ricky awakened with a start the moment he started to doze off.

The pill that Dr. Anderson had given him was beginning to take effect. Though sleep seemed more and more attrac-tive to him with each passing moment, Ricky knew that it would provide only the illusion of escape. As long as he was on board the *Atlantic Princess* in the middle of the ocean, there really was nowhere he could go to escape.

Keiko heard the people in the cabins dreaming. But that was just the beginning. The *Atlantic Princess* could not contain her. Keiko's consciousness leapt from the ship to plumb the dark waters, where she mingled with the spirits of creatures that exist only to hunt and kill.

"You are like them now," Nicoletta said, rocking gently as she continued to cradle Keiko's head against her breast.

Keiko's mind was reaching farther, grasping for knowledge. In the next moment her awareness entered the bathhouse where her Yakuza overlord was having his way with a pretty young girl, the same tariff he had exacted from Keiko to seal their secret partnership. He would pay for the liberties he'd taken—they all would pay, everyone who had ever looked at her sideways or spoken to her with the slightest degree of condescension because she was a woman and a Japanese!

Like Nicoletta, she would make them all pay.

Keiko's consciousness spiraled downward into the inner workings of her body, where with each cell the secret substance she'd ingested along with Nicoletta's blood was working minute changes in her body. The next moment she was going in the opposite direction, her intellect flying upward, outward, away from the earth to explore the clockwork of the solar system, the galaxy, the universe itself. It was as if Nicoletta had lifted up the top of God's head, permitting Keiko to look inside and see how everything worked.

Suddenly it was all too much. Keiko wanted no more of Nicoletta's breast, yet the princess held her fast. Keiko was burning up, her skin on fire as the genetic code in each of her cells was remade in the image of a different species, her bones glowing like coals pulled from a fire. Keiko felt herself caught by the edge of the dark vortex, a whirlpool that spun faster and faster, sucking her down into the depths of its whirling black heart. Keiko thought she was going to die, and since death meant escape from her present agony, she welcomed it.

When Keiko awoke, Nicoletta was sitting in a chair watching her, smiling.

Keiko opened her eyes and looked about with stunned amazement.

"It is wonderful, is it not, *amore mio*? You see colors as you have never seen them and hear sounds as you have never heard them. Listen to them going at it in the adjoining *appartements de grand luxe*. Monsieur Salahuddin insists on taking his lover in a most unnatural fashion, does he not?"

It was true! Keiko *could* hear them, and see into their minds as easily as she might look through a window. A wonderful power it was, but disorienting. So many voices, so many thoughts. Keiko pressed her fingertips to her temples.

"You can shut out the voices, my dear. Just turn them off and on at will. You have only to think to make it so."

Incredibly, Keiko could!

"I have much to tell you," Principessa Nicoletta said, standing and holding out her hand to help Keiko rise. "However, my delicious cherry blossom, now you must feed the Hunger so that you may grow strong."

Keiko had not noticed it before, but she *was* hungry. Yet it was not hunger of the ordinary sort, but a more primal, insistent sort of hunger—the *Hunger*. Keiko ran her tongue between her lip and her gum and discovered the sharp tips of two teeth she had not had before.

Nicoletta, who had dressed Keiko while she was unconscious, ushered her toward the door. "Do not worry, *amore mio*. You will know what to do. That is why I chose you. You are no weakling who must be taught how to kill."

Kill? The word hung in the air a moment but quickly dissipated. Of course Keiko would kill to feed the Hunger. What did the life of an ordinary human being matter to her now that she was immortal?

"Go forth, *amore mio,* and kill tonight to your heart's desire. The more you feed, the stronger you will become. Make other immortals if you find any who are worthy. You will have that power for the next few nights, while my blood is strong in you. Leave it to me to take care of any complications that may arise from your actions. And do not waste time thinking about David. You are the one I will go away with when we are done amusing ourselves with this ship of doomed fools."

They stopped at the door. Keiko turned to Nicoletta and looked into her eyes, eyes that seemed filled with fathomless wisdom and insurmountable strength.

"There will be time for us later," Nicoletta whispered into Keiko's ear as they held each other. "Go enjoy your new powers while it is still night. You are young and unable to resist the sun. You must be back in your cabin by dawn."

After a final tender kiss from her lover, from her *Vampiri* mother, Keiko turned and went out into the night to hunt.

# 18

✧

# Nicoletta's Diary VII

**I**HAVE HEARD priests talk about salvation, about how God's grace can descend to bleach white the sinner's blackened soul in an instant, in a heartbeat between the stirrup and the ground, if the evildoer has the proper intention in her heart. The other thing—I will not call it damnation, for it is not that—comes with equal speed, but it is not so much a gift as an awakening, an enlightenment. In a heartbeat between the stirrup and the ground comes a transformation that is infinitely more significant than mere salvation.

I stood looking down on Gareloch's crumpled form, witnessing the consequence of my cruel new pleasures, and I felt the terrible joy rising in my heart for the first time. My eyes had been opened, and I looked upon *everything* with a ferocious clarity. I knew what I had done, and what it meant, and even though it was wicked, it brought me great pleasure.

My faithful servant, my friend, my Rubicon. Gareloch alone had stood by me through my final mortal illness, and I had repaid her loyalty with death. After all these centuries, she is still the only mortal I have ever killed whose death I regretted.

And yet . . .

And yet so overwhelming was the epiphany that came upon me in that moment that it made me forget my grief and my guilt in an instant. Deliverance descended upon me the way the priests said it would, in a heartbeat between the stirrup and the ground, in the time it took my eyes to register how sweetly Death had loosened her limbs and robbed the light from her staring eyes. In draining Gareloch of her blood I had fed upon forbidden fruit. I had consecrated my immortality by consuming the *Vampiri* sacraments of flesh and blood—not bread as flesh and wine as blood, but human flesh and human blood. It had cleansed me, freeing me forever from the petty constraints of simple mortal morality.

> For God doth know that in the day ye eat thereof, then your eyes shall be opened, and ye shall be as gods, knowing good and evil.

Knowledge made Eve cower—naked, fearful, too meek to seize the opportunity. Is there any wonder she was driven from the Garden? Had Principessa Nicoletta Vittorini di Medusa been there with Adam in the beginning, a different history would have been written.

My cloistered upbringing had left me blind to fully half the universe. I had been day without night, sun without moon, sweet without bitter. But that night in the Carpathian Mountains, in a heartbeat between the stirrup and the ground, my understanding of the world was completed for me as I stood looking down on my poor servant's lifeless body.

Gareloch's death joined me to the *Vampiri* in spirit as well as flesh. I had become *as a god, knowing good and evil,* my enlightenment releasing upon the world a deathless being free to dispense death freely.

The metamorphosis was complete.

And so I came to be evil—or evil in the eyes of mortal society. A merciless killer, an enemy of humankind, wanton, depraved, licentious. Entirely ruthless, entirely unforgiven, entirely unrepentant.

I am not ashamed to call myself evil. Why should I be? *Evil* is simply a label, a classification contrived from drawing distinctions between like objects, a differentiation that serves best to triangulate the observer's position relative to the object being observed. Whether Vienna is east or west is a question of being in Paris or Budapest, not upon an *eastness* or *westness* inherent to the nature of the Austrian capital. Good and bad, east and west—these terms are too subjective and imprecise to define the mystery of gods, vampires, and other immortal creatures.

I make no excuses for myself.

Modern apologists will no doubt assign the blame for my fall (unconscious to the imprecision of calling it a *fall*) on those who wronged me—my uncle and the other men in Bellaria who refused to follow me into battle because I was a woman; the pigs who robbed and raped me, selling me into bondage. How insulting to infer that *men* made me what I am! Credit or blame for what I am is mine alone.

As for the sea change in my nature—good to evil, princess to predator—it is simply proof that the seed had been sleeping within me all along, as it is in all mortals, awaiting the mysterious signal calling it to awaken and grow—dark, malignant, bristling with poisonous thorns; seductive, powerful, and free.

I turned King Radu's hunting lodge into a funeral pyre for Gareloch, racing through the Hammer's rooms with a torch in my hands, swinging it in broad arcs, watching the ancient oak timbers sweep upward in sheets of crackling flame the moment open fire kissed them. The noise, the heat, the piercing golden-white light—a frightful combination for even a vampire to endure. I threw the torch behind me into the flames, feeding fire with fire, and ran outside into the waiting arms of a screaming mountain blizzard.

I would have perished in a matter of minutes had I still been human, but the cold had no effect on my immortal form. I set off through the deeply drifted snow barefoot, wearing nothing but a woolen nightgown. I had to squeeze shut my eyes against the stinging ice crystals, but it mattered little, for I could see where I was going even without the limited vision one's eyes afford.

The forest surrounding the lodge was thickly populated with timber wolves, intelligent beasts that loitered in the vicinity through the harsh winter months, hopeful for scraps left behind by hunters, if not a meal of the hunters themselves. I had heard the wolves howling in my fever dreams as I lay ill, my mortal body dying. Even now their lonely, menacing song is etched vividly into my memory. I sensed them in their lairs, and they sensed me, and by mutual consent we agreed, one predator to the other, to leave one another alone that snowy night.

I was crossing a frozen river when Aedon materialized before me, a pagan goddess taking form in the wilderness, beautiful and alone, an apparition in the dark, swirling snows. She held a fur cloak about her. A diadem of holly boughs crowned her head, the wind lifting her long fair hair so that it seemed to float, a halo, a penumbra, a soft silver aura.

"Aedon!" I cried, rushing forward.

She did not speak but opened her arms.

"I have so many questions!"

"There will be time for that, my *Principessa*, but later. Look to the east: The dawn is nearly upon us." She knew what I wanted to ask even as the thought took form within my mind. "I will teach you to protect yourself from the sun, little one, but for now we must get inside or you will be burned."

We flew through the forest as if we were angels beating the air with invisible wings, streaking through the trees, up narrow passes, over dizzying precipices. It seemed impossible, yet on we flew, faster and faster, until we reached a woodcutter's cottage, where we were offered safe haven from the storm.

I sat before the fire for a few minutes, enjoying the warmth without feeling that I especially needed it to restore me. Indeed, I required something else entirely. Our flight through the forest had filled me with a tremendous longing that was suddenly upon me. I leapt to my feet and drained the woodcutter and his wife of their blood almost before I knew what I was doing. If the couple had had children, I would have killed them, too—though it has been my practice never to harm children—for I could not get enough blood to slake my thirst that first fledgling night. Aedon said nothing, but stood in the shadows, watching. She had known what I would need and had been careful to provide it, a good mother to her bloodthirsty daughter.

We caught up with the bard three nights later and remained with him for several years, until he became too infirm to continue our wanderings. Aedon offered him the gift, but he refused it, the first of only two mortals I have ever known to reject the opportunity to become a god. Aedon and I continued on together then, two seeming sheep who never tired of turning the tables on the would-be wolves who thought they could have their ways with us. Aedon taught me the secret ways of the *Vampiri* and to play the lute, and I taught her to read and write.

It was a wonderful time to be a vampire, and as years became decades, we were very happy together. Sometimes we killed for pleasure, but more often we killed out of mercy, or to bring a rare bit of justice into the mortal world. At a time when people were either brutally oppressed or brutal oppressors, it was never difficult to find someone who richly deserved to die—and more often than not the most deserving victims proved to be men.

All things pass with time. Aedon became fascinated with the strange scales and dissonant tonalities of the Eastern music she heard for the first time from a band of Persian silk traders. One night she told me of her plans to journey to India and find a master who would teach her the ragas. She invited me to go with her, but I am sure she already sensed that I was making other plans.

Perhaps Aedon is living still in India, a devotee of the sitar. I never saw her again, not even during the ten years I lived in New Delhi during the reign of the British Raj.

* * *

I retraced my footsteps to Bellaria, intending to settle old scores along the way.

Zonguldak had fallen into Muslim hands by the time I returned to that Sodom on the Black Sea. The only man I knew still living in the city was Themistius, who was now elderly and had adopted the Muslim religion and a name to go with it as the price for continuing to do business in the seaport. When I found the Greek, his body and mind were ravaged with venereal disease. He was blind from cataracts and half insane, his body covered with oozing chancres, flies swarming around his open sores, suppurating wounds crawling with maggots.

"Hello, Themistius. I promised to one day repay you for all you had done."

The Greek shuddered on his pallet at the sound of my voice, disturbing the vermin that lived in the reeking straw beneath his rotting body.

"Clear your mind of its infirmity so that I may show you everything I am, and every boon I might grant you, were I so disposed."

I restored the Greek's eyes and his intellect, and arrested his mortal fears so that he might more perfectly envision the rich possibilities before him: his health and youth restored; wealth beyond his wildest imagining; life everlasting; the indomitable strength, power, and grace of the *Vampiri*. Then I showed Themistius an alternate version of the future, one that involved death, but at least a death that was quick and merciful compared to what he could otherwise expect.

"Can it really be *you*?" Themistius croaked, propped up by the psychic strength I supplied him.

I nodded gravely.

"For the love of God, Nicoletta . . ."

That made me laugh out loud.

"Pleeeze," he said, drawing the word out in a way I found almost unbearably pathetic. "Have mercy on me, *Principessa*."

"Oh, but I shall," I said with a sardonic grin. "I shall

give three pieces of silver to the leper begging outside your door to ensure that you have a few sips of water and some gruel forced down your throat at regular intervals. I would not want you to expire prematurely due to a lack of proper care."

"I would rather you killed me and had done with it!"

"Perhaps, but only if you grovel."

"I beg of you, *Principessa*! Do not leave me here to suffer in my own filth."

"You shall have to do better than that."

"I beg of you, Nicoletta. Please find it in your heart to forgive me. It was all a horrible mistake. You must believe me when I say that I wanted only to help you, to save you from the Turkish brothels. I swear it, Nicoletta. I could not stand by and let that happen. You were—you *are*—so lovely."

"Lovely enough for you to rape me as if I were a peasant orphan sold to a traveling whoremonger by her village."

"You misunderstand, *Principessa*. I did not intend to hurt you even when I did." Themistius began to sob. "There is an impossibly great distance between our stations in life, but from the very first time I saw you in the slave market, I knew that I loved—"

"Do not dare utter *that* word! I will not permit you to so debase it."

"Do not hate me, *Principessa*, even though you have ample cause."

"What kind of a fool do you take me for, pimp?"

"I do not take you for a fool at all, *Principessa*. I think of you only as a highborn lady who, though she has been done a very great wrong, is capable of bringing even more honor on her name by forgiving those who have sinned against her."

"Now you are entertaining me," I said, showing my delight. "Who but you could mistake a vampire for Lady Bountiful? I would sooner defile my father's grave than forgive you."

"If you are a vampire, *Principessa*, kill me now. I beg of you: End my life."

Themistius began to blink rapidly, vainly trying to preserve his sight, which I was allowing to fail again.

"*Principessa?* Are you still there? *Principessa?*"

I was halfway out the door, leaving Themistius lying in his own excrement, calling after me, distraught and already nearly inchoate.

The leper made an excellent nurse, and it took the Greek a long, long time to die.

After I had fed Themistius's body to a pack of starving dogs outside the city gates, I cured the leper of his disease and made him a wealthy man. I later heard that he had returned to his native Sardinia, where he founded a hospital and became a revered holy man. He was canonized as a saint after he died—all because of the generosity of a *vampire*!

The years had changed Bellaria almost beyond recognition. The outlines of the island's natural profile remained, but everything else—the city, the people—had changed.

The surviving Christians fled the island after my family's fall. After that, the Khalisa spread out of its former boundaries and enveloped the entire city, which was no longer called Misilmari, but Khalisa. The local caliph had remade Castle Misilmari in the image of the Alhambra. Nearly everything was different, though the groves of fruit trees that my father had planted were still tended with loving care.

On the first night of my return to Bellaria, I stood amid the fruit trees in the moonlight, taking apart a Valencia orange with my fingers to help myself remember—and mourn for the last time—my loss.

I slipped a wedge of orange in my mouth and closed my eyes, conjuring a vision of an earnest young princess-philosopher. She remained in my mind a moment before the virgin's image wavered and became indistinct, fading like a cloud driven apart by the winds.

The people of Bellaria had forgotten the di Medusa

family, and so had I. I had become someone else, something else. My ties with the past were severed. The philosopher-princess was dead; long live the vampire princess.

The next morning I bought a ship and sailed away from Bellaria forever.

I settled in the Palazzo Calixtus, a beautiful classical edifice Pope Calixtus III had built. The interior courtyard enclosed a luxuriant garden, at its center a fountain where black marble dolphins rode an endless wave through the flower-perfumed air. My secretary, a former diplomat named Niccolo, negotiated the palazzo's purchase for me. Calixtus had belonged to the same Spanish-Italian family that bore Cesare Borgia, the prince of Florence, who occasionally employed Niccolo to conspire in minor intrigues with other Italian principalities.

Though there were things about Niccolo I did not admire—his ugly hook nose, his passion for politics—his connections with the best families and most brilliant artists and artisans were invaluable. Niccolo knew everybody in Florence, along with their secrets, their scandals, their strengths, weaknesses, passions, and fears. He was my entree to the highest echelon of Florentine society.

I did not, however, share Niccolo's high opinion of the prince. Cesare Borgia embodied all the traits I admire least in a man: He was so full of himself that I would have expected him to become trapped in front of the first gilded mirror he passed. Villainy ran deep in Cesare Borgia's family. His father and most powerful ally, Pope Alexander VI, was even more sinister than his illegitimate son. And Lucretia Borgia, the prince's sister, was the most evil mortal woman I had ever known.

Lucretia Borgia was her brother's lover, which shocked Italian society to its foundation—no mean feat, at a time when popes kept mistresses, fathered illegitimate children, and sold ecclesiastical offices to the highest bidders. But incest was only where Lucretia's amorality started. In collusion with her brother and father, she took Florence's richest men to bed and poisoned them, her family confiscating the murdered men's estates to replenish coffers depleted by the Borgias' twin obsessions—art and debauchery.

How like one of the *Vampiri* Lucretia Borgia was! Little wonder I loved her enough to share my immortality with her, though it proved to be a serious mistake. Lucretia immediately passed the gift to her shallow brother, which was doubly insulting, since this proved that she loved him more than me.

Cesare Borgia was a poor candidate for the *Vampiri*. He abused his immortal power so much that the nobility and the church banded together to oppose him. Borgia might have overcome either enemy singly, but combined they were able to drive even a *Vampiri* prince out of Florence and into exile. Borgia was soon forced to disappear from the mortal realm, supposedly while fighting for the King of Navarre at Viana—as if Cesare Borgia would ever fight for anyone except himself!

Lucretia disappeared with her brother. They have spent the ensuing centuries turning unworthy miscreants into vampires in order to aid Borgia in his failed efforts to take over the mortal world by becoming shadow ruler of various benighted countries. I have spoken to Lucretia only once since she left Florence. Fate brought us together at a party on the terrace of a chalet in Berchtesgaden, Germany, in 1939.

"As you can see, my brother's plans are at long last coming to flower," Lucretia bragged, beaming.

Adolf Hitler was the latest of Cesare Borgia's protégés. I found *der Führer* to be a despicable cockroach of a man. Gaining *Vampiri* powers from Cesare Borgia had turned Hitler into a spellbinding orator, but the little corporal had a petty, twisted mind filled with foolish racist delusions and a tortured sense of inadequacy.

"I fail to understand your enthusiasm, Lucretia. Herr Hitler is not even a good watercolorist. What makes you think he could conquer Europe?"

"Europe will be only the beginning!"

Disgusted, I turned away and left the party without saying good-bye to my odious host. I left Germany that night and continued traveling until I reached South America, where I remained until 1945.

How I abhor war! To soak the ground with the blood of millions of men, women, and children for shallow enjoyment of a few self-important politicians—who could conceive of any greater obscenity?

"I do not understand my new prince's unhappiness with me. I bring him every secret."

Poor Niccolo. Dismissed, imprisoned, tortured. It had been a year since his beloved prince, Cesare Borgia, had been driven from Florence. The Medici family had returned to power, and Niccolo suddenly found himself very much in disfavor, along with the Borgias' other retainers. I might have done something to smooth Niccolo's difficulties with the Medicis, but he had been rather rude to me the day I decided to side against the Borgias. I decided he needed to be taught a lesson. I let him languish in Sforza prison, thinking that the wrathful Medicis were solely to blame for his incarceration. A few visits to the rack would make him a better servant.

"It is only prudent of Giuliano de' Medici to be harsh with you and anybody else who was allied with his family's enemies," I said to Niccolo. "When a prince seizes a state, he ought to determine all the injuries that he will need to inflict and inflict them once and for all—quickly, efficiently, ruthlessly—to ensure that his allies will remain loyal and his enemies fearful. To do otherwise, because he is timid or through poor advice, will force the prince to have the knife always ready in his hand."

"Where is the virtue in such a policy?"

"Virtue is of no use to a prince, Niccolo, unless it is used to mislead his enemies. This is not heaven but earth, my friend. Princes who let virtue rather than expediency guide them will only come to a bad end. The far wiser course is for the prince to understand that he is surrounded by people to whom virtue is nothing, and to act accordingly."

Niccolo nodded and drifted off into one of the long, brooding silences to which he had become subject. At one time I had considered making him immortal, but I had since decided that I could never put up with his insufferable moodiness.

"Pray do not continue in this vein, Niccolo," I said, becoming impatient with his heavy sighs. "Take action against your misfortunes instead of whining about them."

"What recourse have I against the powerful Medicis?"

"You were given a good mind, Niccolo. Use it!"

"To intrigue against the prince?"

The shock in Niccolo's face reminded me that the de' Medicis employed talented torturers. That was a mark in their favor, but only one of many. The de' Medicis were patrons to my favorite artists—Brunelleschi, Donatello, Ghiberti, Botticelli, and Raphael. Giuliano de' Medici had only recently brought Michelangelo back to Florence; the artist had been forced to spend the years of Cesare Borgia's rule lying on his back in Rome, painting the ceiling of the Sistine Chapel for Pope Julius.

"I would instead advise you to curry favor with the de' Medicis. Perhaps you could take the notes you've written during my discourses on worldly power and cast them in the form of a treatise. The prince will no doubt find my ideas edifying, especially if you dedicate the book to him. Perhaps it will win you back into his good graces."

Niccolo used my ideas and often my exact words. I did not object, since I thought my precepts merited dissemination, though I had no desire to attract the notoriety authorship would draw. Unfortunately for Niccolo, *The Prince* failed to impress the de' Medicis, and he was never permitted to return to public life. Niccolo lived out his final years on his estate, writing history, poetry, and plays. Though it failed to achieve its objective, his treatise—*my* treatise—on *Realpolitik* proved to be Niccolo Machiavelli's one claim to immortality.

* * *

My closest mortal friend in Florence after Niccolo Machiavelli was the great Leonardo da Vinci, the only human being I have ever known whose brilliance nearly equaled that of an immortal. With the single exception of Professor Einstein, the human beings I have known since Leonardo have been dolts and dullards.

"Look at this, *Principessa*!" Leonardo would cry in his excited voice whenever I visited his studio. And whatever it was—a painting, invention, or discovery—would keep us talking excitedly far into the night, our conversations covering art, mechanics, city planning, botany, about how birds flew, the properties of flowing water—everything under the sun. I often helped him in his work, sometimes providing gentle coaching. It was I who first took Leonardo to the hospital of the Santa Maria Nuova, where we dissected corpses in the morgue in order to study anatomy. The lessons he learned from the dead allowed Leonardo to paint figures in a fuller, fleshier, more realistic manner, a style soon copied by Michelangelo and Raphael.

"Look at this, *Principessa*!"

Leonardo ran ahead of me up the stairs to the rooftop with a lamp. He called his latest mechanical contraption an ornithopter. It consisted of a wooden frame, a pair of movable batlike wings covered in a finely woven, lightweight fabric, and an approximation of a swallow's tail. The ornithopter sat perched on a set of wooden tracks that sloped toward the edge of the roof, where they abruptly ended out over the open air beyond the rooftop.

"It's a flying machine. You get into my ornithopter in a prone position, headfirst. Pull the release—there—and you are catapulted into the air. The wings are driven by the arms and legs, the mechanical energy transferred through this gearing mechanism."

But there was a problem, Leonardo confessed.

"It takes an extremely powerful man to propel the drive mechanism at a rate sufficient to maintain flight. This is one of two models I have built. My assistant, Ludovico, who as you know is very strong, flew this ornithopter this morning. He was able to stay aloft for a very short time. Piero tried to fly the second model after lunch and crashed straight to the street. It is a miracle he was not killed."

Leonardo rested a hand on his invention and smiled sadly. "I myself do not have the strength to drive its wings."

"I would like to try your invention. I am stronger than I look."

Leonardo's smile lost its humor when he realized I was serious.

"You cannot possibly operate the ornithopter, Nicoletta. Ludovico exhausted himself trying to remain aloft long enough to keep from breaking his neck. It would be suicide."

"Perhaps you are right." I turned away from the ornithopter and looked up in the sky. "It is such a lovely night. It would be pleasant to drink a glass of wine up here and discuss what manner of device might be contrived to aid the human eye in bringing the moon more closely into view."

The moment Leonardo disappeared to summon a servant, I got into the ornithopter and pulled the release lever. The machine skidded forward, faster and faster, the runners scraping against the wooden rails. And then—silence, and a sensation of exhilarating weightlessness!

The ornithopter moved through the night sky in a quirky fashion, but I had the strength and reflexes to make the machine do as I wished, rising over Florence like an angel of death. Below me the palazzos, cathedrals, and squares became miniature models of themselves. The churches were the easiest buildings to pick out at night, below me passing Santa Maria del Fiore, Santa Croce, Santa Maria Novella, and San Lorenzo. I found the lights in the opened windows of the Pitti Palace and the Palazzo Vecchio. On I flew, leaving the city behind, soaring out over the Tuscan countryside, high above the mountains and hills, high above the

Chianti vineyards before I finally decided to return to Florence.

Leonardo was waiting for me on the rooftop when I returned. I could tell that he hardly believed I could fly the ornithopter, but since he had searched the street and neighboring rooftops, it was the only explanation left.

The time had come for Leonardo and me to come to an understanding. His genius made it possible for him to hear my story without the hysterical fear I would expect in an ordinary man. (I did not tell him *everything*, of course. There would be time for that later.)

Leonardo was fascinated, as I had expected. He wanted to know all about the transformation and my new needs. He even asked to see my blood teeth! I showed him my fangs, though it required every bit of my self-control to keep from burying them in his delicious neck.

"You are too brilliant for your intellect to be lost through illness or age, Leonardo. I am sharing my secret with you because I want you to become one of us. Join with the *Vampiri* and you will have eternity to pursue your every interest."

Leonardo listened thoughtfully to my proposal, then asked more about the specific agents and reactions involved in the transformation. Through all of this he maintained his usual childlike eagerness for information, hungry for knowledge, wanting to know far more than I could tell him.

"What agent leads to this change, Nicoletta? Certainly there must be some generative power atomized in the vampire's kiss."

I could only confess my ignorance. He was of course correct, though it would be three centuries before a curious vampire identified the mysterious virus that is responsible for our rebirth, a third genetic parent after our biological ones.

"What you offer is quite intriguing, Nicoletta," Leonardo said after taking a moment to think. "Join me for supper tomorrow and I will give you my answer."

His answer, to my astonishment, was no.

Leonardo explained that he was not afraid to become a vampire. And it was not that he had some religious concern about losing his soul, even though I wondered if he had perhaps worked out that there was more to being a vampire than I had admitted. His ultimate reason for rejecting my offer was complicated, and I am not sure that I understand it exactly even now. The world, Leonardo said, is analogous to a vast, finely integrated clockwork in which every sentient being has its role to fulfill. Since he had been born a human being, he could conclude only that it was necessary for him to remain a mortal man, to fulfill his purpose in the cosmic engine.

"Besides, Nicoletta," Leonardo added, "joining with the *Vampiri* would make it impossible for me to investigate the greatest scientific puzzle of them all."

"What could you possibly know as a man but not as a vampire?"

"Death," Leonardo answered with an enigmatic smile, unafraid to die when the time came, even if it was at that moment, at my hand. "And the beyond," he said after a moment.

Being a vampire would have allowed Leonardo to become intimate with death, though I did not say so, for I knew it was not the side of death he wished to explore. Though Leonardo would have no doubt learned to love to hunt and kill, I realized that transforming him might reduce him in some irreversible way. A large measure of Leonardo's charm was the childlike wonder with which he regarded the world. (I could have thought the same thing about a certain philosopher-princess, but there was no going back for *me* at that point.) Without his innocence, Leonardo would not be Leonardo. Transformed, he could be something incomparably wonderful—or very sad.

"Will you reconsider your decision?"

"I am sorry, Nicoletta, but no."

I loved Leonardo too much to become angry at his decision, though ours was not a physical love, but one of two sympathetic intellects. Perhaps it would have been different had we been actual lovers, but Leonardo was not interested in women in that way. (Why has almost no one noticed that the enigmatic *Mona Lisa* is in fact a self-portrait of Leonardo da Vinci dressed as a woman?)

"You understand, my dear Leonardo, that everything I have revealed about myself must remain a secret between us," I said, looking at him over the rim of my wineglass.

I had considered what to do if Leonardo rejected my offer without reaching any conclusion. It would have been the worst sort of folly for me to permit a mortal to live knowing the truth about me, yet I knew I could not kill Leonardo. I could have left Florence, but I hated the idea of that. There was nowhere I wanted to go just then. I had given Queen Isabella the money to pay for Columbus's trip, thinking he might find an easy passage to India and Aedon; unfortunately, the expedition had ended in disaster, the explorer bumbling onto a bleak and cultureless New World I had no present interest in visiting.

"You know your secrets are safe with me, Nicoletta," Leonardo said, showing no sign he feared my power, which I found strangely flattering.

"Excuse me for pushing the conversation away from its center, Nicoletta, but I have recently received an invitation from King Francis to join his court. He has promised me a castle in Cloux and all the funds I require for my research. I am seriously considering leaving Florence, but only if you grant me your leave."

I did not know whether to laugh or cry. Would that the world had given us more men of Leonardo's sensitivity and insight!

"The thought of you leaving Florence pains me greatly, Leonardo," I said, setting down my wineglass, "but let us discuss the matter logically . . ."

After Leonardo left I began to drift, slowly and pleasantly, through the years, intent mainly on following the hunt, floating upon the bloody current of my own dark nature.

Florence soon became a dark star, collapsing inward on itself from the weight of its own success. The time for my visit there had ended. The Renaissance had flowered, nurtured by its loving though bloodthirsty *Vampiri* gardener, and the bloom was now off the rose, as the saying goes. I wandered around Europe, traveling to Germany to meet Martin Luther, helping foment the Protestant revolt against the corrupt and oppressive Catholic Church, doing a little bit of good to vary my diet of otherwise unremitting evil.

I had begun hearing about sublime tragedies being staged at the Globe Theatre, so in 1595 I went to see them for myself. In England I met Will Shakespeare, who worked harder than any mortal man I had ever met. I told him the story of two star-crossed lovers I had known in Florence, which he turned into *Romeo and Juliet*. First Machiavelli and then Shakespeare—what an inspiration I was to the *literati*! But that is not where the parallel between Niccolo and Will ended.

Shakespeare was an avid synthesist, incorporating—perhaps unconsciously, perhaps not—almost anything he came upon that he could use in his plays. I left my diary lying open in a tavern one day and was startled to find him standing over the table. Fortunately, he did not divine the significance of what he had read, but that did not keep part of that day's entry from turning up in *Hamlet*.

*What a piece of work is the Vampiri! how noble in reason! how infinite in faculty! in form and moving how express and admirable! in action how like an angel! in apprehension how like a God! the beauty of the world! the paragon of animals!*

Shakespeare substituted *man* for *Vampiri*, but otherwise quoted the rest verbatim. It is said that plagiarism is the sincerest form of flattery, which I suppose is good, as long as the plagiarist doesn't know about the existence of vampires.

I befriended Sir Francis Bacon during my English years,

briefly rekindling my old interest in philosophy. How we argued about the relative merits of induction and deduction in the early days of our friendship! Nevertheless, it was difficult for me to stay interested for long. My days as a philosopher were far behind me. When Sir Francis invited me to visit him to discuss *The New Atlantis*, his fable about political philosophy, I killed him, sparing myself from another evening of tedium.

I sat across the table from Sir Francis's corpse and opened a letter from a scholarly acquaintance on the Continent.

Galileo, the letter informed me, had invented a microscope. Johannes Kepler had proposed his third law of planetary motion. I dropped the letter into the fire without reading further, already bored nearly to tears with the monotonous parade of discoveries and inventions. Thanks to science, novelty had to cease to be novel.

The only thing that did interest me my final year in England—aside from my seductions and murders—was George Sandys's translation of *Metamorphoses*, Ovid's pornographic poem. English was a foreign tongue to me, but I thought that I could do a far better job with Ovid's hexameters than Sandys, though I soon tired of this project, too, and set it aside in favor of the truer poetry of the hunt.

Increasingly I came to understand that I existed for one purpose and one purpose alone, that there was nothing in mortal society worthy of diverting my interest. Perhaps Leonardo had been right and the world was a colossal clockwork, each of us having a place where we fit into the machinery, cogs that played an integral role in keeping the universe's wheels turning. There was no confusion about the role I was cast to play. Between the stirrup and the ground on a snowy Transylvanian night, I had looked down on poor dead Gareloch and embraced what mortals call evil.

If a leper can become a saint, then it logically follows that a princess can become an executioner, a reaper sent into the field to reap sheaves of golden wheat when they are ripest for the harvesting. The saints stand on one side of the scale, the *Vampiri* on the other, good and evil perfectly balanced, neither one able to exist without its opposite.

# PART III

✧

# Noblesse Oblige

# 19

✦

# The Epicurean

**K**EIKO STOOD ON the deck outside Nadja's suite, listening to her and Captain Franchini's quiet breathing in the bedroom beyond the suite's formal stateroom. It was amazing what she could hear since Nicoletta's magical kiss, her perceptual acuity increased at least one hundred-fold. Keiko breathed in a complex aroma through the heavy fireproof door: perfume, sweat, two brands of cigarettes, men's cologne, Swedish vodka, sex.

Keiko put her hand on the metal latch and tried to turn it. The door was locked. Soon it would be dawn.

Inside Nadja's bedroom, Franchini rolled over and began to snore. Nadja sighed in her sleep and rolled away from the captain to the delicious sound of silk rustling against bare skin.

Keiko gripped the latch and pressed it downward. The metalwork in the lock complained, then abruptly broke free with a brittle snap. The door swung silently open into the darkened suite. The naked lovers did not awaken at the sound, or at Keiko's footsteps as she slipped into the bedroom and stood looking down on them. They had both been drunk when they fucked, she realized with a smirk, and were sleeping the comatose sleep of the drugged. Still, sleep made Nadja appear more innocent than she really was, a kitten instead of a voluptuous tigress bent on devouring everything she desired.

Franchini snorted, rubbing the back of his hand against his nose, and went back to snoring. He was wearing his *socks*! Keiko saw with disgust. The captain truly was a pig. His mouth was hung open in a most graceless manner, spittle glistening on his bottom lip. In another minute he would begin to drool upon the satin pillowcase.

"Your choice in men leaves much to be desired," Keiko said.

Keiko wanted the actress to hear her voice in her sleep, and she did. Nadja sat straight up in bed and stared at Keiko with a startled expression, unable to make out the vampire's form in the darkness. Franchini continued to snore, oblivious of the intrusion.

"You should not give your flower to such unworthy scum."

Nadja's eyes fastened on the dark shape standing next to her bed. "What the hell are you doing in my cabin?" she demanded, her accent thickening the way it did when she was upset. Nadja snapped on the lamp beside the bed, jerking the satin sheet around her—and off the captain—as she leapt out of bed.

The disappointing stretch marks on the actress's famous breasts were sadly evident to Keiko even in the dark as Nadja wrapped the sheet more tightly about herself. The cameramen who photographed Nadja's trademark sex scenes obviously knew how to disguise signs of the actress's aging.

"I asked you a question," Nadja said, so angry that she actually spat on Keiko when she spoke. "What is the meaning of this unforgivable invasion of my privacy?"

Franchini stirred and raised himself up on one elbow, blinking stupidly in the darkness. Still stinking drunk, Keiko realized. Some captain Lord Godwin had hired! Franchini began to root around in the tangle of clothes on the floor for his boxer shorts.

"Answer me," Nadja demanded in a shrill voice, "you slant-eyed bitch!"

Nadja struck Keiko across the face, hard, with her open hand. Keiko smiled slowly, the pain a delicious warmth against her cheek, a stinging caress.

"I find your characterization of me to be rather crude," Keiko said as her hand flashed out, grabbing the sheet where it crossed the actress's breasts. Nadja tried to twist away, but the vampire's grip was far too strong for her to break.

"I believe, darling Nadja, that what you need is someone . . ."

Keiko's slap stunned Nadja, ending her futile struggle.

". . . to teach you some manners."

Keiko struck the opposite side of Nadja's face with the back of her hand, hitting her firmly but not too hard, conscious that she could take the woman's head off if she wasn't careful.

"You see, the only thing that you lack, my dear Nadja . . ."

Keiko slapped Nadja again with her palm. The actress reeled unsteadily and would have fallen if the vampire hadn't held her upright.

". . . is some discipline. You *round-eyed* bitch!"

Keiko put some strength into her swing this time, and the sound of her hand against Nadja's cheek cracked like a gunshot. A long, slow parabola of blood and saliva floated across the room and splattered on the wall.

Franchini bolted for the door. He was an absurd figure, wearing only his underwear and carrying his shoes and the rest of his clothes.

Keiko threw the now-unconscious actress backward onto the bed and grabbed the captain's arm just as he reached the bedroom door. Keiko could read Franchini's thoughts. His brain, even in its intoxicated state, had realized that no human being could possibly move as fast as Keiko had moved. The captain knew something was wrong, most ominously wrong, but he couldn't quite grasp it yet.

"You are a coward to leave a lady in such distressing circumstances," Keiko said, spinning Franchini around to face her. Her eyes lowered, then came back up to meet his again. "And not a very well-endowed coward at that."

Franchini cringed when Keiko raised her hand, but she

did not intend to strike him. Instead, she brushed the fingernail of her index finger along his neck, barely touching his skin. Keiko took a step backward, regarding the captain with her head tipped to one side, as if examining a curiosity.

Franchini pulled his hands to his throat the moment arterial blood began to spray from his carotid artery. The captain's eyes bulged as he clamped his hands around his neck in the vain attempt to keep his life from running out of him with his blood.

"Who is Mandy Robsard, and what makes you think that I killed her earlier tonight?" Keiko asked, reading Franchini's frantic dying thoughts. "I didn't kill her. At least, I don't think I did," she added with a little laugh. "I've killed so many people that it's difficult to keep them straight."

Captain Franchini pitched forward onto the floor.

The sight of so much beautiful blood set the Hunger to howling again inside Keiko. Nicoletta had been right: The Hunger was fierce on Keiko's first night as fledgling vampire.

"Tonight I'm insatiable," she said to Franchini's prone form in a merry voice. "Like you, Captain, I cannot get enough of it."

Captain Franchini was already beyond hearing her taunts.

Keiko got down on all fours, thinking it fortunate Franchini had not fallen on one of her antique Persian rugs Lord Godwin had paid so much money for. Keiko lowered her lips to the crimson pool spreading out across the parquet floor and began to lap at his blood like a dog.

Behind Keiko on the bed, Nadja struggled into a sitting position, saw what was transpiring at the foot of her bed, and began to retch. Keiko did not look up from her treat. Blood was good only when it was fresh, Nicoletta had told her. The retching sound had stopped. Nadja was slipping quietly out of bed, hugging the far wall, trying to get out of the room without being noticed.

"You should join me," Keiko said, looking up at Nadja, her grin smeared with blood. "It is most *delicious*."

Keiko let Nadja get all the way to the outside door before she grabbed her by the hair and threw her down to the floor, jumping onto the actress, straddling her. Keiko pinned Nadja's hands against the carpet so that she couldn't struggle.

"Quiet, my darling."

The panic—but not the fear—suddenly went out of Nadja's eyes, and she stopped fighting against her immortal assailant. Such a face! A few light slaps and Nadja's right eye was black and swollen shut, her lip split, both cheeks bruised an ugly shade of purple.

"You look as if one of my associates in the Yakuza has worked your face over with a rubber hose, poor darling."

Nadja said nothing, but, keeping her eyes locked onto Keiko's, turned her head to offer her jugular vein to the vampire.

"There is only one intimate act you have left to experience, darling Nadja," Keiko said, leaning lower.

Keiko smelled Franchini on Nadja's skin. Enraged, she sank her teeth savagely into Nadja's throat.

Carrie heard the footsteps of a faster runner gaining on her.

"Hello there."

Oh, no, Carrie thought as Alexander Fox slowed to match her pace.

"Mind if I run along with you for a bit?"

She did mind, but she was too polite to say so. "I wouldn't have taken you for a runner, Mr. Fox."

"No?"

"I would have guessed you were the sort of man whose idea of exercise is playing computer games."

"A nerd with a plastic pocket protector?"

"Well, since you said so." She glanced up at Fox and grinned; it was not a friendly grin.

"And glasses mended with white surgical tape?"

"Now you've got the picture."

"I hate computer games. In fact, at this point in my life I hate computers period. Sometimes I think I'll throw up if I ever see another, but I can't seem to get away from them. The damned things are everywhere."

"Thanks in part to you."

"Touché."

"Computers have their place. They make it a lot easier to keep track of reservations on the *Atlantic Princess*, for example."

"Do I detect a hidden agenda in your comments, Dr. Anderson?"

"I didn't mean anything at all, Mr. Fox." There wasn't any point in causing a scene. "Well, that's it for me today." Carrie stopped running, lifting her left hand to wave goodbye.

"Me, too." Fox pulled up beside her. He nodded to the juice bar outside the men's gym. "Let's get something to drink."

"No, thanks, Mr. Fox. I need to get to back to the infirmary."

"You don't like me very much, do you, Dr. Anderson?"

Carrie put her hands on her hips. "If you're going to put me on the spot, Mr. Fox, no, I don't particularly like you."

"Is it my aftershave or my witty repartee? Or do you just have a thing about people who have a lot of money?"

"I don't like dishonest people, Mr. Fox."

"Neither do I."

"You must find it difficult to like yourself."

"Is this going someplace, Dr. Anderson?"

"I know how you got your reservation aboard the *Atlantic Princess*. You might have thought it was a game to hack your way into our computer system and bump somebody out of their reservations, but it was a dishonest thing to do."

"It's not a game, it's wire fraud. But only if you can prove it," Fox added with a grin.

"Do you think this is funny?"

"Lighten up, Doctor. Tell me that you've never bent the rules."

"Good-bye, Mr. Fox," Carrie said, turning away.

"I know who murdered Mandy Robsard."

Carrie's Nikes stopped her so abruptly on the decking that she nearly lost her balance and fell forward.

"If you'll have a carrot juice with me, I'll tell you what I know."

Carrie turned slowly, her face filled with wariness. "Make it apple juice."

"Only if I can call you Carrie. You can call me Alex. Or Fox. It doesn't matter which. Just don't call me Alexander. I hate that."

"Lord Godwin speaking."

The telephone receiver Lord Godwin held to his ear was filled with the most ungodly mechanical racket.

"This is O'Conner," the chief engineer bellowed. "We got trouble down here. Hear that?" O'Conner held the receiver away from his face for Lord Godwin's edification.

"I am not sure, Mr. O'Conner," Lord Godwin said when the chief engineer came back on the line. "What precisely was it that I'm supposed to hear?"

"A low howl with a steady screech every couple of seconds. Come on down if you like. You can hear it plenty well enough in the starboard after engine room."

"I'll defer to your judgment in the matter, Mr. O'Conner. What is the significance of this noise?"

"Oh, it's only the fucking main bearings burning up in the outboard starboard screw."

Lord Godwin winced, deploring Bob O'Conner's unfortunate tendency to use profanity when things weren't going as planned. He started to say something but checked himself, turning instead to refer to the framed sectional plan of the *Atlantic Princess* on the wall of his stateroom. He was familiar enough with the ship's running gear, in a general way. Four monstrous propellers, or screws, drove the *Atlantic Princess* through the water. There were two propellers on either side of the hull, an "inboard" and an "outboard" screw, to use the nautical term, as Lord Godwin tried to always remember to do. Each screw connected to an enormous shaft that rotated within a tunnel upon a series of bearings, attaching finally to a complicated series of reduction gears leading off the ship's main turbines.

"I told you we should have rebuilt those son-of-a-bitching main bearings," O'Conner shouted above the roar.

Lord Godwin had wanted to rebuild the main bearings as much as O'Conner had, but that would have meant delaying the *Atlantic Princess*'s maiden cruise. And, of course, Keiko Matsuoka had been quite insistent about *that*.

"We shall rebuild the bearings," Lord Godwin said, squeezing the bridge of his nose between thumb and forefinger, "during the *Princess*'s first scheduled maintenance layover, Mr. O'Conner."

"I've got news for you, Godwin. Those bearings aren't going to last that goddamned long. They're not going to last the goddamned day."

"Can't you lubricate them?" Lord Godwin asked brusquely, his now-chronic heartburn kicking in.

"We've been lubricating the hell out of them for the past twelve hours. Shit!"

"What is it?" Lord Godwin demanded, standing up at his desk.

"They've started squealing. Hear it?"

Lord Godwin *could* hear it. Rising over the din of the turbines was a metallic shriek that even to Lord Godwin sounded like machinery on the verge of failure.

"I don't have any choice," O'Conner yelled into the phone. "I'm shutting her down."

"You're shutting down the turbines?" Lord Godwin felt a moment of panic. The image of the gigantic ocean liner wallowing without power in the North Atlantic nauseated him. Even if they managed to tow the ship halfway across the ocean to a safe port, Lord Godwin wouldn't be able to give away tickets on the ship, much less sell them at an undiscounted rate of $10,000 per passenger.

"Not the turbines, damn it!" O'Conner roared. "I'm shutting down the starboard screw. If I don't, she'll seize up."

"Can we maintain speed without it?"

"I'll have to shut down the outboard port screw, too, to maintain balance."

The noise coming through the receiver was muffled as O'Conner covered the mouthpiece with his hand. Still, Lord Godwin could hear O'Conner shout orders to shut down both outboard screws immediately. The background noise began to fall off with a low, fading moan.

"I asked, Mr. O'Conner, if we can maintain our speed in order to make port on schedule."

"Only if we increase the RPMs to the inboard screws. Under the circumstances, I would hardly recommend it. It would only add stress to the inboard screws, and to the turbines."

"What does Captain Franchini say?"

"I tried to raise him on the bridge, but they haven't seen him. He's probably still lying in bed with one of the female passengers from last night, getting his pipes cleaned. Sorriest excuse for a captain I've ever shipped with."

"I want you to do whatever is necessary to maintain our normal cruising speed, Mr. O'Conner."

"That's damned stupid," O'Conner said, after a beat adding, "sir."

"Perhaps, Mr. O'Conner, but it is an order."

Lord Godwin slammed down the telephone in a rare display of anger.

Keiko would be furious, but it was her own bloody fault. She shouldn't have insisted that he defer part of the ship's overhaul simply to keep them on schedule. There was also the shocking matter of Mandy Robsard's death to discuss. Something told Lord Godwin that learning about the murder would not upset his partner nearly as much as the mechanical trouble—not so long as they could manage to keep the killing from becoming generally known.

Lord Godwin pulled back his French cuff and checked his watch. He was supposed to have breakfast with Keiko, but she was late. She must have decided to sleep in, too, which was just as well. He only hoped she wasn't with Captain Franchini. That man was unreliable enough, and Lord Godwin had already decided to get rid of him at the first possible opportunity.

Lord Godwin reached for the intercom to buzz the steward to bring him some tea and two hard-boiled eggs. That was all his stomach could handle. The stress of getting the *Atlantic Princess* through its maiden voyage was giving him an ulcer.

"About a year and a half ago I figured to hell with it. It was time to enjoy life. I sold my company, which gave me more money than I could ever possibly spend. I bought a Harley-Davidson and rode it from Maine to Baja. I'd always wanted to do that. Then I went mountain climbing in Wyoming, and white-water rafting on the Colorado River. I'd always wanted to do that, too. I flew to Europe with my girlfriend and did the grand tour. My girlfriend and I broke up in Paris in the spring, which isn't really supposed to be the way it works, is it?"

"Is it ever?" Carrie said, instantly wishing she hadn't offered an opinion about romance when she hardly knew anything about it.

"I guess not," Fox said. "I came home and learned how to scuba dive. Scuba diving was cool, except for the part where the shark tried to eat me in the Bahamas. I was lying on a beach in Cancún, bored out of my skull, when I decided that getting away from it all is great, but only if there was something to get away from—and back to."

"You life story is really very interesting, Alex, but what does it have to do with your telling me who killed Mandy?"

"A lot, actually," Fox said with a grin. "There I was in Cancún, reading mystery novels on the beach, all the time in the back of my head thinking about going back to work.

The question was: What kind of work? The idea of writing computer codes again gave me a migraine. I decided that whatever I was going to do, it wouldn't have anything to do with computers, at least not directly. I had the money to try my hand at whatever I wanted. So after several days of careful consideration and numerous gin and tonics, I decided to fly back to the States and buy a detective agency."

"I was afraid that's where your story was leading," Carrie said, looking away.

"I know what you're thinking, and you're right. I'm a rank amateur in way over my head." Fox held up his hands in a gesture of surrender. "I confess it's true. But I also do happen to know who strangled Mandy Robsard and hacked out her tongue."

Carrie's glare was icy. "Mandy Robsard's death is not public knowledge, and the details you just mentioned are confidential. Where did you get your information? I suppose you tapped into the ship's computer network while I was typing out the death certificate on my word processor."

"No, it didn't have anything to do with computers. Let's just say I have my sources."

Carrie started to leave.

"Wait! Hear the whole story before you decide that a hacker and an amateur detective is wasting your time. I need your help stopping a serial killer. His victims tend to be attractive young females. I don't mean to alarm you, Carrie, but you're exactly the sort of woman he preys upon."

Carrie gave Fox a hard look but sat back down.

"I bought Fitzgerald and Associates, in Chicago, which is where I lived before moving to Silicon Valley. It's a middling-size agency. The guy who owned it, Ray Fitzgerald, is a retired police detective. He agreed to come in one afternoon a week to keep me from running the business into the ground the first year. I got my private investigator's license and—*voilà*!—instant detective.

"Running a detective agency is a lot less exciting than

they make it out to be in the movies. However, every once in a while something interesting comes along. Which brings me to Clarice Luce.

"Six weeks ago a big-shot Chicago attorney named Frederick Luce came into the office. His daughter, Clarice, was killed two years ago in a fall while traveling in Germany. It was supposedly an accident, one of those commonplace tragedies you hope happens to the other guy. Luce had her buried in Hillside, a Chicago suburb filled with cemeteries, where the dead outnumber the living.

"Two months ago Luce was having lunch at an Italian restaurant on the North Side, when he ran into an old tennis buddy who has been living out on the West Coast. It was the first time they'd seen each other since Luce's daughter's wedding. They had a drink, and the conversation worked its way around to Clarice. The friend mentioned that he'd seen Clarice's husband in Munich the day after she fell to her death. Luce's buddy didn't know that Clarice and her husband were separated at the time of her death. In fact, Clarice had filed for divorce. She'd gone to Germany alone, or that's what her father had thought. Luce is no dummy. He knew it was a pretty big coincidence that his daughter's estranged husband was seen close to where she had died in a supposedly accidental fall. After his suspicions ate at him for a couple of weeks, Luce hired me to check up on his late daughter's husband."

"Wait a minute, Fox. Lawyers work with detective agencies all the time. If he's such a big-shot Chicago attorney, why would he hire an amateur like you?"

"You really know how to hurt a guy, Carrie. To tell you the truth, Luce wanted an outsider. The daughter's husband came from one of the richest families in Chicago. He didn't want it to get back to them that he was checking up on their boy. The other thing was that the husband had, for all intents and purposes, vanished into thin air. Which is really where I come in. Since I took over the agency, we've started to specialize in electronic missing-persons traces. You'd be surprised at the computerized trail people leave behind them, even when they try to keep a very low profile. Credit cards, utility bills, hotel reservations, parking tickets—even library cards are computerized these days. Luce had heard about what I could do.

"Our guy's trail was easy to follow, at least at first. He moved to Las Vegas after splitting with his wife. He lived in a rented house on the edge of the desert. The neighbors never saw him. They figured he was a recluse or a gambler who spent all night in the casinos and slept all day. Then, not long before his wife died, our guy decided to visit Germany. He used his American Express card in a shop less than ten miles from the place where Clarice's body was found on the day she died. But the weird thing is, he went to Germany *before* his wife."

"It almost sounds as if she went to Germany to follow him."

"That's exactly what I thought, though I haven't been able to prove anything definite. At any rate, he was hardly a grieving widower. Instead of coming back to Chicago for Clarice's funeral—she was still his wife, after all—he went to Bayreuth for the Wagner Festival. When he finally did come back to the States, he settled in New York City and married a Russian ballerina, Tatiana something—I've got her name in my laptop back in the cabin. They didn't stay together long. Tatiana dumped him. I haven't interviewed her yet, so I don't know if she had any idea what he was up to or not. I'd bet money she suspected something was up, especially after the bodies started piling up in New York."

*"Bodies?"*

"About the time our guy arrives in New York, a series of gruesome murders began. The victims were always women, the bodies always mutilated. The killer had a weird obsession with blood—"

" 'Dracula'?"

"That's what the tabloids called him. You've obviously heard about our boy. A very frightening guy. And more fiendishly clever than Jack the Ripper. The police never even got close to catching him. It was very weird, almost as if the killer actually did possess Dracula's supernatural powers."

"He was never caught, was he?"

Fox shook his head. "But at least the killings stopped. The police had various theories: They said that 'Dracula' killed himself or was killed by an accomplice. But he wasn't dead. He just went somewhere else to carry on his sick work."

"Where?" Carrie asked, leaning forward on the table, engrossed in Fox's story.

"About the time the so-called Dracula killings stopped in New York, a series of suspiciously similar murders began in a small southern town, where our guy had, not coincidentally, gone to live. He didn't stay long, though. Something scared him off. I've interviewed people who knew him in Mississippi. I even met a woman, a beautiful blonde named Victoria Buchanan, who didn't do a very good job of disguising the fact that she was in love with him. She doesn't know how lucky she is to be alive.

"After Mississippi our guy spent several months aimlessly wandering the country. My computer traces followed him to New Orleans, San Antonio, Taos, San Francisco, Seattle. During the same time span, there were horrific murders in New Orleans, San Antonio, San Francisco. There were suspicious disappearances in Taos and in Seattle, where a dozen prostitutes vanished during the two weeks he was checked into the best suite in the Metropolitan Hotel. Their bodies are yet to be found. He can be careful when he's in the mood.

"He's also broadened his taste in victims. One of the dead in Mississippi was a gay man. Our guy still preys primarily upon women, but there are men among them. Some of the Seattle prostitutes were male. The male victims are not always homosexual, however."

Fox took a drink and continued.

"After Seattle he moved diagonally across the country and ended up among the millionaires in Palm Beach. There were a half dozen murders in Palm Beach County that matched our guy's style, although he seemed to be trying to maintain a low profile and keep the authorities from noticing any trend. Florida is an excellent place for murderers to operate. Between the Everglades, the orange groves, and the ocean, there are lots of places to dump bodies.

"I was getting ready to fly into West Palm Beach Airport when I found out about his reservations aboard the *Atlantic Princess*. I came close to missing him, though. The reservations were in the name of the woman he's traveling with."

"And now you think 'Dracula' killed Mandy?"

"I'm sure of it."

"Why haven't you gone to the police with this information?"

"I have, and they always tell me the same thing: The fact that somebody happens to be in town when a crime is committed isn't evidence you can take to a grand jury. The fact that somebody is in a half dozen towns when the same sorts of crimes are committed makes the scenario somewhat more interesting, but it's still only circumstantial evidence. And keeping on the move is a damned smart tactic. Police are too busy, and their budgets too limited, to chase phantoms who have already disappeared from their jurisdiction by the time they become suspects.

"There's also an ugly social component at work. Being from a wealthy family provides camouflage for our guy. People are myopic when it comes to rich criminals. You can get a cop to consider the possibility that a transient farm worker who travels the country in a beat-up pickup is a serial killer. Tell the same story about a socialite who travels by jet or in his Jaguar convertible, and they look at you like you're crazy."

Fox sighed. "The only way this bastard will ever be caught is if a lone investigator gets mad enough to make a crusade out of nailing him."

"That's where you come in."

"That's right," Fox said, and grinned. "Frederick Luce thinks—and I concur—that if I follow our guy long enough, he'll make a mistake and I'll get something on him. That's why I scammed reservations for this voyage. Hell, Carrie, I know it was wrong, but it was the only way I could get on the ship. I didn't have a choice."

Fox thought he saw Carrie's dislike for him soften slightly.

"The person you need to tell all this to is Jack Ketch, our chief of security."

"I already did. He told me to, and I quote, 'fuck off.'"

"You're kidding."

"He has the typical cop mentality about private investigators: We're inept amateurs who aren't worth the time of day. I don't know that he's entirely wrong, but I would think he'd be at least mildly interested in following up on a tip that 'Dracula' was aboard the *Atlantic Princess*. But he's not. And that's where *you* come in."

"Me?"

"I know the general details about what happened last night, but Ketch won't share any of the hard evidence recovered from the crime scene."

"I'm sorry, but I can't help you there."

"I know I'm asking you to go out on a limb and share confidential information, but this psychopath will continue killing if we don't stop him."

"You misunderstand me, Alex. I can't tell you about the evidence, because except for the body, there isn't any. Ketch didn't collect any, as far as I know."

"You're kidding."

"I wish I were."

"There's always evidence. Crime scene sketches, interviews, notes on—"

"There aren't," Carrie said, cutting him off. "The only thing Jack Ketch was interested in last night was cleaning up the scene before it attracted a crowd. Ketch isn't a policeman anymore; he's Lord Godwin's public relations man. To my knowledge he hasn't talked to anybody but the boy who found the body and his grandparents. They've all been asked to keep absolutely quiet about the incident, supposedly to prevent panic. Of course, what they're really worried about is a scandal that will make people afraid to book reservations. It's amazing how successful they've been at keeping a lid on this."

"Jesus," Fox said, looking out in the direction of where the sun was climbing up over the waves. The light on the water was too blinding to look into for more than a few seconds.

"Who is it, Alex? Is the killer someone I might know?"

"Oh, you know the killer all right," Fox said. "We sat at the same table with him last night at supper, although he didn't say much. The serial killer is Principessa Nicoletta's boyfriend, David Parker."

"Take a look at these, Chief."

Chief Burnham put down his coffee and accepted the clipboard from Seaman Rameriz.

"The winds and currents are running stronger than normal."

"I can see that, Rameriz. Your little monster seems to have up a pretty good head of steam."

"The satellite mass readout is on the next page."

"Hmmm." Burnham scratched his head. "For an ice cube, it sure isn't melting very fast."

"Nope. Check out the thermographs on the next page. See there how that finger of the Labrador Current curlicues around to the northeast, pushing into the Gulf Stream? I haven't worked out the math on it yet, but there's got to be an exponential increase in speed when you get both currents pushing M-27 along. We'd better put out a supplemental advisory to ships in the lane."

"That's an affirmative," Chief Burnham said, handing the clipboard back to Seaman Rameriz. "I still don't think that 'berg will be a problem unless some fool wanders far out of the shipping lane while running completely blind."

Chief Burnham snorted and picked up his coffee cup.

"It's hard to imagine anybody not spotting a floating ice

mountain on their radar. It would be easier to sail into the Rock of Gibraltar without noticing it first."

Nicoletta sat at the vanity, brushing out her hair with the antique silver brush that had once belonged to Marie Antoinette. It would be nice to have a comely young woman in her service again to help with such chores. She thought of how Gareloch had spent hours combing her hair while she worked by candlelight in Castle Vlachs. So long ago, and yet it might have been only the night before.

Nicoletta pulled a handful of hair around her shoulder, brushing it against her breast. A strange word, "friend." Nicoletta had lovers and companions, but not since Aedon and Leonardo had she had a friend. David? No, she had started out with high hopes for him, but he had left her sadly disappointed. It was best to be alone. Unlike the weaklings who flocked to the *Illuminati* for the safety of the herd—as David had, before she stole him away from them—Nicoletta had preferred to remain a solitary vampire, moving through the years with only a lover for companionship. But alas, love had never proven to be immortal for her, unless it was her love for Gareloch, who was dead, or Aedon, who had gone away, or Leonardo, who had been beyond reach of her feminine charms and was dead now, too.

Nicoletta gathered another section of hair with her nimble white fingers and began to brush it. When she was back in her villa overlooking the Mediterranean, Nicoletta thought, she would find a servant, someone suitable, someone with the proper combination of beauty, manners, intelligence, and loyalty. A comely youth or perhaps a girl Nicoletta could take to her bed when the impulse so moved her. Someone with whom Nicoletta could, perhaps, share the kiss of immortality.

Nicoletta's brush found a tangle. She worked it out, thinking about David Parker.

She was certain she would not enjoy the dubious pleasure of David's company much longer, though his brilliant talent at the piano never failed to bring back sweet memories of her beloved minstrel, Aedon. Nicoletta had tried to help David come to know his *Vampiri* nature, but he was too stubborn, too stuck between the mortal and immortal worlds. Nicoletta had grown tired of David even as he had grown tired of his own pathetic existence. He would pass from her life soon, one way or the other.

The time had come to consider future arrangements. A new servant and also a new lover. Perhaps a woman, this time. Nicoletta pulled the brush savagely through her hair now, enjoying the pain because it helped distract her from things she would rather not think about.

Keiko Matsuoka would never do. Nicoletta had transformed Keiko only to torment David and wreak havoc aboard the *Atlantic Princess*. Keiko was unsuitable, a greedy woman whose soul would remain constrained by its petty acquisitiveness even now that she was immortal. Indeed, she was exactly the kind of vampire who would be attracted to Cesare Borgia with his petty grasping after power. Such trifles were beneath a vampire's interest. Wealth was everywhere in the world. When a vampire needed or desired something, she simply took it.

Dr. Carrie Anderson—now, there was an interesting prospect! The young physician's hungry mind and independent spirit reminded the *principessa* of herself as a young woman. Dr. Anderson would make a fitting consort for a philosopher-turned-vampire. Unfortunately, Nicoletta suspected that Carrie would have as much trouble as David learning to enjoy the pleasures of the hunt.

Nicoletta put the brush down next to her diary. For a moment she stared balefully at the crimson leather volume whose antique pages were filled with the painful recent recollections of her early life. How foolish of her, the vampire princess, to feel such regret! Was it not enough to have an eternity to go wherever she wanted and do whatever she wished?

The world was indeed a curious place. Her disciple Machiavelli had been correct in saying that hatred is acquired by good actions as easily as bad. As it is impossible for anyone to be entirely good, true *virtu* lies in knowing how best to be evil.

Nicoletta's eyes flashed when she looked at herself in the mirror. She would forever have the face of a fifteen-year-old girl; the innocence she could so effortlessly conjure was an excellent disguise. She was no longer innocent of anything. Nor was she any longer a Stoic. Looking at herself in the mirror, Principessa Nicoletta Vittorini di Medusa realized that the centuries had transformed her into an Epicurean. The purpose of life was pleasure—her immortal *Vampiri* pleasure!

Nicoletta deposited her diary in a necessaries box carved from rosewood and engraved with the *Atlantic Princess* insignia. She would burn it later. The past was past, and the future glorious, for countless delicious *occasione* awaited her aboard the *Atlantic Princess* as it reached the midway point in its passage across the Atlantic Ocean.

In the coming bacchanal, the immortal epicure would drown her melancholia beneath a tide of blood!

# 20

✧

# Delirium

LIEUTENANT JAMES PORTEHAY preferred the night watch for bridge duty aboard the *Atlantic Princess*. There were no tours or sunbathers to distract the officers as there were during the day, only a few joggers running by unseen in the darkness below on the Sports Deck.

Except for the running lights, the area in front of the bridge was kept dark at night to make it easier for officers to spot hazards in the water. Though radar and the Navstar global satellite positioning system were infinitely more important than eyesight in piloting an ocean liner in open sea, those old-fashioned precautions made perfect sense to the by-the-book ex–Royal Navy officer. It took a long time to turn the gargantuan ship, and even longer to stop it, so the officers had to be alert to potential trouble at all times. Lieutenant James Portehay had heard of small wooden vessels getting in under a ship's radar and being run down. Such accidents, which involved almost criminal negligence in Lieutenant Portehay's opinion, would never happen on board one of *his* ships.

Thanks to computerization, it was possible to man the bridge with only two officers during night watch, the lieutenant, who as Officer of the Deck was in command of the ship while the captain was off duty, and a junior ensign serving as pilot. Lieutenant Portehay's pilot for the *Atlantic Princess*'s first transatlantic crossing was a young officer from Bristol named Jackson. Since the autopilot handled any minute course corrections that became necessary,

269

Jackson's duties were limited to standing before the radar-scope, shifting his eyes back and forth between the horizon and the scope at prescribed ten-second intervals.

Lieutenant Portehay was noting the hourly longitude and latitude on the bridge's plotting table, when the door opened behind him. Portehay spun smartly around, looking past the two women, expecting to see Captain Franchini close on their heels, come to show off for the ladies. Lieutenant Portehay had already come to the conclusion that the captain was unfit to command the *Atlantic Princess*. Franchini was far more interested in socializing with the passengers than in the ship's operations. Unlike Captain Franchini, whose experience had been limited to pleasure cruises in the Caribbean and Mediterranean, Lieutenant Portehay had spent the past fifteen years of his life sailing the Atlantic Ocean. The Atlantic was a dangerous place. Trouble could come up out of almost nowhere on the Atlantic, and it was often deadly. A ship sailing the Atlantic needed a captain, not a social director, standing between the passengers and quick death by hypothermia in the ocean's frigid waters.

Captain Franchini wasn't with the women, which was a surprise, because he'd already made it his habit to visit the bridge with whatever woman he was trying to impress.

"Sorry, ladies, but this is a restricted area except during regularly scheduled tours."

Lieutenant Portehay felt a jolt of recognition as the taller woman came toward him. It was Nadja Bisou, the motion picture actress. She seemed even younger in appearance than she did on the screen, though Portehay knew she had to be at least forty. Apparently being at sea agreed with her.

Ignoring Lieutenant Portehay, the second woman—an attractive Japanese lady in a red minidress—pulled the bridge door closed behind her.

"I thought you might be able to make an exception," Nadja Bisou purred. "We wanted to see where you drive the ship."

"I would like to accommodate you, Miss Bisou, but regulations expressly forbid it." Lieutenant Portehay felt himself beginning to perspire. The movie star was standing so close to him that he could feel her body heat radiating through her tight black dress.

"Not even as a special favor for me?" Nadja pouted. "Come on, Lieutenant. What would be the harm?"

Lieutenant Portehay had to drag his eyes away from Nadja to shoot Ensign Jackson a rebuking glare. Jackson didn't notice his superior's disapproval, however. Keiko Matsuoka was down on her knees in front of him, busy unfastening the ensign's pants.

"Stop right th—"

Nadja's hand touched Lieutenant Portehay in a very surprising place. "You must be a very skillful sailor to control such a big ship," she said, her lips nearly touching Portehay's.

Lieutenant Portehay put his hands against Nadja's bare arms to push her away, but some unaccountable loss of will stopped him short. Her skin was smooth and dry but feverish to the touch. How exciting it would be to feel Nadja Bisou's hot naked flesh against his own!

"I really must order you to leave the bridge immediately," Lieutenant Portehay said, struggling to regain a measure of his usual self-control. "The smallest lapse of attention by the bridge officers puts the ship into jeopardy."

"But we're in the middle of the ocean, Lieutenant," Nadja said in a voice that seemed to caress him even as her hand did. "What possible danger could there be in the middle of the Atlantic?"

"If you refuse to leave, I'll have to call Security."

"Do you really want to invite more men to the bridge, Lieutenant? There's enough of Keiko and me to go around, but do you really want to *share*?"

Some mysterious quality in Nadja's voice caused an invisible barrier to dissolve in Lieutenant Portehay's mind. What did it matter? The *Atlantic Princess* was so automated that it could practically sail herself. And they were, after all, in the middle of the Atlantic—almost exactly in the middle, according to the coordinates Lieutenant Portehay had been plotting when the visitors arrived.

"You can stay," Lieutenant Portehay said, thinking that his voice sounded strange and faraway, "but only for a little while."

Nadja Bisou's mouth was suddenly all over his mouth, her hands all over his body. She opened his shirt, his pants, in a hurry to have him. Portehay let himself be pushed down upon the bridge deck. As Nadja hiked up her skirt to straddle him, he saw that she wasn't wearing any underwear.

"My God," he gasped as she mounted him.

Nadja tightened and relaxed the muscles between her legs, the sensation driving Lieutenant Portehay wild, squeezing him so tight that it almost hurt before releasing the pressure.

And then suddenly it *did* hurt.

She relaxed.

Portehay began to moan and grabbed his lover by her hips, thrusting upward to meet her, wanting to bring her quickly along with him to the brink. He wouldn't be able to hold himself back much longer if she kept using her lover's trick. She'd suck it right out of him—if she didn't rip it off first!

Jackson screamed.

"Not so loud, Ensign!" Portehay ordered in an irritable whisper. If anybody caught them, their careers would be finished.

Keiko turned toward Lieutenant Portehay and spat something onto the deck. Her face was smeared with dark liquid. Blood, Portehay realized, but it was almost as if he could not believe what he was seeing. Blood that ran from her mouth and down her chin in a long, thick drool, blood that sprayed from the wound in Jackson, splattering her hair, her face.

Lieutenant Portehay tried to sit up, but he couldn't. Nadja Bisou had him pinned against the deck so that it was impossible to do more than struggle.

On the other side of the bridge, Keiko Matsuoka loudly sucked the blood hemorrhaging from Ensign Jackson. Jackson collapsed backward, but Keiko stayed with him, her blood teeth fastened deep into his torn flesh.

Lieutenant Portehay's own pain was suddenly excruciating. He'd managed to pull his hands free and smashed his fists against Nadja, but he might as well have been striking the foremast. She held him pinned flat against the deck, her body as immovable as if it were part of the ship itself. Portehay did not know whether he heard or only felt the awful tearing away of the flesh between his legs. He heard his disembodied screams fill the bridge until Nadja buried her teeth in his throat.

After that, all was silence.

Ricky McCormick was lying in bed on his stomach with his head hanging over the edge, reading a comic book open on the floor. He'd stuck close to his grandparents' suite since finding the body. It was probably silly to think that Mandy Robsard's killer was looking for him, but he wasn't taking any chances.

"Ricky?"

He rolled over and sat up in a single movement. "What's up, Grandpa?"

George McCormick put his finger to his lips. "Grandma's napping. Would you mind running down to the pharmacy when they call back to pick up my Naprosin prescription?"

"Is your back hurting again, Grandpa?"

The old man smiled painfully.

Ricky glanced at the window. The curtains were pulled, but he knew it was dark. Not that Ricky was scared of the dark. And it wasn't late. There would be lots of people out. Besides, Ricky had felt a lot safer ever since Mr. Ketch told them he already knew who killed that woman. The bad guy was her boyfriend, a cook in the kitchen, and the ship's police were watching him closely. The cook would probably be arrested as soon as they landed in England, Mr. Ketch said. Getting to the pharmacy would be easy enough: down the Sun Deck to the No. 3 stack, take the elevator six flights down to the D Deck. The pharmacy was just beyond the infirmary, where Dr. Anderson would be working. Ricky could stop in and say hello if she was on duty. He liked Dr. Anderson. She was pretty and she didn't treat him like a little kid.

"Sure thing, Gramps."

"Thanks, Ricky. You're a good boy."

The sailor sat sprawled on the floor in the corner of the radio room. Monsieur Salahuddin was on his knees in front of the man, leaning forward, his face buried in the radioman's neck. The pale skin on the inside of the corpse's bare arms was beginning to pucker by the time Salahuddin struggled to his feet, wiping his blood-smeared lips on his black dinner-jacket sleeve.

"That, my young friend, is the benefit of wearing basic black," Salahuddin said, his words deeply slurred. "It's the only color that hides bloodstains. Ask any junkie. *Me*, for instance."

Salahuddin giggled and rubbed his hands together, the warmth from the friction sending a delicious sensation up his arms and down his torso into his legs.

Blood was an infinitely greater pop than the excellent Iranian heroin Salahuddin injected into his veins four times a day. A steady supply of the best smack was one of the many perquisites resulting from his clandestine business dealings with certain factions in Tehran.

Would he still crave the junk now that he was—*changed*? Salahuddin doubted heroin would have much effect on him. But what if he pumped someone full of heroin and drank their blood? Would the high be doubly magnified? Perhaps Cheri would help him find out. The black-and-blue woman back in his *appartement de grand luxe* was always willing to put up with his cruelty as long as he gave her the junk she needed to feed her greedy habit. He had had to beat Cheri on several occasions to remind her not to use too much of his stash. Tonight, however, he would let her have her fill. And after she had shot all of the junk she could handle into the purple, needle-scarred vein in her thigh, Salahuddin would prepare a real fix for her. How sweet it would be to rip open Cheri's neck and drink her heroin-laced blood even as she went into convulsions from her overdose!

Salahuddin's gaze fell on the dead radioman. "But first things first," he said to himself. Monsieur Salahuddin had never been able to resist an attractive sailor in uniform.

The arms dealer was rolling the dead man onto his stomach when the hazard-to-navigation warning concerning iceberg M-27 began to print on the radio room's laser printer. The copy tray was full, so the iceberg alert spilled out onto the floor, landing in the puddle of blood spreading slowly from the wound in the dead man's neck. The paper blotted the blood so that it would have been impossible to read, had there been anyone there who wanted to try.

Lord Godwin slipped out of dinner early and went down to the engine room to check on things. His popularity was at a low ebb with the black gang, judging from the cold stares.

"How are things holding up, Chief?" Lord Godwin hollered as O'Conner pulled off the sound-deadening headphones the crew members wore to protect their hearing around the deafening turbines.

"Our luck's held so far."

"Super!"

"At the RPMs we're turning, we won't get any warning. A turbine spinning this fast doesn't seize up. It explodes."

"Just make sure that doesn't happen," Lord Godwin snapped, and turned away.

"Yes, your lordship!" O'Conner shouted after Godwin. "Whatever your lordship orders."

Lord Godwin kept walking, pretending not to hear O'Conner's sarcasm. A scene in front of the crew was the last thing he needed at this point. He took the elevator to the Promenade Deck and strolled toward the bow at a leisurely pace, stopping at regular intervals to speak with passengers leaving the *grande salle à manger* after supper. He considered it an important part of his job to survey passengers' likes and dislikes, and he kept copious notes toward future improvements in the service aboard the *Atlantic Princess*. Lord Godwin was careful not to let the passengers see his fatigue. The long days and stress had taken a toll on his energy, he thought, dragging himself up the stairs to the bridge. Perhaps at the end of the *Atlantic Princess*'s maiden voyage he would take a brief vacation. Only not a cruise, he thought, smiling to himself as he reached for the brass door handle so highly polished that it gleamed even in the darkness. He'd finally had his fill of ships!

Lord Godwin glanced through the window as he reached for the handle to the bridge door.

"Bloody hell!"

The bridge was *deserted*.

It was only when he angrily jerked open the bridge door that Lord Godwin saw the mutilated bodies of Lieutenant Portehay and Ensign Jackson.

Ricky slipped his Swiss Army penknife into the run-through pocket of his Umbro soccer pullover and headed for the door.

"Back in a few minutes, Grandpa."

"All right, Ricky," McCormick said, checking his watch, "but promise me no detours. It's too late for exploring."

"Sure thing, Grandpa."

Ricky stepped out onto the Sun Deck in time to see a woman in a long evening dress chase a man out of sight where the deck curved beneath the bridge at the front of the ship. It was supposed to be the other way around, Ricky thought with a grin, the man chasing the woman.

Ricky hurried toward the elevator. The dreaded helipad was above him. He ran a little until he was past the steps leading up to it.

"Don't be such a chicken," Ricky said out loud to himself, slowing to a quick walk.

A woman's shrieks came through the windows of the Grande Lounge. It sounded like someone in serious trouble—which was silly, of course, Ricky told himself sternly. Just an adult who had had too much to drink. He'd seen a lot of that on board the *Atlantic Princess*.

Ricky hopped into the elevator and pushed the D Deck button. The red numerals in the digital readout above the door reported his progress: Promenade Deck, Main Deck, A Deck, B Deck.

The car stopped prematurely on C Deck. The doors opened, but nobody got into the elevator.

Ricky stuck his head out of the elevator and looked up and down the hallway. The corridor—brightly lit and empty except for the tropical plants and artwork on the walls—was empty. Ricky pulled his head back in as the elevator doors closed.

"Jokers," Ricky said to himself as the car began to move again.

The boy hopped out of the elevator when it stopped at D Deck, but he immediately stopped. The peculiar quality that something was not quite right hung in the air like a building charge of static electricity. He could not identify its source, but Ricky sensed something weird, a disturbing presence on the D Deck. It was almost as if someone were watching him, waiting. The hair stood up on the back of Ricky's neck as he slowly looked over his shoulder.

There was no one behind him, at least no one he could see. Looking toward the ship's stern, he had an unobstructed view of the corridor for fifty feet, all the way to the swinging doors that came out of the bulkhead set just ahead of the big aft ventilator. A stained-glass window was set into each door. Although the swirling colored glass made it impossible to be certain, Ricky was almost sure that someone's eye was pressed up against the window in the right door, watching him.

Fortunately, that was not the way Ricky needed to go.

The boy turned and began to walk swiftly past doors displaying brass numbers: D 140, D 141, D 142. Quarters for the ship's medical staff, Ricky knew, throwing a glance back over his shoulder. Whoever was watching him through the window in the door—if it was anyone at all—had not come after him. Not that they could catch him now, he thought with false bravado, puffing up his courage.

The brass letters on the door said PHARMACY. One door down was the infirmary, where Dr. Anderson would be if she was working.

Ricky took one more look back down the corridor at the doors. Did the right door just move slightly, as if inadvertently bumped, or was it only his imagination?

Maybe Ricky could invent some pretext to get Dr. Anderson to walk him back to his grandparents' suite. He couldn't imagine heading back down the hallway alone toward the haunted doors with only his grandfather's prescription for company, for protection.

The electronic buzzer hummed when Ricky pushed open the pharmacy door, warning the pharmacist that a customer had arrived. The waiting room had four chairs arranged around a low table, upon it an array of magazines fanned out for passengers to read while they waited. At the far end of the room was a counter, and behind it row after row of shelves filled with bottles and boxes and jars of medicine.

"Hello there," the smiling woman said as she appeared from behind the shelves.

"Hi. I'm Ricky McCormick. I came down to pick up a prescription for my grandpa. His name is George McCormick."

"I was just getting it ready," the pretty woman said, and gave Ricky a big smile. "Say, I know you. You're the boy who found the"—she checked herself—"you're the boy who made that unfortunate discovery last night on the helipad."

Being reminded of *that* sent a chill through Ricky's body, a feeling like a skeleton running its cold, bony forefinger down his spine.

"Sorry, but I'm not supposed to talk about it."

"That's okay, Ricky. My name is Brooke Morris. I'm one of the nurses on the *Atlantic Princess*. Dr. Anderson told me all about it. She said you were very brave. I'm just helping out in the pharmacy tonight," she added.

"Dr. Anderson is really nice, for a doctor." Ricky felt a blush rising. "I mean—"

"I know exactly what you mean. How are you holding up? That must have been quite a shock for you."

"Oh, I'm okay," Ricky said, shrugging one shoulder.

"Really? You look pale. Come closer and let me feel your forehead."

As the pretty nurse came through the swinging door at the end of the counter to meet Ricky, the boy saw a man's shoe and part of a leg sticking out from behind one of the shelves. He began to fumble with the pocketknife inside his pullover, but he was too nervous to get it open.

"I declare, Ricky McCormick," Brooke said, her smile becoming even brighter, "you are becoming more pallid even as I look at you."

Ricky froze, like a deer caught in an oncoming truck's headlights. Brooke put her hand on his forehead. Ricky thought the nurse's palm felt unnaturally hot against his skin, but maybe that was just because his own blood had suddenly turned to ice.

Maybe what he'd seen was a fake leg. Ricky had seen fake legs in drugstores.

"Are you sure you're really all right?" Brooke's face was filled with gentle concern.

A nervous nod was all Ricky could manage.

A fake leg, Ricky thought. Brooke's smile disarmed his fear. It was time he stopped being such a baby. His eyes focused on the white enameled end piece of one of the shelves. It took a few seconds for his brain to register the image. It was a handprint. The perfect outline of a man's hand, in blood, was streaked at the bottom from when the man who had made it sank toward the floor.

"Hey, look at that."

"What?" the vampire asked, turning her head.

Ricky could hardly believe his luck. The diversion had worked! He sprinted for the door.

"Come back, boy!" Brooke screeched.

Ricky was reaching for the infirmary door when she caught him by the arm, jerking him around to face her, holding him so hard that it made tears well up in his eyes.

"You're going into shock, child. Hush. Let me warm you in my arms."

"Help! Help, Dr. Anderson!"

The vampire was far too strong for Ricky to resist. With a serpentine hiss, the neophyte opened her mouth so that the boy could see a pair of fangs as long as his little finger suddenly appear beneath her upper lip, their blue-white enamel so thin that the teeth were nearly transparent.

"Don't struggle, Ricky. I promise you're going to like this."

The mixture of pain and pleasure that flooded into Ricky McCormick as the vampire sank her teeth into his neck was so overpowering that it was reflex alone that made the boy throw his arms around her. As if directed by a force outside the semiconscious child, he plunged the blade of his pocket-knife deep into the vampire's eye.

Ricky flew backward through the air. He crashed through the pharmacy door and landed in a heap on the hallway carpet. Dazed, he crawled to the wall and steadied himself against it as he struggled to his feet. The vampire stumbled out into the hall and collapsed, her body compressed into a compact, writhing ball that thrashed back and forth, both hands covering her wounded eye.

Ricky started to back away.

The vampire got up on her knees, swaying back and forth, pulled the knife from her eye, and dropped it, a dull thud against the carpeted floor. Brooke slowly took her bloody hands away from her wounded eye. Despite the blood and innerocular jelly smeared down the right side of her face, the eye seemed to have miraculously healed itself. The neophyte let loose a screech of laughter, no less amazed than Ricky at her body's supernatural ability to heal itself.

The vampire jumped to her feet and closed the distance between herself and Ricky before he could even think about running.

"No more tricks, my young friend," she said, wrapping her arms around him as if with affection.

Something exploded behind Ricky. The vampire dropped him abruptly to the floor.

"Back away from the boy," said a man's voice, a voice with an English accent. "Stand off or I'll put the next slug in your belly."

Feeling as if he were dreaming, Ricky rolled over to see Max Burr, the ship's purser, a revolver in his hand. Ricky glanced back toward the vampire. The vampire's head was tilted forward so that her chin rested against her chest; she looked malevolently at Ricky through her eyebrows.

"Get away from the boy! I won't warn you again."

The vampire's hand streaked out and grabbed Ricky's ankle and started to drag him to her.

"Don't let her get me!" Ricky screamed.

Max Burr's gun exploded again, and a black circle appeared in Brooke's nurse's uniform just above her belly button, an aureole of red spreading away from the hole. She let Ricky go and put her hands over her stomach.

"You shot me," Brooke said in disbelief.

Ricky scrambled to his feet and ran to Burr.

"There's a brave lad," Burr said, dropping the revolver into his jacket pocket as the vampire fell backward onto the floor and was still.

"There's a body in the pharm—"

The vampire was suddenly on her feet and upon them both, slamming into them, knocking them to the floor, holding Ricky with one hand and Burr with the other.

"Leave them both alone," said a calm voice.

The man standing over them had the most peculiar expression on his face. More than anything else, he appeared to be bored. Ricky knew who he was—the man who was traveling with the Italian princess, the musical composer. *He* wouldn't be able to save them, Ricky thought with despair, looking at the man's thin, powerless body. It would take someone far stronger than David Parker to save him and Max Burr from the vampire.

"You're a cute one," Brooke said, rising up to face the luckless interloper. "I think I'll kill you first."

"I don't think so," David Parker said. He raised an eyebrow and Brooke Morris flew backward and hit the wall, propelled by an invisible force. The neophyte remained against the wall, shaking, pinned, the blood pumping again from the wound in her stomach.

"Go back to the one who made you, Miss Morris, and tell her I forbid you to harm any more of the passengers or crew aboard this ship. Should you make the mistake of defying me, I promise you the repercussions will be extremely unpleasant."

The neophyte moaned as a trickle of blood began to flow from her nose, and another from her ear.

"Now leave us," the man commanded.

The vampire's body went slack against the wall, the invisible force that had been holding her there withdrawn. She ran past Ricky and slammed through the doors down the corridor.

"Are you all right, young man?"

"She bit me." Ricky rubbed his neck. It was sore, but there was only a trace of blood on his fingers when he brought his hand away.

"You will be fine. And so will your brave friend." The man nodded at Max. "He's suffered a minor concussion. He'll be around in a minute or two. Dr. Anderson should have a look at him."

"How did you stop her, Mr. Parker?"

"That is something you would be better off not knowing, Ricky. At any rate, some things are best forgotten. Look into my eyes, Ricky."

Ricky suddenly felt like stretching out on the carpet next to Max Burr and going to sleep.

"I want you to—"

There was a bloodcurdling scream from somewhere down the corridor, past the double doors, in the direction the vampire had run.

"Damn!" David Parker said, turning to run toward the cry for help.

"Don't leave me!" Ricky cried desperately. He followed for a few steps, but knew he couldn't keep up with the man who flew down the hall at an impossible speed and disappeared through the swinging doors. Besides, what was on the other side of those doors scared the boy more than being left alone with the unconscious Mr. Burr.

"Ricky?"

Carrie stepped out of the elevator, her medical bag in her left hand, seeing Ricky and Max Burr, seeing the vampire's blood on the carpet and splattered upon the walls.

"What's going on, Ricky?" the physician asked, rushing forward. "What happened to Max? Are you hurt?"

"Dr. Anderson!" Ricky was too frightened to feel embarrassed when he began to cry.

"I can't believe none of you can find Ketch," Lord Godwin snapped at the security officer, a Welshman named Burton.

"I can't believe it either, governor. I'm sure there must be a perfectly good explanation."

Lord Godwin was as close to fury as he'd ever been in his life. Ketch and the other senior officers were technically on duty around the clock when they were at sea. Wandering off without taking his pager or leaving word where he could be found was a gross breach of his contract with Godwin Lines, Ltd.

Lord Godwin began to nervously twist the signet ring he wore on the pinkie of his left hand. "What the hell is happening?" he asked Burton. "First that unfortunate young woman on the heliport, and now this."

"The killer is an extremely disturbed individual, your lordship. I never saw men mutilated like that in my twenty years at the Yard. A psychopathic homosexual would be my guess."

"It is inexcusable that Ketch has picked such a time to pair off with a lady friend. There will be hell to pay, Burton."

"No doubt, sir," Burton agreed, nodding grimly. "I'll organize a team to go cabin by cabin, warning the passengers to stay inside with their doors locked until we apprehend the lunatic."

"You will do nothing of the sort!" Lord Godwin shouted. The others on the bridge looked at Lord Godwin as if he had lost his mind, but for once he was too distracted to care what other people thought of him. "Listen to me, Burton: I will not have you start a panic aboard my ship."

"It's your boat, governor," the Welshman said, and shrugged. "How do you think it best to proceed, sir?"

"Take some men and find Ketch. And Captain Franchini. I can hardly believe it possible that I hired as my senior officers two individuals capable of such dereliction. I'll have them both swinging by their balls from the mainmast yardarm if they don't turn up shortly. Inform the security officers that they will remain on duty all night, Burton. Draft whatever level-one and -two officers you can lay your hands on to help."

An Australian sailor wiping blood off the radarscope was watching Lord Godwin rant and failed to realize that he was pressing the pressure switches controlling the system's range setting. The ominous mass of bright light creeping into the scope's northeast sector disappeared as the sailor inadvertently switched the radar into its long-range mode.

"What do you want us to do, governor, aside from finding Mr. Ketch and Captain Franchini?"

"How the hell should I know, man? Patrol the decks. Keep your eyes and ears open for anything suspicious. Maybe we'll get lucky and catch the murderer before morning. But do not—I repeat, do *not*—do anything that will start a panic among the passengers. We must avoid that at all cost."

"Right-o, sir."

The young officer hurrying onto the bridge was still buttoning his tunic as he squeezed past Burton in the doorway. "How may I be of assistance, sir?"

"Lieutenant—" Godwin stopped to check the name tag on the lieutenant's jacket. "Piersen."

"Yes, sir?"

"You are in command of the *Atlantic Princess* until I say otherwise or a senior officer appears on the bridge to relieve you. Do you understand that, Lieutenant?"

"Aye-aye, sir," Piersen, the ship's most junior lieutenant, said, managing to look excited, frightened, and confused all at the same time.

"That sailor cleaning up over there will serve for the time being as your ensign."

"Yes, sir!" the sailor said, smearing blood on his forehead as he smartly saluted Lord Godwin.

"Lock the door to the bridge when I leave, Lieutenant Piersen, and keep it locked. If you can do that and keep this ship on course until you are relieved, I assure you that you both will be well rewarded for doing your duty. Do you understand, Lieutenant?"

"We'll do our level best, sir."

Lord Godwin left the men on the bridge, trying not to notice that Lieutenant Piersen's new ensign was staring dubiously at the radarscope as if it were a strange piece of equipment from another planet.

Alex Fox sat in the infirmary, staring at his shoes. Ricky and Max were side by side on the examining table, both looking the worse for wear. Ricky and Max were staring at Fox, as was Dr. Anderson, who leaned against the wall, her hands crossed over her chest, stethoscope dangling from her right hand.

When Fox finally looked up, the others straightened, alert, eager to hear what he had to say.

"It's the most preposterous story I've ever heard," Fox said, slapping his hands on his knees and standing. "You're a doctor, Carrie. What do you make of this? Some kind of mass hallucination—if two people can be considered a 'mass'—or somebody has dumped LSD in the *Atlantic Princess*'s water supply."

"A hallucination doesn't account for the blood in the passageway," Carrie said.

"True," Fox agreed.

"I know what I saw with my own two eyes, boss."

"Boss?" Carrie asked.

Fox shot Burr a sour look, then shrugged. "Max works for me."

"Max is the ship's purser. In what sense could you regard him as your employee?"

"In the sense that I needed to get somebody on the crew to help keep an eye on David Parker. When what's-his-name got killed—"

"Cyril Ogden."

"Max was perfectly well qualified to fill Ogden's job, which is why I hired him to work for the agency for the duration of the cruise, and made sure he got the position on board this ship. His specialty before he retired from Scotland Yard was investigating bank fraud. He is a chartered accountant."

"That I am, ma'am."

Carrie's face darkened. "Oh, I get it. Since you were able to break into the Godwin Line's computer system to steal a reservation, I suppose it wasn't any great feat to do whatever electronic fiddling it took to make Max seem more qualified than the other candidates."

"Something like that, Carrie."

"You are despicable. You, too, Max. I'm appalled."

"And I'm appalled you expect me to play by the rules against a monster."

"And exactly which monster are we talking about, Fox? Not David Parker. He's the one who came to Ricky and Max's rescue. That hardly makes him sound like a killer."

"I don't know, Carrie," Fox said, throwing up his hands. "I thought I knew, but there's obviously more going on aboard this ship than I understand. What do you think, Max?"

"Dashed if I know, sir."

"It's like I told you, Mr. Fox. The *Atlantic Princess* is infested with vampires."

"You're old enough to know there is no such thing as a vampire, Ricky."

"But she bit me—here."

"You've seen that there are clear signs of puncture wounds, Fox," Carrie said, lightly touching the boy's neck again. "They continue to fade even as we speak."

"I put a slug true enough into her brisket, sir. No ordinary human being gets up after being gut shot. And I don't remember the last time I was tackled by a lady, not that it unduly wounded my pride."

"And how do you explain the way David Parker threw the nurse against the wall using only the force of his mind, making blood run from her ear and nose?"

"I don't know, Ricky," Fox said, shaking his head. "I just don't know."

"You're convinced Parker is a serial killer. Maybe he's a serial killer *and* a vampire."

"That's ridiculous, Carrie."

"There's nothing ridiculous about Horace Latkin's body in the pharmacy," she replied. The pharmacist's murder only increased her anxieties about two other crew members, though she would wait until Ricky was gone to share those with Fox. Dr. Hunt and his nurse were inexplicably missing from the infirmary. Carrie had been called out earlier to treat a seasick passenger after the infirmary's regular night crew proved unavailable. The senior physician and his nurse weren't in their cabins and hadn't answered their pages. Given what had been happening on board the *Atlantic Princess*, their unexplained absences seemed ominous.

"Let's apply some logic to this," Carrie went on. "I don't believe in vampires any more than I believe in the tooth fairy, but once you throw out the explanations that don't fit, the remaining explanation, no matter how bizarre, must be the one that holds."

Fox stared at Carrie, incredulous. "You're not saying that you don't believe in vampires. You're saying that you *do* believe in them."

"Maybe, Alex. At this point I'm not sure what I believe. Whatever is going on here, there must be a scientific—as opposed to a supernatural—explanation. That being said, I think we must assume for the sake of argument that something extremely unusual and perhaps unprecedented is happening on board the *Atlantic Princess*. I am ready to accept as a working hypothesis that something happened to Brooke to transform her into what we might as well call, for lack of a better term, a vampire."

Fox groaned.

"I'm also ready to accept the proposition—judging from what Ricky witnessed—that David Parker possesses similar powers, but to a far greater extreme. I'm proposing that Brooke Morris is a vampire, that David Parker is a vampire, and that there may well be other vampires on board the *Atlantic Princess*, also."

"That means the 'Dracula' serial killings in New York were the work of a real-life Dracula," Burr said.

"I hadn't thought about that," Carrie said, giving Fox a frightened look.

"You'd better think about it," Fox said. "We'd all better think about it. If Parker really does have some kind of supernormal powers, we're in a hell of a lot of trouble, especially if he's been busily making more vampires. We're what, two and a half days from England?"

Burr nodded.

"So what do we do now, Doc? You seem to be the one with all the ideas."

Carrie looked at Fox, recognizing the push-pull energy between them. Under normal circumstances she could imagine learning to deeply dislike Alexander Fox—or to love him. The voyage had become strange and disturbing on so many different levels. Two nights earlier she had been feeling old, her heart filled with anxiety over having missed her chance to find love, to have a family. Now the bizarre danger aboard the *Atlantic Princess* made her feel extremely young—too young to die. There was still time for love, and perhaps with Alex Fox, but only if she survived.

"For starters," Carrie said, "let's have Max take Ricky up to his grandparents and get them to stay locked inside their suite until daylight."

"You think daylight will stop the vampires, ma'am?"

"Who knows, Max? It does in the movies." She turned to Fox. "Meanwhile, we'd better go have a talk with Ketch."

Fox laughed bitterly. "A lot of good that will do."

"I'll make him listen, Alex."

"If anybody can get through to Ketch, you can. You've almost got *me* believing in vampires."

# 21

✧

# Pandemonium

THOUGH IT WAS approaching midnight, early aboard the *Atlantic Princess*, the ship was curiously deserted. Carrie and Fox found the security office shut and locked. They walked on to the Forward Bar and Observation Lounge, hoping to find someone from Security who could tell them where to locate Ketch.

Ketch was in the bar. Behind it, in fact. The room was otherwise deserted.

"What are you doing?"

"Just trying to make myself useful, Carrie. With this virus going around the ship, half the damn crew is laid up."

Carrie and Fox exchanged a look. "What virus?"

"How can you not know about it, Carrie? Dr. Hunt has been running himself ragged tonight."

"That at least explains where he's been," Fox said.

"We couldn't find Phil or Della anywhere," Carrie explained. "I was pretty worried about them."

"Did you think they fell overboard?"

"Something like that."

"As long as you're behind the bar, Ketch, give me a double Chivas."

"What about you, Doc?"

"Nothing, thanks. We've been looking for you, Jack. There's been another murder."

"You don't say," Ketch said, his back to them, reaching for the Scotch. "Up or on the rocks, Mr. Fox?"

"Up."

"Horace Latkin. He was found dead in the pharmacy. I locked the door so that nothing would be disturbed."

"Good for you," was all Ketch said.

"You don't seem overly concerned, Jack," Carrie said, suddenly angry. "Or perhaps murders have become too much a part of the routine aboard the *Atlantic Princess* for you to pay them much notice."

Ketch turned and set the Scotch before Fox. "The first thing a policeman learns about homicide, Dr. Anderson, is not to panic. I would think the same applied to physicians."

"Jesus Christ, Jack, I'm not panicking. I just want to know if you're going to continue to play bartender, or if you're going to go do something about it."

"I'll have a look, of course," Ketch said, but he made no indication that he was planning to do so anytime soon. "Was Latkin strangled like Mandy?"

"His throat was torn out," Fox said in a flat voice. "He looks like some sort of wild animal killed him."

Carrie nodded when Ketch looked at her for confirmation. Ketch frowned thoughtfully and put his hands in the pockets of his dinner jacket. "How odd."

"Odd?" Fox exclaimed. "It's a hell of a lot more than 'odd.' "

"I suppose you, in your capacity as a private investigator, have a theory about who did it."

"I'll ignore your tone of voice."

"How gentlemanly of you."

"I don't understand your attitude," Carrie said, struggling to constrain her anger.

"As a matter of fact, I do have an idea about who killed the pharmacist," Fox said. He glanced at Carrie. "That is, we do."

"Oh, super. I suppose it's David Parker again. Your psychopathic killer is certainly branching out, targeting pharmacists now as well as attractive young women."

"Actually, I don't think Parker had anything to do with killing the pharmacist, though I still think he killed Mandy."

"I hate to be the one to break the news to you," Ketch

said, leaning against the bar, "but David Parker didn't have anything to do with killing Mandy Robsard, although I have been perfectly content to let you think he did. Perhaps you'd like me to enlighten you."

Fox returned Ketch's hostile stare but said nothing.

"Who killed her?" Carrie demanded.

Jack Ketch shifted his stare to Carrie. There was something peculiar about his eyes. They were glassy and remote, the eyes of someone burning up with fever. Carrie guessed that Ketch had become infected with the virus he'd mentioned earlier.

"Mandy Robsard was aboard the *Atlantic Princess* under false pretenses," Ketch said. "It seems the woman Lord Godwin hired to edit our on-board newspaper was not as detached from her job at the *New York Post* as we were led to believe."

"Mandy was working undercover on a story?"

"Now you've got it, Fox," Ketch said, cocking one eyebrow. "She was researching a story purporting to detail the numerous corners Lord Godwin had been forced to cut when he ran into money and time problems with the *Atlantic Princess*. Her working thesis was that this ship, in its present condition, is unseaworthy."

"Sounds like a motive for murder to me," Fox said, swirling the Scotch in his glass. "A story like that would be a public relations disaster for the Godwin Lines."

"You might make a detective yet, Mr. Fox."

"Is it?"

"Is it what, Carrie?"

"Is the *Atlantic Princess* unseaworthy?"

"It passed all inspections. The ship is seaworthy, in a legal sense."

"And in a real sense?"

"There are certain *issues*," Ketch said with a crooked smile. "Even taken in aggregate, they're probably nothing that put us in jeopardy of actually sinking."

"I can't believe Lord Godwin would act that irresponsibly."

"Certain compromises become a lot more palatable when hundreds of millions of dollars are at stake."

"So you think Lord Godwin found out that Mandy Robsard was working on a story that would ruin him, and killed her," Fox said.

Ketch laughed derisively. "Now you begin to betray your status as an amateur detective. Bryce Godwin is incapable of murdering anyone. He gave up fox hunting—no pun intended, Mr. Fox—because he couldn't bear to witness what happened when the hounds caught up with their prey. Keiko Matsuoka is not nearly so squeamish."

"Who?" Fox asked.

"The Japanese woman who sat at Lord Godwin's table during the captain's dinner," Carrie said. "She runs an investment group that put up the money to finish the *Atlantic Princess* when overruns forced Lord Godwin to bring in a new partner."

"Keiko plays hardball," Ketch said approvingly. "She has ties to the Yakuza—the Japanese Mafia, you know—although Godwin didn't know *that* when he got mixed up with her. I could have told him, if he'd bothered to ask me."

"And Keiko killed Mandy Robsard to protect her investment?"

"Not hardly, Fox. Keiko is far too intelligent to dirty her own hands with that kind of housekeeping chore."

"Then her Yakuza henchman?"

"In a manner of speaking, Fox." Ketch dropped his voice to a confiding whisper. "If you both really must know who did the foul deed . . ."

Carrie and Fox leaned forward on the bar, waiting.

"I killed the bitch myself."

"That's not funny," Carrie snapped.

"And I cut out her tongue as a special warning to any of her friends in whom she might have confided," Ketch said, looking straight into Carrie's eyes. "I'd seen you two chatting before the captain's dinner. I thought she might be telling you her dirty little secrets, though it seems I was mistaken."

"You son of a bitch!"

"I'm merely a professional doing a job, Carrie."

"I'll see that you pay for this, Ketch."

"Not likely, Fox. If I were you, I'd keep my ear cocked for the sound of baying hounds. I do not think your chances of eluding them on this ship are at all good now that the hunt is on. Or yours either, Carrie."

Ketch smiled so that Carrie and Fox could see the fangs distending from his upper gum line.

"Jesus, Alex!" Carrie said, her fingernails digging into Fox's arm as she dragged him backward from the bar. "He's one of them!"

There was a commotion at the door as a half dozen passengers made their noisy entrance to the lounge. When Carrie and Fox turned back toward the bar, Ketch had already vanished.

"Come in."

George McCormick opened the cabin door and stepped through it, closing it gently behind him.

"I'm in here," the woman called.

McCormick hesitated a moment, then went through the stateroom and into the candlelit bedroom.

Nadja Bisou was lying on her circular bed wearing a long nightdress made of red silk. The sleeping gown was held up with spaghetti straps, cut to show off her famous breasts. Her nipples were hard beneath the material, which only increased McCormick's discomfort.

"You must have read my mind last night at supper, darling. I was just lying here, fantasizing about you. Mature men have always been one of my passions."

"That's an enormously flattering thing to say to an old man, Nadja. But that's not why I am here."

"No?" Her voice was hurt.

"Please don't be offended. You are an extraordinarily attractive woman. I will do anything for you—anything—and pay any price if only you can help me."

"Then come sit by me and tell me what favors you would have of me," Nadja said, patting the bed.

George McCormick slowly crossed the bedroom and sat down next to the beautiful woman. "It's my wife. Nancy has Alzheimer's. She's fast slipping away from me. There is no cure, no way to reverse the symptoms."

Nadja took his hand and placed it on her breast, smiling wickedly. "I will help you forget."

"I'm sure a night with so beautiful a woman would make me forget," he said, gently withdrawing his hand. "Although I am too old to truly please you in bed, Nadja, I will gladly try if you can only help my wife."

"How can I help her?"

"I have heard things tonight, crazy things, impossible things. And not just from my grandson. From Dr. Anderson and others. I myself saw things on my way here that—I'm sorry, Nadja. I'm not making very much sense, am I?"

Nadja looked up at him with her lovely eyes, eyes half veiled with seduction and the promise of pleasures beyond imagining. For a moment George McCormick actually forgot why he had come to visit her.

Suddenly there were tears rimming the old man's eyes.

"I haven't always been the best husband. There were other women, many of them, I'm afraid, when I was producing on Broadway. That's part of the reason I gave all that up. You see, I can't bear the idea of being without Nancy. I can't let her slip away from me. I'll do anything I can to keep her. Anything."

McCormick paused long enough to gather his emotions.

"I've come here to ask you to give my wife the gift you gave to the nurse. Make her whole again for me. I'm willing to do anything, even become eternally damned if it will keep me together with the only woman I have ever truly loved."

Nadja sat slowly up in bed and looked closely at George McCormick.

"That is the most beautiful thing I have ever heard, darling," Nadja said.

"Only do not hurt the boy."

"Of course not!" the vampire exclaimed, shocked. She put her hand lightly on his shoulder and leaned toward him as if to kiss his lips.

"I will share the gift with you first, then your wife. You will be together forever."

"I will never be able to thank you enough, my dear friend."

"Nonsense," Nadja said, lowering her lips to his neck. "Only this is payment enough."

George McCormick closed his eyes and held his breath, wondering whether it would hurt. The old man gasped when the vampire locked onto his neck with her teeth. Wave after wave of ecstatic pleasure rolled through him, making his entire body tremble. McCormick sank backward against the bed. Without releasing him, Nadja slid on top of him as she drank.

The unexpected darkness moved quickly toward George McCormick, the black tide of nothingness rising higher and higher, threatening to drown him. Animal fear made him want to struggle, but he was too weak by then to even move. The darkness was swallowing him. This was not what he had asked for. Nadja Bisou had lied to him so convincingly that he realized it only when it was too late.

George McCormick had made a terrible mistake. He had bargained with the devil and gotten exactly what he should have expected to get. Now he was going to die, leaving no one to protect his wife, no one to protect his grandson from the monstrous predators loose aboard the *Atlantic Princess*.

The last thing George McCormick heard before he died was Nadja Bisou's gurgling laughter.

Bob O'Conner sat on a stool in front of the control panel in the engine room, drinking the last swallow of cold coffee from a white porcelain mug. Reassuring himself with a final glance at the gauges, the chief engineer headed off toward the cot in his glass-walled office on the catwalk between the forward and after engine rooms.

O'Conner hadn't left the Engineering Deck since he'd ordered the outboard screws shut down. He had his meals brought down to him so that he could stay on duty around the clock, napping for a few hours when he became too exhausted to keep his eyes open. He would personally supervise the Engineering Deck crew until they were close enough to port to back off the turbines, which, at Lord Godwin's irresponsible insistence, continued to turn at dangerously fast RPMs.

Countless things could go wrong when a ship as old as the *Esprit de France* was brought back into service, O'Conner thought, stretching out on his back on the rough woolen blanket without bothering to take off his boots. They'd already burned up the main bearing in the port outboard screw shaft. The No. 2 turbine had been giving him fits, but he'd been able to keep her in service. A naval officer who ran his ship as irresponsibly as Lord Godwin would end up in a court-martial, O'Conner thought. A civilian, unfortunately, had a far greater latitude to be stupid.

O'Conner closed his eyes and fell instantly into a dreamless sleep.


Ricky sat in his bedroom with all the lights and the television on, determined to stay awake until dawn. He was so startled by the sound of someone rapping on the exterior door that he literally jumped up off his bed. Picking up the golden crucifix he'd borrowed from his grandmother's jewelry box, he padded barefoot into the stateroom.

The knock came again, sharper this time, insistent.

Ricky stood on his tiptoes and looked through the peephole.

"Grandpa!"

He hurried to unfasten the chain and unlock the latch. The door refused to open. Then he remembered—the dead bolt. It took both hands to turn the heavy lock.

"What are you doing outside, Grandpa? We were all supposed to stay in, with the doors locked."

Ricky's grandfather stared straight through him. He
didn't say anything and he didn't come into the cabin suite.

"What's wrong, Grandpa?"

The man's skin was a pasty shade of white, his hair
messed. It was only as George McCormick began to fall
face forward into the cabin that Ricky saw the two angry
red holes in his grandfather's neck.

"I knew you were too intelligent a child to open the door
to a stranger."

Nadja Bisou, the movie star, had somehow gotten into the
cabin and was standing behind Ricky, though he couldn't explain how she could have moved through the open door so
quickly that he hadn't even seen her. She was still wearing
the red silk nightdress, which clung to her breasts and hips
like a second layer of skin.

"I am afraid that your grandfather is no longer among
the living," Nadja said, stepping around Ricky to drag the
limp body into the cabin suite and close the door. "There is
no reason to cry, child. Nobody lives forever. Unless, of
course, they happen to be a vampire."

Ricky took a single step backward but stopped when the
vampire turned to look down on him.

"What about you, Ricky? Would you like to live forever?"

Ricky shook his head.

"I see you are admiring my body. It is a nice body, isn't
it? I have used it to get everything I have ever needed.
Come closer. I will show you."

"Stay away from me!" Ricky shouted, holding the
golden crucifix up as if it were a shield.

Nadja shrieked and threw her arms up in front of her
face. But then she looked out from between her arms, the
fear in her face dissolving.

"Give me that!" Nadja snatched the crucifix from the
boy's hands and held it up before her eyes, grinning. "It's
just an old wives' tale, you see," she said, fastening the

chain around her neck, positioning the crucifix between her breasts.

"Crucifixes can't hurt us. We are far too powerful. And we don't sleep in coffins. Keiko already told me that. Another old wives' tale."

She lowered her head and looked at Ricky, commanding him in a smoky voice: "Now come to me, Ricky McCormick. Now!"

Against his will, his right leg slid stiffly forward, then his left.

"You are stupid not to want to become one of us. It is nothing like you think."

She put her hands on the boy's shoulders. He tried to shrink from her touch, but his body no longer obeyed him.

"Have you ever been kissed on your lips by a woman?" Nadja's voice was a whisper. "I mean, really kissed. Or here on your neck? I promise you will find it a singularly pleasurable experience."

He had been kissed there, by the nurse. It had been inexpressibly delightful—and horrible, both at the same time.

Ricky closed his eyes as Nadja's lips brushed against his neck. He grimaced, fighting the strange pleasure her touch gave him. It was all a trick, he knew, a vampire's trick to keep you from fighting. He tried to pull away, but she held him tight, laughing quietly.

"Good-bye, Ricky," the vampire whispered. "Perhaps I'll see you again one day in hell."

"Who are you people?"

Ricky opened his eyes. "Grandma! Run!"

"What are you doing in my house at this hour of the night? You, boy! What's your name? And who is that lying on my floor? Is he *drunk*?"

Oh, my God, Ricky thought. His grandmother was having one of her spells. They were the worst when she woke up, before she became oriented.

"I want you out of here this minute or I will call the police."

"Shut the fuck up, old woman," Nadja snarled.

"Help!" Nancy McCormick yelled, disappearing back into the bedroom. "Burglars! Help! Someone call the sheriff!"

"How pathetic," Nadja said, turning her attention back to Ricky. "And now, my dear young lad . . ."

Ricky's grandmother ran out of the bedroom holding a small traveling iron in her right hand. The scene was so completely bizarre that Ricky had no idea what his grandmother was planning to do. He almost expected his grandmother to get down on her hands and knees and begin trying to press the shirt her dead husband wore with the cold iron. She started in the direction of Ricky's grandfather, but she veered off at the last moment and smashed the vampire in the forehead with the iron's pointed front.

The force of the unexpected blow spun Nadja around. Blood sprayed from the triangular wound in her forehead as she crumpled to the ground.

"Oh, dear," Nancy McCormick said. "George, I think I've killed the burglar."

"Come on, Grandma!" Ricky said, grabbing her by the wrist. "She's not dead. We've got to run."

"Let go of my arm, boy!" she said, slapping at him with her free arm.

Ricky saw a crimson form rise up in the corner of his eye.

"Please, Grandma! We've got to get away! We've got to run!"

Nadja was suddenly at his grandmother's side, her hand clamped on the old woman's arm. The vampire's face was a welter of blood and brain tissue. Ricky thought he was going to vomit.

"You're first, old woman," the vampire said, throwing Nancy McCormick down on the couch and leaping on top of her.

Ricky threw himself at the vampire, beating her back furiously with his fists and knees. Nadja gave no sign she was aware the boy was attacking her. She sank her teeth into the old woman. Trembling with ecstasy, Nadja gave herself completely over to the frenzy. She jerked her head this way and that, like a dog shaking a cat in its jaws. The vampire's teeth kept tearing free from her victim's tissue, making it necessary for her to bite the old woman again and again, creating great gashing wounds, spraying arterial blood everywhere.

Splattered with his grandmother's blood, Ricky jumped back in horror. His grandmother was obviously beyond help. Even if he could get the vampire off her, she would bleed to death, if she wasn't dead already.

Ricky began to back toward the door. Without looking he reached behind himself and found the handle. Nadja did not seem to notice. The vampire continued to thrash about on the couch with her victim.

Ricky turned the handle and pulled the door open a few inches.

Still the vampire ignored him.

Ricky opened the door and ran for his life.

O'Conner opened his eyes and stared at the ceiling, listening hard.

He didn't hear anything out of the ordinary, yet something had startled him awake from a dead sleep. He looked at his watch. He'd been out less than half an hour.

But it was a feeling, not a sound, that had awakened him. The cot sat on the bare metal floor in the office, which was located on a catwalk suspended between the forward and after engine rooms. That catwalk was like a huge tuning fork, sensitive enough to pick up vibrations too subtle to be noticed elsewhere. O'Conner realized he was probably the first to notice the low, almost imperceptible vibration that came up through the cot's metal framework.

The chief engineer jumped to his feet and looked down through the window. The graveyard crew was going about its usual business. None of the men showed any outward sign of concern. They didn't *know*.

"Sweet Jesus," O'Conner said, a curse as well as a prayer. With a little luck, there would be enough time to forestall a catastrophe. But there was no more luck for the black gang aboard the *Atlantic Princess*.

A vibration coming from the metal floor intensified to the point that he could feel it in his feet. He saw the engineers in the after engine room freeze as they felt the same vibration and the low, menacing rumble rising out of it. One of the men—an old hand named Wilson—had time to look up at the engineer's office and catch O'Conner's eye.

Wilson knew what was about to happen.

So did O'Conner.

A loud metallic scream split the air, followed by a deafening explosion that pitched O'Conner violently backward, shaking the entire ship. The windows in the engineer's office imploded, showering O'Conner with broken chunks of safety glass as he crashed into a filing cabinet and fell forward. The temperature in the engineer's office instantly shot up thirty degrees.

The No. 2 turbine had seized up and ruptured.

Inside each turbine were thousands of knife-blade-thin alloy turbine blades the length of airplane propellers mounted on a central spindle designed to turn at high speeds, withstanding the heat and stress of the superpressurized steam that drove them. The moment the No. 2 turbine seized up, the blades began to sheer from their spindle, flying loose inside the turbine housing. Though the heavy steel housing was designed to contain the loose blades, inevitably in a complete seizure dozens of blades cut through the metal casing, like hot knives through butter, and became missiles.

The steam escaping from the ruptured turbine sounded like an angry dragon, and, slicing through it, the distinctive brittle *ping* of the lethal turbine blades flying free in the engine room. Spine-chilling shrieks rising from the after engine room marked each man found by a missile or scalding steam.

But that was just the prelude.

The pressurized steam couldn't escape fast enough through the missile breaches in the housing. After another ten seconds the No. 2 turbine exploded, shaking the entire ship. O'Conner covered his head with his arms as hundreds of missiles careened around the after engine room with lethal fury, scouring it of life, piercing the metal floor and walls of the engineer's office but miraculously missing the ship's chief engineer.

And then, a few seconds later, there was only the sound of low-pressure steam leaking into the air.

O'Conner got to his feet and tried vainly to see through the thick steam.

"Shut down *all* the fucking boilers!" O'Conner yelled, cupping his hands in front of his mouth.

The noise of the turbines began to fade as they went into automatic shutdown mode. At least something aboard the *Atlantic Princess* was working correctly, O'Conner thought bitterly.

Another vibration rose up through O'Conner's feet. Another turbine was going to blow.

"Take cover!" he shouted, wondering if there was anybody left alive on the Engineering Deck to hear as he threw himself to the floor.

O'Conner was wrong. It wasn't another turbine blowing, but the reduction gears locking up, the mammoth transmission gearing thrown out of synchronization when the No. 2 turbine went. There was a noise like a dozen semitrailers colliding head-on as the huge mechanical clockwork that linked the turbines to the screw-drive shafts ground into tons of twisted scrap metal.

"That's the fucking ball game," O'Conner said to himself, sitting up in the almost unbearably hot, wet darkness to brush the safety glass out of the creases in his shirt and trousers. The *Atlantic Princess* would be dead in the water as soon as it lost its forward momentum.

"Get me some auxiliary power!"

"Yes, sir, chief!" a faraway voice shouted.

It was good to hear a voice. At least all of O'Conner's men weren't dead.

* * *

Max Burr was napping in the tiny servants' cabin aft of the McCormicks' suite when the explosion woke him. He jumped out of bed and flipped on the lights, but they wouldn't come on. He opened the door and peered cautiously outside. The entire ship was plunged into darkness.

All was quiet on the Sun Deck, which had only the *appartements de grand luxe*, but beneath him Burr could hear people coming out onto the lower decks. He heard men shouting in alarm and fear and women crying. The passengers must be terrified, Burr thought. Bloody hell, *he* was terrified.

What had exploded? Was the ship about to sink into the icy North Atlantic on its maiden voyage? It was the *Titanic* all over again!

A few far-spaced lights flickered on, went out, then came back on again, shining dimly. At least the emergency lighting system worked.

A barefoot boy dashed out onto the Sun Deck and ran past Burr as fast as he could.

"Ricky!"

The boy did not stop.

"Balls!" Burr muttered. But before he could take out after the boy, someone else emerged from the McCormicks' suite. There was just enough light from the flickering emergency lights that were coming on for Burr to recognize Nadja Bisou as she turned after Ricky. Her face and breast were smeared with blood. And her eyes—there was no mistaking the predatory evil Burr saw in Nadja Bisou's mad eyes.

Nadja began to run toward Burr, but he knew it was the boy she was after.

Without thinking about it—there was no time for such luxuries—Max Burr stuck out his leg as the vampire ran by. Nadja was running so fast that she did a somersault, rolled over three times, and landed on her feet, facing Burr, her face a vision of seething hatred.

Max Burr could see what was going to happen with remarkable clarity. The vampire would kill him first, then the boy.

When Nadja started toward Burr, he put down his head and drove hard at her midsection, the way he had when he played rugby with his mates, clamping his arms around her as they collided. The vampire's fingernails tore at his back like knives, but he didn't let go, not even when they crashed into the railing. There was a brief sickening moment of hanging suspended in a failing balance, and then Max Burr was falling toward the black water, his arms around the screeching vampire, waiting for the shock of the frigid water.

But it was not water Max and the vampire hit, but a chunk of free ice, its surface as jagged and deadly as a bed of spikes.

Bob O'Conner had not been exaggerating when he told Carrie there was nothing she could do for the injured men on the Engineering Deck. All that was left of the after engine room crew was a random dispersal of body parts, most recognizable only as bits of bloody flesh and bone. Carrie left two paramedics to the grim task of gathering up the fragments in plastic garbage bags. No doubt the families would insist that the men's remains be sorted out in some fashion, though there hardly seemed any point.

Feeling queasy, Carrie went to check in on Ricky. She intended to reassure herself that the boy and his grandparents were safe and then find Fox, who had gone off in search of Lord Godwin and Captain Franchini. With the *Atlantic Princess* dead in the water, they would have to convince Godwin and the others of the need to organize a defense against the monsters roaming the ship until help arrived. Even their rescue would be complicated by the need to quarantine passengers to prevent the spread of the bizarre vampire disease. It had to be a disease, Carrie thought, because she didn't believe in supernatural agencies. Her theory was that the condition was caused by a fast-acting retrovirus transmitted via blood-to-blood contact with those bitten but not killed. It would hardly be the first time a legend turned out to be grounded in scientific or historical fact.

Carrie had climbed the midship stairs to the C Deck when someone—or something—several flights above her unleashed an animal howl. Taking the stairs back down two and three at a time, she retreated to the D Deck, desperately considering alternate routes topside. It wouldn't matter that she survived until dawn if she let herself get trapped below-decks, where she couldn't seek out the sunlight's protection—assuming the sunlight would provide any protection from the killers.

D Deck was completely without power, but Carrie managed to find her way safely through the darkness to the stairwell nearest the ship's stern. She crept up the stairs and stepped out onto the deserted Main Deck adjacent to the outdoor swimming pool, which looked down upon the fantail one deck below. The air was sharp with predawn chill and the thickening fog descending on the drifting ship was so dense that Carrie could barely make out the stern navigation lights flickering weakly from the overtaxed backup power system.

The fog swirled and parted, clearing just enough for Carrie to see that there was at least one other person on the deck. The figure of a tall, thin man materialized out of the mist, standing in his shirtsleeves on the fantail below Carrie, looking into the water beyond the railing. Apparently sensing that she was watching him, the man turned and looked up at Carrie.

It was David Parker.

Carrie's heart nearly stopped, yet she did not turn and flee, though Fox believed that David was the most bloodthirsty killer of them all.

David put one foot upon the railing.

"Don't!" Carrie called. She immediately realized the absurdity of her request. David Parker was responsible for the nightmare the *Atlantic Princess* had sailed into. Why in the name of God would she try to stop Parker from killing himself, when his suicide might be the one thing that could stop vampires from completely overrunning the *Atlantic Princess* as she drifted helplessly in the Atlantic?

David turned and again looked up at Carrie, his smile the saddest she had ever seen. "Your impressions about me are entirely mistaken, Dr. Anderson."

David's voice carried easily across the distance—a calm, clear voice, steady despite its sadness. Carrie realized that she was not hearing him with her ears. He was speaking inside her head.

"I have never knowingly hurt a human being," David said, looking up at Carrie, beseeching her to believe him, to understand him, to forgive him for whatever role he had played in the tragedies during the voyage and preceding it. "I want at least one person to know that before I die. I have never harmed anyone."

Carrie nodded. She had no reason to believe him, and yet for some reason she did.

"I know that it is not easy to understand what I have become, Dr. Anderson, though as a physician you can perhaps be more dispassionate in your judgment of me than most. We are peculiar creatures, driven by terrible needs, yet we need not kill to satisfy the Hunger. I do not kill. Killing and violence disgust me. I have never indulged in my darker urges. And in answer to your unspoken question, it does require a conscious effort to infect someone with the virus that makes us what we are."

Carrie nodded. It did not seem to be a trick. He approached no closer, remaining beside the railing. It was compassion that the vampire wanted of her, not blood.

"The unspeakable things Alexander Fox believes I did in New York City—" David broke off as if too overcome with depression to continue.

"Yes?" Carrie said.

"I am incapable of committing such crimes. That was the work of another vampire, a lunatic I followed to Mississippi and killed to stop him from hurting more innocents."

Carrie saw David's chest rise and fall in a heavy sigh.

"Unfortunately, I lost my way after that. I turned my back on my true friends, allowing myself to be seduced by someone who is very old, very powerful, and very, very evil."

David's voice fell to a grieving whisper.

"She has tried to force me to do things—terrible things—that I can never do. I have refused to bend to her will, Carrie, but I am weakening. Of late I find myself subject to violent urges and bloody fantasies. My tormentor says that dedicating myself to killing is the only thing that will bring me into harmony with my true nature. She says it's the only thing that will grant me any measure of peace. Perhaps she is right."

The look David gave Carrie made her tremble. She knew David was thinking about all the things he could do with her, and to her, before leaving her body cold and lifeless. But then his expression softened, and Carrie saw that good had won out over evil in the battle for David's soul—at least for the present.

The vampire looked out at the dark and rolling sea and almost imperceptibly nodded his head, as if in agreement with some thought or conclusion.

"The Hunger rages within me even at this moment, Dr. Anderson, yet I find it impossible even to take the few small swallows of blood I need to keep the beast within me at bay. Why? Because I no longer trust myself. I am not sure I could make myself stop—or that I would want to."

David looked up again at Carrie, his eyes filled with undisguised anguish.

"I have given up being human; I can no longer continue doing the things I must to live as a vampire."

He replaced his foot on the railing.

"And so, Dr. Anderson, I ask you to witness the honorable end to a dishonorable life."

"Please don't," Carrie said, her voice shaking. "Take what you need of me. I offer it freely."

"Do not tempt me, Carrie. Your face has a simple beauty I find almost unbearably attractive, but your mind interests me even more. Like me, you have let opportunities for love escape while you pursued other things. You must not continue to make this mistake, Carrie, or you truly will one day find yourself old and alone."

"I am offering you a bargain, David. I will give you what you need, but you must help us save ourselves from the killers aboard this ship."

"If only it were that simple," the vampire said, looking completely lost. "I could not guarantee that I could stop the others."

"You are our only hope, David."

"You fail to understand. I have spent so much time wanting to kill the woman who has become the authoress of my misery that the impulse to murder has grown strong in me. No doubt this is as she planned it. If so, I walked into the black widow's web with my eyes shut and now find myself completely ensnared and bitten." David shut his eyes. "I can feel the poison moving through me, getting close to my heart."

"You can resist your baser impulses, David. I have faith in you. You've got to have faith in yourself."

He shook his head.

"I'm willing to take that risk. Please, David. I need your help to save Ricky and the others. Come up here. Take what you need from me."

"No!" David said with such sudden sharpness that it made Carrie's heart palpitate. "I am the one you should fear most, Carrie. I, the doomed romantic who could find it so easy to love you, but easier still to kill you."

The vampire turned back toward the fantail railing.

"David, wait—"

"Good-bye, Carrie."

David Parker was over the railing before she could speak.

"Do not trouble yourself wondering whether you have any further obligation to save David Parker's life. He is now entirely beyond the help of you or anybody else. And pray do not mourn him. He was a pathetic weakling. His self-pity would have proven as insufferable to you as it has to me."

Carrie continued to stare at the empty space on the deck that David Parker had occupied, unable to make herself turn around and face Principessa Nicoletta Vittorini di Medusa.

# 22

## "Nearer, My God, to Thee"

**"C**HAMPAGNE?"

Carrie nodded. She usually avoided alcohol, but under the circumstances a drink might actually calm her jagged nerves enough to marginally improve her reaction time.

The wine steward appeared out of the darkness, carrying a silver tray with two champagne flutes and a bottle of Dom Pérignon. He made his way around the overturned tables and smashed chairs littering the *grande salle à manger*. There were no bodies evident, but the bloody smears visible in the dimly lit room told Carrie all that she needed to know about what had happened there. The horror had taken possession of the *Atlantic Princess* to a far greater degree than even she had imagined.

There was plainly something wrong with the wine steward, Carrie realized, seeing the lobotomized glaze in Edwin Decastille's eyes. He did not blink when the cork popped from the bottle's neck, narrowly missing his head, or seem to notice the fountain of champagne that spewed from the bottle's neck. It was as if he'd been turned into a—

"Edwin is no zombie," Nicoletta said, reading Carrie's thoughts and interrupting them even before they took final form. "A zombie is a walking corpse. Edwin is as alive as you are. And, no, I have not drugged him. Why must you be so quick to always think the worst of me, *amore mio*?"

Carrie forced a weak smile. "What am I to think, *Principessa*? I know very little about you and your power.

311

I have only my own limited frame of reference to draw upon."

"Quite so," the vampire said with a smile. "You have a logical mind. I mean that as a compliment, of course."

Anything Carrie could learn about Nicoletta would be useful if—she choked off the thought before it could further coalesce. She must observe everything closely, but she had to be careful not to *think* about it. The vampire could obviously read her mind.

"To life everlasting," Nicoletta said, raising her glass.

"To life," Carrie said, touching the vampire's glass.

"Yes, vampires enjoy drinking champagne," Nicoletta said, again reading Carrie's mind, "but only if it is the very best champagne and chilled ice cold."

"What about food?"

Nicoletta laughed. "You have seen me eat. We were together at the captain's dinner. Oh, now I see what you mean. No, it was no trick, *amore mio*. We immortals eat and drink the same as you." Her eyes sparkled. "Although we do require additional sustenance."

Edwin topped their glasses.

"That will be all," Nicoletta said, waving him away. "Allow me to pay you another compliment, Dr. Anderson," she then said, giving Carrie her most charming smile. "Most mortals have feeble minds, but you, dear doctor, possess an impressive intelligence."

"Thank you. Do you enjoy knowing what people are thinking, or is it a burden?"

"What I enjoy, Dr. Anderson, is your curiosity," Nicoletta said, smiling at Carrie in a way that made her distinctly uncomfortable. "How could it be a burden to know what is on someone's mind?"

"Some things are better left unsaid, *Principessa*. I would think that it is often unpleasant to know what people are really thinking."

"I can shut it out whenever I wish. I often do. Ordinary mortals' minds tend to be filled with petty, venal, jealous, and lustful thoughts. I find it all rather tedious. Do you like music, Dr. Anderson? Perhaps we should have some music to accompany our conversation."

The candelabrum on the orchestra stage burst into flame, the flickering candles only serving to emphasize the crepuscular gloom in the cavernous room. A woman was seated at the piano, inexplicably dressed in only a bra and panties. The man standing beside her holding a violin wore a tuxedo with the left sleeve torn away. Both musicians stared off into space, their minds as disconnected as the wine steward's.

"Play," Nicoletta said softly. The jerky tango that echoed through the *grande salle à manger* sounded macabre and sinister instead of exotic and sensual, a dance not of love, but of death.

"Do you tango, Doctor?"

Carrie shook her head.

"I shall teach you."

"I would prefer not, if you don't mind, *Principessa*. Certainly you can understand that I am in no mood to dance after all that I have witnessed tonight."

"Such a pity! But as you wish. You must think me a monster, Doctor."

Carrie looked deep into the vampire's eyes, trying not to let herself be mesmerized by the mystery and cruel beauty there. "I am a physician, *Principessa*. Your disregard for life is hardly something I can endorse."

"That goes without saying, Dr. Anderson. But are you not interested in learning more about the strange and frightening secret that can turn an innocent and studious young philosopher into a vampire princess?"

"Since you can see into my mind, you know that I am."

The vampire leaned toward Carrie and spoke in a low, seductive voice. "Then become what I am, Doctor, and you shall learn this and much more. Become one of us and you will gain more knowledge than you imagined possible!"

Carrie shrank back from the small white hand reaching

out to caress her face. "I would rather die," Carrie said, her voice shaking.

" 'Tis a pity," Nicoletta said, her voice filled with what seemed to be genuine regret. "You and I are so much alike. We could be very happy together."

"I am nothing like you, Nicoletta."

"Oh, but you are, *amore mio*. Fiercely intelligent, independent, hungry for knowledge about the world and everything in it."

"I have dedicated myself to preserving lives, *Principessa*, not destroying them."

"Such delusions you suffer!" Nicoletta's laugh was scornful. "You may preserve a life, but for how long? Ten years? Thirty? Fifty? The best case is no more than the blink of an eye in the vast expanse of eternity. 'Preserving lives' is exactly the right way to phrase it. You preserve life, but only temporarily. And what a life at that! Mortal life is a miserable, lonely existence filled with struggle, unhappiness, and treachery."

There was fire in Nicoletta's eyes, and while it was as dangerous as the fire she had seen in David Parker's eyes, this flame burned far more seductively.

"When I save a life, *amore mio*, I save it for all eternity. The transformation brought on by my kiss brings immortality and the power to fully experience the senses—and develop new ones unimagined by mere mortals. So tell me, my dear doctor, whose work is permanent, and whose is as ephemeral as the fog that surrounds this ship tonight but will blow away with the first breeze?"

The vampire sat back in her chair.

"Does it not anger you that despite your excellent mind and strong will, men treat you as if you were a second-class citizen, a plaything, a toy best suited to providing a few idle hours of amusement?"

"Not all men are like that."

"Oh, yes, dear doctor, they are. I have lived long and seen much. Perhaps someday I will trust you enough to tell you my story. Then you would understand as well as I."

The vampire looked off into the darkness, her eyes far away. "You can scarcely imagine the indignities, the insults to the body, the mind, the spirit."

The music on the distant stage stopped with an ugly screech of the violinist's bow against his strings. The violinist had placed the tip of his bow beneath his chin as if it were the point of a rapier. While the pianist stared straight ahead, lost in her trance, the violinist walked around in a backward circle as if trying to escape himself, his head thrown back in terror, in pain.

"What are you doing?"

"Sometimes," Nicoletta said, her eyes narrowed to slits, "I think that I want to annihilate every last man on this planet!"

Carrie looked away as the violinist rammed the tip of his bow through his lower jaw and up into his skull. Carrie shut her eyes to the sound of splintering wood. The man collapsed on the stage, followed by a brief commotion as he kicked his legs and threw his arms about, the death spasm. In the quietness that draped itself over the room like a pall, Carrie could hear the waves outside the ship. Somewhere in the distance, a woman screamed.

The service door banged open.

"Well, this is a surprise, Nicoletta!"

Carrie looked up in horrified fascination at her friend Brooke. Instead of a nurse's uniform she wore a full-length gown. She kept her eyes on Carrie as she came up behind Nicoletta and rested her hands on the *principessa*'s bare shoulders.

"Let me have her!" Brooke whispered into Nicoletta's ear.

"Don't give in to it, Brooke," Carrie said, hearing the frightened quaver in her own voice. "You don't have to kill to satisfy the Hunger."

"Oh, do shut up, Carrie!" Brooke cried. "Please let me have her, *Principessa*?" Brooke begged as plaintively as a little girl begging for a treat. "Let me drain her."

"Not just yet, *amore mio.* Besides, there is a man here who is dying to dance with you. Oh, Edwin!"

The wine steward shuffled out of the shadows.

"See if you can teach Edwin to enjoy dancing with a woman, Brooke. It would be a new experience for him."

Showing no sign she was conscious of the dead violinist at her feet, the pianist picked up the tango where she had left off. Brooke and Edwin moved gracefully across the deserted dance floor, the sinuous motion of the vampire and the man somehow one of the more obscene things Carrie had ever witnessed.

"Are you certain that you wish to refuse me? I offer you my friendship, my protection, my immortality."

"Kill me if you must, or allow me to be killed, but I will never willingly become what you are."

The tango had reached its finale. Edwin Decastille stood with his arms around Brooke, embracing her body as he bent it far backward toward the dance floor. His back stiffened when Brooke sank her teeth in the wine steward's neck. They collapsed in a heap on the floor, Edwin on top. The vampire's arms remained wrapped around Edwin, whose own arms and legs flapped spastically.

"What shall I do with you, dearest Carrie? I confess that I suspected you might prove a difficult convert. You are so much like me that it seems a shame to kill you."

"I am nothing like you."

"Oh, yes, you are, only the world has yet to teach you its ugliest lessons. I think that I shall let you live a bit longer," Nicoletta said with a wave of the hand. "Perhaps you shall eventually come around."

Carrie got to her feet and began to back away from the table.

"Call it noblesse oblige, if you like," the vampire princess said with a small, tight smile. "It will be interesting to visit you in a year, or in ten years, to see if you still have the same optimistic ideas about your place in a society dominated by men."

The pianist began to reprise the awful tango, but Carrie did not take her eyes away from Nicoletta.

"Of course you realize, *amore mio*, my offer may no longer stand when next we meet. You will never be as beautiful as you are tonight. If you disappoint me too much in your struggle to make something of yourself in the world, I will probably cut you down without a moment's mercy."

"Good-bye, Nicoletta," Carrie said, finding the courage to turn and walk quickly toward the dining room door.

"Good-bye, Dr. Anderson, but pray do not go that way. I sense a gathering of my unholy children beyond the outer door. Go the way Brooke came. And do avoid the Promenade Deck whatever you do."

Carrie ran from the *grande salle à manger* so fast that she was halfway to the McCormicks' suite before it occurred to her that perverse as it seemed, she should have thanked the vampire princess.

Carrie found the door to the McCormicks' quarters hanging half open.

"Ricky!" she cried, peering into the cabin's dark interior. There was no answer.

Carrie ignored the potential danger and plunged into the darkness. She did not bother to check either George or Nancy McCormick. Even in the dim light filtering in through the open door and windows, it was obvious that they had both been savagely murdered.

"Ricky?"

Maybe Max got Ricky out before the vampires got to his grandparents. Carrie found a candle and conducted a room-to-room search, looking in closets, under beds, and behind chairs. Ricky was nowhere to be found.

Carrie was coming back into the stateroom, when a figure blocked the door, which she hadn't bothered to close. A flashlight flipped on and shined in her face, blinding her so that she could see nothing but the light.

"Looks like the McCormicks didn't make it."

"Fox!" Carrie shielded her eyes with her hands. "You scared me half to death. Put down that damned light."

"You scared me, too, but I'm the one with the weapon." Fox set down on the couch the fire ax he'd looted from an alarm box, propping the flashlight beside it. He ducked back outside long enough to retrieve an aluminum briefcase, then kicked the door shut.

"Things have degenerated aboard the *Atlantic Princess* a lot quicker than I ever expected."

"I know," Fox said grimly. "Any sign of the boy?"

"No," Carrie said, her voice breaking.

"He's a pretty resourceful child, Carrie. Don't give up hope."

"I won't. What about Lord Godwin and the captain?"

"They're either hiding somewhere or dead. I found the bodies of two crew members on the bridge. Their throats—" Fox's face became gray.

"I know. David Parker is dead."

At first Fox didn't seem to register Carrie's words. "How?" he asked finally.

"He took his own life. He jumped overboard. I saw it."

"Are you absolutely certain?"

Carrie nodded. "I spoke with him before he killed himself. He denied being responsible for the killings."

"Right."

"I believe him, Fox. He was depressed but extremely lucid. The murders in New York were the work of another vampire, a psychopath he said he followed to Mississippi and killed. That's why they were both in the same places at the same times. He was trailing the real killer."

"And what about the murders in Florida and on board the *Atlantic Princess*?"

"Principessa Nicoletta Vittorini di Medusa is responsible."

"Parker's girlfriend?"

"I just left her. She admitted as much. She's utterly insane, Alex, and extremely dangerous."

Fox frowned, having trouble believing it.

"We can debate it later. We've got to go look for Ricky."

"It would be a lot smarter to lock the door and stay inside."

"Alex!"

"All right."

"And we've got to figure out a way to call for help."

"The equipment in the radio room has been smashed, but I think I've got it covered." Fox pointed to the briefcase. "I've got my laptop and traveling toolbox. If I can make it up to the satellite dishes, I can tap in and upload a distress call, assuming one hasn't been sent."

"I wouldn't assume anything. I'm glad all your nerd knowledge is good for something besides stealing reservations," Carrie said, but she was smiling.

"Like I said earlier, Carrie, I'm sick of computers, but I can't get away from them no matter how hard I try."

"Nicoletta said to stay off the Promenade Deck."

"And you trust *her*?"

"She said the Promenade Deck wasn't safe."

"If we're going to be systematic about looking for Ricky, we have to do it a deck at a time."

"I guess you're right. It seems weird that nobody is out wandering around, trying to figure out why the engines have—"

A man staggered out onto the Promenade, carrying Brooke Morris piggyback, her teeth locked onto his neck from behind. He managed to take several steps forward—his hands outstretched, beseeching Carrie and Fox to help him—before he collapsed, ridden down dead onto the deck by the vampire.

"Don't try to be a hero," Carrie whispered, holding Fox by the arm. "He's already dead. Let's get out of here while we can."

"What a delicious couple. I had no idea you two were an item."

Keiko was six feet behind them, Monsieur Salahuddin at her side. Salahuddin had lost his jacket somewhere; the front of his white tuxedo shirt was soaked in blood, as were his arms up past the elbows.

"Which of them do you prefer?"

"The choice is most intriguing," Salahuddin said. "I think I prefer the woman."

"Leaving Alexander Fox for me."

Carrie screamed as Brooke's fingernails brushed against her back.

"You can have her, Salahuddin," Brooke said, "but you'll have to share her with me."

Carrie raised her hands to her face, turning in a circle in her futile search for a way to escape Brooke and Salahuddin. Their feverish murderers' hands roamed over her face, her arms, her back, her breasts. Fox fared no better. Keiko had her arms around him and was backing him toward the railing.

"Leave us alone!" Carrie said desperately. The vampires responded with cruel laughter. Just get it over with, she thought, closing her eyes. Her tormentors' hands became more insistent. Carrie cringed as they began to kiss and lick her wherever her flesh was exposed.

"Since you pray for a quick death, we will kill you very slowly," Salahuddin said, his breath like the odor of a dead snake found under a rock.

"Monsieur knows some excellent tricks from his days with Savak," Brooke whispered in Carrie's ear. "Monsieur the Monster, they called him."

"Get away from me, you pig!" Carrie slapped Salahuddin and shoved away the surprised Brooke. "Nicoletta! Help me!"

Salahuddin grabbed Carrie from behind, clenching a painful tangle of hair in either fist. "Nicoletta will not come to your aid," he sneered. "She is busy elsewhere."

"Your death need not be hard, Carrie." Brooke held her face so close that Carrie thought the vampire was going to kiss her. Unlike the Iranian, Brooke's breath was sweet, smelling vaguely of cherries. "Perhaps I shall take you off alone and kill you with exquisite sweetness."

Carrie looked into Brooke's dead eyes and saw no hint of the friend who had worked beside her. She spat in the vampire's face.

"As you wish!" Brooke snarled, drawing back her upper lip in a terrible grimace as her blood teeth distended and locked into place with a dull click of interlocking cartilage and bone snapping to full extension.

Carrie screamed as the vampire lowered her teeth to her throat, but her cry of terror disappeared beneath the ear-splitting shriek as a huge stiletto of ice pierced the ship's plate-steel hull. It almost seemed that it was the sound rather than the collision that sent the ocean liner pitching wildly to starboard as the *Atlantic Princess* and M-27 rammed into each other.

Carrie was slammed down onto the deck. She felt herself separate miraculously from the vampires' grasp as she tumbled violently across the Promenade Deck, rolling so hard that it knocked the breath out of her. Almost before she knew it, her feet were kicking against the black void of the North Atlantic night. Carrie reached out and managed to grab the railing before it got past her.

The *Atlantic Princess* had hit something in the water, something big enough to knock the titanic ship halfway on its side. They must have collided with another ship, and if not a ship, then—

"My God!" Carrie gasped.

Fox sat on the slanting deck, trying to blink his eyes back into focus. Something warm and wet was running down his face. He gingerly touched his fingers to his forehead and brought them away red with blood. He must have been unconscious for a moment, for there was now no sign of his attackers.

"Carrie!"

Fox scrambled across the deck and grabbed Carrie's wrists.

"Don't let me fall!"

"Not in a million years," Fox said, fighting back a

sudden wave of dizziness that made him glad he had the railing to lean against for support. He had to shut his eyes to fight off the nauseating corkscrew of the vertigo spinning around in his head and gut. Terrified voices were emerging all around him. Fox could only hope it was the passengers, waking up in horror to discover the *Atlantic Princess* was sinking, and not vampires.

Fox opened his eyes and saw that the ship was about to capsize. Carrie hung at a forty-five-degree angle from the ship, which steepened to fifty degrees in the time it took Fox to register the image of the *Atlantic Princess* rolling over on them. Fox threw a look over his shoulder and saw the passengers boiling out of their cabins, so terrified that none of them offered to help save Carrie.

"Pull, damn it!" Fox ordered, straining against Carrie's weight, leaning backward, putting first one foot and then the other against the railing as the ship continued to yaw to starboard. The waves rolling past were so near now that Fox felt the icy salt spray against his hands and face, making the gash in his head burn.

"What do we do now?" Carrie asked, clearing the rail and huddling her shivering body against Fox's.

"Get to a lifeboat," Fox said, trying to sound braver than he felt.

An unnatural wail rose up from the sea itself, a hideous sound that Fox felt in his teeth. "Cold water hitting boilers," he said, having to yell to make himself heard.

But Fox was wrong. The scream was the sound of the fog-shrouded iceberg withdrawing its lethal fingertip from the steel hull, leaving behind a ragged tear in the port side stretching from the foremast all the way back past the No. 1 stack. As the iceberg pulled away from the ship, the *Atlantic Princess* unexpectedly lurched to port as radically as it had yawed to starboard.

"There it is!" Fox shouted. Looking up through the parting mists, they could see M-27 towering above the *Atlantic Princess*, a floating mountain of ice.

"Just like the *Titanic*," Carrie said in a stunned voice.

A vampire jumped down from the deck above, falling on a passenger's back.

"Only worse," Fox said.

A second vampire fell on the man, then a third. In the next moment there seemed to be as many vampires as humans on the Promenade Deck, the killers dispatching their victims with a speed that was equaled only by the ferocity of their attacks. The monsters were not killing to feed the Hunger, but for the diabolical joy of killing.

"Come on!" Fox grabbed Carrie's arm and pulled her backward toward an open cabin. "If we stay here, we're going to die."

Carrie resisted Fox, but not enough to keep him from pulling her to safety. He slammed the door and snapped the dead bolt shut, dubious that it would keep out any vampire who was determined to get in.

Fox pulled back the curtain and looked out.

"Maybe we're already dead and in hell . . ." he said, his voice trailing off.

The scene outside the cabin quickly dissolved into a whirling vortex of panic and violence. Some passengers flung themselves into the Atlantic, choosing a quick death over a contest to see whether the beasts or the sinking ship would be first to claim their lives.

"We'll have to wait here for dawn," Carrie said. "We've got to hope the ship stays afloat until dawn. It's our only chance."

Fox turned and looked at her, surprised at the eerie control in her voice. She was calling on an unexpected reserve of strength. No, not completely unexpected, Fox thought. Carrie Anderson was a physician. She had been trained to keep her head in life-or-death situations, even when death seemed unbeatable. He might be playing detective, but she was the one with real guts.

"I believe I shall have to enjoy you al fresco, though it hardly seems fitting, considering your reputation as a great chef."

Nicoletta was in the enormous kitchen that serviced the *Atlantic Princess*'s *grande salle à manger*. The ship's galley was as elaborately appointed as the kitchen in any five-star Michelin restaurant in France. Everywhere were gleaming stainless steel stoves and appliances. Brilliantly polished copper cookware hung from the ceiling like offerings to druid gods; of course, the pots and pans hung at unnatural angles now that the ship listed like a drunk about to collapse in an alley.

"If I had time, I might impose upon you to make me a nice blood pudding," Nicoletta said. "They are not much in fashion these days, but I rather like one from time to time."

Chef Charles L'Ouverture was stretched out on the stainless steel preparation table, his body trembling as Nicoletta removed his starched white hat and stroked his damp brow.

"Do not let them worry you," she said, indicating the bodies littering the room with a sweep of her hand. "I will show you the proper respect. Good chefs are almost impossible to find nowadays."

Yet Nicoletta found herself out of patience when Chef Charles began to cry and plead for his life. As much as she hated arrogant men, she was equally intolerant of weak men. Nicoletta tore open the chef's throat and sucked the life out of him as easily and quickly as she might crush a moth.

The vampire wiped her bloody mouth on a linen napkin. "*Très bien*. Now, perhaps a nice dessert wine."

Nicoletta opened the door to the walk-in cooler, where the survivors among the kitchen staff were caged. Seeing them cower back against the far wall almost put her off her appetite. Were no real men left in the world? Such whimpering, effeminate fops were hardly fit objects for her immortal rage.

"I am afraid I have some rather bad news for you all. The ship has hit an iceberg and is sinking rapidly. I should think that you all would be most eager to get up on deck. Would any of you like to leave? You have only to get past me."

None of the men moved.

"What a brave crew sails upon this ship! Come on, boys. I am, after all, only a woman," Nicoletta taunted, laughing at her own joke. The sharp smell of ammonia assaulted her nose. "Oh, brave sailors indeed. Which one of you has wet himself?"

Her question elicited no response.

"What year were you born, sailor?"

She compelled the trembling baker to answer. "Nineteen fifty-eight."

Nicoletta grabbed the man and pulled him to her so quickly that the others saw only a blur of motion. She sank her teeth but briefly into the baker's neck, opening her lips and breathing in through her mouth to discern better the more delicate nuances present in the blood.

"Not a very impressive year, it seems," she said.

She clamped her teeth more tightly onto the baker's neck and drained him almost instantly, letting his body fall dead and empty at her feet.

"What about you?" Nicoletta said, pointing to the nearest man. "What year were you born? Step forward and declare your vintage."

Carrie sat hunkered down in the darkness, her knees drawn up beneath her chin. She was glad that Fox was there to put his arm around her, to pool his courage with hers. This must have been how their ancestors cowered in dark caves while wild beasts scavenged the savanna for their less fortunate brethren. Though Carrie had always abhorred weapons of any sort, she made a silent pact with herself to get a gun, a powerful handgun, and learn to use it if she survived the *Atlantic Princess*'s first and final voyage. A big-bore handgun might not be of any use against vampires, but anything would be better than the awful helplessness she felt.

The noise of killing on the deck outside the cabin had gradually subsided as dawn approached. The ship's listing to port was not so obvious in the dark, in the absence of visual clues. Carrie would have never imagined herself able to sleep at such a time, but her experience during the night had left her so utterly drained that when she rested her forehead against her knees and closed her eyes, she fell quickly into a mercifully dreamless slumber.

Carrie awoke with a start, alone.

"Alexander?"

"I asked you not to call me that," Fox's voice said somewhere in the darkness.

Carrie scrambled to her feet, completely disoriented. The floor was slanting much more than she had remembered. The ship had tipped even further over on its side while she dozed.

"Alex?" she asked, hating the fear in her voice. "Where are you?"

A dim light appeared above her in the ceiling. No, not the ceiling. It was the circular window in the door. If the ship leaned much further, she'd be on all fours.

"It's getting light outside. Do you want to chance it?"

Carrie could see the dim outline of Fox's smiling face in the pale light. Crossing the stateroom to him was like walking up a steep hill. When Fox held out his hand she didn't hesitate to take it. Fox squeezed her hand; she squeezed back.

"We're going to make it, Carrie."

"Sure we are," Carrie said, wondering if she believed it, wondering if Fox believed it.

Carrie pushed her face up to the glass and looked both ways. The Promenade Deck was deserted. Beyond the railing, where the rolling Atlantic swells should have been, there was only gray and pink sky. The fog had turned into the sort of hazy overcast that would burn off before the sun got very high in the sky.

"Okay. What's the plan?"

"I think we should get to a lifeboat before the barge rolls over and goes under."

"What about the other passengers?"

"We'll help anybody we can," Fox said. "I'm going to

go out on the deck now and make some noise. We've got to find out whether those freaks can come outside in the sunlight."

"Don't you think you'd better wait? The sun isn't over the horizon yet."

"It's getting light fast now. The sun might actually be up and we can't see it because of the angle."

"I don't think so, Alex."

"Listen: We can't wait another hour just to be sure. The ship isn't going to last that long."

"Let's give it another ten minutes, and we'll both run for it. We'll have to make it over to the other side of the ship. I doubt lifeboats can be launched from this side due to the angle."

Fox heaved open the cabin door and helped Carrie climb out onto the steeply tipping deck. She crawled to the railing and held it with one hand, cupping the other hand to her mouth.

"Come on out, you bastards!" Carrie screamed. "Come out and get me, if you can."

Fox, looking very pale, said nothing, but stood by her, ready to face whatever was to come next.

Nothing happened.

"Come out and kill me, if you can!"

Still nothing.

"I think we're in the clear."

Fox smiled.

"Listen up!" Carrie shouted. "My name is Dr. Carrie Anderson. Any ship's officers who can hear me should come out onto the deck. Now!"

There was no response. Carrie's heart sank. What if she was the only officer left alive?

"Attention, all passengers within hearing!" Carrie tried again, shouting so loudly that it hurt her throat. "Come out of your cabins. The ship is sinking. We've got to get to the lifeboats. We don't have much time."

Still there was no response. Carrie stood hanging from

the rail, hearing the waves slapping against the gently rocking ship, waves that would, before long, close over its hull and commend it into the cold and lightless depths. For a sickening moment Carrie wondered if she and Fox were the only ones left alive aboard the *Atlantic Princess*—the only mortals.

"They can't come out in the sunlight!" Fox shouted.

That seemed to do the trick, for Carrie immediately heard a door latch rattle somewhere down the deck.

"Come out and save yourselves! The killers can't come out in the sunlight! We've all got to get to the lifeboats on the other side of the ship!"

A dozen doors slowly opened.

"What if it's *them*?" Fox asked under his breath.

Carrie had no opportunity to answer before a balding, middle-aged man with streaks of gray in his hair pulled himself warily onto the deck. His fear appeared genuine enough.

"Come on!" Carrie said, waving with her free hand. "We won't hurt you. We've got to get to the lifeboats."

The man turned back toward the cabin and nodded. A woman in a nightgown and robe dragged herself around the doorjamb. Trembling, she looked up and down the deck before reaching back into the cabin. A little girl appeared, clinging to her mother's leg so that the woman had to practically drag her.

"I've got to find Ricky, Alex."

"We'll search as we go. Head around to the other side of the ship and get a lifeboat lowered into the water," Fox told the man.

"How am I supposed to do that?"

"You can read, can't you?" Carrie asked, mustering her most reassuring bedside smile. "The directions are spelled out plain as day. All you have to do is follow them."

The man looked dubious. Carrie could hear the sound of doors opening up and down, above and below them on other decks.

"Come on," she urged the man. "There are others to

help. You can help one another. Hurry, people! There isn't much time."

Carrie and Fox pounded on doors, then moved along the slanting Promenade Deck. Perhaps Ricky was hiding in one of these cabins. "Get to the lifeboats! The ship is sinking."

Carrie banged on the door, then jiggled the handle. It was unlocked, so she opened it, only to find herself backing away from a grinning Jack Ketch and Brooke Morris.

"I've wanted to do you ever since I first laid eyes on you," Ketch said, baring his fangs. Then the pain hit him. Ketch's entire body began to tremble as if he'd come in contact with a powerful electric current. White smoke rose up from his exposed skin, filling the air with the sickeningly sweet smell of burning flesh.

"I'm burning!" Brooke screeched, hiding her face in her hands.

The vampires spun away from Carrie, their skin already blistered with third-degree burns. Ketch made it back into the cabin, but Brooke was not so lucky.

"You bitch!" a passenger shouted, hitting Brooke in the head with the carry-on bag into which she had stuffed the few possessions she hoped to rescue from the sinking ship. Brooke fell to the deck and pulled herself into the fetal position, the smoke and wisps of flame continuing to rise from her burning flesh. Passengers formed an angry circle around the fallen monster.

"She killed my husband!" the woman who had knocked Brooke to the deck cried, then kicked the vampire in the kidneys. The others swarmed over the fallen vampire, kicking and stomping, mad with fear and a lust for revenge against the monster.

"There isn't time for this!" Carrie yelled, trying futilely to pull a woman away from the mob. "Save yourselves!"

The vengeful passengers had already reduced Brooke's body to a smoldering mass of flesh. Here and there bits of bloody bone protruded—a bit of femur, a length of ulna. Not even a vampire could survive that, Carrie thought, letting Fox turn her away from the terrible sight.

* * *

Nicoletta opened a case of Dom Pérignon, stripped off her clothes standing in the midst of her victims' corpses, and bathed in champagne. She had known women who had bathed their skin in milk, others in blood. While she had tried both of these treatments, there was nothing quite as refreshing as a shower of good champagne.

The galley was dark but for the candles Nicoletta had taken from the dining room and scattered around the room. Most of these had guttered and gone out, drowning in their own melted wax as the ship leaned farther over on its wounded side. She stood on tiptoe and lifted the first bottle high over her head with both hands, holding up her face to the effervescent shower, her postprandial refreshment. The champagne was as icy as spring water welling up from the ancient earth, loosening the clotted blood in her hair and on her face. She opened her mouth and took a swallow of what seemed the most heavenly of elixirs—champagne combined with the subtle blend of a dozen men's blood.

*Prosit!*

Nicoletta toweled herself with a tablecloth, then stood naked in the darkness, waiting. She scarcely had to listen at all to hear the whispers behind the heavily insulated steel door.

"Is she gone?"

"We've got to get out of here before we sink!"

"Quiet, you idiot! Do you want her to hear us?"

"Ain't no way she could hear us, man."

The ship gave off a low, resonant groan, the death moan of the Titan, or perhaps the angel Lucifer at the moment of his defeat, when he realized he was about to be cast into the howling depths. A vibration began as a low hum and grew into a shudder that made it difficult to stand. Pots fell to the floor. The hanging copper pans began to swing madly back and forth, dissonant wind chimes, pendulums on a clock whose hands were both pointing straight up to the final hour of doom.

And then the rumbling stopped.

The men in the cooler began to scream and pound on the door. The *Atlantic Princess* didn't have much time left, nor did those who sailed upon it, unless they beat a hasty retreat to one of the lifeboats.

"Let us out!" the men screamed almost in unison. Strange how their minds were galvanized by that single thought. The pounding grew louder still. They were kicking the door at the same time. Nicoletta also heard the brittle scraping of men actually trying to claw their way through the steel door with now-bloody fingernails!

"I regret that I cannot let you gentlemen out," Nicoletta sang, pulling a fresh tablecloth around her shoulders. "We must obey the age-old maxim of seafaring disaster: Women and children first. As sailors, you must certainly understand."

The men cried in despair as Nicoletta left them, stepping gingerly over the bodies on the floor, pausing to blow out the sole remaining candle on her way out of the galley.

The people rushing madly back and forth when she stepped out onto the deck paid her not the least attention. The calamity that had befallen them—and the worse one that would come the moment the ship gave up the struggle to stay afloat—left them preoccupied with the question of their own survival. A woman clothed only in a tablecloth was hardly anything the panicking mortals felt occasion to pause and comment upon.

The sun felt warm and even pleasant upon her skin. Nicoletta made a mental note to spend more time hunting during daylight hours. Though it had been many centuries since she had learned to control her body well enough to keep the sun's rays from harming her, she had nevertheless remained a creature of the night. Still, nothing but habit held her to the patterns she had established when she was an apprentice to immortality. Perhaps this was but one last chain for her to throw off in her quest for absolute freedom.

Nicoletta made her way to her cabin, which was in a shambles, and dressed in a blue traveling suit. Then she packed two small suitcases. The deck around the lifeboats on the ship's port side was swarming with people. Two lifeboats were already in the water. A half dozen others were in various stages of being lowered, orange spiders dropping down from the web on metal cables. There was no panic evident in the lines of people queued up to get into the remaining lifeboats. The remaining crew members and a few heroic passengers had done an excellent job of calming the others.

Nicoletta looked down on this orderly scene and sighed. It would have been great fun to swoop down on this herd, sending them bleating for cover like sheep fleeing from a ravenous wolf. Alas, there was no time left for such diversions. The *Atlantic Princess*, so supremely elegant and graceful before Nicoletta had begun her spree, was wallowing on its side like a great fat cow floundering in a farm pond. Any moment now and she would roll over on her back and expire.

The captain's launch still swung suspended from cables near the bridge. The launch was set one deck higher and somewhat forward from the passenger lifeboats. It was intended to serve the senior officers, who were to supervise the evacuation and then scamper away at the last minute, if possible, gunning the launch's powerful inboard engines to escape the whirlpool the sinking liner would create. Fortunately for Principessa Nicoletta, there were no senior officers left aboard the *Atlantic Princess*. Not live ones, at any rate.

Nicoletta put the suitcases into the boat and busied herself with preparing to launch the craft. It was a little like leaving Bellaria, she thought. Only this time when she made landfall, it would not be Nicoletta who was at the mercy of the people she met, but just the reverse.

"Nicoletta!"

Keiko Matsuoka pressed her face against the porthole opposite Nicoletta, squinting against the sun, vainly trying to shield her burning flesh with a hand towel. Keiko was forced to pull away from the window a second later, shrieking in agony. Nicoletta could remember what it was like to be at the mercy of the sun's burning rays. And Nicoletta *could* help Keiko if she so desired, lending her a little of her ancient strength.

"Help me!" Keiko cried in a plaintive, begging voice.

Dear Keiko. Not since John Wilkes Booth had Principessa Nicoletta had such a promising apprentice. Unfortunately, Nicoletta had become extremely weary of her playmates aboard the *Atlantic Princess*. Carrie had refused to join in her fun, and David Parker had, of course, left a completely sour taste in her mouth—so to speak! Like a gourmet getting up after a long and elaborate feast, where course after course of the most exotic delicacies had been served, the only appetite remaining in Principessa Nicoletta Vittorini di Medusa was for quiet and solitude.

*I am so very sorry*, amore mio.

Keiko's screams were all in vain as Nicoletta pushed the button that set the electronic motors turning to lower her motor launch safely toward the water.

"Come on, Carrie."

Carrie stood scanning the ship, which loomed above them like a mountain that threatened to fall on them at any moment. The iceberg, which had drifted slowly into the distance since colliding with the ship, looked menacing but hardly capable of dealing a death blow to such an enormous vessel. It was a trick of perspective. M-27 was much larger than the *Atlantic Princess*, though it seemed to grow smaller as it floated toward the horizon. The immediate threat was the ship itself. It leaned so far to port that waves were breaking onto the A Deck. The *Atlantic Princess* could not possibly list much more without rolling over on its back.

"Ricky!"

"He might be in one of the other boats," Fox said, ignoring the fear and impatience of the people waiting for them both aboard the last remaining lifeboat.

"I checked the other boats. Ricky!"

A door banged open on the deck above them and a figure leaned over the railing immediately above.

Carrie and Fox looked up with hope, but it was not Ricky McCormick. It was Jack Ketch. The vampire burst into flames as he stood at the railing, looking down at Carrie with an expression of deathless hatred in his eyes. Ketch hurled himself into the ocean. His burning body hit the water with a sizzling splash and disappeared.

That was all that one of the passengers aboard the last lifeboat could stand. "Come on, lady," the passenger screamed hysterically at Carrie, "or we're leaving you!"

"Carrie." Fox gently took her arm. "You've got to think of the others now. We've got to get clear before the ship capsizes."

Carrie allowed herself to be led aboard the lifeboat. The moment it reached the safety of the water, the grief and shock rolled over her. She hid her eyes behind her hands and began to cry. Fox's arm was around her again, comforting her.

"Is anybody going to rescue us?" Carrie heard a man ask.

"I bounced up an SOS signal last night to the satellite uplink," Fox said. "I'll be surprised if help doesn't arrive by noon."

Ricky McCormick ran down the darkened interior corridor as fast as he could. Nicoletta was chasing him. He'd learned that night the princess was a vampire who could have caught him in an instant, but she was toying with him. She got close enough for him to feel her corpse breath on the back of his neck, reaching out to claw at him with her fingernails.

Ricky screamed and spurted ahead, but he knew he would never escape her.

He spun around a corner and suddenly realized he had a chance. He threw himself into the door and it crashed open, slamming back against the metal exterior wall with an explosive *clang*. The sunlight blinded Ricky. He tripped over the threshold and sprawled out onto the deck.

The vampire howled like an animal caught in a trap.

The sunlight! he thought.

But where was everybody? Had they abandoned the ship without him? He couldn't believe Dr. Anderson and Alex would have left him. Something didn't make sense. He looked up. None of the lifeboats were gone. But of course they weren't, not on the starboard side; it would have been impossible to launch them. The people were all on the other side of the ship! The boy started to run down the deck, moving with a crab-legged motion on the slanted surface.

"Ricky!"

The boy jerked to a stop, eyes wide.

"Ricky! You're alive! Thank God!"

"Grandma?"

Inside the open cabin door, standing back in the shadows, was his grandmother.

"Come here, darling!" she cried, holding out her arms.

Ricky took a tentative step forward and saw his grandpa was there, too, standing behind his grandmother.

"Is that you, Grandpa?"

"Come here, child, and we'll all be together again." His smile broadened so that Ricky could see his fangs as he added, "Forever."

Ricky's scream woke him from the nightmare. He was kicking his feet and throwing his hands, banging them against the metal interior of the crow's nest, scraping the knuckles of his left hand. The pain brought it all back into terrible focus. His grandparents were gone—gone past even becoming vampires.

Ricky had played a deadly game of hide-and-seek with the vampires until one of them—a middle-aged woman with an ugly hooked nose—nearly pulled him down the fore hatch. He would have been history if the iceberg hadn't appeared out of the fog and smashed into the ship. Ricky had managed to climb into the crow's nest to hide. For a long time he sat and watched the iceberg as it drifted away from the ship. After a while he became tired and cold, so he sat down and drew himself up in a ball, falling asleep.

Ricky blinked the sleep from his eyes. The *Atlantic Princess* had lurched so far to one side that Ricky was practically lying on the wall!

The boy pulled himself up and was stunned to see that the towering crow's nest was now no more than ten feet out of the water. Ricky knew how to swim, and the water didn't *look* cold, but he knew that he'd die of hypothermia within minutes. He fought back the tears. He didn't want to die. It wasn't fair.

A lifeboat emerged from behind the bridge. Ricky leaned out of the crow's nest, waving his arms and screaming frantically for them to rescue him. Anybody in a lifeboat had to be safe, he thought, since no vampire could go out in the sunlight.

At first Ricky thought the lifeboat was going to go past him, but the boat's engines cut, then increased a notch as the ship rode up one swell and down the other side, wallowing heavily in the ocean. The lifeboat drifted slowly up to the crow's nest. A hatch in the front of the covered boat popped open.

Something made Ricky shrink back then. He'd had too many close calls during the past few days and nights to believe that rescuers could so conveniently arrive to save him at the last possible moment. What if the lifeboat contained not his friends but Principessa Nicoletta, come not to save him but to kill him? A vision of startling clarity came to Ricky then—the image of Nicoletta alone in a lifeboat, the vampire princess more than willing to pick up a mortal boy to keep her company there in the middle of the North Atlantic.

"Ricky!"

"Dr. Anderson!"

Ricky McCormick had never been so glad to see anyone in all his life.

* * *

The lifeboats were tied together and drifted silently on the sea, rising and falling on the gentle swells. The covers to the crafts were propped open, as were the hatches at the front and back of each boat. It had become hot after the sun burned off the early morning haze. Almost all of the people, completely exhausted and in varying degrees of shock after the previous night, had fallen asleep in the warmth.

"What are you thinking about?"

Fox spoke in a low voice. He sat on the floor, across from Carrie, whose arm was around Ricky, who slept with his head resting on her shoulder.

"Nicoletta. I can't believe she's dead."

"Can't or don't?"

Carrie shrugged with her eyebrows.

"I wouldn't put too much stock in Ricky's so-called vision, Carrie. I don't believe in ESP. If she was aboard the *Atlantic Princess*, Carrie, she's dead, because she's sure as hell not in any of these lifeboats. You saw the ship go down. Nobody, not even Nicoletta, could have gotten away from that."

Carrie thought about how the ocean liner had begun to shudder and moan the moment they rescued Ricky. Dozens of vampires appeared on the upper decks, shrieking like lost souls as their bodies spontaneously combusted. Some of them jumped into the water and tried to swim for the lifeboats, but none of them could withstand the sun long enough to get very far, their bodies sinking in circles of water brought to boiling by the ferocious oxidation of their own skin and bones. Keiko had been one of the last. For as long as Carrie lived, she would remember the awful terror on the vampire's contorted face. She had run across the deck, leaping over the railing like a high hurdler, her body exploding into a fireball that arced toward the water trailing a cloud of acrid smoke and a spine-tingling wail. And yet she was a woman—or had been until she stepped on board the *Atlantic Princess*.

The ship had then rolled over on its back, sending out a huge rolling wave that terrified the passengers aboard the lifeboats. Carrie and Fox's lifeboat was nearly a mile away when the stern rose suddenly in the air, exposing the four gigantic, motionless propellers—screws, Carrie reminded herself, substituting the proper nautical term. The entire hull had then slipped beneath the waves faster than Carrie would have thought possible. The sinking created a frightening whirlpool, but even that disappeared in a few minutes. After that there was only the sound of the waves slapping against the lifeboats' hulls.

"What do you suppose happened to Lord Godwin?"

"Assuming he was still alive at the end, Carrie, my guess is that he decided to go down with his ship."

"As was fitting," she said a little bitterly.

Carrie looked out at the expanse of water that now covered the *Atlantic Princess* and the monstrous evil locked forever within its hull at the bottom of the sea. Was it possible that an entity who could release so much satanic power within the course of a few short nights could be so simply and completely dispatched? Carrie found it difficult to believe that Principessa Nicoletta Vittorini di Medusa could survive the challenge of so many centuries, only to allow herself to perish along with a doomed ocean liner. Not that Carrie wished that Nicoletta was anything other than dead. She wanted very much to believe that Nicoletta would not be able to make good on her promise to pay Carrie a visit in the future.

The flow of flotsam and jetsam from the *Atlantic Princess*, dense at first, had thinned considerably during the past hour. As Carrie sat staring out at the water, something floating near the boat caught her attention. A wooden cigar or jewelry box decorated with the *Atlantic Princess*'s logo. It floated closer still, as if drawn by some unusual magnetic attraction. Carrie reached down and plucked it from the water.

"What have you got?" Fox asked, whispering so as not to disturb the others.

Carrie put the dripping box on the bench beside her. Her left arm still around Ricky, she opened it with her free hand. The box had sealed well enough to keep the salt water from getting to the only object it held, a curious antique book. Carrie worked the book out of the box and opened it to the title page.

"You look as if you've just seen a ghost."

"I have. It's Principessa Nicoletta's diary," she said finally.

"Throw the damned thing back into the ocean!"

Several of the passengers stirred in their sleep.

But Carrie didn't do as Fox urged. Instead, she sat holding the infernal book, wondering which was the more dangerous course: to keep the vampire princess's diary, or to commend it into the fathomless depths without learning its secrets, leaving it to lie forever at the bottom of the sea near the *Atlantic Princess* and the doomed souls forever entombed there.

# POSTSCRIPTUM

✧

## To the Light

THE COLD AND darkness were welcome companions, a comforting postlude after so much abject misery. To have one's life cast down in the dust, in the blood, in the lightless depths of the oceans that were the mother of us all—what did any of it matter in the end? No one is truly immortal. Not even the sun will burn forever. In the end we all must return to the mystery from whence we came, enveloped in eternity's dark, comforting embrace, again one with the void.

Death was not unwelcome. We run very hard to stay ahead of the weariness, but eventually it catches us, and when it does, we discover, very much to our surprise, that we are relieved.

It was not entirely as expected. There was still the sense of having a body, of being a corporeal entity, though all the other senses were greatly numbed. The overall impression was that of floating, slowly floating, with neither direction nor destination.

There would be plenty of time to think, to reflect over a life poorly lived. And what then? A reunion with God, a welcoming into heaven accompanied by angels blowing golden trumpets? Or would the soul be cast into hell, as was more likely what was deserved when one's sins and virtues were weighed in the balance and the deficit noted. Or perhaps it wasn't the end but only a passage. Perhaps there would be another chance at life, a rebirth, with the opportunity to expiate karma accumulated in the previous life. Or maybe this was only the last bit of individual consciousness, an echo that would slowly extinguish after a final chance to reflect.

At length a dim light could be perceived in the distance. So it *was* like people had reported after near-death experiences. There was a light, and the light showed you the way.

To the light!

All it took was wishing to make it so. The light grew quickly brighter—the distant shimmering glow becoming a fiery golden beacon, a lighthouse showing life's lost sailors the way into the safe harbor, to the home the soul had sought through all the painful years of its odyssey.

To the light!

David Parker's face broke free from the water.

The light was no divine beacon, but the sun. David brought his hands up to his face in horror and saw that the salt water had not even wrinkled his immortal skin after many weeks of floating in the ocean's depths. Seaweed was stuck between his fingers, and his fingernails had grown to be grotesquely long and mossy.

Yet he had not died.

He *could* not die.

A rising swell lifted David mockingly toward the sun, then brought him low again in the trough between the waves. Whether floating on the surface or deep in the cold depths, the silent currents would push David inexorably toward land. It might take a month or two, but eventually the sea, too, would cast him out, an eternal wanderer unable to find refuge even in death, a Cain.

David lifted up his hands to the sun as if it had the power to release him from his eternity of torment. His anguished cry echoed across the rolling waters, a terrible wail of despair and loneliness. There was no one to hear David, or to answer, but only the sea and its endless rocking motion, carrying him inexorably back into the world.

Surrender to the thrill
of TERROR, the ecstasy
of the unseen....

Read MICHAEL ROMKEY'S
first two vampire
books, sure to steal
the light from your
days and seep into
your dreams....

# I, VAMPIRE

Living forever, he dwells among us mortals. Connoisseur of the finest in life—beautiful women, well-aged wine, and classical composers—he has no need of guilt. For he is neither good nor bad, neither angel nor devil. This is his story.

# THE VAMPIRE PAPERS

An invitation to study the life of the *Vampiri,* those creatures who are joined by blood and cursed to live out their days in lonely immortality. Discover the world of pleasureable pain and everlasting yearning. Feel the power of infinite strength. But pay attention as you read: You never know when you will be called upon to use this information....